For an instant the light held him—lounging against the wall in his spaceman's leather, the burns upon it, the tatters, ray-gun in its holster low on his thigh, and the brown scarred face turned to hers, eyes the colorless color of pale steel narrowed into the glare. It was a typical face. It belonged here, on the Venusian waterfront, in these dark and dangerous streets. It belonged to the type that frequents such places, those lawless men who ride the spaceways and live by the rule of the ray-gun, recklessly, warily outside the Patrol's jurisdiction. But there was more than that in the scarred brown face turned to the light. She must have seen it as she held the flash unwavering, some deep-buried trace of breeding and birth that made his cultured accents not incongruous.

NORTHWEST SMITH

NORTHWEST SMITH

C. L. MOORE

ACE BOOKS, NEW YORK

NORTHWEST SMITH

The contents of this book appeared in hardcover under the title *Scarlet Dream*, published by Donald M. Grant, Kingston, R.I.

An Ace Book

Published by arrangement with the author.

First Ace Printing: October 1982
Published simultaneously in Canada

ISBN: 0-441-58613-9

Manufactured in the United States of America

Ace Books, 200 Madison Avenue, New York, New York 10016

ACKNOWLEDGMENTS

Shambleau, copyright 1933 by Popular Fiction Publishing Company, for *Weird Tales*, November 1933.

Black Thirst, copyright 1934 by Popular Fiction Publishing Company for *Weird Tales*, April 1934.

The Tree of Life, copyright 1936 by Popular Fiction Publishing Company for *Weird Tales*, October 1936.

Scarlet Dream, copyright 1934 by Popular Fiction Publishing Company for *Weird Tales*, May 1934.

Dust of the Gods, copyright 1934 by Popular Fiction Publishing Company for *Weird Tales*, August 1934.

Lost Paradise, copyright 1936 by Popular Fiction Publishing Company for *Weird Tales*, July 1936.

Julhi, copyright 1935 by Popular Fiction Publishing Company for *Weird Tales*, March 1935.

The Cold Gray God, copyright 1935 by Popular Fiction Publishing Company for *Weird Tales*, October 1935.

Yvala, copyright 1936 by Popular Fiction Publishing Company for *Weird Tales*, February 1936.

Song in a Minor Key, copyright 1957 by King-Size Publications, Inc., for *Fantastic Universe*, June 1957.

SHAMBLEAU

MAN has conquered Space before. You may be sure of that. Somewhere beyond the Egyptians, in that dimness out of which come echoes of half-mythical names–Atlantis, Mu–somewhere back of history's first beginnings there must have been an age when mankind, like us today, built cities of steel to house its star-roving ships and knew the names of the planets in their own native tongues–heard Venus' people call their wet world "Sha-ardol" in that soft, sweet, slurring speech and mimicked Mars' guttural "Lakkdiz" from the harsh tongues of Mars' dryland dwellers. You may be sure of it. Man has conquered Space before, and out of that conquest faint, faint echoes run still through a world that has forgotten the very fact of a civilization which must have been as mighty as our own. There have been too many myths and legends for us to doubt it. The myth of the Medusa, for instance, can never have had its roots in the soil of Earth. That tale of the snake-haired Gorgon whose gaze turned the gazer to stone never originated about any creature that Earth nourished. And those ancient Greeks who told the story must have remembered, dimly and half believing, a tale of antiquity about some strange being from one of the outlying planets their remotest ancestors once trod.

"Shambleau! Ha . . . Shambleau!" The wild hysteria of the mob rocketed from wall to wall of Lakkdarol's narrow streets and the storming of heavy boots over the slag-red pavement made an ominous undernote to that swelling bay, "Shambleau! Shambleau!"

Northwest Smith heard it coming and stepped into the nearest doorway, laying a wary hand on his heat-gun's grip, and his colorless eyes narrowed. Strange sounds were common enough in the streets of Earth's latest colony on Mars—a raw, red little town where anything might happen, and very often did. But Northwest Smith, whose name is known and respected in every dive and wild outpost on a dozen wild planets, was a cautious man, despite his reputation. He set his back against the wall and gripped his pistol, and heard the rising shout come nearer and nearer.

Then into his range of vision flashed a red running figure, dodging like a hunted hare from shelter to shelter in the narrow street. It was a girl—a berry-brown girl in a single tattered garment whose scarlet burnt the eyes with its brilliance. She ran wearily, and he could hear her gasping breath from where he stood. As she came into view he saw her hesitate and lean one hand against the wall for support, and glance wildly around for shelter. She must not have seen him in the depths of the doorway, for as the bay of the mob grew louder and the pounding of feet sounded almost at the corner she gave a despairing little moan and dodged into the recess at his very side.

When she saw him standing there, tall and leather-brown, hand on his heat-gun, she sobbed once, inarticulately, and collapsed at his feet, a huddle of burning scarlet and bare, brown limbs.

Smith had not seen her face, but she was a girl, and sweetly made and in danger; and though he had not the reputation of a chivalrous man, something in her hopeless huddle at his feet touched that chord of sympathy for the underdog that stirs in every Earthman, and he pushed her gently into the corner behind him and jerked out his gun, just as the first of the running mob rounded the corner.

It was a motley crowd, Earthmen and Martians and a sprinkling of Venusian swampmen and strange, nameless denizens of unnamed planets—a typical Lakkdarol mob. When the first of them turned the corner and saw the empty street before them there was a faltering in the rush and the foremost spread out and began to search the doorways on both sides of the street.

"Looking for something?" Smith's sardonic call sounded clear above the clamor of the mob.

They turned. The shouting died for a moment as they took in the scene before them—tall Earthman in the space-explorer's leathern garb, all one color from the burning of savage suns save for the sinister pallor of his no-colored eyes in a scarred and resolute face, gun in his steady hand and the scarlet girl crouched behind him, panting.

The foremost of the crowd—a burly Earthman in tattered leather from which the Patrol insignia had been ripped away—stared for a moment with a strange expression of incredulity on his face overspreading the savage exultation of the chase. Then he let loose a deep-throated bellow, "Shambleau!" and lunged forward. Behind him the mob took up the cry again. "Shambleau! Shambleau! Shambleau!" and surged after.

Smith, lounging negligently against the wall, arms folded and gun-hand draped over his left forearm, looked incapable of swift motion, but at the leader's first forward step the pistol swept in a practised half-circle and the dazzle of blue-white heat leaping from its muzzle seared an arc in the slag pavement at his feet. It was an old gesture, and not a man in the crowd understood it. The foremost recoiled swiftly against the surge of those in the rear, and for a moment there was confusion as the two tides met and struggled. Smith's mouth curled into a grim curve as he watched. The man in the mutilated Patrol uniform lifted a threatening fist and stepped to the very edge of the deadline, while the crowd rocked to and fro behind him.

"Are you crossing that line?" queried Smith in an ominously gentle voice.

"We want that girl!"

"Come and get her!" Recklessly Smith grinned into his face. He saw danger there, but his defiance was not the foolhardy gesture it seemed. An expert psychologist of mobs from long experience, he sensed no murder here. Not a gun had appeared in any hand in the crowd. They desired the girl with an inexplicable bloodthirstiness he was at a loss to understand, but toward himself he sensed no such fury. A mauling he might expect, but his life was in no danger. Guns would have appeared before now if they were coming out at all. So he grinned in the man's angry face and leaned lazily against the wall.

Behind their self-appointed leader the crowd milled impatiently, and threatening voices began to rise again. Smith heard the girl moan at his feet.

"What do you want with her?" he demanded.

"She's Shambleau! Shambleau, you fool! Kick her out of there—we'll take care of her!"

"I'm taking care of her," drawled Smith.

"She's Shambleau, I tell you! Damn your hide, man, we never let those things live! Kick her out here!"

The repeated name had no meaning to him, but Smith's innate stubbornness rose defiantly as the crowd surged forward to the very edge of the arc, their clamor growing louder. "Shambleau! Kick her out here! Give us Shambleau! Shambleau!"

Smith dropped his indolent pose like a cloak and planted both feet wide, swinging up his gun threateningly. "Keep back!" he yelled. "She's mine! Keep back!"

He had no intention of using that heat-beam. He knew by now that they would not kill him unless he started the gunplay himself, and he did not mean to give up his life for any girl alive. But a severe mauling he expected, and he braced himself instinctively as the mob heaved within itself.

To his astonishment a thing happened then that he had never known to happen before. At his shouted defiance the foremost of the mob—those who had heard him clearly—drew back a little, not in alarm but evidently surprised. The ex-Patrolman said, "Yours! She's *yours?*" in a voice from which puzzlement crowded out the anger.

Smith spread his booted legs wide before the crouching figure and flourished his gun.

"Yes," he said. "And I'm keeping her! Stand back there!"

The man stared at him wordlessly, and horror and disgust and incredulity mingled on his weather-beaten face. The incredulity triumphed for a moment and he said again,

"Yours!"

Smith nodded defiance.

The man stepped back suddenly, unutterable contempt in his very pose. He waved an arm to the crowd and said loudly, "It's—his!" and the press melted away, gone silent, too, and the look of contempt spread from face to face.

The ex-Patrolman spat on the slag-paved street and turned his back indifferently. "Keep her, then," he advised briefly over one shoulder. "But don't let her out again in this town!"

Smith stared in perplexity almost open-mouthed as the suddenly scornful mob began to break up. His mind was in a whirl. That such bloodthirsty animosity should vanish in a breath he could not believe. And the curious mingling of contempt and disgust on the faces he saw baffled him even more. Lakkdarol was anything but a puritan town—it did not enter his head for a moment that his claiming the brown girl as his own had caused that strangely shocked revulsion to spread through the crowd. No, it was something deeper-rooted than that. Instinctive, instant disgust had been in the faces he saw—they would have looked less so if he had admitted cannibalism or *Pharol*-worship.

And they were leaving his vicinity as swiftly as if whatever unknowing sin he had committed were contagious. The street was emptying as rapidly as it had filled. He saw a sleek Venusian glance back over his shoulder as he turned the corner and sneer, "Shambleau!" and the word awoke a new line of speculation in Smith's mind. Shambleau! Vaguely of French origin, it must be. And strange enough to hear it from the lips of Venusian and Martian drylanders, but it was their use of it that puzzled him more. "We never let those things live," the ex-Patrolman had said. It reminded him dimly of something . . . an ancient line from some writing in his own tongue . . . "Thou shalt not suffer a witch to live." He smiled to himself at the similarity, and simultaneously was aware of the girl at his elbow.

She had risen soundlessly. He turned to face her, sheathing his gun and stared at first with curiosity and then in the entirely frank openness with which men regard that which is not wholly human. For she was not. He knew it at a glance, though the brown, sweet body was shaped like a woman's and she wore the garment of scarlet—he saw it was leather—with an ease that few unhuman beings achieve toward clothing. He knew it from the moment he looked into her eyes, and a shiver of unrest went over him as he met them. They were frankly green as young grass, with slit-like, feline pupils that pulsed unceasingly, and there was a look of dark, animal wisdom in their depths—that look of the beast which sees more than man.

There was no hair upon her face—neither brows nor lashes, and he would have sworn that the tight scarlet turban bound around her head covered baldness. She had three fingers and a thumb, and her feet had four digits apiece too, and all sixteen of them were tipped with round claws that sheathed back into the flesh like a cat's. She ran her tongue over her lips—a thin, pink, flat tongue as feline as her eyes—and spoke with difficulty. He felt that that throat and tongue had never been shaped for human speech.

"Not—afraid now," she said softly, and her little teeth were white and pointed as a kitten's.

"What did they want you for?" he asked her curiously. "What have you done? Shambleau . . . is that your name?"

"I—not talk your—speech," she demurred hesitantly.

"Well, try to—I want to know. Why were they chasing you? Will you be safe on the street now, or hadn't you better get indoors somewhere? They looked dangerous."

"I—go with you." She brought it out with difficulty.

"Say you!" Smith grinned. "What are you, anyhow? You look like a kitten to me."

"Shambleau." She said it somberly.

"Where d'you live? Are you a Martian?"

"I come from—from far—from long ago—far country—"

"Wait!" laughed Smith. "You're getting your wires crossed. You're not a Martian?"

She drew herself up very straight beside him, lifting the turbaned head, and there was something queenly in the pose of her.

"Martian?" she said scornfully. "My people—are—are—you have no word. Your speech—hard for me."

"What's yours? I might know it—try me."

She lifted her head and met his eyes squarely, and there was in hers a subtle amusement—he could have sworn it.

"Some day I—speak to you in—my own language," she promised, and the pink tongue flicked out over her lips, swiftly, hungrily.

Approaching footsteps on the red pavement interrupted Smith's reply. A dryland Martian came past, reeling a little and exuding an aroma of *segir*-whisky, the Venusian brand. When he caught the red flash of the girl's tatters he turned his head sharply, and as his *segir*-steeped brain took in the fact of her presence he lurched toward the recess unsteadily, bawling, "Shambleau, by *Pharol!* Shambleau!" and reached out a clutching hand.

Smith struck it aside contemptuously.

"On your way, drylander," he advised.

The man drew back and stared, bleary-eyed.

"Yours, eh?" he croaked. "*Zut!* You're welcome to it!" And like the ex-Patrolman before him he spat on the pavement and turned away, muttering harshly in the blasphemous tongue of the drylands.

Smith watched him shuffle off, and there was a crease between his colorless eyes, a nameless unease rising within him.

"Come on," he said abruptly to the girl. "If this sort of thing is going to happen we'd better get indoors. Where shall I take you?"

"With—you," she murmured.

He stared down into the flat green eyes. Those ceaselessly pulsing pupils disturbed him, but it seemed to him, vaguely, that behind the animal shallows of her gaze was a shutter—a closed barrier that might at any moment open to reveal the very deeps of that dark knowledge he sensed there.

Roughly he said again, "Come on, then," and stepped down into the street.

She pattered along a pace or two behind him, making no effort to keep up with his long strides, and though Smith—as men know from Venus to Jupiter's moons—walks as softly as a cat, even in spacemen's boots, the girl at his heels slid like a shadow over the rough pavement, making so little sound that even the lightness of his footsteps was loud in the empty street.

Smith chose the less frequented ways of Lakkdarol, and somewhat shamefacedly thanked his nameless gods that his lodgings were not far away, for the few pedestrians he met turned and stared after the two with that by now familiar mingling of horror and contempt which he was as far as ever from understanding.

The room he had engaged was a single cubicle in a lodging-house on the edge of the city. Lakkdarol, raw camptown that it was in those days, could have furnished little better anywhere within its limits, and Smith's errand there was not one he wished to advertise. He had slept in worse places than this before, and knew that he would do so again.

There was no one in sight when he entered, and the girl slipped up the stairs at his heels and vanished through the door, shadowy, unseen by anyone in the house. Smith closed the door and leaned his broad shoulders against the panels, regarding her speculatively.

She took in what little the room had to offer in a glance—frowsy bed, rickety table, mirror hanging unevenly and cracked against the wall, unpainted chairs—a typical camp-town room in an Earth settlement abroad. She accepted its poverty in that single glance, dismissed it, then crossed to the window and leaned out for a moment, gazing across the low roof-tops toward the barren countryside beyond, red slag under the late afternoon sun.

"You can stay here," said Smith abruptly, "until I leave town. I'm waiting here for a friend to come in from Venus. Have you eaten?"

"Yes," said the girl quickly. "I shall—need no—food for—a while."

"Well—" Smith glanced around the room. "I'll be in sometime tonight. You can go or stay just as you please. Better lock the door behind me."

With no more formality than that he left her. The door closed and he heard the key turn, and smiled to himself. He did not expect, then, ever to see her again.

He went down the steps and out into the late-slanting sunlight with a mind so full of other matters that the brown girl receded very quickly into the background. Smith's errand in Lakkdarol, like most of his errands, is better not spoken of. Man lives as he must, and Smith's living was a perilous affair outside the law and ruled by the ray-gun only. It is enough to say that the shipping-port and its cargoes outbound interested him deeply just now, and that the friend he awaited was Yarol the Venusian, in that swift little Edsel ship the *Maid* that can flash from world to world with a derisive speed that laughs at Patrol boats and leaves pursuers floundering in the ether far behind. Smith and Yarol and the *Maid* were a trinity that had caused the Patrol leaders much worry and many gray hairs in the past, and the future looked very bright to Smith himself that evening as he left his lodging-house.

Lakkdarol roars by night, as Earthmen's camp-towns have a way of doing on every planet where Earth's outposts are, and it was beginning lustily as Smith went down among the awakening lights toward the center of town. His business there does not concern us. He mingled with the crowds where the lights were brightest, and there was the click of ivory counters and the jingle of silver, and red *segir* gurgled invitingly from black Venusian bottles, and much later Smith strolled homeward under the moving moons of Mars, and if the street wavered a little under his feet now and then—why, that is only understandable. Not even Smith could drink red *segir* at every bar from the *Martian Lamb* to the *New Chicago* and remain entirely steady on his feet. But he found his way back with very little difficulty—considering—and spent a good five minutes hunting for his key before he remembered he had left it in the inner lock for the girl.

He knocked then, and there was no sound of footsteps from within, but in a few moments the latch clicked and the door swung open. She retreated soundlessly before him as he entered, and took up her favorite place against the window, leaning back on the sill and outlined against the starry sky beyond. The room was in darkness.

Smith flipped the switch by the door and then leaned back against the panels, steadying himself. The cool night air had sobered him a little and his head was clear enough—liquor went to Smith's feet, not his head, or he would never have come this far along the lawless way he had chosen. He lounged against the door now and regarded the girl in the sudden glare of the bulbs, blinding a little as much at the scarlet of her clothing as at the light.

"So you stayed," he said.

"I—waited," she answered softly, leaning farther back against the sill and clasping the rough wood with slim, three-fingered hands, pale brown against the darkness.

"Why?"

She did not answer that, but her mouth curved into a slow smile. On a woman it would have been reply enough—provocative, daring. On Shambleau there was something pitiful and horrible in it—so human on the face of one half-animal. And yet . . . that sweet brown body curving so softly from the tatters of scarlet leather—the velvety texture of that brownness—the white-flashing smile. . . . Smith was aware of a stirring excitement within him. After all—time would be hanging heavy now until Yarol came. . . . Speculatively he allowed the steel-pale eyes to wander over her, with a slow regard that missed nothing. And when he spoke he was aware that his voice had deepened a little. . . .

"Come here," he said.

She came forward slowly, on bare clawed feet that made no slightest sound on the floor, and stood before him with downcast eyes and mouth trembling in that pitifully human smile. He took her by the shoulders—velvety soft shoulders, of a creamy smoothness that was not the texture of human flesh. A little tremor went over her, perceptibly, at the contact of his hands. Northwest Smith caught his breath suddenly and dragged her to him . . . sweet yielding brownness in the circle of his arms . . . heard her own breath catch and quicken as her velvety arms closed about his neck. And then he was looking down into her face, very near, and the green animal eyes met his with the pulsing pupils and the flicker of—something—deep behind their shallows—and through the rising clamor of his blood, even as he stooped his lips to hers, Smith felt something deep within him shudder away—inexplicable, instinctive, revolted. What it might be he had no words to tell, but the very touch of her was suddenly loathsome—so soft and velvet and unhuman—and it might have been an animal's face that lifted itself to his mouth—the dark knowledge looked hungrily from the darkness of those slit pupils—and for a mad instant he knew that same wild, feverish revulsion he had seen in the faces of the mob. . . .

"God!" he gasped, a far more ancient invocation against evil than he realized, then or ever, and he ripped her arms from his neck, swung her away with such a force that she reeled half across the room. Smith fell back against the door, breathing heavily, and stared at her while the wild revolt died slowly within him.

She had fallen to the floor beneath the window, and as she lay there against the wall with bent head he saw, curiously, that her turban had slipped—the turban that he had been so sure covered baldness—and a lock of scarlet hair fell below the binding leather, hair as scarlet as her garment, as unhumanly red as her eyes were unhumanly green. He stared, and shook his head dizzily and stared again, for it seemed to him that the thick lock of crimson had moved, *squirmed* of itself against her cheek.

At the contact of it her hands flew up and she tucked it away with a very human gesture and then dropped her head again into her hands. And from the deep shadow of her fingers he thought she was staring up at him covertly.

Smith drew a deep breath and passed a hand across his forehead. The inexplicable moment had gone as quickly as it came—too swiftly for him to understand or analyze it. "Got to lay off the *segir*," he told himself unsteadily. Had he imagined that scarlet hair? After all, she was no more than a pretty brown girl-creature from one of the many half-human races peopling the planets. No more than that, after all. A pretty little thing, but animal. . . . He laughed, a little shakily.

"No more of that," he said. "God knows I'm no angel, but there's got to be a limit somewhere. Here." He crossed to the bed and sorted out a pair of blankets from the untidy heap tossing them to the far corner of the room. "You can sleep there."

Wordlessly she rose from the floor and began to rearrange

the blankets, the uncomprehending resignation of the animal eloquent in every line of her.

Smith had a strange dream that night. He thought he had awakened to a room full of darkness and moonlight and moving shadows, for the nearer moon of Mars was racing through the sky and everything on the planet below her was endued with a restless life in the dark. And something . . . some nameless, unthinkable *thing* . . . was coiled about his throat . . . something like a soft snake, wet and warm. It lay loose and light about his neck . . . and it was moving gently, very gently, with a soft, caressive pressure that sent little thrills of delight through every nerve and fiber of him, a perilous delight—beyond physical pleasure, deeper than joy of the mind. That warm softness was caressing the very roots of his soul and with a terrible intimacy. The ecstasy of it left him weak, and yet he knew—in a flash of knowledge born of this impossible dream—that the soul should not be handled. . . . And with that knowledge a horror broke upon him, turning the pleasure into a rapture of revuslion, hateful, horrible—but still most foully sweet. He tried to lift his hands and tear the dream-monstrosity from his throat—tried but half-heartedly; for though his soul was revolted to its very deeps, yet the delight of his body was so great that his hands all but refused the attempt. But when at last he tried to lift his arms a cold shock went over him and he found that he could not stir . . . his body lay stony as marble beneath the blankets, a living marble that shuddered with a dreadful delight through every rigid vein.

The revulsion grew strong upon him as he struggled against the paralyzing dream—a struggle of soul against sluggish body—titanically, until the moving dark was streaked with blankness that clouded and closed about him at last and he sank back into the oblivion from which he had awakened.

Next morning, when the bright sunlight shining through Mars' clear thin air awakened him, Smith lay for a while trying to remember. The dream had been more vivid than reality, but he could not now quite recall . . . only that it had been more sweet and horrible than anything else in life. He lay puzzling for a while, until a soft sound from the corner aroused him from his thoughts and he sat up to see the girl lying in a cat-like coil on her blankets, watching him with round, grave eyes. He regarded her somewhat ruefully.

"Morning," he said. "I've just had the devil of a dream. . . . Well, hungry?"

She shook her head silently, and he could have sworn there was a covert gleam of strange amusement in her eyes.

He stretched and yawned, dismissing the nightmare temporarily from his mind.

"What am I going to do with you?" he inquired, turning to more immediate matters. "I'm leaving here in a day or two and I can't take you along, you know. Where'd you come from in the first place?"

Again she shook her head.

"Not telling? Well, it's your business. You can stay here until I give up the room. From then on you'll have to do your own worrying."

He swung his feet to the floor and reached for his clothes.

Ten minutes later, slipping the heat-gun into its holster at his thigh, Smith turned to the girl. "There's food-concentrate in that box on the table. It ought to hold you until I get back. And you'd better lock the door again after I've gone."

Her wide, unwavering stare was his only answer, and he was not sure she had understood, but at any rate the lock clicked after him as before, and he went down the steps with a faint grin on his lips.

The memory of last night's extraordinary dream was slipping from him, as such memories do, and by the time he had reached the street the girl and the dream and all of yesterday's happenings were blotted out by the sharp necessities of the present.

Again the intricate business that had brought him here claimed his attention. He went about it to the exclusion of all else, and there was a good reason behind everything he did from the moment he stepped out into the street until the time when he turned back again at evening; though had one chosen to follow him during the day his apparently aimless rambling through Lakkdarol would have seemed very pointless.

He must have spent two hours at the least idling by the space-port, watching with sleepy, colorless eyes the ships that came and went, the passengers, the vessels lying at wait, the cargoes—particularly the cargoes. He made the rounds of the town's saloons once more, consuming many glasses of varied liquors in the course of the day and engaging in idle conversation with men of all races and worlds, usually in their own languages, for Smith was a linguist of repute among his contemporaries. He heard the gossip of the spaceways, news from a dozen planets of a thousand different events. He heard the latest joke about the Venusian Emperor and the latest report on the Chino-Aryan war and the latest song hot from the lips of Rose Robertson, whom every man on the civilized planets adored as "the Georgia Rose." He passed the day quite profitably, for his own purposes, which do not concern us now, and it was not until late evening, when he turned homeward again, that the thought of the brown girl in his room took definite shape in his mind, though it had been lurking there, formless and submerged, all day.

He had no idea what comprised her usual diet, but he bought a can of New York roast beef and one of Venusian frog-broth and a dozen fresh canal-apples and two pounds of that Earth lettuce that grows so vigorously in the fertile canal-soil of Mars. He felt that she must surely find something to her liking in this broad variety of edibles, and—for his day had been very satisfactory—he hummed *The Green Hills of Earth* to himself in a surprisingly good baritone as he climbed the stairs.

The door was locked, as before, and he was reduced to kicking the lower panels gently with his boot, for his arms were full. She opened the door with that softness that was characteristic of her and stood regarding him in the semidarkness as he stumbled to the table with his load. The room was unlit again.

"Why don't you turn on the lights?" he demanded irritably after he had barked his shin on the chair by the table in an effort to deposit his burden there.

"Light and—dark—they are alike—to me," she murmured.

"Cat eyes, eh? Well, you look the part. Here, I've brought you some dinner. Take your choice. Fond of roast beef? Or how about a little frog-broth?"

She shook her head and backed away a step.

"No," she said. "I can not—eat your food."

Smith's brows wrinkled. "Didn't you have any of the food-tablets?"

Again the red turban shook negatively.

"Then you haven't had anything for—why, more than twenty-four hours! You must be starved."

"Not hungry," she denied.

"What can I find for you to eat, then? There's time yet if I hurry. You've got to eat, child."

"I shall—eat," she said softly. "Before long—I shall—feed. Have no—worry."

She turned away then and stood at the window, looking out over the moonlit landscape as if to end the conversation. Smith cast her a puzzled glance as he opened the can of roast beef. There had been an odd undernote in that assurance that, undefinably, he did not like. And the girl had teeth and tongue and presumably a fairly human digestive system, to judge from her human form. It was nonsense for her to pretend that he could find nothing that she could eat. She must have had some of the food concentrate after all, he decided, prying up the thermos lid of the inner container to release the long-sealed savor of the hot meat inside.

"Well, if you won't eat you won't," he observed philosophically as he poured hot broth and diced beef into the dish-like lid of the thermos can and extracted the spoon from its hiding-place between the inner and outer receptacles. She turned a little to watch him as he pulled up a rickety chair and sat down to the food, and after a while the realization that her green gaze was fixed so unwinkingly upon him made the man nervous, and he said between bites of creamy canal-apple, "Why don't you try a little of this? It's good."

"The food—I eat is—better," her soft voice told him in its hesitant murmur, and again he felt rather than heard a faint undernote of unpleasantness in the words. A sudden suspicion struck him as he pondered on that last remark—some vague memory of horror-tales told about campfires in the past—and he swung round in the chair to look at her, a tiny, creeping fear unaccountably arising. There had been that in her words—in her unspoken words, that menaced. . . .

She stood up beneath his gaze demurely, wide green eyes with their pulsing pupils meeting his without a falter. But her mouth was scarlet and her teeth were sharp. . . .

"What food do you eat?" he demanded. And then, after a pause, very softly, "Blood?"

She stared at him for a moment, uncomprehending; then something like amusement curled her lips and she said scornfully, "You think me—vampire, eh? No—I am Shambleau!"

Unmistakably there were scorn and amusement in her voice at the suggestion, but as unmistakably she knew what he meant—accepted it as a logical suspicion—vampires! Fairy-tales—but fairy-tales this unhuman, outland creature was most familiar with. Smith was not a credulous man, nor a superstitious one, but he had seen too many strange things himself to doubt that the wildest legend might have a basis of fact. And there was something namelessly strange about her. . . .

He puzzled over it for a while between deep bites of the canal-apple. And though he wanted to question her about a great many things, he did not, for he knew how futile it would be.

He said nothing more until the meat was finished and

another canal-apple had followed the first, and he had cleared away the meal by the simple expedient of tossing the empty can out of the window. Then he lay back in the chair and surveyed her from half-closed eyes, colorless in a face tanned like saddle-leather. And again he was conscious of the brown, soft curves of her, velvety—subtle arcs and planes of smooth flesh under the tatters of scarlet leather. Vampire she might be, unhuman she certainly was, but desirable beyond words as she sat submissive beneath his low regard, her red-turbaned head bent, her clawed fingers lying in her lap. They sat very still for a while, and the silence throbbed between them.

She was so like a woman—an Earth woman—sweet and submissive and demure, and softer than soft fur, if he could forget the three-fingered claws and the pulsing eyes—and that deeper strangeness beyond words. . . . (Had he dreamed that red lock of hair that moved? Had it been *segir* that woke the wild revulsion he knew when he held her in his arms? Why had the mob so thirsted for her?) He sat and stared, and despite the mystery of her and the half- suspicions that thronged his mind—for she was so beautifully soft and curved under those revealing tatters—he slowly realized that his pulses were mounting, became aware of a kindling within . . . brown girl-creature with downcast eyes . . . and then the lids lifted and the green flatness of a cat's gaze met his, and last night's revulsion woke swiftly again, like a warning bell that clanged as their eyes met—animal, after all, too sleek and soft for humanity, and that inner strangeness. . . .

Smith shrugged and sat up. His failings were legion, but the weakness of the flesh was not among the major ones. He motioned the girl to her pallet of blankets in the corner and turned to his own bed.

From deeps of sound sleep he awoke much later. He awoke suddenly and completely, and with that inner excitement that presages something momentous. He awoke to brilliant moonlight, turning the room so bright that he could see the scarlet of the girl's rags as she sat up on her pallet. She was awake, she was sitting with her shoulder half turned to him and her head bent, and some warning instinct crawled coldly up his spine as he watched what she was doing. And yet it was a very ordinary thing for a girl to do—any girl, anywhere. She was unbinding her turban. . . .

He watched, not breathing, a presentiment of something horrible stirring in his brain, inexplicably. . . . The red folds loosened, and—he knew then that he had not dreamed—again a scarlet lock swung down against her cheek . . . a hair, was it? a lock of hair? . . . thick as a thick worm it fell, plumply, against that smooth cheek . . . more scarlet than blood and thick as a crawling worm . . . and like a worm it crawled.

Smith rose on an elbow, not realizing the motion, and fixed an unwinking stare, with a sort of sick, fascinated incredulity, on that—that lock of hair. He had not dreamed. Until now he had taken it for granted that it was the *segir* which had made it seem to move on that evening before. But now . . . it was lengthening, stretching, moving of itself. It must be hair, but it *crawled;* with a sickening life of its own it squirmed down against her cheek, caressingly, revoltingly, impossibly. . . . Wet, it was, and round and thick and shining. . . .

She unfastened the last fold and whipped the turban off. From what he saw then Smith would have turned his eyes away—and he had looked on dreadful things before, without flinching—but he could not stir. He could only lie there on elbow staring at the mass of scarlet, squirming—worms, hairs, what?—that writhed over her head in a dreadful mockery of ringlets. And it was lengthening, falling, somehow growing before his eyes, down over her shoulders in a spilling cascade, a mass that even at the beginning could never have been hidden under the skull-tight turban she had worn. He was beyond wondering, but he realized that. And still it squirmed and lengthened and fell, and she shook it out in a horrible travesty of a woman shaking out her unbound hair—until the unspeakable tangle of it—twisting, writhing, obscenely scarlet—hung to her waist and beyond, and still lengthened, an endless mass of crawling horror that until now, somehow, impossibly, had been hidden under the tight-bound turban. It was like a nest of blind, restless red worms . . . . it was—it was like naked entrails endowed with an unnatural aliveness, terrible beyond words.

Smith lay in the shadows, frozen without and within in a sick numbness that came of utter shock and revulsion.

She shook out the obscene, unspeakable tangle over her shoulders, and somehow he knew that she was going to turn in a moment and that he must meet her eyes. The thought of that meeting stopped his heart with dread, more awfully than anything else in this nightmare horror; for nightmare it must be, surely. But he knew without trying that he could not wrench his eyes away—the sickened fascination of that sight held him motionless, and somehow there was a certain beauty. . . .

Her head was turning. The crawling awfulness rippled and squirmed at the motion, writhing thick and wet and shining over the soft brown shoulders about which they fell now in obscene cascades that all but hid her body. Her head was turning. Smith lay numb. And very slowly he saw the round of her cheek foreshorten and her profile come into view, all the scarlet horrors twisting ominously, and the profile shortened in turn and her full face came slowly round toward the bed—moonlight shining brilliantly as day on the pretty girl-face, demure and sweet, framed in tangled obscenity that crawled. . . .

The green eyes met his. He felt a perceptible shock, and a shudder rippled down his paralyzed spine, leaving an icy numbness in its wake. He felt the goose-flesh rising. But that numbness and cold horror he scarcely realized, for the green eyes were locked with his in a long, long look that somehow presaged nameless things—not altogether unpleasant things—the voiceless voice of her mind assailing him with little murmurous promises. . . .

For a moment he went down into a blind abyss of submission; and then somehow the very sight of that obscenity in eyes that did not then realize they saw it, was dreadful enough to draw him out of the seductive darkness . . . the sight of her crawling and alive with unnamable horror.

She rose, and down about her in a cascade fell the squirming scarlet of—of what grew upon her head. It fell in a long, alive cloak to her bare feet on the floor, hiding her in a wave of dreadful, wet, writhing life. She put up her hands and like a swimmer she parted the waterfall of it, tossing the masses back over her shoulders to reveal her own brown body, sweetly curved. She smiled exquisitely, and in starting waves back from her forehead and down about her in a hideous background writhed the snaky wetness of her living tresses. And Smith knew that he looked upon Medusa.

The knowledge of that—the realization of vast backgrounds reaching into misted history—shook him out of his frozen horror for a moment, and in that moment he met her eyes again, smiling, green as glass in the moonlight, half hooded under drooping lids. Through the twisting scarlet she held out her arms. And there was something soul-shakingly desirable about her, so that all the blood surged to his head suddenly and he stumbled to his feet like a sleeper in a dream as she swayed toward him, infinitely graceful, infinitely sweet in her cloak of living horror.

And somehow there was beauty in it, the wet scarlet writhings with moonlight sliding and shining along the thick, worm-round tresses and losing itself in the masses only to glint again and move silvery along writhing tendrils—an awful, shuddering beauty more dreadful than any ugliness could be.

But all this, again, he but half realized, for the insidious murmur was coiling again through his brain, promising, caressing, alluring, sweeter than honey; and the green eyes that held his were clear and burning like the depths of a jewel, and behind the pulsing slits of darkness he was staring into a greater dark that held all things. . . . He had known—dimly he had known when he first gazed into those flat animal shallows that behind them lay this—all beauty and terror, all horror and delight, in the infinite darkness upon which her eyes opened like windows, paned with emerald glass.

Her lips moved, and in a murmur that blended indistinguishably with the silence and the sway of her body and the dreadful sway of her—her hair—she whispered—very softly, very passionately, "I shall—speak to you now—in my own tongue—oh, beloved!"

And in her living cloak she swayed to him, the murmur swelling seductive and caressing in his innermost brain—promising, compelling, sweeter than sweet. His flesh crawled to the horror of her, but it was a perverted revulsion that clasped what it loathed. His arms slid round her under the sliding cloak, wet, wet and warm and hideously alive—and the sweet velvet body was clinging to his, her arms locked about his neck—and with a whisper and a rush the unspeakable horror closed about them both.

In nightmares until he died he remembered that moment when the living tresses of Shambleau first folded him in their embrace. A nauseous, smothering odor as the wetness shut around him—thick, pulsing worms clasping every inch of his body, sliding, writhing, their wetness and warmth striking through his garments as if he stood naked to their embrace.

All this in a graven instant—and after that a tangled flash of conflicting sensation before oblivion closed over him for he remembered the dream—and knew it for nightmare reality now, and the sliding, gently moving caresses of those wet, warm worms upon his flesh was an ecstasy above words—that deeper ecstasy that strikes beyond the body and beyond the mind and tickles the very roots of soul with unnatural delight. So he stood, rigid as marble, as helplessly stony as any of Medusa's victims in ancient legends were, while the terrible pleasure of Shambleau thrilled and shuddered through every fiber of him; through every atom of his body and the intangible atoms of what men call the soul, through all that was Smith the dreadful pleasure ran. And it was truly dreadful. Dimly he knew it, even as his body answered to the root-deep ecstasy, a foul and dreadful wooing from which his very soul shuddered away—and yet in the innermost depths of that soul some grinning traitor shivered with delight. But deeply, behind all this, he knew horror and revulsion and despair beyond telling, while the intimate caresses crawled obscenely in the secret places of his soul—knew that the soul should not be handled—and shook with the perilous pleasure through it all.

And this conflict and knowledge, this mingling of rapture and revulsion all took place in the flashing of a moment while the scarlet worms coiled and crawled upon him, sending deep, obscene tremors of that infinite pleasure into every atom that made up Smith. And he could not stir in that slimy, ecstatic embrace—and a weakness was flooding that grew deeper after each succeeding wave of intense delight, and the traitor in his soul strengthened and drowned out the revulsion—and something within him ceased to struggle as he sank wholly into a blazing darkness that was oblivion to all else but that devouring rapture. . . .

The young Venusian climbing the stairs to his friend's lodging-room pulled out his key absent-mindedly, a pucker forming between his fine brows. He was slim, as all Venusians are, as fair and sleek as any of them, and as with most of his countrymen the look of cherubic innocence on his face was wholly deceptive. He had the face of a fallen angel, without Lucifer's majesty to redeem it; for a black devil grinned in his eyes and there were faint lines of ruthlessness and dissipation about his mouth to tell of the long years behind him that had run the gamut of experiences and made his name, next to Smith's, the most hated and the most respected in the records of the Patrol.

He mounted the stairs now with a puzzled frown between his eyes. He had come into Lakkdarol on the noon liner—the *Maid* in her hold very skillfully disguised with paint and otherwise—to find in lamentable disorder the affairs he had expected to be settled. And cautious inquiry elicited the information that Smith had not been seen for three days. That was not like his friend—he had never failed before, and the two stood to lose not only a large sum of money but also their personal safety by the inexplicable lapse on the part of Smith. Yarol could think of one solution only: fate had at last caught up with his friend. Nothing but physical disability could explain it.

Still puzzling, he fitted his key in the lock and swung the door open.

In that first moment, as the door opened, he sensed something very wrong. . . . The room was darkened, and for a while he could see nothing, but at the first breath he scented a strange, unnamable odor, half sickening, half sweet. And deep stirrings of ancestral memory awoke within him—ancient swamp-born memories from Venusian ancestors far away and long ago. . . .

Yarol laid his hand on his gun, lightly, and opened the door wider. In the dimness all he could see at first was a curious mound in the far corner. . . . Then his eyes grew accustomed to the dark, and he saw it more clearly, a mound that somehow heaved and stirred within itself. . . . A mound of—he caught his breath sharply—a mound like a mass of entrails, living, moving, writhing with an unspeakable aliveness. Then a hot Venusian oath broke from his lips and he cleared the door-sill in a swift stride, slammed the door and set his back against it, gun ready in his hand, although his flesh crawled—for he *knew*. . . .

"Smith!" he said softly, in a voice thick with horror.

The moving mass stirred—shuddered—sank back into crawling quiescence again.

"Smith! Smith!" The Venusian's voice was gentle and insistent, and it quivered a little with terror.

An impatient ripple went over the whole mass of aliveness in the corner. It stirred again, reluctantly, and then tendril by writhing tendril it began to part itself and fall aside, and very slowly the brown of a spaceman's leather appeared beneath it, all slimed and shining.

"Smith! Northwest!" Yarol's persistent whisper came again, urgently, and with a dream-like slowness the leather garments moved . . . a man sat up in the midst of the writhing worms, a man who once, long ago, might have been Northwest Smith. From head to foot he was slimy from the embrace of the crawling horror about him. His face was that of some creature beyond humanity—dead-alive, fixed in a gray stare, and the look of terrible ecstasy that overspread it seemed to come from somewhere far within, a faint reflection from immeasurable distances beyond the flesh. And as there is mystery and magic in the moonlight which is after all but a reflection of the everyday sun, so in that gray face turned to the door was a terror unnamable and sweet, a reflection of ecstasy beyond the understanding of any who have known only earthly ecstasy themselves. And as he sat there turning a blank, eyeless face to Yarol the red worms writhed ceaselessly about him, very gently, with a soft, caressive motion that never slacked.

"Smith . . . come here! Smith . . . get up . . . Smith, Smith!" Yarol's whisper hissed in the silence, commanding, urgent—but he made no move to leave the door.

And with a dreadful slowness, like a dead man rising, Smith stood up in the nest of slimy scarlet. He swayed drunkenly on his feet, and two or three crimson tendrils came writhing up his legs to the knees and wound themselves there, supportingly, moving with a ceaseless caress that seemed to give him some hidden strength, for he said then, without inflection.

"Go away. Go away. Leave me alone." And the dead ecstatic face never changed.

"Smith!" Yarol's voice was desperate. "Smith, listen! Smith, can't you hear me?"

"Go away," the monotonous voice said. "Go away. Go away. Go—"

"Not unless you come too. Can't you hear? Smith! Smith! I'll—"

He hushed in mid-phrase, and once more the ancestral prickle of race-memory shivered down his back, for the scarlet mass was moving again, violently, rising. . . .

Yarol pressed back against the door and gripped his gun, and the name of a god he had forgotten years ago rose to his lips unbidden. For he knew what was coming next, and the knowledge was more dreadful than any ignorance could have been.

The red, writhing mass rose higher, and the tendrils parted and a human face looked out—no, half human, with green cat-eyes that shone in that dimness like lighted jewels, compellingly. . . .

Yarol breathed "Shar!" again, and flung up an arm across his face, and the tingle of meeting that green gaze for even an instant went thrilling through him perilously.

"Smith!" he called in despair. "Smith, can't you hear me?"

"Go away," said that voice that was not Smith's. "Go away."

And somehow, although he dared not look, Yarol knew that the—the other—had parted those worm-thick tresses and stood there in all the human sweetness of the brown, curved woman's body, cloaked in living horror. And he felt the eyes upon him, and something was crying insistently in his brain to lower that shielding arm. . . . He was lost—he knew it, and the knowledge gave him that courage which comes from despair. The voice in his brain was growing, swelling, deafening him with a roaring command that all but swept him before it—command to lower that arm—to meet the eyes that opened upon darkness—to submit—and a promise, murmurous and sweet and evil beyond words, of pleasure to come. . . .

But somehow he kept his head—somehow, dizzily, he was gripping his gun in his upflung hand—somehow, incredibly, crossing the narrow room with averted face, groping for Smith's shoulder. There was a moment of blind fumbling in emptiness, and then he found it, and gripped the leather that was slimy and dreadful and wet—and simultaneously he felt something loop gently about his ankle and a shock of repulsive pleasure went through him, and then another coil, and another, wound about his feet. . . .

Yarol set his teeth and gripped the shoulder hard, and his hand shuddered of itself, for the feel of that leather was slimy as the worms about his ankles, and a faint tingle of obscene delight went through him from the contact.

That caressive pressure on his legs was all he could feel, and the voice in his brain drowned out all other sounds, and his body obeyed him reluctantly—but somehow he gave one heave of tremendous effort and swung Smith, stumbling, out of that nest of horror. The twining tendrils ripped loose with a little sucking sound, and the whole mass quivered and reached after, and then Yarol forgot his friend utterly and turned his whole being to the hopeless task of freeing himself. For only a part of him was fighting, now—only a part of him struggled against the twining obscenities, and in his innermost brain the sweet, seductive murmur sounded, and his body clamored to surrender. . . .

"Shar! Shar y'danis . . . Shar mor'la-rol–" prayed Yarol, gasping and half unconscious that he spoke, boy's prayers that he had forgotten years ago, and with his back half turned to the central mass he kicked desperately with his heavy boots at the red, writhing worms about him. They gave back before him, quivering and curling themselves out of reach, and though he knew that more were reaching for his throat from behind, at least he could go on struggling until he was forced to meet those eyes. . . .

He stamped and kicked and stamped again, and for one instant he was free of the slimy grip as the bruised worms curled back from his heavy feet, and he lurched away dizzily, sick with revulsion and despair as he fought off the coils, and then he lifted his eyes and saw the cracked mirror on the wall. Dimly in its reflection he could see the writhing scarlet horror behind him, cat face peering out with its demure girl-smile, dreadfully human, and all the red tendrils reaching after him. And remembrance of something he had read long ago swept incongruously over him, and the gasp of relief and hope that he gave shook for a moment the grip of the command in his brain.

Without pausing for a breath he swung the gun over his shoulder, the reflected barrel in line with the reflected horror in the mirror, and flicked the catch.

In the mirror he saw its blue flame leap in a dazzling spate across the dimness, full into the midst of that squirming, reaching mass behind him. There was a hiss and a blaze and a high, thin scream of inhuman malice and despair—the flame cut a wide arc and went out as the gun fell from his hand, and Yarol pitched forward to the floor.

Northwest Smith opened his eyes to Martian sunlight streaming thinly through the dingy window. Something wet and cold was slapping his face, and the familiar fiery sting of *segir*-whisky burnt his throat.

"Smith!" Yarol's voice was saying from far away. "N.W.! Wake up, damn you! Wake up!"

"I'm—awake," Smith managed to articulate thickly. "Wha's matter?"

Then a cup-rim was thrust against his teeth and Yarol said irritably, "Drink it, you fool!"

Smith swallowed obediently and more of the fire-hot *segir* flowed down his grateful throat. It spread a warmth through his body that awakened him from the numbness that had gripped him until now, and helped a little toward driving out the all-devouring weakness he was becoming aware of slowly. He lay still for a few minutes while the warmth of the whisky went through him, and memory sluggishly began to permeate his brain with the spread of the *segir*. Nightmare memories . . . sweet and terrible . . . memories of—

"God!" gasped Smith suddenly, and tried to sit up. Weakness smote him like a blow, and for an instant the room wheeled as he fell back against something firm and warm—Yarol's shoulder. The Venusian's arm supported him while the room steadied, and after a while he twisted a little and stared into the other's black gaze.

Yarol was holding him with one arm and finishing the mug of *segir* himself, and the black eyes met his over the rim and crinkled into sudden laughter, half hysterical after that terror that was passed.

"By *Pharol!*" gasped Yarol, choking into his mug. "By *Pharol*, N.W.! I'm never gonna let you forget this! Next time you have to drag me out of a mess I'll say—"

"Let it go," said Smith. "What's been going on? How—"

"Shambleau," Yarol's laughter died. "Shambleau! What were you doing with a thing like that?"

"What was it?" Smith asked soberly.

"Mean to say you didn't know? But where'd you find it? How—"

"Suppose you tell me first what you know," said Smith firmly. "And another swig of that *segir*, too. I need it."

"Can you hold the mug now? Feel better?"

"Yeah—some. I can hold it—thanks. Now go on."

"Well—I don't know just where to start. They call them Shambleau—"

"Good God, is there more than one?"

"It's a—a sort of race, I think, one of the very oldest. Where they come from nobody knows. The name sounds a little French, doesn't it? But it goes back beyond the start of history. There have always been Shambleau."

"I never heard of 'em."

"Not many people have. And those who know don't care to talk about it much."

"Well, half this town knows. I hadn't any idea what they were talking about, then. And I still don't understand,—"

"Yes, it happens like this, sometimes. They'll appear, and the news will spread and the town will get together and hunt them down, and after that—well, the story doesn't get around very far. It's too—too unbelievable."

"But—my God, Yarol!—what was it? Where'd it come from? How—"

"Nobody knows just where they come from. Another

planet—maybe some undiscovered one. Some say Venus—I know there are some rather awful legends of them handed down in our family—that's how I've heard about it. And the minute I opened that door, awhile back—I—I think I knew that smell. . . ."

"But—what *are* they?"

"God knows. Not human, though they have the human form. Or that may be only an illusion . . . or maybe I'm crazy. I don't know. They're a species of the vampire—or maybe the vampire is a species of—of them. Their normal form must be that—that mass, and in that form they draw nourishment from the—I suppose the life-forces of men. And they take some form—usually a woman form, I think, and key you up to the highest pitch of emotion before they—begin. That's to work the life-force up to intensity so it'll be easier. . . . And they give, always, that horrible, foul pleasure as they—feed. There are some men who, if they survive the first experience, take to it like a drug—can't give it up—keep the thing with them all their lives—which isn't long—feeding it for that ghastly satisfaction. Worse than smoking *ming* or—or 'praying to *Pharol*.' "

"Yes," said Smith. "I'm beginning to understand why that crowd was so surprised and—and disgusted when I said—well, never mind. Go on."

"Did you get to talk to—to it?" asked Yarol.

"I tried to. It couldn't speak very well. I asked it where it came from and it said—'from far away and long ago'—something like that."

"I wonder. Possibly some unknown planet—but I think not. You know there are so many wild stories with some basis of fact to start from, that I've sometimes wondered—mightn't there be a lot more of even worse and wilder superstitions we've never even heard of? Things like this, blasphemous and foul, that those who know have to keep still about? Awful, fantastic things running around loose that we never hear rumors of at all!

"These things—they've been in existence for countless

ages. No one knows when or where they first appeared. Those who've seen them, as we saw this one, don't talk about it. It's just one of those vague, misty rumors you find half hinted at in old books sometimes. . . . I believe they are an older race than man, spawned from ancient seed in times before ours, perhaps on planets that have gone to dust, and so horrible to man that when they are discovered the discoverers keep still about it—forget them again as quickly as they can.

"And they go back to time immemorial. I suppose you recognized the legend of Medusa? There isn't any question that the ancient Greeks knew of them. Does it mean that there have been civilizations before yours that set out from Earth and explored other planets? Or did one of the Shambleau somehow make its way into Greece three thousand years ago? If you think about it long enough you'll go off your head! I wonder how many other legends are based on things like this—things we don't suspect, things we'll never know.

"The Gorgon, Medusa, a beautiful woman with—with snakes for hair, and a gaze that turned men to stone, and Perseus finally killed her—I remembered this just by accident, N.W., and it saved your life and mine—Perseus killed her by using a mirror as he fought to reflect what he dared not look at directly. I wonder what the old Greek who first started that legend would have thought if he'd known that three thousand years later his story would save the lives of two men on another planet. I wonder what that Greek's own story was, and how he met the thing, and what happened. . . .

"Well, there's a lot we'll never know. Wouldn't the records of that race of—of *things,* whatever they are, be worth reading! Records of other planets and other ages and all the beginnings of mankind! But I don't suppose they've kept any records. I don't suppose they've even any place to keep them—from what little I know, or anyone knows about it, they're like the Wandering Jew, just bobbing up here and there at long intervals, and where they stay in the meantime I'd give my eyes to know! But I don't believe that terribly hypnotic power they have indicates any superhuman intelligence. It's their means of getting food—just like a frog's long tongue or a carnivorous flower's odor. Those are physical because the frog and the flower eat physical food. The Shambleau uses a—a mental reach to get mental food. I don't quite know how to put it. And just as a beast that eats the bodies of other animals acquires with each meal greater power over the bodies of the rest, so the Shambleau, stoking itself up with the life-forces of men, increases its power over the minds and the souls of other men. But I'm talking about things I can't define—things I'm not sure exist.

"I only know that when I felt—when those tentacles closed around my legs—I didn't want to pull loose, I felt sensations that—that—oh, I'm fouled and filthy to the very deepest part of me by that—pleasure—and yet—"

"I know," said Smith slowly. The effect of the *segir* was beginning to wear off, and weakness was washing back over him in waves, and when he spoke he was half meditating in a low voice, scarcely realizing that Yarol listened. "I know it—much better than you do—and there's something so indescribably awful that the thing emanates, something so utterly at odds with everything human—there aren't any words to say it. For a while I was a part of it, literally, sharing its thoughts and memories and emotions and hungers, and—well, it's over now and I don't remember very clearly, but the only part left free was that part of me that was all but insane from the—the obscenity of the thing. And yet it was a pleasure so sweet—I think there must be some nucleus of utter evil in me—in everyone—that needs only the proper stimulus to get complete control; because even while I was sick all through from the touch of those—things—there was something in me that was—was simply gibbering with delight. . . . Because of that I saw things—and knew things—horrible, wild things I can't quite remember—visited unbelievable places, looked backward through the memory of that—creature—I was one with, and saw—God, I wish I could remember!"

"You ought to thank your God you can't," said Yarol soberly.

• • •

His voice roused Smith from the half-trance he had fallen into, and he rose on his elbow, swaying a little from weakness. The room was wavering before him, and he closed his eyes, not to see it, but he asked, "You say they—they don't turn up again? No way of finding—another?"

Yarol did not answer for a moment. He laid his hands on the other man's shoulders and pressed him back, and then sat staring down into the dark, ravaged face with a new, strange, undefinable look upon it that he had never seen there before—whose meaning he knew, too well.

"Smith," he said finally, and his black eyes for once were steady and serious, and the little grinning devil had vanished from behind them, "Smith, I've never asked your word on anything before, but I've—I've earned the right to do it now, and I'm asking you to promise me one thing."

Smith's colorless eyes met the black gaze unsteadily. Irresolution was in them, and a little far of what that promise might be. And for just a moment Yarol was looking, not into his friend's familiar eyes, but into a wide gray blankness that held all horror and delight—a pale sea with unspeakable pleasures sunk beneath it. Then the wide stare focused again and Smith's eyes met his squarely and Smith's voice said, "Go ahead. I'll promise."

"That if you ever should meet a Shambleau again—ever, anywhere—you'll draw your gun and burn it to hell the instant you realize what it is. Will you promise me that?"

There was a long silence. Yarol's somber black eyes bored relentlessly into the colorless ones of Smith, not wavering. And the veins stood out on Smith's tanned forehead. He never broke his word—he had given it perhaps half a dozen times in his life, but once he had given it, he was incapable of breaking it. And once more the gray seas flooded in a dim tide of memories, sweet and horrible beyond dreams. Once more Yarol was staring into blankness that hid nameless things. The room was very still.

The gray tide ebbed. Smith's eyes, pale and resolute as steel, met Yarol's levelly.

"I'll—try," he said. And his voice wavered.

BLACK THIRST

Northwest Smith leant his head back against the warehouse wall and stared up into the black night-sky of Venus. The waterfront street was very quiet tonight, very dangerous. He could hear no sound save the eternal slap-slap of water against the piles, but he knew how much of danger and sudden death dwelt here voiceless in the breathing dark, and he may have been a little homesick as he stared up into the clouds that masked a green star hanging lovely on the horizon—Earth and home. And if he thought of that he must have grinned wryly to himself in the dark, for Northwest Smith had no home, and Earth would not have welcomed him very kindly just then.

He sat quietly in the dark. Above him in the warehouse wall a faintly lighted window threw a square of pallor upon the wet street. Smith drew back into his angle of darkness under the slanting shaft, hugging one knee. And presently he heard footsteps softly on the street.

He may have been expecting footsteps, for he turned his head alertly and listened, but it was not a man's feet that came so lightly over the wooden quay, and Smith's brow furrowed. A woman, here, on this black waterfront by night? Not even the lowest class of Venusian street-walker dared come along the waterfronts of Ednes on the nights when the space-liners were not in. Yet across the pavement came clearly now the light tapping of a woman's feet.

Smith drew farther back into the shadows and waited. And presently she came, a darkness in the dark save for the triangular patch of pallor that was her face. As she passed under the light falling dimly from the window overhead he understood suddenly how she dared walk here and who she was. A long black cloak hid her, but the light fell upon her face, heart-shaped under the little three-cornered velvet cap that Venusian women wear, fell on ripples of half-hidden bronze hair; and by that sweet triangular face and shining hair he knew her for one of the Minga maids—those beauties that from the beginning of history have been bred in the Minga stronghold for loveliness and grace, as race-horses are bred on Earth, and reared from earliest infancy in the art of charming men. Scarcely a court on the three planets lacks at least one of these exquisite creatures, long-limbed, milk-white, with their bronze hair and lovely brazen faces—if the lord of that court has the wealth to buy them. Kings from many nations and races have poured their riches into the Minga gateway, and girls like pure gold and ivory have gone forth to grace a thousand palaces, and this has been so since Ednes first rose on the shore of the Greater Sea.

This girl walked here unafraid and unharmed because she wore the beauty that marked her for what she was. The heavy hand of the Minga stretched out protectingly over her bronze head, and not a man along the wharf-fronts but knew what dreadful penalties would overtake him if he dared so much as to lay a finger on the milk-whiteness of a Minga maid—terrible penalties, such as men whisper of fearfully over *segir*-whisky mugs in the waterfront dives of many nations—mysterious, unnamable penalties more dreadful than any knife or gun-flash could inflict.

And these dangers, too, guarded the gates of the Minga castle. The chastity of the Minga girls was proverbial, a trade boast. This girl walked in peace and safety more sure than that attending the steps of a nun through slum streets by night on Earth.

But even so, the girl went forth very rarely from the gates of the castle, never unattended. Smith had never seen one before, save at a distance. He shifted a little now, to catch a better glimpse as she went by, to look for the escort that must surely walk a pace or two behind, though he heard no footsteps save her own. The slight motion caught her eye. She stopped. She peered closer into the dark, and said in a voice as sweet and smooth as cream.

"How would you like to earn a goldpiece, my man?"

A flash of perversity twisted Smith's reply out of its usual slovenly dialect, and he said in his most cultured voice, in his most perfect High Venusian,

"Thank you, no."

For a moment the woman stood quite still, peering through the darkness in a vain effort to reach his face. He could see her own, a pale oval in the window light, intent, surprised. Then she flung back her cloak and the dim light glinted on the case of a pocket flash as she flicked the catch. A beam of white radiance fell blindingly upon his face.

For an instant the light held him—lounging against the wall in his spaceman's leather, the burns upon it, the tatters, ray-gun in its holster low on his thigh, and the brown scarred face turned to hers, eyes the colorless color of pale steel narrowed to the glare. It was a typical face. It belonged here, on the waterfront, in these dark and dangerous streets. It belonged to the type that frequents such places, those lawless men who ride the spaceways and live by the rule of the ray-gun, recklessly, warily outside the Parol's jurisdiction. But there was more than that in the scarred brown face turned to the light. She must have seen it as she held the flash unwavering, some deep-buried trace of breeding and birth that made the cultured accents of the High Venusian not incongruous. And the colorless eyes derided her.

"No," she said, flicking off the light. "Not one goldpiece, but a hundred. And for another task that I meant."

"Thank you," said Smith, not rising. "You must excuse me."

"Five hundred," she said without a flicker of emotion in her creamy voice.

In the dark Smith's brows knit. There was something fantastic in the situation. Why—?

She must have sensed his reaction almost as he realized it himself, for she said.

"Yes, I know. It sounds insane. You see—I knew you in the light just now. Will you?—can you?—I can't explain here on the street. . . ."

Smith held the silence unbroken for thirty seconds, while a lightning debate flashed through the recesses of his wary mind. Then he grinned to himself in the dark and said,

"I'll come." Belatedly he got to his feet. "Where?"

"The Palace Road on the edge of the Minga. Third door from the central gate, to the left. Say to the door-warden—'Vaudir.' "

"That is—?"

"Yes, my name. You will come, in half an hour?"

An instant longer Smith's mind hovered on the verge of refusal. Then he shrugged.

"Yes."

"At the third bell, then." She made the little Venusian gesture of parting and wrapped her cloak about her. The blackness of it, and the softness of her footfalls, made her seem to melt into the darkness without a sound, but Smith's trained ears heard her footsteps very softly on the pavement as she went on into the dark.

He sat there until he could no longer detect any faintest sound of feet on the wharf. He waited patiently, but his mind was a little dizzy with surprise. Was the traditional inviolability of the Minga a fraud? Were the close-guarded girls actually allowed sometimes to walk unattended by night, making assignations as they pleased? Or was it some elaborate hoax? Tradition for countless centuries had declared the gates in the Minga wall to be guarded so relentlessly by strange dangers that not even a mouse could slip through without the knowledge of the Alendar, the Minga's lord. Was it then by order of the Alendar that the door would open to him when he whispered "Vaudir" to the warden? Or would it open? Was the girl perhaps the property of some Ednes lord, deceiving him for obscure purposes of her own? He shook his head a little and grinned to himself. After all, time would tell.

He waited a while longer in the dark. Little waves lapped the piles with sucking sounds, and once the sky lit up with the long, blinding roar of a space-ship splitting the dark.

At last he rose and stretched his long body as if he had been sitting there for a good while. Then he settled the gun on his leg and set off down the black street. He walked very lightly in his spaceman's boots.

A twenty-minute walk through dark byways, still and deserted, brought him to the outskirts of that vast city-within-a-city called the Minga. The dark, rough walls of it towered over him, green with the lichen-like growths of the Hot Planet. On the Palace Road one deeply-sunk central gateway opened upon the mysteries within. A tiny blue light burned over the arch. Smith went softly through the dimness to the left of it, counting two tiny doors half hidden in deep recesses. At the third he paused. It was painted a rusty green, and a green vine spilling down the wall half veiled it, so that if he had not been searching he would have passed it by.

Smith stood for a long minute, motionless, staring at the green panels deep-sunk in rock. He listened. He even sniffed the heavy air. Warily as a wild beast he hesitated in the dark. But at last he lifted his hand and tapped very lightly with his fingertips on the green door.

It swung open without a sound. Pitch-blackness confronted him, an archway of blank dark in the dimly seen stone wall. And a voice queried softly, *"Qu'a lo' val?"*

"Vaudir," murmured Smith, and grinned to himself involuntarily. How many romantic youths must have stood at these doors in nights gone by, breathing hopefully the names of bronze beauties to doormen in dark archways! But unless tradition lied, no man before had ever passed. He must be the first in many years to stand here invited at a little doorway in the Minga wall and hear the watchman murmur, "Come."

Smith loosened the gun at his side and bent his tall head under the arch. He stepped into blackness that closed about him like water as the door swung shut. He stood there with quickened heart-beats, hand on his gun, listening. A blue light, dim and ghostly, flooded the place without warning and he saw the doorman had crossed to a switch at the far side of the tiny chamber wherein he stood. The man was one of the Minga eunuchs, a flabby creature, splendid in crimson velvet. He carried a cloak of purple over his arm, and made a splash of royal colors in the dimness. His sidelong eyes regarded Smith from under lifted brows, with a look that the Earthman could not fathom. There was amusement in it, and a touch of terror and a certain reluctant admiration.

Smith looked about him in frank curiosity. The little entry was apparently hollowed out of the enormously thick wall itself. The only thing that broke its bareness was the ornate bronze door set in the far wall. His eyes sought the eunuch's in mute inquiry.

The creature came forward obsequiously, murmuring, "Permit me—" and flung the purple cloak he carried over Smith's shoulders. Its luxurious folds, faintly fragrant, swept about him like a caress. It covered him, tall as he was, to the very boot-soles. He drew back in faint distaste as the eunuch lifted his hands to fasten the jeweled clasp at his throat. "Please to draw up the hood also," murmured the creature without apparent resentment, as Smith snapped the fastening himself. The hood covered his sun-bleached hair and fell in thick folds about his face, casting it into deep shadow.

The eunuch opened the bronze inner door and Smith stared down a long hallway curving almost imperceptibly to the right. The paradox of elaborately decorated simplicity was illustrated in every broad polished panel of the wall, so intricately and exquisitely carved that it gave at first the impression of a strange, rich plainness.

His booted feet sank sensuously into the deep pile of the carpet at every step as he followed the eunuch down the hall. Twice he heard voices murmuring behind lighted doors, and his hand lay on the butt of the ray-gun under the folds of his robe, but no door opened and the hall lay empty and dim before them. So far it had been amazingly easy. Either tradition lied about the impregnability of the Minga, or the girl Vaudir had bribed with incredible lavishness or—that thought again, uneasily—it was with the Alendar's consent that he walked here unchallenged. But why?

They came to a door of silver grille at the end of the curved corridor, and passed through it into another hallway slanting up, as exquisitely voluptuous as the first. A flight of stairs wrought from dully gleaming bronze curved at the end of it. Then came another hall lighted with rosy lanterns that swung from the arched ceiling, and beyond another stairway, this time of silvery metal fretwork, spiraling down again.

And in all that distance they met no living creature. Voices hummed behind closed doors, and once or twice strains of music drifted faintly to Smith's ears, but either the corridors had been cleared by a special order, or incredible luck was attending them. And he had the uncomfortable sensation of eyes upon his back more than once. They passed dark hallways and open, unlighted doors, and sometimes the hair on his neck bristled with the feeling of human nearness, inimical, watching.

For all of twenty minutes they walked through curved corridors and up and down spiral stairs until even Smith's keen senses were confused and he could not have said at what height above the ground he was, or in what direction the corridor led into which they at last emerged. At the end of that time his nerves were tense as steel wire and he restrained himself only by force from nervous, over-the-shoulder glances each time they passed an open door. An air of languorous menace brooded almost visibly over the place, he thought. The sound of soft voices behind doors, the feel of eyes, of whispers in the air, the memory of tales half heard in waterfront dives about the secrets of the Minga, the nameless dangers of the Minga. . . .

Smith gripped his gun as he walked through the splendor and the dimness, every sense assailed by voluptuous appeals, but his nerves strained to wire and his flesh crawled as he passed unlighted doors. This was too easy. For so many centuries the tradition of the Minga had been upheld, a byword of impregnability, a stronghold guarded by more than swords, by greater dangers than the ray-gun—and yet here he walked, unquestioned, into the deepest heart of the place, his only disguise a velvet cloak, his only weapon a holstered gun, and no one challenged him, no guards, no slaves, not even a passer-by to note that a man taller than any dweller here should be strode unquestioned through the innermost corridors of the inviolable Minga. He loosened the ray-gun in its sheath.

The eunuch in his scarlet velvet went on confidently ahead. Only once did he falter. They had reached a dark passageway, and just as they came opposite its mouth the sound of a soft, slithering scrape, as of something over stones, draggingly, reached their ears. He saw the eunuch start and half glance back, and then hurry on at a quicker pace, nor did he slacken until they had put two gates and a length of lighted corridor between them and that dark passage.

So they went on, through halls half lighted, through scented air and empty dimness where the doorways closed upon murmurous mysteries within or opened to dark and the feel of watching eyes. And they came at last, after endless, winding progress, into a hallway low-ceilinged and paneled in mother-of-pearl, pierced and filigreed with carving, and all the doors were of silver grille. And as the eunuch pushed open the silver gate that led into this corridor the thing happened that his taut nerves had been expected ever since the start of the fantastic journey. One of the doors opened and a figure stepped out and faced them.

Under the robe Smith's gun slid soundlessly from its holster. He thought he saw the eunuch's back stiffen a little, and his step falter, but only for an instant. It was a girl who had come out, a slave-girl in a single white garment, and at the first glimpse of the tall, purple-robed figure with hooded face, towering over her, she gave a little gasp and slumped to her knees as if under a blow. It was obeisance, but so shocked and terrified that it might have been a faint. She laid her face to the very carpet, and Smith, looking down in amazement on the prostrate figure, saw that she was trembling violently.

The gun slid back into its sheath and he paused for a moment over her shuddering homage. The eunuch twisted round to beckon with soundless violence, and Smith caught a glimpse of his face for the first time since their journey began. It was glistening with sweat, and the sidelong eyes were bright and shifting, like a hunted animal's. Smith was oddly reassured by the sight of the eunuch's obvious panic. There was danger then—danger of discovery, the sort of peril he knew and could fight. It was that creeping sensation of eyes watching, of unseen things slithering down dark passages, that had strained his nerves to painfully. And yet, even so, it had been too easy. . . .

The eunuch had paused at a silver door half-way down the hall and was murmuring something very softly, his mouth against the grille. A panel of green brocade was stretched across the silver door on the inside, so they could see nothing within the room, but after a moment a voice said, "Good!" in a breathing whisper, and the door quivered a little and swung open six inches. The eunuch genuflected in a swirl of scarlet robes, and Smith caught his eye swiftly, the look of terror not yet faded, but amusement there too, and a certain respect. And then the door opened wider and he stepped inside.

He stepped into a room green as a sea-cave. The walls were paneled in green brocade, low green couches circled the room, and, in the center, the blazing bronze beauty of the girl Vaudir. She wore a robe of green velvet cut in the startling Venusian fashion to loop over one shoulder and swathe her body in tight, molten folds, and the skirt of it was slit up one side so that at every other motion the long white leg flashed bare.

He saw her for the first time in a full light, and she was lovely beyond belief with her bronze hair cloudy on her shoulders and the pale, lazy face smiling. Under deep lashes the sidelong black eyes of her race met his.

He jerked impatiently at the hampering hood of the cloak. "May I take this off?" he said. "Are we safe here?"

She laughed with a short, metallic sound. "Safe!" she said ironically. "But take it off if you must. I've gone too far now to stop at trifles."

And as the rich folds parted and slid away from his leather brownness she in turn stared in quickened interest at what she had seen only in a half-light before. He was almost laughably incongruous in this jewel-box room, all leather and sunburn and his scarred face keen and wary in the light of the lantern swinging from its silver chain. She looked a second time at that face, its lean, leathery keenness and the scars that ray-guns had left, and the mark of knife and talon, and the tracks of wild years along the spaceways. Wariness and resolution were instinct in that face, there was ruthlessness in every line of it, and when she met his eyes a little shock went over her. Pale, pale as bared steel, colorless in the sunburnt face. Steady and clear and no-colored, expressionless as water. Killer's eyes.

And she knew that this was the man she needed. The name and fame of Northwest Smith had penetrated even into these mother-of-pearl Minga halls. In its way it had spread into stranger places than this, by strange and devious paths and for strange, devious reasons. But even had she never heard the name (nor the deed she connected it with, which does not matter here), she would have known from this scarred face, these cold and steady eyes, that here stood the man she wanted, the man who could help her if any man alive could.

And with that thought, others akin to it flashed through her mind like blades crossing, and she dropped her milkwhite lids over the sword-play to hide its deadliness, and said, "Northwest . . . Smith," in a musing murmur.

"To be commanded," said Smith in the idiom of her own tongue, but a spark of derision burned behind the courtly words.

Still she said nothing, but looked him up and down with slow eyes. He said at last.

"Your desire—?" and shifted impatiently.

"I had need of a wharfman's services," she said, still in that breathing whisper. "I had not seen you, then. . . . There are many wharfmen along the seafront, but only one of you, oh man of Earth—" and she lifted her arms and swayed toward him exactly as a reed sways to a lake breeze, and her arms lay lightly on his shoulders and her mouth was very near. . . .

Smith looked down into the veiled eyes. He knew enough of the breed of Venus to guess the deadly swordflash of motive behind anything a Venusian does, and he had caught a glimpse of that particular sword-flash before she lowered her lids. And if her thoughts were sword-play, his burnt like heat-beams straight to their purpose. In the winking of an eye he knew a part of her motive—the most obvious part. And he stood there unanswering in the circle of her arms.

She looked up at him, half incredulous not to feel a leather embrace tighten about her.

"*Qu'a lo'val?*" she murmured whimsically. "So cold, then, Earthman? Am I not desirable?"

Wordlessly he looked down at her, and despite himself the blood quickened in him. Minga girls for too many centuries had been born and bred to the art of charming men for Northwest Smith to stand here in the warm arms of one and feel no answer to the invitation in her eyes. A subtle fragrance rose from her brazen hair, and the velvet molded a body whose whiteness he could guess from the flash of the long bare thigh her slashed skirt showed. He grinned a little crookedly and stepped away, breaking the clasp of her hands behind his neck.

"No," he said. "You know your art well, my dear, but your motive does not flatter me."

She stood back and regarded him with a wry, half-appreciative smile.

"What do you mean?"

"I'll have to know much more about all this before I commit myself as far as—that."

"You fool," she smiled. "You're in over your head now, as deeply as you could ever be. You were the moment you crossed the door-sill at the outer wall. There is no drawing back."

"Yet it was so easy—so very easy, to come in," murmured Smith.

She came forward a step and looked up at him with narrowed eyes, the pretense of seduction dropped like a cloak.

"You saw that, too?" she queried in a half-whisper. "It seemed so—to you? Great Shar, if I could be *sure*. . . ." And there was terror in her face.

"Suppose we sit down and you tell me about it," suggested Smith practically.

She laid a hand—white as cream, soft as satin—on his arm and drew him to the low divan that circled the room. There was inbred, generations-old coquetry in the touch, but the white hand shook a little.

"What is it you fear so?" queried Smith curiously as they sank to the green velvet. "Death comes only once, you know."

She shook her bronze head contemptuously.

"Not that," she aid. "At least—no, I wish I knew just what it is I do fear—and that is the most dreadful part of it. But I wish—I wish it had not been so easy to get you here."

"The place was deserted," he said thoughtfully. "Not a soul along the halls. Not a guard anywhere. Only once did we see any other creature, and that was a slave-girl in the hall jut outside your door."

"What did she—do?" Vaudir's voice was breathless.

"Dropped to her knees as if she'd been shot. You might have thought me the devil himself by the way she acted."

The girl's breath escaped in a sigh.

"Safe, then," she said thankfully. "She must have thought you the—the Alendar." Her voice faltered a little over the name, as if she half feared to pronounce it. "He wears a cloak like that you wore when he comes through the halls. But he comes so very seldom. . . ."

"I've never seen him," said Smith, "but, good Lord, is he such a monster? The girl dropped as if she'd been hamstrung."

"Oh, hush, hush!" Vaudir agonized. "You mustn't speak of him so. He's—he's—of course she knelt and hid her face. I wish to heaven I had. . . ."

Smith faced her squarely and searched the veiled dark eyes with a gaze as bleak as empty seas. And he saw very clearly behind the veils the stark, nameless terror at their depths.

"What is it?" he demanded.

She drew her shoulders together and shivered a little, and her eyes were furtive as she glanced around the room.

"Don't you feel it?" she asked in that half-whisper to which her voice sank so caressingly. And he smiled to himself to see how instinctively eloquent was the courtezan in her—alluring gestures though her hands trembled, soft voice huskily seductive even in its terror. "—always, always!" she was saying. "The soft, hushed, hovering menace! It haunts the whole place. Didn't you feel it as you came in?"

"I think I did," Smith answered slowly. "Yes—that feel of something just out of sight, hiding in dark doorways . . . a sort of tensity in the air. . . ."

"Danger," she whispered, "terrible, nameless danger . . . oh, I feel it wherever I go . . . it's soaked into me and through me until it's a part of me, body and soul. . . ."

Smith heard the note of rising hysteria in her voice, and said quickly.

"Why did you come to me?"

"I didn't, consciously." She conquered the hysteria with

an effort and took up her tale a little more calmly. "I was really looking for a wharfman, as I said, and for quite another reason than this. It doesn't matter, now. But when you spoke, when I flashed my light and saw your face, I knew you. I'd heard of you, you see, and about the—the Lakkmanda affair, and I knew in a moment that if anyone alive could help me, it would be you."

"But what is it? Help you in what?"

"It's a long story," she said, "and too strange, almost, to believe, and too vague for you to take seriously. And yet I *know*. . . . Have you heard the history of the Minga?"

"A little of it. It goes back very far."

"Back into the beginning—and farther. I wonder if you can understand. You see, we on Venus are closer to our beginnings than you. Life here developed faster, of course, and along lines more different than Earthmen realize. On Earth, civilization rose slowly enough for the—the elementals—to sink back into darkness. On Venus—oh, it's bad, *bad* for men to develop too swiftly! Life rises out of dark and mystery and things too strange and terrible to be looked upon. Earth's civilization grew slowly, and by the time men were civilized enough to look back they were sufficiently far from their origins not to see, not to know. But we here who look back see too clearly, sometimes, too nearly and vividly the black beginning. . . . Great Shar defend me, what I have seen!"

White hands flashed up to hide sudden terror in her eyes, and hair in a brazen cloud fell fragrantly over her fingers. And even in that terror was an inbred allure as natural as breathing.

In the little silence that followed, Smith caught himself glancing furtively over his shoulder. The room was ominously still. . . .

Vaudir lifted her face from her hands, shaking back her hair. The hands trembled. She clasped them on her velvet knee and went on.

"The Minga," she said, and her voice was resolutely

steady, "began too long ago for anyone to name the date. It began before dates. When Far-thursa came out of the seafog with his men and founded this city at the mountain's foot he built it around the walls of a castle already here. The Minga castle. And the Alendar sold Minga girls to the sailors and the city began. All that is myth, but the Minga had always been here.

"The Alendar dwelt in his stronghold and bred his golden girls and trained them in the arts of charming men, and guarded them with—with strange weapons—and sold them to kings at royal prices. There has always been an Alendar. I have seen him, once. . . .

"He walks the halls on rare occasions, and it is best to kneel and hide one's face when he comes by. Yes, it is best. . . . But I passed him one day, and—and—he is tall, tall as you, Earthman, and his eyes are like—the space between the worlds. I looked into his eyes under the hood he wore—I was not afraid of devil or man, then. I looked him in the eyes before I made obeisance, and I—I shall never be free of fear again. I looked into evil as one looks into a pool. Blackness and blankness and raw evil. Impersonal, not malevolent. Elemental . . . the elemental dreadfulness that life rose from. And I know very surely, now, that the first Alendar sprang from no mortal seed. There were races before man. . . . Life goes back very dreadfully through many forms and evils, before it reaches the well-spring of its beginning. And the Alendar had not the eyes of a human creature, and I met them—and I am damned!"

Her voice trailed softly away and she sat quiet for a space, staring before her with remembering eyes.

"I am doomed and damned to a blacker hell than any of Shar's priests threaten," she resumed. "No, wait—this is not hysteria. I haven't told you the worst part. You'll find it hard to believe, but it's truth—truth—Great Shar, if I could hope it were not!

"The origin of it is lost in legend. But why, in the beginning, did the first Alendar dwell in the misty sea-edge castle, alone and unknown, breeding his bronze girls?—not for sale, then. Where did he get the secret of producing the invariable type? And the castle, legend says, was age-old when Farthursa found it. The girls had a perfected, consistent beauty that could be attained only by generations of effort. How long had the Minga been built, and by whom? Above all, why? What possible reason could there be for dwelling there absolutely unknown, breeding civilized beauties in a world half-savage? Sometimes I think I have guessed the reason. . . ."

Her voice faded into a resonant silence, and for a while she sat staring blindly at the brocaded wall. When she spoke again it was with a startling shift of topic.

"Am I beautiful, do you think?"

"More so than any I have ever seen before," answered Smith without flattery.

Her mouth twisted.

"There are girls here now, in this building, so much lovelier than I that I am humbled to think of them. No mortal man has ever seen them, except the Alendar, and he—is not wholly mortal. No mortal man will ever see them. They are not for sale. Eventaully they will disappear. . . .

"One might think that feminine beauty must reach an apex beyond which it can not rise, but this is not true. It can increase and intensify until—I have no words. And I truly believe that there is no limit to the heights it can reach, in the hands of the Alendar. And for every beauty we know and hear of, through the slaves that tend them, gossip says there are as many more, too immortally lovely for mortal eyes to see. Have you ever considered that beauty might be refined and intensified until one could scarcely bear to look upon it? We have tales here of such beauty, hidden in some of the secret rooms of the Minga.

"But the world never knows of these mysteries. No monarch on any planet known is rich enough to buy the loveliness hidden in the Minga's innermost rooms. It is not for sale. For countless centuries the Alendars of the Minga have been breeding beauty, in higher and higher degrees, at infinite labor and cost—beauty to be locked in secret chambers, guarded most terribly, so that not even a whisper of it passes the outer walls, beauty that vanishes, suddenly, in a breath—like that! Where? Why? How? No one knows.

"And it is that I fear. I have not a fraction of the beauty I speak of, yet a fate like that is written for me—somehow I know. I have looked into the eyes of the Alendar, and—I know. And I am sure that I must look again into those blank black eyes, more deeply, more dreadfully. . . . I know—and I am sick with terror of what more I shall know, soon. . . .

"Something dreadful is waiting for me, drawing nearer and nearer. Tomorrow, or the next day, or a little while after, I shall vanish, and the girls will wonder and whisper a little, and then forget. It has happened before. Great Shar, what shall I do?"

She wailed it, musically and hopelessly and sank into a little silence. And then her look changed and she said reluctantly,

"And I have dragged you in with me. I have broken every tradition of the Minga in bringing you here, and there has been no hindrance—it has been too easy, too easy. I think I have sealed your death. When you first came I was minded to trick you into committing yourself so deeply that perforce you must do as I asked to win free again. But I know now that through the simple act of asking you here I have dragged you in deeper than I dreamed. It is a knowledge that has come to me somehow, out of the air tonight. I can feel knowledge beating upon me—compelling me. For in my terror to get help I think I have precipitated damnation upon us both. I know now—I have known in my soul since you entered so easily, that you will not go out alive—that—*it*—will come for me and drag you down too. . . . Shar, Shar, what have I done!"

"But what, what?" Smith struck his knee impatiently. "What is it we face? Poison? Guards? Traps? Hypnotism? Can't you give me even a guess at what will happen?"

He leaned forward to search her face commandingly, and saw her brows knit in an effort to find words that would cloak the mysteries she had to tell. Her lips parted irresolutely.

"The Guardians," she said. "The—Guardians. . . ."

And then over her hesitant face swept a look of such horror that his hand clenched on his knee and he felt the hairs rise along his neck. It was not horror of any material thing, but an inner dreadfulness, a terrible awareness. The eyes that had met his glazed and escaped his commanding stare without shifting their focus. It was as if they ceased to be eyes and became dark windows—vacant. The beauty of her face set like a mask, and behind the blank windows, behind the lovely set mask, he could sense dimly the dark command flowing in. . . .

She put out her hands stiffly and rose. Smith found himself on his feet, gun in hand, while his hackles lifted shudderingly and something pulsed in the air as tangibly as the beat of wings. Three times that nameless shudder stirred the air, and then Vaudir stepped forward like an automaton and faced the door. She walked in her dream of masked dreadfulness, stiffly, through the portal. As she passed him he put out a hesitant hand and laid it on her arm, and a little stab of pain shot through him at the contact, and once more he thought he felt the pulse of wings in the air. Then she passed by without hesitation, and his hands fell.

He made no further effort to arouse her, but followed after on cat-feet, delicately as if he walked on eggs. He was crouching a little, unconsciously, and his gun-hand held a tense finger on the trigger.

They went down the corridor in a breathing silence, an empty corridor where no lights showed beyond closed doors, where no murmur of voices broke the live stillness. But little shudders seemed to shake in the air somehow, and his heart was pounding suffocatingly.

Vaudir walked like a mechanical doll, tense in a dream of horror. When they reached the end of the hall he saw that the silver grille stood open, and they passed through without pausing. But Smith noted with a little qualm that a gateway opening to the right was closed and locked, and the bars across it were sunk firmly into wall-sockets. There was no choice but to follow her.

The corridor slanted downward. They passed others branching to right and left, but the silver gateways were closed and barred across each. A coil of silver stairs ended the passage, and the girl went stiffly down without touching the rails. It was a long spiral, past many floors, and as they descended, the rich, dim light lessened and darkened and a subtle smell of moisture and salt invaded the scented air. At each turn where the stairs opened on successive floors, gates were barred across the outlets; and they passed so many of these that Smith knew, as they went down and down, that however high the green jewel-box room had been, by now they were descending deep into the earth. And still the stair wound downward. The stories that opened beyond the bars like honeycomb layers became darker and less luxurious, and at last ceased altogether and the silver steps wound down through a well of rock, lighted so dimly at wide intervals that he could scarcely see the black polished walls circling them in. Drops of moisture began to appear on the dark surface, and the smell was of black salt seas and dank underground.

And just as he was beginning to believe that the stairs went on and on into the very black, salt heart of the planet, they came abruptly to the bottom. A flourish of slim, shining rails ended the stairs, at the head of a hallway, and the girl's feet turned unhesitatingly to follow its dark length. Smith's pale eyes, searching the dimness, found no trace of other life than themselves; yet eyes were upon him—he knew it surely.

They came down the black corridor to a gateway of wrought metal set in bars whose ends sank deep into the stone walls. She went through, Smith at her heels raking the dark with swift, unresting eyes like a wild animal's, wary in a strange jungle. And beyond the great gates a door hung with sweeping curtains of black ended the hall. Somehow Smith felt that they had reached their destination. And nowhere along the whole journey had he had any choice but to follow Vaudir's unerring, unseeing footsteps. Grilles had been locked across every possible outlet. But he had his gun. . . .

Her hands were white against the velvet as she pushed aside the folds. Very bright she stood for an instant—all green and gold and white—against the blackness. Then she passed through and the folds swept to behind her—candle-flame extinguished in dark velvet. Smith hesitated the barest instant before he parted the curtains and peered within.

He was looking into a room hung in black velvet that absorbed the light almost hungrily. That light radiated from a single lamp swinging from the ceiling directly over an ebony table. It shone softly on a man—a very tall man.

He stood darkly under it, very dark in the room's darkness, his head bent, staring up from under level black brows. His eyes in the half-hidden face were pits of blackness, and under the lowered brows two pinpoint gleams stabbed straight—not at the girl—but at Smith hidden behind the curtains. It held his eyes as a magnet holds steel. He felt the narrow glitter plunging blade-like into his very brain, and from the keen, burning stab something within him shuddered away involuntarily. He thrust his gun through the curtains, stepped through quietly, and stood meeting the sword-gaze with pale, unwavering eyes.

Vaudir moved forward with a mechanical stiffness that somehow could not hide her grace—it was as if no power existing could ever evoke from that lovely body less than loveliness. She came to the man's feet and stopped there. Then a long shudder swept her from head to foot and she dropped to her knees and laid her forehead to the floor.

Across the golden loveliness of her the man's eyes met Smith's, and the man's voice, deep, deep, like black waters flowing smoothly, said,

"I am the Alendar."

"Then you know me," said Smith, his voice harsh as iron in the velvet dimness.

"You are Northwest Smith," said the smooth, deep voice dispassionately. "An outlaw from the planet Earth. You have broken your last law, Northwest Smith. Men do not come here uninvited—and live. You perhaps have heard tales. . . ."

His voice melted into silence, lingeringly.

Smith's mouth curled into a wolfish grin, without mirth, and his gun hand swung up. Murder flashed bleakly from his steel-pale eyes. And then with stunning abruptness the world dissolved about him. A burst of coruscations flamed through his head, danced and wheeled and drew slowly together in a whirling darkness until they were two pinpoint sparks of light—a dagger stare under level brows. . . .

When the room steadied about him he was standing with slack arms, the gun hanging from his fingers, an apathetic numbness slowly withdrawing from his body. A dark smile curved smoothly on the Alendar's mouth.

The stabbing gaze slid casually away, leaving him dizzy in sudden vertigo, and touched the girl prostrate on the floor. Against the black carpet her burnished bronze curls sprayed out exquisitely. The green robe folded softly back from the roundness of her body, and nothing in the universe could have been so lovely as the creamy whiteness of her on the dark floor. The pit-black eyes brooded over her impassively. And then, in his smooth, deep voice the Alendar asked, amazingly, matter-of-factly,

"Tell me, do you have such girls on Earth?"

Smith shook his head to clear it. When he managed an answer his voice had steadied, and in the receding of that dizziness even the sudden drop into casual conversation seemed not unreasonable.

"I have never seen such a girl anywhere," he said calmly.

The sword gaze flashed up and pierced him.

"She has told you," said the Alendar. "You know I have beauties here that outshine her as the sun does a candle. And yet . . . she has more than beauty, this Vaudir. You have felt it, perhaps?"

Smith met the questioning gaze, searching for mockery, but finding none. Not understanding—a moment before the man had threatened his life—he took up the conversation.

"They all have more than beauty. For what other reason do kings buy the Minga girls?"

"No—not that charm. She has it too, but something more subtle than fascination, much more desirable than loveliness. She has courage, this girl. She has intelligence. Where she got it I do not understand. I do not breed my girls for such things. But I looked into her eyes once, in the hallway, as she told you—and saw there more arousing things than beauty. I summoned her—and you come at her heels. Do you know why? Do you know why you did not die at the outer gate or anywhere along the hallways on your way in?"

Smith's pale stare met the dark one questioningly. The voice flowed on.

"Because there are—interesting things in your eyes too. Courage and ruthlessness and a certain—power, I think. Intensity is in you. And I believe I can find a use for it, Earthman."

Smith's eyes narrowed a little. So calm, so matter-of-fact, this talk. But death was coming. He felt it in the air—he knew that feel of old. Death—and worse things than that, perhaps. He remembered the whispers he had heard.

On the floor the girl moaned a little, and stirred. The Alendar's quiet, pinpoint eyes flicked her, and he said softly, "Rise." And she rose, stumbling, and stood before him with bent head. The stiffness was gone from her. On an impulse Smith said suddenly, "Vaudir!" She lifted her face and met his gaze, and a thrill of horror rippled over him. She had regained consciousness, but she would never be the same frightened girl he had known. Black knowledge looked out of her eyes, and her face was a strained mask that covered horror barely—barely! It was the face of one who has walked through a blacker hell than any of humanity's understanding, and gained knowledge there that no human soul could endure knowing and live.

She looked him full in the face for a long moment, silently, and then turned away to the Alendar again. And Smith thought, just before her eyes left his, he had seen in them one wild flash of hopeless, desperate appeal. . . .

"Come," said the Alendar.

He turned his back— Smith's gun-hand trembled up and then fell again. No, better wait. There was always a bare hope, until he saw death closing in all around.

He stepped out over the yielding carpet at the Alendar's heels. The girl came after with slow steps and eyes downcast in a horrible parody of meditation, as if she brooded over the knowledge that dwelt so terribly behind her eyes.

The dark archway at the opposite end of the room swallowed them up. Light failed for an instant—a breathstopping instant while Smith's gun leaped up involuntarily, like a live thing in his hand, futilely against invisible evil, and his brain rocket at the utter blackness that enfolded him. It was over in the wink of an eye, and he wondered if it had ever been as his gun-hand fell again. But the Alendar said across one shoulder.

"A barrier I have placed to guard my—beauties. A mental barrier that would have been impassable had you not been with me, yet which—but you understand now, do you not, my Vaudir?" And there was an indescribable leer in the query that injected a note of monstrous humanity into the inhuman voice.

"I understand," echoed the girl in a voice as lovely and toneless as a sustained musical note. And the sound of those two inhuman voices proceeding from the human lips of his companions sent a shudder thrilling along Smith's nerves.

They went down the long corridor thereafter in silence, Smith treading soundlessly in his spaceman's boots, every fiber of him tense to painfulness. He found himself wondering, even in the midst of his strained watchfulness, if any other creature with a living human soul had ever gone down this corridor before—if frightened golden girls had followd the Alendar thus into blackness, or if they too had been drained of humanity and steeped in that nameless horror before their feet followed their master through the black barrier.

The hallway led downward, and the salt smell became clearer and the light sank to a glimmer in the air, and in a silence that was not human they went on.

Presently the Alendar said—and his deep, liquid voice did nothing to break the stillness, blending with it softly so that not even an echo roused,

"I am taking you into a place where no other man than the Alendar has ever set foot before. It pleases me to wonder just how your unaccustomed senses will react to the things you are about to see. I am reaching an—an age"—he laughed softly—"where experiment interests me. Look!"

Smith's eyes blinked shut before an intolerable blaze of sudden light. In the streaked darkness of that instant while the glare flamed through his lids he thought he felt everything shift unaccountably about him, as if the very structure of the atoms that built the walls were altered. When he opened his eyes he stood at the head of a long gallery blazing with a soft, delicious brilliance. How he had got there he made no effort even to guess.

Very beautifully it stretched before him. The walls and floor and ceiling were of sheeny stone. There were low couches along the walls at intervals, and a blue pool broke the floor, and the air sparkled unaccountably with golden light. And figures were moving through that champagne sparkle. . . .

Smith stood very still, looking down the gallery. The Alendar watched him with a subtle anticipation upon his face, the pinpoint glitter of his eyes sharp enough to pierce the Earthman's very brain. Vaudir with bent head brooded over the black knowledge behind her drooping lids. Only Smith of the three looked down the gallery and saw what moved through the golden glimmer of the air.

They were girls. They might have been goddesses—angels haloed with bronze curls, moving leisurely through a golden heaven where the air sparkled like wine. There must have been a score of them strolling up and down the gallery in twos and threes, lolling on the couches, bathing in the pool. They wore the infinitely graceful Venusian robe with its looped shoulder and slit skirt, in soft, muted shades of violet and blue and jewel-green, and the beauty of them was breath-stopping as a blow. Music was in every gesture they made, a flowing, singing grace that made the heart ache with its sheer loveliness.

He had thought Vaudir lovely, but here was beauty so exquisite that it verged on pain. Their sweet, light voices were pitched to send little velvety burrs along his nerves, and from a distance the soft sounds blended so musically that they might have been singing together. The loveliness of their motion made his heart contract suddenly, and the blood pounded in his ears. . . .

"You find them beautiful?" The Alendar's voice blended into the humming lilt of voices as perfectly as it has blended with silence. His dagger-glitter of eyes was fixed piercingly on Smith's pale gaze, and he smiled a little faintly. "Beautiful? Wait!"

He moved down the gallery, tall and very dark in the rainbow light. Smith, following after, walked in a haze of wonder. It is not given to every man to walk through heaven. He felt the air tingle like wine, and a delicious perfume caressed him and the haloed girls drew back with wide, amazed eyes fixed on him in his stained leather and heavy boots as he passed. Vaudir paced quietly after, her head bent, and from her the girls turned away their eyes, shuddering a little.

He saw now that their faces were as lovely as their bodies, languorously, colorfully. They were contented faces, unconscious of beauty, unconscious of any other existence than their own—soulless. He felt that instinctively. Here was beauty incarnate, physically, tangibly; but he had seen in Vaudir's face—before—a sparkle of daring, a tenderness of remorse at having brought him here, that gave her an indefinable superiority over even this incredible beauty, soulless.

They went down the gallery in a hush as the musical voices fell silent from very amazement. Apparently the Alendar was a familiar figure here, for they scarcely glanced at him, and from Vaudir they turned away in a shuddering revulsion that preferred not to recognize her existence. But Smith was the first man other than the Alendar whom they had ever seen, and the surprise of it struck them dumb.

They went on through the dancing air, and the last lovely, staring girls fell behind, and an ivory gateway opened before them without a touch. They went downstairs from there, and along another hallway, while the tingle died in the air and a hum of musical voices sprang up behind them. They passed beyond the sound. The hallway darkened until they were moving again through dimness.

Presently the Alendar paused and turned.

"My more costly jewels," he said, "I keep in separate settings. As here—"

He stretched out his arm, and Smith saw that a curtain hung against the wall. There were others, farther on, dark blots against the dimness. The Alendar drew back black folds, and light from beyond flowed softly through a pattern of bars to cast flowery shadows on the opposite wall. Smith stepped forward and stared.

He was looking through a grille window down into a room lined with dark velvet. It was quite plain. There was a low couch against the wall opposite the window, and on it—Smith's heart gave a stagger and paused—a woman lay. And if the girls in the gallery had been like goddesses, this woman was lovelier than men have ever dared to imagine even in legends. She was beyond divinity—long limbs white against the velvet, sweet curves and planes of her rounding under the robe, bronze hair spilling like lava over one shoulder, and her face calm as death with closed eyes. It was a passive beauty, like alabaster shaped perfectly. And charm, a fascination all but tangible, reached out from her like a magic spell. A sleeping charm, magnetic, powerful. He could not wrench his eyes away. He was like a wasp caught in honey. . . .

The Alendar said something across Smith's shoulder, in a vibrant voice that thrilled the air. The closed lids rose. Life and loveliness flowed into the calm face like a tide, lighting it unbearably. That heady charm wakened and brightened to a dangerous liveness—tugging, pulling. . . . She rose in one long glide like a wave over rocks; she smiled (Smith's senses reeled to the beauty of that smile) and then sank in a deep salaam, slowly, to the velvet floor, her hair rippling and falling all about her, until she lay abased in a blaze of loveliness under the window.

The Alendar let the curtain fall, and turned to Smith as the dazzling sight was blotted out. Again the pinpoint glitter stabbed into Smith's brain. The Alendar smiled again.

"Come," he said, and moved down the hall.

They passed three curtains, and paused at a fourth. Afterward Smith remembered that the curtain must have been drawn back and he must have bent forward to stare through the window bars, but the sight he saw blasted every memory of it from his mind. The girl who dwelt in this velvet-lined room was stretching on tiptoe just as the drawn curtain caught her, and the beauty and grace of her from head to foot stopped Smith's breath as a ray-stab to the heart would have done. And the irresistible, wrenching charm of her drew him forward until he was clasping the bars with white-knuckled hands, unaware of anything but her compelling, soul-destroying desirability. . . .

She moved, and the dazzle of grace that ran like a song through every motion made his senses ache with its pure, unattainable loveliness. He knew, even in his daze of rapture, that he might hold the sweet, curved body in his arms for ever, yet hunger still for the fulfilment which the flesh could never wring from her. Her loveliness aroused a hunger in the soul more maddening than the body's hunger could ever be. His brain rocked with the desire to possess that intangible, irresistible loveliness that he knew he could never possess, never reach with any sense that was in him. That bodiless desire raged like madness through him, so violently that the room reeled and the white outlines of the beauty unattainable as the stars wavered before him. He caught his breath and choked and drew back from the intolerable, exquisite sight.

The Alendar laughed and dropped the curtain.

"Come," he said again, the subtle amusement clear in his voice, and Smith in a daze moved after him down the hall.

They went a long way, past curtains hanging at regular intervals along the wall. When they paused at last, the curtain before which they stopped was faintly luminous about the edges, as if something dazzling dwelt within. The Alendar drew back the folds.

"We are approaching," he said, "a pure clarity of beauty, hampered only a little by the bonds of flesh. Look."

One glance only Smith snatched of the dweller within. And the exquisite shock of that sight went thrilling like torture through every nerve of him. For a mad instant his reason staggered before the terrible fascination beating out from that dweller in waves that wrenched at his very soul—incarnate loveliness tugging with strong fingers at every sense and every nerve and intangibly, irresistibly, at deeper things than these, groping among the roots of his being, dragging his soul out. . . .

Only one glance he took, and in the glance he felt his soul answer that dragging, and the terrible desire tore futilely through him. Then he flung up an arm to shield his eyes and reeled back into the dark, and a wordless sob rose to his lips and the darkness reeled about him.

The curtain fell. Smith pressed the wall and breathed in long shuddering gasps, while his heart-beats slowed gradually and the unholy fascination ebbed from about him. The Alendar's eyes were glittering with a green fire as he turned from the window, and a nameless hunger lay shadowy on his face. He said,

"I might show you others, Earthman. But it could only drive you mad, in the end—you were very near the brink for a moment just now—and I have another use for you. . . . I wonder if you begin to understand, now, the purpose of all this?"

The green glow was fading from that dagger-sharp gaze as the Alendar's eyes stabbed into Smith's. The Earthman gave his head a little shake to clear away the vestiges of that devouring desire, and took a fresh grip on the butt of his gun. The familiar smoothness of it brought him a measure of reassurance, and with it a reawakening to the peril all around. He knew now that there could be no conceivable mercy for him, to whom the innermost secrets of the Minga had been unaccountably revealed. Death was waiting—strange death, as soon as the Alendar wearied of talking—but if he kept his ears open and his eyes alert it might not—please God—catch him so quickly that he died alone. One sweep of that blade-blue flame was all he asked, now. His eyes, keen and hostile, met the dagger-gaze squarely. The Alendar smiled and said.

"Death in your eyes, Earthman. Nothing in your mind but murder. Can that brain of yours comprehend nothing but battle? Is there no curiosity there? Have you no wonder of why I brought you here? Death awaits you, yes. But a not unpleasant death, and it awaits all, in one form or another. Listen, let me tell you—I have reason for desiring to break through that animal shell of self-defense that seals in your mind. Let me look deeper—if there are depths. Your death will be—useful, and in a way, pleasant. Otherwise—well, the black beasts hunger. And flesh must feed them, as a sweeter drink feeds me. . . . Listen."

Smith's eyes narrowed. A sweeter drink. . . . Danger, danger—the smell of it in the air—instinctively he felt the peril of opening his mind to the plunging gaze of the Alendar, the force of those compelling eyes beating like strong lights into his brain. . . .

"Come," said the Alendar softly, and moved off soundlessly through the gloom. They followed, Smith painfully alert, the girl walking with lowered, brooding eyes, her mind and soul afar in some wallowing darkness whose shadow showed so hideously beneath her lashes.

The hallway widened to an arch, and abruptly, on the other side, one wall dropped away into infinity and they stood on the dizzy brink of a gallery opening on a black, heaving sea. Smith bit back a startled oath. One moment before the way had led through low-roofed tunnels deep underground; the next instant they stood on the shore of a vast body of rolling darkness, a tiny wind touching their faces with the breath of unnamable things.

Very far below, the dark waters rolled. Phosphorescence lighted them uncertainly, and he was not even sure it was water that surged there in the dark. A heavy thickness seemed to be inherent in the rollers, like black slime surging.

The Alendar looked out over the fire-tinged waves. He waited for an instant without speaking, and then, far out in the slimy surges, somehing broke the surface with an oily splash, something mercifully veiled in the dark, then dived again, leaving a wake of spreading ripples over the surface.

"Listen," said the Alendar, without turning his head. "Life is very old. There are older races than man. Mine is one. Life rose out of the black slime of the sea-bottoms and grew toward the light along many diverging lines. Some reached maturity and deep wisdom when man was still swinging through the jungle trees.

"For many centuries, as mankind counts time, the Alendar has dwelt here, breeding beauty. In later years he has sold some of his lesser beauties, perhaps to explain to mankind's satisfaction what it could never understand were it told the truth. Do you begin to see? My race is very remotely akin to those races which suck blood from man, less remotely to those which drink his life-forces for nourishment. I refine taste even more than that. I drink—beauty. I live on beauty. Yes, literally.

"Beauty is as tangible as blood, in a way. It is a separate, distinct force that inhabits the bodies of men and women. You must have noticed the vacuity that accompanies perfect beauty in so many women . . . the force so strong that it drives out all other forces and lives vampirishly at the expense of intelligence and goodness and conscience and all else.

"In the beginning, here—for our race was old when this world began, spawned on another planet, and wise and ancient—we woke from slumber in the slime, to feed on the beauty force inherent in mankind even in cave-dwelling days. But it was meager fare, and we studied the race to determine where the greatest prospects lay, then selected specimens for breeding, built this stronghold and settled down to the business of evolving mankind up to its limit of loveliness. In time we weeded out all but the present type. For the race of man we have developed the ultimate type of loveliness. It is interesting to see what we have accomplished on other worlds, with utterly different races. . . .

"Well, there you have it. Women, bred as a spawning-ground for the devouring force of beauty on which we live.

"But—the fare grows monotonous, as all food must without change. Vaudir I took because I saw in her a sparkle of something that except in very rare instances has been bred out of the Minga girls. For beauty, as I have said, eats up all other qualities but beauty. Yet somehow intelligence and courage survived latently in Vaudir. It decreases her beauty, but the tang of it should be a change from the eternal sameness of the rest. And so I thought until I saw you.

"I realized then how long it had been since I tasted the beauty of man. It is so rare, so different from female beauty, that I had all but forgotten it existed. And you have it, very subtly, in a raw, harsh way. . . .

"I have told you all this to test the quality of that—that harsh beauty in you. Had I been wrong about the deeps of your mind, you would have gone to feed the black beasts, but I see that I was not wrong. Behind your animal shell of self-preservation are depths of that force and strength which nourish the roots of male beauty. I think I shall give you a while to let it grow, under the forcing methods I know, before I—drink. It will be delightful. . . ."

The voice trailed away in a murmurous silence, the pin-point glitter sought Smith's eyes. And he tried half-heartedly to avoid it, but his eyes turned involuntarily to the stabbing gaze, and the alertness died out of him, gradually, and the compelling pull of those glittering points in the pits of darkness held him very still.

And as he stared into the diamond glitter he saw its brilliance slowly melt and darken, until the pinpoints of light had changed to pools that dimmed, and he was looking into black evil as elemental and vast as the space between the worlds, a dizzying blankness wherein dwelt unnamable horror . . . deep, deep . . . all about him the darkness was clouding. And thoughts that were not his own seeped into his mind out of that vast, elemental dark . . . crawling, writhing thoughts . . . until he had a glimpse of that dark place where Vaudir's soul wallowed, and something sucked him down and down into a waking nightmare he could not fight. . . .

Then somehow the pull broke for an instant. For just that instant he stood again on the shore of the heaving sea and gripped a gun with nerveless fingers—then the darkness closed about him again, but a different, uneasy dark that had not quite the all-compelling power of that other nightmare—it left him strength enough to fight.

And he fought, a desperate, moveless, soundless struggle in a black sea of horror, while worm-thoughts coiled through his straining mind and the clouds rolled and broke and rolled again about him. Sometimes, in the instants when the pull slackened, he had time to feel a third force struggling here between that black, blind downward suck that dragged at him and his own sick, frantic effort to fight clear, a third force that was weakening the black drag so that he had moments of lucidity when he stood free on the brink of the ocean and felt the sweat roll down his face and was aware of his laboring heart and how gaspingly breath tortured his lungs, and he knew he was fighting with every atom of himself, body and mind and soul, against the intangible blackness sucking him down.

And then he felt the force against him gather itself in a final effort—he sensed desperation in that effort—and come rolling over him like a tide. Bowled over, blinded and dumb and deaf, drowning in utter blackness, he floundered in the deeps of that nameless hell where thoughts that were alien and slimy squirmed through his brain. Bodiless he was, and unstable, and as he wallowed there in the ooze more hideous than any earthly ooze, because it came from black, inhuman souls and out of ages before man, he became aware that the worm-thoughts a-squirm in his brain were forming slowly into monstrous meanings—knowledge like a formless flow was pouring through his bodiless brain, knowledge so dreadful that consciously he could not comprehend it, though subconsciously every atom of his mind and soul sickened and writhed futilely away. It was flooding over him, drenching him, permeating him through and through with the very essence of dreadfulness—he felt his mind melting away under the solvent power of it, melting and running fluidly into new channels and fresh molds—horrible molds. . . .

And just at that instant, while madness folded around him and his mind rocked on the verge of annihilation, something snapped, and like a curtain the dark rolled away, and he stood sick and dizzy on the gallery above the black sea. Everything was reeling about him, but they were stable things that shimmered and steadied before his eyes, blessed black rock and tangible surges that had form and body—his feet pressed firmness and his mind shook itself and was clean and his own again.

And then through the haze of weakness that still shrouded him a voice was shrieking wildly, "Kill! . . . kill!" and he saw the Alendar staggering against the rail, all his outlines unaccountably blurred and uncertain, and behind him Vaudir with blazing eyes and face wrenched hideously into life again, screaming "Kill!" in a voice scarcely human.

Like an independent creature his gun-hand leaped up—he had gripped that gun through everything that happened—and he was dimly aware of the hardness of it kicking back against his hand with the recoil, and of the blue flash flaming from its muzzle. It struck the Alendar's dark figure full, and there was a hiss and a dazzle. . . .

Smith closed his eyes tight and opened them again, and stared with a sick incredulity; for unless that struggle had unhinged his brain after all, and the worm-thoughts still dwelt slimily in his mind, tingeing all he saw with unearthly horror—unless this was true, he was looking not at a man just rayed through the lungs, and who should be dropping now in a bleeding, collapsed heap to the floor, but at—at—God, what *was* it? The dark figure had slumped against the rail, and instead of blood gushing, a hideous, nameless, formless black poured sluggishly forth—a slime like the heaving sea below. The whole dark figure of the man was melting, slumping farther down into the pool of blackness forming at his feet on the stone floor.

Smith gripped his gun and watched in numb incredulity, and the whole body sank slowly down and melted and lost all form—hideously, gruesomely—until where the Alendar had stood a heap of slime lay viscidly on the gallery floor, hideously alive, heaving and rippling and striving to lift itself into a semblance of humanity again. And as he watched, it lost even that form, and the edges melted revoltingly and the mass flattened and slid down into a pool of utter horror, and he became aware that it was pouring slowly through the rails into the sea. He stood watching while the whole rolling, shimmering mound melted and thinned and trickled through the bars, until the floor was clear again, and not even a stain marred the stone.

A painful constriction of his lungs roused him, and he realized he had been holding his breath, scarcely daring to realize. Vaudir had collapsed against the wall, and he saw her knees give limply, and staggered forward on uncertain feet to catch her as she fell.

"Vaudir, Vaudir!" he shook her gently. "Vaudir, what's happened? Am I dreaming? Are we safe now? Are you—awake again?"

Very slowly her white lids lifted, and the black eyes met his. And he saw shadowily there the knowledge of that wallowing void he had dimly known, the shadow that could never be cleared away. She was steeped and foul with it. And the look of her eyes was such that involuntarily he released her and stepped away. She staggered a little and then regained her balance and regarded him from under bent brows. The level inhumanity of her gaze struck into his soul, and yet he thought he saw a spark of the girl she had been, dwelling in torture amid the blackness. He knew he was right when she said, in a far-away, toneless voice,

"Awake? . . . No, not ever now, Earthman. I have been down too deeply into hell . . . he had dealt me a worse torture than he knew, for there is just enough humanity left within me to realize what I have become, and to suffer. . . .

"Yes, he is gone, back into the slime that bred him. I have been a part of him, one with him in the blackness of his soul, and I know. I have spent eons since the blackness came upon me, dwelt for eternities in the dark, rolling seas of his mind, sucking in knowledge . . . and I was one with him, and he now gone, so shall I die; yet I will see you safely out of here if it is in my power, for it was I who dragged you in. If I can remember—if I can find the way. . . ."

She turned uncertainly and staggered a step back along the way they had come. Smith sprang forward and slid his free arm about her, but she shuddered away from the contact.

"No, no—unbearable—the touch of clean human flesh—and it breaks the chord of my remembering. . . . I can not look back into his mind as it was when I dwelt there, and I must, I must. . . ."

She shook him off and reeled on, and he cast one last look at the billowing sea, and then followed. She staggered along the stone floor on stumbling feet, one hand to the wall to support herself, and her voice was whispering gustily, so that he had to follow close to hear, and then almost wished he had not heard.

"—black slime—darkness feeding on light—everything wavers so—slime, slime and a rolling sea—he rose out of it, you know, before civilization began here—he is age-old—there never has been but one Alendar. . . . And somehow

—I could not see just how, or remember why—he rose from the rest, as some of his race on other planets had done, and took the man-form and stocked his breeding-pens. . . ."

They went on up the dark hallway, past curtains hiding incarnate loveliness, and the girl's stumbling footsteps kept time to her stumbling, half-incoherent words.

"—has lived all these ages here, breeding and devouring beauty—vampire-thirst, a hideous delight in drinking in that beauty-force—I felt it and remembered it when I was one with him—wrapping black layers of primal slime about—quenching human loveliness in ooze, sucking—blind black thirst. . . . And his wisdom was ancient and dreadful and full of power—so he could draw a soul out through the eyes and sink it in hell, and drown it there, as he would have done mine if I had not had, somehow, a difference from the rest. Great Shar, I wish I had not! I wish I were drowned in it and did not feel in every atom of me the horrible uncleanness of—what I know. But by virtue of that hidden strength I did not surrender wholly, and when he had turned his power to subduing you I was able to struggle, there in the very heart of his mind, making a disturbance that shook him as he fought us both—making it possible to free you long enough for you to destroy the human flesh he was clothed in—so that he lapsed into the ooze again. I do not quite understand why that happened—only that his weakness with you assailing him from without and me struggling strongly in the very center of his soul was such that he was forced to draw on the power he had built up to maintain himself in the man form, and weakened it enough so that he collapsed when the man-form was assailed. And he fell back into the slime again—whence he rose—black slime—heaving—oozing. . . ."

Her voice trailed away in murmurs, and she stumbled, all but falling. When she regained her balance she went on ahead of him at a greater distance, as if his very nearness were repugnant to her, and the soft babble of her voice drifted back in broken phrases without meaning.

Presently the air began to tingle again, and they passed the silver gate and entered that gallery where the air sparkled like champagne. The blue pool lay jewel-clear in its golden setting. Of the girls there was no sign.

When they reached the head of the gallery the girl paused, turning to him a face twisted with the effort at memory.

"Here is the trail," she said urgently. "If I can remember—" She seized her head in clutching hands, shaking it savagely. "I haven't the strength, now—can't—can't—" the piteous little murmur reached his ears incoherently. Then she straightened resolutely, swaying a little, and faced him, holding out her hands. He clapsed them hesitantly, and saw a shiver go through her at the contact, and her face contort painfully, and then a shudder communicated itself through that clasp and he too winced in revolt. He saw her eyes go blank and her face strain in lines of tensity, and a fine dew broke out on her forehead. For a long moment she stood so, her face like death, and strong shudders went over her body and her eyes were blank as the void between the planets.

And as each shudder swept her it went unbroken through the clasping of their hands to him, and they were black waves of dreadfulness, and again he saw the heaving sea and wallowed in the hell he had fought out of on the gallery, and he knew for the first time what torture she must be enduring who dwelt in the very deeps of that uneasy dark. The pulses came faster, and for moments together he went down into the blind blackness and the slime, and felt the first wriggling of the worm-thoughts tickling the roots of his brain. . . .

And then suddenly a clean darkness closed round them and again everything shifted unaccountably, as if the atoms of the gallery were changing, and when Smith opened his eyes he was standing once more in the dark, slanting corridor with the smell of salt and antiquity heavy in the air.

Vaudir moaned softly beside him, and he turned to see her reeling against the wall and trembling so from head to foot that he looked to see her fall the next moment.

"Better—in a moment," she gasped. "It took—nearly all

my strength to—to get us through—wait. . . ."

So they halted there in the darkness and the dead salt air, until the trembling abated a little and she said, "Come," in her little whimpering voice. And again the journey began. It was only a short way, now, to the barrier of black blankness that guarded the door into the room where they had first seen the Alendar. When they reached the place she shivered a little and paused, then resolutely held out her hands. And as he took them he felt once more the hideous slimy waves course through him, and plunged again into the heaving hell. And as before the clean darkness flashed over them in a breath, and then she dropped his hands and they were standing in the archway looking into the velvet-hung room they had left—it seemed eons ago.

He watched as waves of blinding weakness flooded over her from that supreme effort. Death was visible in her face as she turned to him at last.

"Come—oh, come quickly," she whispered, and staggered forward.

At her heels he followed, across the room, past the great iron gateway, down the hall to the foot of the silver stairs. And here his heart sank, for he felt sure she could never climb the long spiral distances to the top. But she set her foot on the step and went upward resolutely, and as he followed he heard her murmuring to herself.

"Wait—oh, wait—let me reach the end—let me undo this much—and then—no, no! Please Shar, not the black slime again. . . . Earthman, Earthman!"

She paused on the stair and turned to face him, and her haggard face was frantic with desperation and despair.

"Earthman, promise—do not let me die like this! When we reach the end, ray me! Burn me clean, or I shall go down for eternity into the black sinks from which I dragged you free. Oh, promise!"

"I will," Smith's voice said quietly. "I will."

And they went on. Endlessly the stairs spiraled upward and endlessly they climbed. Smith's legs began to ache intolerably, and his heart was pounding like a wild thing, but Vaudir seemed not to notice weariness. She climbed steadily and no more unsurely than she had come along the halls. And after eternities they reached the top.

And there the girl fell. She dropped like a dead woman at the head of the silver spiral. Smith thought for a sick instant that he had failed her and let her die uncleansed, but in a moment or two she stirred and lifted her head and very slowly dragged herself to her feet.

"I will go on—I will, I will," she whispered to herself. "—come this far—must finish—" and she reeled off down the lovely, rosily-lit hallway paneled in pearl.

He could see how perilously near she was to her strength's end, and he marveled at the tenacity with which she clung to life though it ebbed away with every breath and the pulse of darkness flowed in after it. So with bulldog stubbornness she made her wavering way past door after door of carven shell, under rosy lights that flushed her face with a ghastly mockery of health, until they reached the silver gateway at the end. The lock had been removed from it by now, and the bar drawn.

She tugged open the gate and stumbled through.

And the nightmare journey went on. It must be very near morning, Smith thought, for the halls were deserted, but did he not sense a breath of danger in the still air? . . .

The girl's gasping voice answered that half-formed query as if, like the Alendar, she held the secret of reading men's minds.

"The—Guardians—still rove the halls, and unleashed now—so keep your ray-gun ready, Earthman. . . ."

After that he kept his eyes alert as they retraced, stumbling and slow, the steps he had taken on his way in. And once he heard distinctly the soft slither of—something—scraping over the marble pavement, and twice he smelt with shocking suddenness in this scented air a whiff of salt, and his mind flashed back to a rolling black sea. . . . But nothing molested them.

Step by faltering step the hallways fell behind them, and he began to recognize landmarks, and the girl's footsteps staggered and hesitated and went on gallantly, incredibly, beating back oblivion, fighting the dark surges rolling over her, clinging with tenacious fingers to the tiny spark of life that drove her on.

And at long last, after what seemed hours of desperate effort, they reached the blue-lit hallway at whose end the outer door opened. Vaudir's progress down it was a series of dizzy staggers, interspersed with pauses while she hung to the carven doors with tense fingers and drove her teeth into a bloodless lip and gripped that last flicker of life. He saw the shudders sweep over her, and knew what waves of washing dark must be rising all about her, and how the worm-thoughts writhed through her brain. . . . But she went on. Every step now was a little tripping, as if she fell from one foot to the other, and at each step he expected that knee to give way and pitch her down into the black deeps that yawned for her. But she went on.

She reached the bronze door, and with a last spurt of effort she lifted the bar and swung it open. Then that tiny spark flickered out like a lamp. Smith caught one flash of the rock room within—and something horrible on the floor—before he saw her pitch forward as the rising tide of slimy oblivion closed at last over her head. She was dying as she fell, and he whipped the ray-gun up and felt the recoil against his palm as a blue blaze flashed forth and transfixed her in midair. And he could have sworn her eyes lighted for a flickering instant and the gallant girl he had known looked forth, cleansed and whole, before death—clean death—glazed them.

She slumped down in a huddle at his feet, and he felt a sting of tears beneath his eyelids as he looked down on her, a huddle of white and bronze on the rug. And as he watched, a film of defilement veiled the shining whiteness of her—decay set in before his eyes and progressed with horrible swiftness, and in less time than it takes to tell he was staring with horrified eyes at a pool of black slime across which green velvet lay bedraggled.

Northwest Smith closed his pale eyes, and for a moment struggled with memory, striving to wrest from it the long-forgotten words of a prayer learned a score of years ago on another planet. Then he stepped over the pitiful, horrible heap on the carpet and went on.

In the little rock room of the outer wall he saw what he had glimpsed when Vaudir opened the door. Retribution had overtaken the eunuch. The body must have been his, for tatters of scarlet velvet lay about the floor, but there was no way to recognize what its original form had been. The smell of salt was heavy in the air, and a trail of black slime snaked across the floor toward the wall. The wall was solid, but it ended there. . . .

Smith laid his hand on the outer door, drew the bar, swung it open. He stepped out under the hanging vines and filled his lungs with pure air, free, clear, untainted with scent or salt. A pearly dawn was breaking over Ednes.

THE TREE OF LIFE

Over time-ruined Illar the searching planes swooped and circled. Northwest Smith, peering up at them with a steel-pale stare from the shelter of a half-collapsed temple, thought of vultures wheeling above carrion. All day long now they had been raking these ruins for him. Presently, he knew, thirst would begin to parch his throat and hunger to gnaw at him. There was neither food nor water in these ancient Martian ruins, and he knew that it could be only a matter of time before the urgencies of his own body would drive him out to signal those wheeling Patrol ships and trade his hard-won liberty for food and drink. He crouched lower under the shadow of the temple arch and cursed the accuracy of the Patrol gunner whose flame-blast had caught his dodging ship just at the edge of Illar's ruins.

Presently it occurred to him that in most Martian temples of the ancient days an ornamental well had stood in the outer court for the benefit of wayfarers. Of course all water in it would be a million years dry now, but for lack of anything better to do he rose from his seat at the edge of the collapsed central dome and made his cautious way by still intact corridors toward the front of the temple. He paused in a tangle of wreckage at the courtyard's edge and looked out across the sun-drenched expanse of pavement toward that ornate well that once had served travelers who passed by here in the days when Mars was a green planet.

It was an unusually elaborate well, and amazingly well preserved. Its rim had been inlaid with a mosaic pattern whose symbolism must once have borne deep meaning, and above it in a great fan of time-defying bronze an elaborate grille-work portrayed the inevitable tree-of-life pattern which so often appears in the symbolism of the three worlds. Smith looked at it a bit incredulously from his shelter, it was so miraculously preserved amidst all this chaos of broken stone, casting a delicate tracery of shadow on the sunny pavement as perfectly as it must have done a million years ago when dusty travelers paused here to drink. He could picture them filing in at noontime through the great gates that—

The vision vanished abruptly as his questing eyes made the circle of the ruined walls. There had been no gate. He could not find a trace of it anywhere around the outer wall of the court. The only entrance here, as nearly as he could tell from the foundations that remained, had been the door in whose ruins he now stood. Queer. This must have been a private court, then, its great grille-crowned well reserved for the use of the priests. Or wait—had there not been a priest-king Illar after whom the city was named? A wizard-king, so legend said, who ruled temple as well as palace with an iron hand. This elaborately patterned well, of material royal enough to withstand the weight of ages, might well have been sacrosanct for the use of that long-dead monarch. It might—

Across the sun-bright pavement swept the shadow of a plane. Smith dodged back into deeper hiding while the ship circled low over the courtyard. And it was then, as he crouched against a crumbled wall and waited, motionless, for the danger to pass, that he became aware for the first time of a sound that startled him so he could scarcely credit his ears—a recurrent sound, choked and sorrowful—the sound of a woman sobbing.

The incongruity of it made him forgetful for a moment of the peril hovering overhead in the sun-hot outdoors. The dimness of the temple ruins became a living and vital place for that moment, throbbing with the sound of tears. He looked about half in incredulity, wondering if hunger and thirst were playing tricks on him already, or if these broken halls might be haunted by a million-year-old sorrow that wept along the corridors to drive its hearers mad. There were tales of such haunters in some of Mars' older ruins. The hair prickled faintly at the back of his neck as he laid a hand on the butt of his force-gun and commenced a cautious prowl toward the source of the muffled noise.

Presently he caught a flash of white, luminous in the gloom of these ruined walls, and went forward with soundless steps, eyes narrowed in the effort to make out what manner of creature this might be that wept alone in time-forgotten ruins. It was a woman. Or it had the dim outlines of a woman, huddled against an angle of fallen walls and veiled in a fabulous shower of long dark hair. But there was something uncannily odd about her. He could not focus his pale stare upon her outlines. She was scarcely more than a luminous blot of whiteness in the gloom, shimmering with a look of unreality which the sound of her sobs denied.

Before he could make up his mind just what to do, something must have warned the weeping girl that she was no longer alone, for the sound of her tears checked suddenly and she lifted her head, turning to him a face no more distinguishable than her body's outlines. He made no effort to resolve the blurred features into visibility, for out of that luminous mask burned two eyes that caught his with an almost perceptible impact and gripped them in a stare from which he could not have turned if he would.

They were the most amazing eyes he had ever met, colored like moonstone, milkily translucent, so that they looked almost blind. And that magnetic stare held him motionless.

In the instant that she gripped him with that fixed, moonstone look he felt oddly as if a tangible bond were taut between them.

Then she spoke, and he wondered if his mind, after all, had begun to give way in the haunted loneliness of dead Illar; for though the words she spoke fell upon his ears in a gibberish of meaningless sounds, yet in his brain a message formed with a clarity that far transcended the halting communication of words. And her milkily colored eyes bored into his with a fierce intensity.

"I'm lost—I'm lost—" wailed the voice in his brain.

A rush of sudden tears brimmed the compelling eyes, veiling their brilliance. And he was free again with that clouding of the moonstone surfaces. Her voice wailed, but the words were meaningless and no knowledge formed in his brain to match them. Stiffly he stepped back a pace and looked down at her, a feeling of helpless incredulity rising within him. For he still could not focus directly upon the shining whiteness of her, and nothing save those moonstone eyes were clear to him.

The girl sprang to her feet and rose on tiptoe, gripping his shoulders with urgent hands. Again the blind intensity of her eyes took hold of his, with a force almost as tangible as the clutch of her hands; again that stream of intelligence poured into his brain, strongly, pleadingly.

"Please, please take me back! I'm so frightened—I can't find my way—oh, please!"

He blinked down at her, his dazed mind gradually realizing the basic facts of what was happening. Obviously her milky unseeing eyes held a magnetic power that carried her thoughts to him without the need of a common speech. And they were the eyes of a powerful mind, the outlets from which a stream of fierce energy poured into his brain. Yet the words they conveyed were the words of a terrified and helpless girl. A strong sense of wariness was rising in him as he considered the incongruity of speech and power, both of which were beating upon him more urgently with every breath. The mind of a forceful and strong-willed woman, carrying the sobs of a frightened girl. There was no sincerity in it.

"Please, please!" cried her impatience in his brain. "Help me! Guide me back!"

"Back where?" he heard his own voice asking.

"The Tree!" wailed that queer speech in his brain, while gibberish was all his ears heard and the moonstone stare transfixed him strongly. "The Tree of Life! Oh, take me back to the shadow of the Tree!"

A vision of the grille-ornamented well leaped into his memory. It was the only tree symbol he could think of just then. But what possible connection could there be between the well and the lost girl—if she was lost? Another wail in that unknown tongue, another anguished shake of his shoulders, brought a sudden resolution into his groping mind. There could be no harm in leading her back to the well, to whose grille she must surely be referring. And strong curiosity was growing in his mind. Much more than met the eye was concealed in this queer incident. And a wild guess had flashed through his mind that perhaps she might have come from some subterranean world into which the well descended. It would explain her luminous pallor, if not her blurriness; and, too, her eyes did not seem to function in the light. There was a much more incredible explanation of her presence, but he was not to know it for a few minutes yet.

"Come along," he said, taking the clutching hands gently from his shoulders. "I'll lead you to the well."

She sighed in a deep gust of relief and dropped her compelling eyes from his, murmuring in that strange, gabbling tongue what must have been thanks. He took her by the hand and turned toward the ruined archway of the door.

Against his fingers her flesh was cool and firm. To the touch she was tangible, but even thus near, his eyes refused to focus upon the cloudy opacity of her body, the dark blur of her streaming hair. Nothing but those burning, blinded eyes were strong enough to pierce the veil that parted them.

She stumbled along at his side over the rough floor of the

temple, saying nothing more, panting with eagerness to return to her incomprehensible "tree." How much of that eagerness was assumed Smith still could not be quite sure. When they reached the door he halted her for a moment, scanning the sky for danger. Apparently the ships had finished with this quarter of the city, for he could see two or three of them half a mile away, hovering low over Illar's northern section. He could risk it without much peril. He led the girl cautiously out into the sun-hot court.

She could not have known by sight that they neared the well, but when they were within twenty paces of it she flung up her blurred head suddenly and tugged at his hand. It was she who led him that last stretch which parted the two from the well. In the sun the shadow tracery of the grille's symbolic pattern lay vividly outlined on the ground. The girl gave a little gasp of delight. She dropped his hand and ran forward three short steps, and plunged into the very center of that shadowy pattern on the ground. And what happened then was too incredible to believe.

The pattern ran over her like garment, curving to the curve of her body in the way all shadows do. But as she stood there striped and laced with the darkness of it, there came a queer shifting in the lines of black tracery, a subtle, inexplicable movement to one side. And with that motion she vanished. It was exactly as if that shifting had moved her out of one world into another. Stupidly Smith stared at the spot from which she had disappeared.

Then several things happened almost simultaneously. The zoom of a plane broke suddenly into the quiet, a black shadow dipped low over the rooftops, and Smith, too late, realized that he stood defenseless in full view of the searching ships. There was only one way out, and that was too fantastic to put faith in, but he had no time to hesitate. With one leap he plunged full into the midst of the shadow of the tree of life.

Its tracery flowed round him, molding its pattern to his body. And outside the boundaries everything executed a queer little sidewise dip and slipped in the most extraordinary manner, like an optical illusion, into quite another scene. There was no intervention of blankness. It was as if he looked through the bars of a grille upon a picture which without warning slipped sidewise, while between the bars appeared another scene, a curious, dim landscape, gray as if with the twilight of early evening. The air had an oddly thickened look, through which he saw the quiet trees and the flower-spangled grass of the place with a queer, unreal blending, like the landscape in a tapestry, all its outlines blurred.

In the midst of this tapestried twilight the burning whiteness of the girl he had followed blazed like a flame. She had paused a few steps away and stood waiting, apparently quite sure that he would come after. He grinned a little to himself as he realized it, knowing that curiosity must almost certainly have driven him in her wake even if the necessity for shelter had not compelled his following.

She was clearly visible now, in this thickened dimness—visible, and very lovely, and a little unreal. She shone with a burning clarity, the only vivid thing in the whole twilit world. Eyes upon that blazing whiteness, Smith stepped forward, scarcely realizing that he had moved.

Slowly he crossed the dark grass toward her. That grass was soft underfoot, and thick with small, low-blooming flowers of a shining pallor. Botticelli painted such spangled swards for the feet of his angels. Upon it the girl's bare feet gleamed whiter than the blossoms. She wore no garment but the royal mantle of her hair, sweeping about her in a cloak of shining darkness that had a queer, unreal tinge of purple in that low light. It brushed her ankles in its fabulous length. From the hood of it she watched Smith coming toward her, a smile on her pale mouth and a light blazing in the deeps of her moonstone eyes. She was not blind now, nor frightened. She stretched out her hand to him confidently.

"It is my turn now to lead you," she smiled. As before, the words were gibberish, but the penetrating stare of those strange white eyes gave them a meaning in the depths of his brain.

Automatically his hand went out to hers. He was a little dazed, and her eyes were very compelling. Her fingers twined in his and she set off over the flowery grass, pulling him beside her. He did not ask where they were going. Lost in the dreamy spell of the still, gray, enchanted place, he felt no need for words. He was beginning to see more clearly in the odd, blurring twilight that ran the outlines of things together in that queer, tapestried manner. And he puzzled in a futile, muddled way as he went on over what sort of land he had come into. Overhead was darkness, paling into twilight near the ground, so that when he looked up he was staring into bottomless deeps of starless night.

Trees and flowering shrubs and the flower-starred grass stretched emptily about them in the thick, confusing gloom of the place. He could see only a little distance through that dim air. It was as if they walked a strip of tapestried twilight in some unlighted dream. And the girl, with her lovely, luminous body and richly colored robe of hair was like a woman in a tapestry too, unreal and magical.

After a while, when he had become a little adjusted to the queerness of the whole scene, he began to notice furtive movements in the shrubs and trees they passed. Things flickered too swiftly for him to catch their outlines, but from the tail of his eye he was aware of motion, and somehow of eyes that watched. That sensation was a familiar one to him, and he kept an uneasy gaze on those shiftings in the shrubbery as they went on. Presently he caught a watcher in full view between bush and tree, and saw that it was a man, a little, furtive, dark-skinned man who dodged hastily back into cover again before Smith's eyes could do more than take in the fact of his existence.

After that he knew what to expect and could make them out more easily: little, darting people with big eyes that shone with a queer, sorrowful darkness from their small, frightened faces as they scuttled through the bushes, dodging always just out of plain sight among the leaves. He could hear the soft rustle of their passage, and once or twice when they passed near a clump of shrubbery he thought he caught the echo of little whispering calls, gentle as the rustle of leaves and somehow full of a strange warning note so clear that he caught it even amid the murmur of their speech. Warning calls, and little furtive hiders in the leaves, and a landscape of tapestried blurring carpeted with a Botticelli flower-strewn sward. It was all a dream. He felt quite sure of that.

It was a long while before curiosity awakened in him sufficiently to make him break the stillness. But at last he asked dreamily.

"Where are we going?"

The girl seemed to understand that without the necessity of the bond her hypnotic eyes made, for she turned and caught his eyes in a white stare and answered.

"To Thag. Thag desire you."

"What is Thag?"

In answer to that she launched without preliminary upon a little singsong monolog of explanation whose stereotyped formula made him faintly uneasy with the thoughts that it must have been made very often to attain the status of a set speech; made to many men, perhaps, whom Thag had desired. And what became of them afterward? he wondered. But the girl was speaking.

"Many ages ago there dwelt in Illar the great King Illar for whom the city was named. He was a magician of mighty power, but not mighty enough to fulfill all his ambitions. So by his arts he called up out of darkness the being known as Thag, and with him struck a bargain. By that bargain Thag was to give of his limitless power, serving Illar all the days of Illar's life, and in return the king was to create a land for Thag's dwelling-place and people it with slaves and furnish a priestess to tend Thag's needs. This is that land. I am that priestess, the latest of a long line of women born to serve Thag. The tree-people are his—his lesser servants.

"I have spoken softly so that the tree-people do not hear, for to them Thag is the center and focus of creation, the end and beginning of all life. But to you I have told the truth."

"But what does Thag want of me?"

"It is not for Thag's servants to question Thag."

"Then what becomes, afterward, of the men Thag desires?" he pursued.

"You must ask Thag that."

She turned her eyes away as she spoke, snapping the mental bond that had flowed between them with a suddenness that left Smith dizzy. He went on at her side more slowly, pulling back a little on the tug of her fingers. By degrees the sense of dreaminess was fading, and alarm began to stir in the deeps of his mind. After all, there was no reason why he need let this blank-eyed priestess lead him up to the very maw of her god. She had lured him into this land by what he knew now to have been a trick; might she not have worse tricks than that in store for him?

She held him, after all, by nothing stronger than the clasp of her fingers, if he could keep his eyes turned from hers. Therein lay her real power, but he could fight it if he chose. And he began to hear more clearly than ever the queer note of warning in the rustling whispers of the tree-folk who still fluttered in and out of sight among the leaves. The twilight place had taken on menace and evil.

Suddenly he made up his mind. He stopped, breaking the clasp of the girl's hand.

"I'm not going," he said.

She swung round in a sweep of richly tinted hair, words jetting from her in a gush of incoherence. But he dared not meet her eyes, and they conveyed no meaning to him. Resolutely he turned away, ignoring her voice, and set out to retrace the way they had come. She called after him once, in a high, clear voice that somehow held a note as warning as that in the rustling voices of the tree-people, but he kept on doggedly, not looking back. She laughed then, sweetly and scornfully, a laugh that echoed uneasily in his mind long after the sound of it had died upon the twilight air.

After a while he glanced back over one shoulder, half expecting to see the luminous dazzle of her body still glowing in the dim glade where he had left her; but the blurred tapestry-landscape was quite empty.

He went on in the midst of a silence so deep it hurt his ears, and in a solitude unhaunted even by the shy presences of the tree-folk. They had vanished with the fire-bright girl, and the whole twilight land was empty save for himself. He plodded on across the dark grass, crushing the upturned flower-faces under his boots and asking himself wearily if he could be mad. There seemed little other explanation for this hushed and tapestried solitude that had swallowed him up. In that thunderous quiet, in that deathly solitude, he went on.

When he had walked for what seemed to him much longer than it should have taken to reach his starting point, and still no sign of an exit appeared, he began to wonder if there were any way out of the gray land of Thag. For the first time he realized that he had come through no tangible gateway. He had only stepped out of a shadow, and—now that he thought of it—there were no shadows here. The grayness swallowed everything up, leaving the landscape oddly flat, like a badly drawn picture. He looked about helplessly, quite lost now and not sure in what direction he should be facing, for there was nothing here by which to know directions. The trees and shrubs and the starry grass still stretched about him, uncertainly outlined in that changeless dusk. They seemed to go on for ever.

But he plodded ahead, unwilling to stop because of a queer tension in the air, somehow as if all the blurred trees and shrubs were waiting in breathless anticipation, centering upon his stumbling figure. But all trace of animate life had vanished with the disappearance of the priestess' white-glowing figure. Head down, paying little heed to where he was going, he went on over the flowery sward.

An odd sense of voids about him startled Smith at last out of his lethargic plodding. He lifted his head. He stood just at the edge of a line of trees, dim and indistinct in the unchanging twilight. Beyond them—he came to himself with a jerk and stared incredulously. Beyond them the grass ran down to nothingness, merging by imperceptible degrees into a streaked and arching void—not the sort of emptiness into which a material body could fall, but a solid *nothing*, curving up toward the dark zenith as the inside of a sphere curves. No physical thing could have entered there. It was too utterly void, an inviolable emptiness which no force could invade.

He stared up along the inward arch of that curving, impassable wall. Here, then, was the edge of the queer land Illar had wrested out of space itself. This arch must be the curving of solid space which had been bent awry to enclose the magical land. There was no escape this way. He could not even bring himself to approach any nearer to that streaked and arching blank. He could not have said why, but it woke in him an inner disquiet so strong that after a moment's staring he turned his eyes away.

Presently he shrugged and set off along the inside of the line of trees which parted him from the space-wall. Perhaps there might be a break somewhere. It was a forlorn hope, but the best that offered. Wearily he stumbled on over the flowery grass.

How long he had gone on along that almost imperceptibly curving line of border he could not have said, but after a timeless interval of gray solitude he gradually became aware that a tiny rustling and whispering among the leaves had been growing louder by degrees for some time. He looked up. In and out among the trees which bordered that solid wall of nothingness little, indistinguishable figures were flitting. The tree-men had returned. Queerly grateful for their presence, he went on a bit more cheerfully, paying no heed to their timid dartings to and fro, for Smith was wise in the ways of wild life.

Presently, when they saw how little heed he paid them, they began to grow bolder, their whispers louder. And among those rustling voices he thought he was beginning to catch threads of familiarity. Now and again a word reached his ears that he seemed to recognize, lost amidst the gibberish of their speech. He kept his head down and his hands quiet, plodding along with a cunning stillness that began to bear results.

From the corner of his eye he could see that a little dark tree-man had darted out from cover and paused midway between bush and tree to inspect the queer, tall stranger. Nothing happened to this daring venturer, and soon another risked a pause in the open to stare at the quiet walker among the trees. In a little while a small crowd of the tree-people was moving slowly parallel with his course, staring with all the avid curiosity of wild things at Smith's plodding figure. And among them the rustling whispers grew louder.

Presently the ground dipped down into a little hollow ringed with trees. It was a bit darker here than it had been on the higher level, and as he went down the slope of its side he saw that among the underbrush which filled it were cunningly hidden huts twined together out of the living bushes. Obviously the hollow was a tiny village where the tree-folk dwelt.

He was surer of this when they began to grow bolder as he went down into the dimness of the place. The whispers shrilled a little, and the boldest among his watchers ran almost at his elbow, twittering their queer, broken speech in hushed syllables whose familiarity still bothered him with its haunting echo of words he knew. When he had reached the center of the hollow he became aware that the little folk had spread out in a ring to surround him. Wherever he looked their small, anxious faces and staring eyes confronted him. He grinned to himself and came to a halt, waiting gravely.

None of them seemed quite brave enough to constitute himself spokesman, but among several a hurried whispering broke out in which he caught the words "Thag" and "danger" and "beware." He recognized the meaning of these words without placing in his mind their origins in some tongue he knew. He knit his sun-bleached brows and concentrated harder, striving to wrest from that curious, murmuring whisper some hint of its original root. He had a smattering of more tongues than he could have counted offhand, and it was hard to place these scattered words among any one speech.

But the word "Thag" had a sound like that of the very

ancient dryland tongue, which upon Mars is considered at once the oldest and most uncouth of all the planet's languages. And with that clue to guide him he presently began to catch other syllables which were remotely like syllables from the dryland speech. They were almost unrecognizable, far, far more ancient than the very oldest versions of the tongue he had ever heard repeated, almost primitive in their crudity and simplicity. And for a moment the sheerest awe came over him, as he realized the significance of what he listened to.

The dryland race today is a handful of semi-brutes, degenerate from the ages of past time when they were a mighty people at the apex of an almost forgotten glory. That day is millions of years gone now, too far in the past to have record save in the vaguest folklore. Yet here was a people who spoke the rudiments of that race's tongue as it must have been spoken in the race's dim beginnings, perhaps, a million years earlier even than that immemorial time of their triumph. The reeling of millenniums set Smith's mind awhirl with the effort at compassing their span.

There was another connotation in the speaking of that tongue by these timid bush-dwellers, too. It must mean that the forgotten wizard king, Illar, had peopled his sinister, twilight land with the ancestors of today's dryland dwellers. If they shared the same tongue they must share the same lineage. And humanity's remorseless adaptability had done the rest.

It had been no kinder here than in the outside world, where the ancient plainsmen who had roamed Mars' green prairies had dwindled with their dying plains, degenerating at last into a shrunken, leather-skinned bestiality. For here that same race root had declined into these tiny, slinking creatures with their dusky skins and great, staring eyes and their voices that never rose above a whisper. What tragedies must lie behind that gradual degeneration!

All about him the whispers still ran. He was beginning to suspect that through countless ages of hiding and murmuring those voices must have lost the ability to speak aloud. And he wondered with a little inward chill what terror it was which had transformed a free and fearless people into these tiny wild things whispering in the underbrush.

The little anxious voices had shrilled into vehemence now, all of them chattering together in their queer, soft, rustling whispers. Looking back later upon that timeless space he had passed in the hollow, Smith remembered it as some curious nightmare—dimness and tapestried blurring, and a hush like death over the whole twilight land, and the timid voices whispering, whispering, eloquent with terror and warning.

He groped back among his memories and brought forth a phrase or two remembered from long ago, an archaic rendering of the immemorial tongue they spoke. It was the simplest version he could remember of the complex speech now used, but he knew that to them it must sound fantastically strange. Instinctively he whispered as he spoke it, feeling like an actor in a play as he mouthed the ancient idiom,

"I—I cannot understand. Speak—more slowly—"

A torrent of words greeted this rendering of their tongue. Then there was a great deal of hushing and hissing, and presently two or three between them began laboriously to recite an involved speech, one syllable at a time. Always two or more shared the task. Never in his converse with them did he address anyone directly. Ages of terror had bred all directness out of them.

"Thag," they said. "Thag, the terrible—That, the omnipotent—Thag, the unescapable. Beware of Thag."

For a moment Smith stood quiet, grinning down at them despite himself. There must not be too much of intelligence left among this branch of the race, either, for surely such a warning was superfluous. Yet they had mastered their agonies of timidity to give it. All virtue could not yet have been bred out of them, then. They still had kindness and a sort of desperate courage rooted deep in fear.

"What is Thag?" he managed to inquire, voicing the archaic syllables uncertainly. And they must have understood the meaning if not the phraseology, for another spate of whispered tumult burst from the clustering tribe. Then, as before, several took up the task of answering.

"Thag—Thag, the end and the beginning, the center of creation. When Thag breathes the world trembles. The earth was made for Thag's dwelling-place. All things are Thag's. Oh, beware! Beware!"

This much he pieced together out of their diffuse whisperings, catching up the fragments of words he knew and fitting them into the pattern.

"What—what is the danger?" he managed to ask.

"Thag—hungers. Thag must be fed. It is we who—feed—him, but there are times when he desires other food than us. It is then he sends his priestess forth to lure—food—in. Oh, beware of Thag!"

"You mean that the priestess brought me in for—food?"

A chorus of grave, murmuring affirmatives.

"Then why did she leave me?"

"There is no escape from Thag. Thag is the center of creation. All things are Thag's. When he calls, you must answer. When he hungers, he will have you. Beware of Thag!"

Smith considered that for a moment in silence. In the main he felt confident that he had understood their warning correctly, and he had little reason to doubt that they knew whereof they spoke. Thag might not be the center of the universe, but if they said he could call a victim from anywhere in the land, Smith was not disposed to doubt it. The priestess' willingness to let him leave her unhindered, yes, even her scornful laughter as he looked back, told the same story. Whatever Thag might be, his power in this land could not be doubted. He made up his mind suddenly what he must do, and turned to the breathlessly waiting little folk.

"Which way—lies Thag?" he asked.

A score of dark, thin arms pointed. Smith turned his head speculatively toward the spot they indicated. In this changeless twilight all sense of direction had long since left him, but he marked the line as well as he could by the formation of the trees, then turned to the little people with a ceremonious farewell rising to his lips.

"My thanks for—" he began, to be interrupted by a chorus of whispering cries of protest. They seemed to sense his intention, and their pleadings were frantic. A panic anxiety for him glowed upon every little terrified face turned up to his, and their eyes were wide with protest and terror. Helplessly he looked down.

"I—I must go," he tried stumblingly to say. "My only chance is to take Thag unawares, before he sends for me."

He could not know if they understood. Their chattering went on undiminished, and they even went so far as to lay tiny hands on him, as if they would prevent him by force from seeking out the terror of their lives.

"No, no, no!" they wailed murmurously. "You do not know what it is you seek! You do not know Thag! Stay here! Beware of Thag!"

A little prickling of unease went down Smith's back as he listened. Thag must be very terrible indeed if even half this alarm had foundation. And to be quite frank with himself, he would greatly have preferred to remain here in the hidden quiet of the hollow, with its illusion of shelter, for as long as he was allowed to stay. But he was not of the stuff that yields very easily to its own terrors, and hope burned strongly in him still. So he squared his broad shoulders and turned resolutely in the direction the tree-folk had indicated.

When they saw that he meant to go, their protests sank to a wail of bitter grieving. With that sound moaning behind him he went up out of the hollow, like a man setting forth to the music of his own dirge. A few of the bravest went with him a little way, flitting through the underbrush and darting from tree to tree in a timidity so deeply ingrained that even when no immediate peril threatened they dared not go openly through the twilight.

Their presence was comforting to Smith as he went on. A futile desire to help the little terror-ridden tribe was rising in him, a useless gratitude for their warning and their friendliness, their genuine grieving at his departure and their odd, paradoxical bravery even in the midst of hereditary terror. But he knew that he could do nothing for them, when he was not at all sure he could even save himself. Something of their panic had communicated itself to him, and he advanced with a sinking at the pit of his stomach. Fear of the unknown is so poignant a thing, feeding on its own terror, that he found his hands beginning to shake a little and his throat going dry as he went on.

The rustling and whispering among the bushes dwindled as his followers one by one dropped away, the bravest staying the longest, but even they failing in courage as Smith advanced steadily in that direction from which all their lives they had been taught to turn their faces. Presently he realized that he was alone once more. He went on more quickly, anxious to come face to face with this horror of the twilight and dispel at least the fearfulness of its mystery.

The silence was like death. Not a breeze stirred the leaves, and the only sound was his own breathing, the heavy thud of his own heart. Somehow he felt sure that he was coming nearer to his goal. The hush seemed to confirm it. He loosened the force-gun at his thigh.

In that changeless twilight the ground was sloping down once more into a broader hollow. He descended slowly, every sense alert for danger, not knowing if Thag was beast or human or elemental, visible or invisible. The trees were beginning to thin. He knew that he had almost reached his goal.

He paused at the edge of the last line of trees. A clearing spread out before him at the bottom of the hollow, quiet in the dim, translucent air. He could focus directly upon no outlines anywhere, for the tapestried blurring of the place. But when he saw what stood in the very center of the clearing he stopped dead-still, like one turned to stone, and a shock of utter cold went chilling through him. Yet he could not have said why.

For in the clearing's center stood the Tree of Life. He had

met the symbol too often in patterns and designs not to recognize it, but here that fabulous thing was living, growing, actually springing up from a rooted firmness in the spangled grass as any tree might spring. Yet it could not be real. Its thin brown trunk, of no recognizable substance, smooth and gleaming, mounted in the traditional spiral; its twelve fantastically curving branches arched delicately outward from the central stem. It was bare of leaves. No foliage masked the serpentine brown spiral of the trunk. But at the tip of each symbolic branch flowered a blossom of bloody rose so vivid he could scarcely focus his dazzled eyes upon them.

This tree alone of all objects in the dim land was sharply distinct to the eye—terribly distinct, remorselessly clear. No words can describe the amazing menace that dwelt among its branches. Smith's flesh crept as he stared, yet he could not for all his staring make out why peril was so eloquent there. To all appearances here stood only a fabulous symbol miraculously come to life; yet danger breathed out from it so strongly that Smith felt the hair lifting on his neck as he stared.

It was no ordinary danger. A nameless, choking, paralyzed panic was swelling in his throat as he gazed upon the perilous beauty of the Tree. Somehow the arches and curves of its branches seemed to limn a pattern so dreadful that his heart beat faster as he gazed upon it. But he could not guess why, though somehow the answer was hovering just out of reach of his conscious mind. From that first glimpse of it his instincts shuddered like a shying stallion, yet reason still looked in vain for an answer.

Nor was the Tree merely a vegetable growth. It was alive, terribly, ominously alive. He could not have said how he knew that, for it stood motionless in its empty clearing, not a branch trembling, yet in its immobility more awfully vital than any animate thing. The very sight of it woke in Smith an insane urging to flight, to put worlds between himself and this inexplicably dreadful thing.

Crazy impulses stirred in his brain, coming to insane birth

at the calling of the Tree's peril—the desperate need to shut out the sight of that thing that was blasphemy, to put out his own sight rather than gaze longer upon the perilous grace of its branches, to slit his own throat that he might not need to dwell in the same world which housed so frightful a sight as the Tree.

All this was a mad battering in his brain. The strength of him was enough to isolate it in a far corner of his consciousness, where it seethed and shrieked half heeded while he turned the cool control which the spaceways life had taught him to the solution of this urgent question. But even so his hand was moist and shaking on his gun-butt, and the breath rasped in his dry throat.

Why—he asked himself in a determined groping after steadiness—should the mere sight of a tree, even so fabulous a one as this, rouse that insane panic in the gazer? What peril could dwell invisibly in a tree so frightful that the living horror of it could drive a man mad with the very fact of its unseen presence? He clenched his teeth hard and stared resolutely at that terrible beauty in the clearing, fighting down the sick panic that rose in his throat as his eyes forced themselves to dwell upon the Tree.

Gradually the revulsion subsided. After a nightmare of striving he mustered the strength to force it down far enough to allow reason's entry once more. Sternly holding down that frantic terror under the surface of consciousness, he stared resolutely at the Tree. And he knew that this was Thag.

It could be nothing else, for surely two such dreadful things could not dwell in one land. It must be Thag, and he could understand now the immemorial terror in which the tree-folk held it, but he did not yet grasp in what way it threatened them physically. The inexplicable dreadfulness of it was a menace to the mind's very existence, but surely a rooted tree, however terrible to look at, could wield little actual danger.

As he reasoned, his eyes were seeking restlessly among the branches, searching for the answer to their dreadfulness.

After all, this thing wore the aspect of an old pattern, and in that pattern there was nothing dreadful. The tree of life had made up the design upon that well-top in Illar through whose shadow he had entered here, and nothing in that bronze grille-work had roused terror. Then why—? What living menace dwelt invisibly among these branches to twist them into curves of horror?

A fragment of old verse drifted through his mind as he stared in perplexity:

What immortal hand or eye
Could frame thy fearful symmetry?

And for the first time the true significance of a "fearful symmetry" broke upon him. Truly a more than human agency must have arched these subtle curves so delicately into dreadfulness, into such an awful beauty that the very sight of it made those atavistic terrors he was so sternly holding down leap in a gibbering terror.

A tremor rippled over the Tree. Smith froze rigid, staring with startled eyes. No breath of wind had stirred through the clearing, but the Tree was moving with a slow, serpentine grace, writhing its branches leisurely in a horrible travesty of voluptuous enjoyment. And upon their tips the blood-red flowers were spreading like cobra's hoods, swelling and stretching their petals out and glowing with a hue so eye-piercingly vivid that it transcended the bounds of color and blazed forth like pure light.

But it was not toward Smith that they stirred. They were arching out from the central trunk toward the far side of the clearing. After a moment Smith tore his eyes away from the indescribably dreadful flexibility of those branches and looked to see the cause of their writhing.

A blaze of luminous white had appeared among the trees across the clearing. The priestess had returned. He watched her pacing slowly toward the Tree, walking with a precise and delicate grace as liquidly lovely as the motion of the

Tree. Her fabulous hair swung down about her in a swaying robe that rippled at every step away from the moonwhite beauty of her body. Straight toward the Tree she paced, and all the blossoms glowed more vividly at her nearness, the branches stretching toward her, rippling with eagerness.

Priestess though she was, he could not believe that she was going to come within touch of that Tree the very sight of which roused such a panic instinct of revulsion in every fiber of him. But she did not swerve or slow in her advance. Walking delicately over the flowery grass, arrogantly luminous in the twilight, so that her body was the center and focus of any landscape she walked in, she neared her horribly eager god.

Now she was under the Tree, and its trunk had writhed down over her and she was lifting her arms like a girl to her lover. With a gliding slowness the flame-tipped branches slid round her. In that incredible embrace she stood immobile for a long moment, the Tree arching down with all its curling limbs, the girl straining upward, her head thrown back and the mantle of her hair swinging free of her body as she lifted her face to the quivering blossoms. The branches gathered her closer in their embrace. Now the blossoms arched near, curving down all about her, touching her very gently, twisting their blazing faces toward the focus of her moon-white body. One poised directly above her face, trembled, brushed her mouth lightly. And the Tree's tremor ran unbroken through the body of the girl it clasped.

The incredible dreadfulness of that embrace was suddenly more than Smith could bear. All his terrors, crushed down with so stern a self-control, without warning burst all bounds and rushed over him in a flood of blind revulsion. A whimper choked up in his throat and quite involuntarily he swung round and plunged into the shielding trees, hands to his eyes in a futile effort to blot out the sight of lovely horror behind him whose vividness was burnt upon his very brain.

Heedlessly he blundered through the trees, no thought in his terror-blank mind save the necessity to run, run, run until he could run no more. He had given up all attempt at reason and rationality; he no longer cared why the beauty of the Tree was so dreadful. He only knew that until all space lay between him and its symmetry he must run and run and run.

What brought that frenzied madness to an end he never knew. When sanity returned to him he was lying face down on the flower-spangled sward in a silence so deep that his ears ached with its heaviness. The grass was cool against his cheek. For a moment he fought the back-flow of knowledge into his emptied mind. When it came, the memory of that horror he had fled from, he started up with a wild thing's swiftness and glared around pale-eyed into the unchanging dusk. He was alone. Not even a rustle in the leaves spoke of the tree-folk's presence.

For a moment he stood there alert, wondering what had roused him, wondering what would come next. He was not left long in doubt. The answer was shrilling very, very faintly through that aching quiet, an infinitesimally tiny, unthinkably far-away murmur which yet pierced his eardrums with sharpness of tiny needles. Breathless, he strained in listening. Swiftly the sound grew louder. It deepened upon the silence, sharpened and shrilled until the thin blade of it was vibrating in the center of his innermost brain.

And still it grew, swelling louder and louder through the twilight world in cadences that were rounding into a queer sort of music and taking on such an unbearable sweetness that Smith pressed his hands over his ears in a futile attempt to shut the sound away. He could not. It rang in steadily deepening intensities through every fiber of his being, piercing him with thousands of tiny music-blades that quivered in his very soul with intolerable beauty. And he thought he sensed in the piercing strength of it a vibration of queer, unnamable power far mightier than anything ever generated by man, the dim echo of some cosmic dynamo's hum.

The sound grew sweeter as it strengthened, with a queer, inexplicable sweetness unlike any music he had ever heard before, rounder and fuller and more complete than any melody made up of separate notes. Stronger and stronger he felt the certainty that it was the song of some mighty power, humming and throbbing and deepening through the twilight until the whole dim land was one trembling reservoir of sound that filled his entire consciousness with its throbbing, driving out all other thoughts and realizations, until he was no more than a shell that vibrated in answer to the calling.

For it was a calling. No one could listen to that intolerable sweetness without knowing the necessity to seek its source. Remotely in the back of his mind Smith remembered the tree-folk's warning, "When Thag calls, you must answer." Not consciously did he recall it, for all his consciousness was answering the siren humming in the air, and, scarcely realizing that he moved, he had turned toward the source of that calling, stumbling blindly over the flowery sward with no thought in his music-brimmed mind but the need to answer that lovely, power-vibrant summoning.

Past him as he went on moved other shapes, little and dark-skinned and ecstatic, gripped like himself in the hypnotic melody. The tree-folk had forgotten even their inbred fear at Thag's calling, and walked boldly through the open twilight, lost in the wonder of the song.

Smith went on with the rest, deaf and blind to the land around him, alive to one thing only, that summons from the siren tune. Unrealizingly, he retraced the course of his frenzied flight, past the trees and bushes he had blundered through, down the slope that led to the Tree's hollow, through the thinning of the underbrush to the very edge of the last line of foliage which marked the valley's rim.

By now the calling was so unbearably intense, so intolerably sweet that somehow in its very strength it set free a part of his dazed mind as it passed the limits of audible things and soared into ecstasies which no senses bound. And though it gripped him ever closer in its magic, a sane part of his brain was waking into realization. For the first time alarm came back into his mind, and by slow degrees the world returned about him. He stared stupidly at the grass moving by under his pacing feet. He lifted a dragging head and saw that the trees no longer rose about him, that a twilit clearing stretched away on all sides toward the forest rim which circled it, that the music was singing from some source so near that—that—

The Tree! Terror leaped within him like a wild thing. The Tree, quivering with unbearable clarity in the thick, dim air, writhed above him, blossoms blazing with bloody radiance and every branch vibrant and undulant to the tune of that unholy song. Then he was aware of the lovely, luminous whiteness of the priestess swaying forward under the swaying limbs, her hair rippling back from the loveliness of her as she moved.

Choked and frenzied with unreasoning terror, he mustered every effort that was in him to turn, to run again like a madman out of that dreadful hollow, to hide himslf under the weight of all space from the menace of the Tree. And all the while he fought, all the while panic drummed like mad in his brain, his relentless body plodded on straight toward the hideous loveliness of that siren singer towering above him. From the first he had felt subconsciously that it was Thag who called, and now, in the very center of that ocean of vibrant power, he knew. Gripped in the music's magic, he went on.

All over the clearing other hypnotized victims were advancing slowly, with mechanical steps and wide, frantic eyes as the tree-folk came helplessly to their god's calling. He watched a group of little, dusky sacrifices pace step by step nearer to the Tree's vibrant branches. The priestess came forward to meet them with outstretched arms. He saw her take the foremost gently by the hands. Unbelieving, hypnotized with horrified incredulity, he watched her lead the rigid little creature forward under the fabulous Tree whose limbs yearned downward like hungry snakes: the great flowers glowing with avid color.

He saw the branches twist out and lengthen toward the sacrifice, quivering with eagerness. Then with a tiger's leap they darted, and the victim was swept out of the priestess' guiding hands up into the branches that darted round like tangled snakes in a clot that hid him for an instant from view. Smith heard a high, shuddering wail ripple out from that knot of struggling branches, a dreadful cry that held such an infinity of purest horror and understanding that he could not but believe that Thag's victims in the moment of their doom must learn the secret of his horror. After that one frightful cry came silence. In an instant the limbs fell apart again from emptiness. The little savage had melted like smoke among their writhing, too quickly to have been devoured, more as if he had been snatched into another dimension in the instant the hungry limbs hid him. Flame-tipped, avid, they were dipping now toward another victim as the priestess paced serenely forward.

And still Smith's rebellious feet were carrying him on, nearer and nearer the writhing peril that towered over his head. The music shrilled like pain. Now he was so close that he could see the hungry flower-mouths in terrible detail as they faced round toward him. The limbs quivered and poised like cobras, reached out with a snakish lengthening, down inexorably toward his shuddering helplessness. The priestess was turning her calm white face toward his.

Those arcs and changing curves of the branches as they neared were sketching lines of pure horror whose meaning he still could not understand, save that they deepened in dreadfulness as he neared. For the last time that urgent wonder burned up in his mind why—*why* so simple a thing as this fabulous Tree should be infused with an indwelling terror strong enough to send his innermost soul frantic with revulsion. For the last time—because in that trembling instant as he waited for their touch, as the music brimmed up with unbearable, brain-wrenching intensity, in that one last moment before the flower-mouths seized him—he saw. He understood.

With eyes opened at last by the instant's ultimate horror, he saw the real Thag. Dimly he knew that until now the thing had been so frightful that his eyes had refused to register its existence, his brain to acknowledge the possibility of such dreadfulness. It had literally been too terrible to see, though his instinct knew the presence of infinite horror. But now, in the grip of that mad, hypnotic song, in the instant before unbearable terror enfolded him, his eyes opened to full sight, and he saw.

That Tree was only Thag's outline, sketched three-dimensionally upon the twilight. Its dreadfully curving branches had been no more than Thag's barest contours, yet even they had made his very soul sick with intuitive revulsion. But now, seeing the true horror, his mind was too numb to do more than register its presence: Thag, hovering monstrously between earth and heaven, billowing and surging up there in the translucent twilight, tethered to the ground by the Tree's bending stem and reaching ravenously after the hypnotized fodder that his calling brought helpless into his clutches. One by one he snatched them up, one by one absorbed them into the great, unseeable horror of his being. That, then, was the reason why they vanished so instantaneously, sucked into the concealing folds of a thing too dreadful for normal eyes to see.

The priestess was pacing forward. Above her the branches arched and leaned. Caught in a timeless paralysis of horror, Smith stared upward into the enormous bulk of Thag while the music hummed intolerably in his shrinking brain—Thag, the monstrous thing from darkness, called up by Illar in those long-forgotten times when Mars was a green planet. Foolishly his brain wandered among the ramifications of what had happened so long ago that time itself had forgotten, refusing to recognize the fate that was upon himself. He knew a tingle of respect for the ages-dead wizard who had dared command a being like this to his services—this vast, blind, hovering thing, ravenous for human flesh, indistinguishable even now save in those terrible outlines that sent panic leaping through him with every motion of the Tree's fearful symmetry.

All this flashed through his dazed mind in the one blinding instant of understanding. Then the priestess' luminous whiteness swam up before his hypnotized stare. Her hands were upon him, gently guiding his mechanical footsteps, very gently leading him forward into—into—

The writhing branches struck downward, straight for his face. And in one flashing leap the moment's infinite horror galvanized him out of his paralysis. Why, he could not have said. It is not given to many men to know the ultimate essentials of all horror, concentrated into one fundamental unit. To most men it would have had that same paralyzing effect up to the very instant of destruction. But in Smith there must have been a bed-rock of subtle violence, an unyielding, inflexible vehemence upon which the structure of his whole life was reared. Few men have it. And when that ultimate intensity of terror struck the basic flint of him, reaching down through mind and soul into the deepest depths of his being, it struck a spark from that inflexible barbarian buried at the roots of him which had force enough to shock him out of his stupor.

In the instant of release his hand swept like an unloosed spring, of its own volition, straight for the butt of his power-gun. He was dragging it free as the Tree's branches snatched him from its priestess' hands. The fire-colored blossoms burnt his flesh as they closed round him, the hot branches gripping like the touch of ravenous fingers. The whole Tree was hot and throbbing with a dreadful travesty of fleshly life as it whipped him aloft into the hovering bulk of incarnate horror above.

In the instantaneous upward leap of the flower-tipped limbs Smith fought like a demon to free his gun-hand from the gripping coils. For the first time Thag knew rebellion in his very clutches, and the ecstasy of that music which had dinned in Smith's ears so strongly that by now it seemed almost silence was swooping down a long arc into wrath, and the branches tightened with hot insistency, lifting the rebellious offering into Thag's monstrous, indescribable bulk.

But even as they rose, Smith was twisting in their clutch to maneuver his hand into a position from which he could blast that undulant tree trunk into nothingness. He knew intuitively the futility of firing up into Thag's imponderable mass. Thag was not of the world he knew; the flame blast might well be harmless to that mighty hoverer in the twilight. But at the Tree's root, where Thag's essential being merged from the imponderable to the material, rooting in earthly soil, he should be vulnerable if he were vulnerable at all. Struggling in the tight, hot coils, breathing the nameless essence of horror, Smith fought to free his hand.

The music that had rung so long in his ears was changing as the branches lifted him higher, losing its melody and merging by swift degrees into a hum of vast and vibrant power that deepened in intensity as the limbs drew him upward into Thag's monstrous bulk, the singing force of a thing mightier than any dynamo ever built. Blinded and dazed by the force thundering through every atom of his body, he twisted his hand in one last, convulsive effort, and fired.

He saw the flame leap in a dazzling gush straight for the trunk below. It struck. He heard the sizzle of annihilated matter. He saw the trunk quiver convulsively from the very roots and the whole fabulous Tree shook once with an ominous tremor. But before that tremor could shiver up the branches to him the hum of the living dynamo which was closing round his body shrilled up arcs of pure intensity into a thundering silence.

Then without a moment's warning the world exploded. So instantaneously did all this happen that the gun-blast's roar had not yet echoed into silence before a mightier sound than the brain could bear exploded outward from the very center of his own being. Before the awful power of it everything reeled into a shaken oblivion. He felt himself falling. . . .

A queer, penetrating light shining upon his closed eyes roused Smith by degrees into wakefulness again. He lifted heavy lids and stared upward into the unwinking eye of Mars' racing nearer moon. He lay there blinking dazedly for a while before enough of memory returned to rouse him. Then he sat up painfully, for every fiber of him ached, and stared round on a scene of the wildest destruction. He lay in the midst of a wide, rough circle which held nothing but powdered stone. About it, rising raggedly in the moving moonlight, the blocks of time-forgotten Illar loomed.

But they were no longer piled one upon another in a rough travesty of the city they once had shaped. Some force mightier than any of man's explosives seemed to have hurled them with such violence from their beds that their very atoms had been disrupted by the force of it, crumbling them into dust. And in the very center of the havoc lay Smith, unhurt.

He stared in bewilderment about the moonlight ruins. In the silence it seemed to him that the very air still quivered in shocked vibrations. And as he stared he realized that no force save one could have wrought such destruction upon the ancient stones. Nor was there any explosive known to man which would have wrought this strange, pulverizing havoc upon the blocks of Illar. That force had hummed unbearably through the living dynamo of Thag, a force so powerful that space itself had bent to enclose it. Suddenly he realized what must have happened.

Not Illar, but Thag himself had warped the walls of space to enfold the twilit world, and nothing but Thag's living power could have held it so bent to segregate the little, terror-ridden land inviolate.

Then when the Tree's roots parted, Thag's anchorage in the material world failed and in one great gust of unthinkable energy the warped space-walls had ceased to bend. Those arches of solid space had snapped back into their original pattern, hurling the land and all its dwellers into—into—His mind balked in the effort to picture what must have happened, into what ultimate dimension those denizens must have vanished.

Only himself, enfolded deep in Thag's very essence, the intolerable power of the explosion had not touched. So when the warped space-curve ceased to be, and Thag's hold upon reality failed, he must have been dropped back out of the dissolving folds upon the spot where the Tree had stood in the space-circled world, through that vanished world-floor into the spot he had been snatched from in the instant of the dim land's dissolution. It must have happened after the terrible force of the explosion had spent itself, before Thag dared move even himself through the walls of changing energy into his own far land again.

Smith sighed and lifted a hand to his throbbing head, rising slowly to his feet. What time had elapsed he could not guess, but he must assume that the Patrol still searched for him. Wearily he set out across the circle of havoc toward the nearest shelter which Illar offered. The dust rose in ghostly, moonlit clouds under his feet.

SCARLET DREAM

Northwest Smith bought the shawl in the Lakkmanda Markets of Mars. It was one of his chiefest joys to wander through the stalls and stands of that greatest of marketplaces whose wares are drawn from all the planets of the solar system, and beyond. So many songs have been sung and so many tales written of that fascinating chaos called the Lakkmanda Markets that there is little need to detail it here.

He shouldered his way through the colorful cosmopolitan throng, the speech of a thousand races beating in his ears, the mingled odors of perfume and sweat and spice and food and the thousand nameless smells of the place assailing his nostrils. Venders cried their wares in the tongues of a score of worlds.

As he strolled through the thick of the crowd, savoring the confusion and the odors and the sights from lands beyond counting, his eye was caught by a flash of that peculiar geranium scarlet that seems to lift itself bodily from its background and smite the eye with all but physical violence.

It came from a shawl thrown carelessly across a carved chest, typically Martian drylander work by the exquisite detail of that carving, so oddly at variance with the characteristics of the harsh dryland race. He recognized the Venusian origin of the brass tray on the shawl, and knew the heap of carved ivory beasts that the tray held as the work of one of the leastknown races on Jupiter's largest moon, but from all his wide experience he could draw no remembrance of any such woven work as that of the shawl. Idly curious, he paused at the booth and asked of its attendant,

"How much for the scarf?"

The man—he was a canal Martian—glanced over his shoulder and said carelessly, "Oh, that. You can have it for half a *cris*—gives me a headache to look at the thing."

Smith grinned and said, "I'll give you five dollars."

"Ten."

"Six and a half, and that's my last offer."

"Oh, take the thing." The Martian smiled and lifted the tray of ivory beasts from the chest.

Smith drew out the shawl. It clung to his hands like a live thing, softer and lighter than Martian "lamb's-wool." He felt sure it was woven from the hair of some beast rather than from vegetable fiber, for the electric clinging of it sparkled with life. And the crazy pattern dazzled him with its utter strangeness. Unlike any pattern he had seen in all the years of his far wanderings, the wild, leaping scarlet threaded its nameless design in one continuous, tangled line through the twilight blue of the background. That dim blue was clouded exquisitely with violet and green—sleepy evening colors against which the staring scarlet flamed like something more sinister and alive than color. He felt that he could almost put his hand between the color and the cloth, so vividly did it start up from its background.

"Where in the universe did this come from?" he demanded of the attendant.

The man shrugged.

"Who knows? It came in with a bale of scrap cloth from

New York. I was a little curious about it myself, and called the market-master there to trace it. He says it was sold for scrap by a down-and-out Venusian who claimed he'd found it in a derelict ship floating around one of the asteroids. He didn't know what nationality the ship had been—a very early model, he said, probably one of the first space-ships, made before the identification symbols were adopted. I've wondered why he sold the thing for scrap. He could have got double the price, anyhow, if he'd made any effort."

"Funny." Smith stared down at the dizzy pattern writhing through the cloth in his hands. "Well, it's warm and light enough. If it doesn't drive me crazy trying to follow the pattern, I'll sleep warm at night."

He crumpled it in one hand, the whole six-foot square of it folding easily into his palm, and stuffed the silky bundle into his pocket—and thereupon forgot it until after his return to his quarters that evening.

He had taken one of the cubicle steel rooms in the great steel lodging-houses the Martian government offers for a very nominal rent to transients. The original purpose was to house those motley hordes of spaceman that swarm every port city of the civilized planets, offering them accommodations cheap and satisfactory enough so that they will not seek the black byways of the town and there fall in with the denizens of the Martian underworld whose lawlessness is a byword among space sailors.

The great steel building that housed Smith and countless others was not entirely free from the influences of Martian byways, and if the police had actually searched the place with any degree of thoroughness a large percentage of its dwellers might have been transferred to the Emperor's prisons—Smith almost certainly among them, for his activities were rarely within the law and though he could not recall at the moment any particularly flagrant sins committed in Lakkdarol, a charge could certainly have been found against him by the most half-hearted searcher. However, the likelihood of a police raid was very remote, and Smith, as he went in under the steel portals of the great door, rubbed shoulders with smugglers and pirates and fugitives and sinners of all the sins that keep the spaceways thronged.

In his little cubicle he switched on the light and saw a dozen blurred replicas of himself, reflected dimly in the steel walls, spring into being with the sudden glow. In that curious company he moved forward to a chair and pulled out the crumpled shawl. Shaking it in the mirror-walled room produced a sudden wild writhing of scarlet patterns over walls and floor and ceiling, and for an instant the room whirled in an inexplicable kaleidoscope and he had the impression that the four-dimensional walls had opened suddenly to undreamed-of vastnesses where living scarlet in wild, unruly patterns shivered through the void.

Then in a moment the walls closed in again and the dim reflections quieted and became only the images of a tall, brown man with pale eyes, holding a curious shawl in his hands. There was a strange, sensuous pleasure in the clinging of the silky wool to his fingers, the lightness of it, the warmth. He spread it out on the table and traced the screaming scarlet pattern with his finger, trying to follow that one writhing line through the intricacies of its path, and the more he stared the more irritatingly clear it became to him that there must be a purpose in that whirl of color, that if he stared long enough, surely he must trace it out. . . .

When he slept that night he spread the bright shawl across his bed, and the brilliance of it colored his dreams fantastically. . . .

That threading scarlet was a labyrinthine path down which he stumbled blindly, and at every turn he looked back and saw himself in myriad replicas, always wandering lost and alone through the pattern of the path. Sometimes it shook itself under his feet, and whenever he thought he saw the end it would writhe into fresh intricacies. . . .

The sky was a great shawl threaded with scarlet lightning that shivered and squirmed as he watched, then wound itself into the familiar, dizzy pattern that became one mighty Word in a nameless writing, whose meaning he shuddered on the verge of understanding, and woke in icy terror just before the significance of it broke upon his brain. . . .

He slept again, and saw the shawl hanging in a blue dusk the color of its background, stared and stared until the square of it melted imperceptibly into the dimness and the scarlet was a pattern incised lividly upon a gate . . . a gate of strange outline in a high wall, half seen through that curious, cloudy twilight blurred with exquisite patches of green and violet, so that it seemed no mortal twilight, but some strange and lovely evening in a land where the air was suffused with colored mists, and no winds blew. He felt himself moving forward, without effort, and the gate opened before him. . . .

He was mounting a long flight of steps. In one of the metamorphoses of dreams it did not surprise him that the gate had vanished, or that he had no remembrance of having climbed the long flight stretching away behind him. The lovely colored twilight still veiled the air, so that he could see but dimly the steps rising before him and melting into the mist.

And now, suddenly, he was aware of a stirring in the dimness, and a girl came flying down the stairs in headlong, stumbling terror. He could see the shadow of it on her face, and her long, bright-colored hair streamed out behind her, and from head to foot she was dabbled with blood. In her blind flight she must not have seen him, for she came plunging downward three steps at a time and blundered full into him as he stood undecided, watching. The impact all but unbalanced him, but his arms closed instinctively about her and for a moment she hung in his embrace, utterly spent, gasping against his broad leather breast and too breathless even to wonder who had stopped her. The smell of fresh blood rose to his nostrils from her dreadfully spattered garments.

Finally she lifted her head and raised a flushed, creamy-brown face to him, gulping in air through lips the color of holly berries. Her dabbled hair, so fantastically golden that it might have been almost orange, shivered about her as she clung to him with lifted, lovely face. In that dizzy moment he saw that her eyes were sherry-brown with tints of red, and the fantastic, colored beauty of her face had a wild tinge of something utterly at odds with anything he had ever known before. It might have been the look in her eyes. . . .

"Oh!" she gasped. "It—it has her! Let me go! . . . Let me—"

Smith shook her gently.

"What has her?" he demanded. "Who? Listen to me! You're covered with blood, do you know it? Are you hurt?"

She shook her head wildly.

"No—no—let me go! I must—not my blood—hers. . . ."

She sobbed on the last word, and suddenly collapsed in his arms, weeping with a violent intensity that shook her from head to foot. Smith gazed helplessly about over the orange head, then gathered the shaking girl in his arms and went on up the steps through the violent gloaming.

He must have climbed for all of five minutes before the twilight thinned a little and he saw that the stairs ended at the head of a long hallway, high-arched like a cathedral aile. A row of low doors ran down one side of the hall, and he turned aside at random into the nearest. It gave upon a gallery whose arches opened into blue space. A low bench ran along the wall under the gallery windows, and he crossed it, gently setting down the sobbing girl and supporting her against his shoulder.

"My sister," she wept. "It has her—oh, my sister!"

"Don't cry, don't cry," Smith heard his own voice saying, surprisingly. "It's all a dream, you know. Don't cry—there never was any sister—you don't exist at all—don't cry so."

She jerked her head up at that, startled out of her sobs for a moment, and stared at him with sherry-brown eyes drowned in tears. Her lashes clung together in wet, starry points. She stared with searching eyes, taking in the leather-brownness of him, his spaceman's suit, his scarred dark face and eyes paler than steel. And then a look of infinite pity softened the strangeness of her face, and she said gently.

"Oh . . . you come from—from—you still believe that you dream!"

"I *know* I'm dreaming," persisted Smith childishly. "I'm lying asleep in Lakkdarol and dreaming of you, and all this, and when I wake—"

She shook her head sadly.

"You will never wake. You have come into a more deadly dream than you could ever guess. There is no waking from this land."

"What do you mean? Why not?" A little absurd pity was starting up in his mind at the sorrow and the pity in her voice, the sureness of her words. Yet this was one of those rare dreams wherein he knew quite definitely that he dreamed. He could not be mistaken. . . .

"There are many dream countries," she said, "many nebulous, unreal half-lands where the souls of sleepers wander, places that have an actual, tenuous existence, if one knows the way. . . . But here—it has happened before, you see—one may not blunder without passing a door that opens one way only. And he who has the key to open it may come through, but he can never find the way into his own waking land again. Tell me—what key opened the door to you?"

"The shawl," Smith murmured. "The shawl . . . of course. That damnable red pattern, dizzy—"

He passed a hand across his eyes, for the memory of it, writhing, alive, searingly scarlet, burned behind his eyelids.

"What was it?" she demanded, breathlessly, he thought, as if a half-hopeless eagerness forced the question from her lips. "Can you remember?"

"A red pattern," he said slowly, "a thread of bright scarlet woven into a blue shawl—nightmare pattern—painted on the gate I came by . . . but it's only a dream, of course. In a few minutes I'll wake. . . ."

She clutched his knee excitedly.

"Can you remember?" she demanded. "The pattern—the red pattern? The Word?"

"Word?" he wondered stupidly. "Word—in the sky? No—no, I don't want to remember—crazy pattern, you know. Can't forget it—but no, I couldn't tell you what it was, or trace it for you. Never was anything like it—thank God. It was on that shawl. . . ."

"Woven on a shawl," she murmured to herself. "Yes, of course. But how you ever came by it, in your world—when it—when *it*—oh!"

Memory of whatever tragedy had sent her flying down the stairs swept back in a flood, and her face crumpled into tears again. "My sister!"

"Tell me what happened." Smith woke from his daze at the sound of her sob. "Can't I help? Please let me try—tell me about it."

"My sister," she said faintly. "It caught her in the hall—caught her before my eyes—spattered me with her blood. Oh! . . .

"It?" puzzled Smith. "What? Is there danger?" and his hand moved instinctively toward his gun.

She caught the gesture and smiled a little scornfully through her tears.

"It," she said. "The—the Thing. No gun can harm it, no man can fight it—It came, and that was all."

"But what is it? What does it look like? Is it near?"

"It's everywhere. One never knows—until the mist begins to thicken and the pulse of red shows through—and then it's too late. We do not fight it, or think of it overmuch—life would be unbearable. For it hungers and must be fed, and we who feed it strive to live as happily as we may know before the Thing comes for us. But one can never know."

"Where did it come from? What is it?"

"No one knows—it has always been here—always will be . . . too nebulous to die or be killed—a Thing out of some alien place we couldn't understand, I suppose—somewhere so long ago, or in some such unthinkable dimension that we will never have any knowledge of its origin. But as I say, we try not to think."

"If it eats flesh," said Smith stubbornly, "it must be vulnerable—and I have my gun."

"Try if you like," she shrugged. "Others have tried—and it still comes. It dwells here, we believe, if it dwells anywhere. We are—taken—more often in these halls than elsewhere. When you are weary of life you might bring your gun and wait under this roof. You may not have long to wait."

"I'm not ready to try the experiment just yet," Smith grinned. "If the Thing lives here, why do you come?"

She shrugged again, apathetically. "If we do not, it will come after us when it hungers. And we come here for—for our food." She shot him a curious glance from under lowered lids. "You wouldn't understand. But as you say, it's a dangerous place. We'd best go now—you will come with me, won't you? I shall be lonely now." And her eyes brimmed again.

"Of course. I'm sorry, my dear. I'll do what I can for you—until I wake." He grinned at the fantastic sound of this.

"You will not wake," she said quietly. "Better not to hope, I think. You are trapped here with the rest of us and here you must stay until you die."

He rose and held out his hand.

"Let's go, then," he said. "Maybe you're right, but—well, come on."

She took his hand and jumped up. The orange hair, too fantastically colored for anything outside a dream, swung about her brilliantly. He saw now that she wore a single white garment, brief and belted, over the creamy brownness of her body. It was torn now, and hideously stained. She made a picture of strange and vivid loveliness, all white and gold and bloody, in the misted twilight of the gallery.

"Where are we going?" she asked Smith. "Out there?" And he nodded toward the blueness beyond the windows.

She drew her shoulders together in a little shudder of distaste. "Oh, no," she said.

"What is it?"

"Listen." She took him by the arms and lifted a serious face to his. "If you must stay here—and you must, for there is only one way out save death, and that is a worse way even than dying—you must learn to ask no questions about the—the Temple. This is the Temple. Here it dwells. Here we—feed.

"There are halls we know, and we keep to them. It is wiser. You saved my life when you stopped me on those stairs—no one has ever gone down into that mist and darkness, and returned. I should have known, seeing you climb them, that you were not of us . . . for whatever lies beyond, wherever that stairway leads—it is better not to know. It is better not to look out the windows of this place. We have learned that, too. For from the outside the Temple looks strange enough, but from the inside, looking out, one is liable to see things it is better not to see. . . . What that blue space is, on which this gallery opens, I do not know—I have no wish to know. There are windows here opening on stranger things than this—but we turn our eyes away when we pass them. You will learn. . . ."

She took his hand, smiling a little.

"Come with me, now."

And in silence they left the gallery opening on space and went down the hall where the blue mist floated so beautifully with its clouds of violet and green confusing the eye, and a great stillness all about.

The hallways led straight, as nearly as he could see, for the floating clouds veiled it, toward the great portals of the Temple. In the form of a mighty triple arch it opened out of the clouded twilight upon a shining day like no day he had ever seen on any planet. The light came from no visible source, and there was a lucid quality about it, nebulous but unmistakable, as if one were looking through the depths of a crystal, or through clear water that trembled a little now and then. It was diffused through the translucent day from a sky as shining and unfamiliar as everything else in this amazing dreamland.

They stood under the great arch of the Temple, looking out over the shining land beyond. Afterward he could never quite remember what had made it so unutterably strange, so indefinably dreadful. There were trees, feathery masses of green and bronze above the bronze-green grass; the bright air shimmered, and through the leaves he caught the glimmer of water not far away. At first glance it seemed a perfectly normal sense—yet tiny details caught his eyes that sent ripples of coldness down his back. The grass, for instance. . . .

When they stepped down upon it and began to cross the meadow toward the trees beyond which water gleamed, he saw that the blades were short and soft as fur, and they seemed to cling to his companion's bare feet as she walked. As he looked out over the meadow he saw that long waves of it, from every direction, were rippling toward them as if the wind blew from all sides at once toward the common center that was themselves. Yet no wind blew.

"It—it's alive," he stammered, startled. "The grass!"

"Yes, of course," she said indifferently.

And then he realized that though the feathery fronds of the trees waved now and then, gracefully together, there was no wind. And they did not sway in one direction only, but by twos and threes in many ways, dipping and rising with a secret, contained life of their own.

When they reached the belt of woodland he looked up curiously and heard the whisper and rustle of leaves above him, bending down as if in curiosity as the two passed beneath. They never bent far enough to touch them, but a sinister air of watchfulness, of aliveness, brooded over the whole uncannily alive landscape, and the ripples of the grass followed them wherever they went.

The lake, like that twilight in the Temple, was a sleepy blue clouded with violet and green, not like real water, for the colored blurs did not diffuse or change as it rippled.

On the shore, a little above the water line, stood a tiny, shrine-like building of some creamy stone, its walls no more than a series of arches open to the blue, translucent day. The girl led him to the doorway and gestured within negligently.

"I live here," she said.

Smith stared. It was quite empty save for two low couches with a blue coverlet thrown across each. Very classic it looked, with its whiteness and austerity, the arches opening on a vista of woodland and grass beyond.

"Doesn't it ever get cold?" he asked. "Where do you eat? Where are your books and food and clothes?"

"I have some spare tunics under my couch," she said. "That's all. No books, no other clothing, no food. We feed at the Temple. It is never any colder or warmer than this."

"But what do you do?"

"Do? Oh, swim in the lake, sleep and rest and wander through the woods. Times passes very quickly."

"Idyllic," murmured Smith, "but rather tiresome, I should think."

"When one knows," she said, "that the next moment may be one's last, life is savored to the full. One stretches the hours out as long as possible. No, for us it is not tiresome."

"But have you no cities? Where are the other people?"

"It is best not to collect in crowds. Somehow they seem to draw—it. We live in twos and threes—sometimes alone. We have no cities. We do nothing—what purpose in beginning anything when we know we shall not live to end it? Why even think too long of one thing? Come down to the lake."

She took his hand and led him across the clinging grass to the sandy brink of the water, and they sank in silence on the narrow beach. Smith looked out over the lake where vague colors misted the blue, trying not to think of the fantastic things that were happening to him. Indeed, it was hard to do much thinking, here, in the midst of the blueness and the silence, the very air dreamy about them . . . the cloudy water lapping the shore with tiny, soft sounds like the breathing of a sleeper. The place was heavy with the stillness and the dreamy colors, and Smith was never sure, afterward, whether in his dream he did not sleep for a while; for presently he heard a stir at his side and the girl reseated herself, clad in a fresh tunic, all the blood washed away. He could not remember her having left, but it did not trouble him.

The light had for some time been sinking and blurring, and imperceptibly a cloudy blue twilight closed about them, seeming somehow to rise from the blurring lake, for it partook of that same dreamy blueness clouded with vague colors. Smith thought that he would be content never to rise again from that cool sand, to sit here for ever in the blurring twilight and the silence of his dream. How long he did sit there he never knew. The blue peace enfolded him utterly, until he was steeped in its misty evening colors and permeated through and through with the tranced quiet.

The darkness had deepened until he could no longer see any more than the nearest wavelets lapping the sand. Beyond, and all about, the dream-world melted into the violet-misted blueness of the twilight. He was not aware that he had turned his head, but presently he found himself looking down on the girl beside him. She was lying on the pale sand, her hair a fan of darkness to frame the pallor of her face. In the twilight her mouth was dark too, and from the darkness under her lashes he slowly became aware that she was watching him unwinkingly.

For a long while he sat there, gazing down, meeting the half-hooded eyes in silence. And presently, with the effortless detachment of one who moves in a dream, he bent down to meet her lifting arms. The sand was cool and sweet, and her mouth tasted faintly of blood.

II

There was no sunrise in that land. Lucid day brightened slowly over the breathing landscape, and grass and trees stirred with wakening awareness, rather horribly in the beauty of the morning. When Smith woke, he saw the girl coming up from the lake, shaking blue water from her orange hair. Blue droplets clung to the creaminess of her skin, and she was laughing and flushed from head to foot in the glowing dawn.

Smith sat up on his couch and pushed back the blue coverlet.

"I'm hungry," he said. "When and what do we eat?"

The laughter vanished from her face in a breath. She gave her hair a troubled shake and said doubtfully,

"Hungry?"

"Yes, starved! Didn't you say you get your food at the Temple? Let's go up there."

She sent him a sidelong, enigmatic glance from under her lashes as she turned aside.

"Very well," she said.

"Anything wrong?" He reached out as she passed and pulled her to his knee, kissing the troubled mouth lightly. And again he tasted blood.

"Oh, no." She ruffled his hair and rose. "I'll be ready in a moment, and then we'll go."

And so again they passed the belt of woods where the trees bent down to watch, and crossed the rippling grassland. From all directions long waves of it came blowing toward them as before, and the fur-like blades clung to their feet. Smith tried not to notice. Everywhere, he was seeing this morning, an undercurrent of nameless unpleasantness ran beneath the surface of this lovely land.

As they crossed the live grass a memory suddenly returned to him, and he said, "What did you mean, yesterday, when you said that there was a way—out—other than death?"

She did not meet his eyes as she answered, in that troubled

voice, "Worse than dying, I said. A way out we do not speak of here."

"But if there's any way at all, I must know of it," he persisted. "Tell me."

She swept the orange hair like a veil between them, bending her head and saying indistinctly, "A way out you could not take. A way too costly. And—and I do not wish you to go, now. . . ."

"I must know," said Smith relentlessly.

She paused then, and stood looking up at him, her sherry-colored eyes disturbed.

"By the way you came," she said at last. "By virtue of the Word. But that gate is impassable."

"Why?"

"It is death to pronounce the Word. Literally. I do not know it now, could not speak it if I would. But in the Temple there is one room where the Word is graven in scarlet on the wall, and its power is so great that the echoes of it ring for ever round and round that room. If one stands before the graven symbol and lets the force of it beat upon his brain he will hear, and know—and shriek the awful syllables aloud—and so die. It is a word from some tongue so alien to all our being that the spoken sound of it, echoing in the throat of a living man, is disrupting enough to rip the very fibers of the human body apart—to blast its atoms asunder, to destroy body and mind as utterly as if they had never been. And because the sound is so disruptive it somehow blasts open for an instant the door between your world and mine. But the danger is dreadful, for it may open the door to other worlds too, and let things through more terrible than we can dream of. Some say it was thus that the Thing gained access to our land eons ago. And if you are not standing exactly where the door opens, on the one spot in the room that is protected, as the center of a whirlwind is quiet, and if you do not pass instantly out of the sound of the Word, it will blast you asunder as it does the one who has pronounced it for you. So you see how impos—" Here she broke off with a little scream and glanced down in half-laughing annoyance, then took two or three little running steps and turned.

"The grass," she explained ruefully, pointing to her feet. The brown bareness of them was dotted with scores of tiny blood-spots. "If one stands too long in one place, barefoot, it will pierce the skin and drink—stupid of me to forget. But come."

Smith went on at her side, looking round with new eyes upon the lovely, pellucid land, too beautiful and frightening for anything outside a dream. All about them the hungry grass came hurrying in long, converging waves as they advanced. Were the trees, then, flesh-eating too? Cannibal trees and vampire grass—he shuddered a little and looked ahead.

The Temple stood tall before them, a building of some nameless material as mistily blue as far-off mountains on the Earth. The mistiness did not condense or clarify as they approached, and the outlines of the place were mysteriously hard to fix in mind—he could never understand, afterward, just why. When he tried too hard to concentrate on one particular corner or tower or window it blurred before his eyes as if the focus were at fault—as if the whole strange, veiled building stood just on the borderland of another dimension.

From the immense triple arch of the doorway, as they approached—a triple arch like nothing he had ever seen before, so irritatingly hard to focus upon that he could not be sure just wherein its difference lay—a pale blue mist issued smokily. And when they stopped within they walked into that twilight dimness he was coming to know so well.

The great hall lay straight and veiled before them, but after a few steps the girl drew him aside and under another archway, into a long gallery through whose drifting haze he could see rows of men and women kneeling against the wall with bowed heads, as if in prayer. She led him down the line to the end, and he saw then that they knelt before small spigots curving up from the wall at regular intervals. She dropped to her knees before one and, motioning him to follow, bent her head and laid her lips to the up-curved spout. Dubiously he followed her example.

Instantly with the touch of his mouth on the nameless substance of the spigot something hot and, strangely, at once salty and sweet flowed into his mouth. There was an acridity about it that gave a curious tang, and the more he drank the more avid he became. Hauntingly delicious it was, and warmth flowed through him more strongly with every draft. Yet somewhere deep within him memory stirred unpleasantly . . . somewhere, somehow, he had known this hot, acrid, salty taste before, and—suddenly suspicions struck him like a bludgeon, and he jerked his lips from the spout as if it burnt. A tiny thread of scarlet trickled from the wall. He passed the back of one hand across his lips and brought it away red. He knew that odor, then.

The girl knelt beside him with closed eyes, rapt avidity in every line of her. When he seized her shoulder she twitched away and opened protesting eyes, but did not lift her lips from the spigot. Smith gestured violently, and with one last long draft she rose and turned a half-angry face to his, but laid a finger on her reddened lips.

He followed her in silence past the kneeling lines again. When they reached the hall outside he swung upon her and gripped her shoulders angrily.

"What was that?" he demanded.

Her eyes slid away. She shrugged.

"What were you expecting? We feed as we must, here. You'll learn to drink without a qualm—if it does not come for you too soon."

A moment longer he stared angrily down into her evasive, strangely lovely face. Then he turned without a word and strode down the hallway through the drifting mists toward the door. He heard her bare feet pattering along behind hurriedly, but he did not look back. Not until he had come out into the glowing day and half crossed the grasslands did he relent enough to glance around. She paced at his heels with bowed head, the orange hair swinging about her face and unhappiness eloquent in every motion. The submission of her touched him suddenly, and he paused for her to catch up, smiling down half reluctantly on the bent orange head.

She lifted a tragic face to his, and there were tears in the sherry eyes. So he had no choice but to laugh and lift her up against his leather-clad breast and kiss the drooping mouth into smiles again. But he understood, now, the faintly acrid bitterness of her kisses.

"Still," he said, when they had reached the little white shrine among the trees, "there must be some other food than—that. Does no grain grow? Isn't there any wild life in the woods? Haven't the trees fruit?"

She gave him another sidelong look from under dropped lashes, warily.

"No," she said. "Nothing but the grass grows here. No living thing dwells in this land but man—and it. And as for the fruit of the trees—give thanks that they bloom but once in a lifetime."

"Why?"

"Better not to—speak of it," she said.

The phrase, the constant evasion, was beginning to wear on Smith's nerves. He said nothing of it then, but he turned from her and went down to the beach, dropping to the sand and striving to recapture last night's languour and peace. His hunger was curiously satisfied, even from the few swallows he had taken, and gradually the drowsy content of the day before began to flow over him in deepening waves. After all, it was a lovely land. . . .

That day drew dreamily to a close, and darkness rose in a mist from the misty lake, and he came to find in kisses that tasted of blood a certain tang that but pointed their sweetness. And in the morning he woke to the slowly brightening day, swam with the girl in the blue, tingling waters of the lake—and reluctantly went up through the woods and across the ravenous grass to the Temple, driven by a hunger greater than his repugnance. He went up with a slight nausea rising within him, and yet strangely eager. . . .

Once more the Temple rose veiled and indefinite under the glowing sky, and once more he plunged into the eternal twilight of its corridors, turned aside as one who knows the way, knelt of his own accord in the line of drinkers along the wall. . . .

With the first draft that nausea rose within him almost overwhelmingly, but when the warmth of the drink had spread through him the nausea died and nothing was left but hunger and eagerness, and he drank blindly until the girl's hand on his shoulder roused him.

A sort of intoxication had wakened within him with the burning of that hot, salt drink in his veins, and he went back across the hurrying grass in a half-daze. Through most of the pellucid day it lasted, and the slow dark was rising from the lake before clearness returned to him.

III

And so life resolved itself into a very simple thing. The days glowed by and the blurred darknesses came and went. Life held little any more but the bright clarity of the day and the dimness of the dark, morning journeys to drink at the Temple fountain and the bitter kisses of the girl with the orange hair. Time had ceased for him. Slow day followed slow day, and the same round of living circled over and over, and the only change—perhaps he did not see it then—was the deepening look in the girl's eyes when they rested upon him, her growing silences.

One evening just as the first faint dimness was clouding the air, and the lake smoked hazily, he happened to glance off across its surface and thought he saw through the rising mists the outline of very far mountains.

He asked curiously, "What lies beyond the lake? Aren't those mountains over there?"

The girl turned her head quickly and her sherry-brown eyes darkened with something like dread.

"I don't know," she said. "We believe it best not to wonder what lies—beyond."

And suddenly Smith's irritation with the old evasions woke and he said violently,

"Damn your beliefs! I'm sick of that answer to every question I ask! Don't you ever wonder about anything? Are you all so thoroughly cowed by this dread of something unseen that every spark of your spirit is dead?"

She turned the sorrowful, sherry gaze upon him.

"We learn by experience," she said. "Those who wonder—those who investigate—die. We live in a land alive with danger, incomprehensible, intangible, terrible. Life is bearable only if we do not look too closely—only if we accept conditions and make the most of them. You must not ask questions if you would live.

"As for the mountains beyond, and all the unknown country that lies over the horizons—they are as unreachable as a mirage. For in a land where no food grows, where we must visit the Temple daily or starve, how could an explorer provision himself for a journey? No, we are bound here by unbreakable bonds, and we must live here until we die."

Smith shrugged. The languor of the evening was coming upon him, and the brief flare of irritation had died as swiftly as it rose.

Yet from that outburst dated the beginning of his discontent. Somehow, despite the lovely languor of the place, despite the sweet bitterness of the Temple fountains and the sweeter bitterness of the kisses that were his for the asking, he could not drive from his mind the vision of those far mountains veiled in rising haze. Unrest had wakened within him, and like some sleeper arising from a lotus-dream his mind turned more and more frequently to the desire for action, adventure, some other use for his danger-hardened body than the exigencies of sleep and food and love.

On all sides stretched the moving, restless woods, farther than the eye could reach. The grasslands rippled, and over the dim horizon the far mountains beckoned him. Even the mystery of the Temple and its endless twilight began to torment his waking moments. He dallied with the idea of exploring those hallways which the dwellers in this lotusland avoided, of gazing from the strange windows that opened upon inexplicable blue. Surely life, even here, must hold some more fervent meaning than that he followed now. What lay beyond the wood and grasslands? What mysterious country did those mountains wall?

He began to harry his companion with questions that woke more and more often the look of dread behind her eyes, but he gained little satisfaction. She belonged to a people without history, without ambition, their lives bent wholly toward wringing from each moment its full sweetness in anticipation of the terror to come. Evasion was the keynote of their existence, perhaps with reason. Perhaps all the adventurous spirits among them had followed their curiosity into danger and death, and the only ones left were the submissive souls who led their bucolically voluptuous lives in this Elysium so shadowed with horror.

In this colored lotus-land, memories of the world he had left grew upon him more and more vividly: he remembered the hurrying crowds of the planets' capitals, the lights, the noise, the laughter. He saw space-ships cleaving the night sky with flame, flashing from world to world through the star-flecked darkness. He remembered sudden brawls in saloons and space-sailor dives when the air was alive with shouts and tumult, and heat-guns slashed their blue-hot blades of flame and the smell of burnt flesh hung heavy. Life marched in pageant past his remembering eyes, violent, vivid, shoulder to shoulder with death. And nostalgia wrenched at him for the lovely, terrible, brawling worlds he had left behind.

Daily the unrest grew upon him. The girl made pathetic little attempts to find some sort of entertainment that would occupy his ranging mind. She led him on timid excursions into the living woods, even conquered her horror of the Temple enough to follow him on timorous tiptoe as he explored a little way down the corridors which did not arouse in her too anguished a terror. But she must have known from the first that it was hopeless.

One day as they lay on the sand watching the lake ripple bluely under a crystal sky, Smith's eyes, dwelling on the faint shadow of the mountains, half unseeingly, suddenly narrowed into a hardness as bright and pale as steel. Muscle ridged his abruptly set jaw and he sat upright with a jerk, pushing away the girl who had been leaning on his shoulder.

"I'm through," he said harshly, and rose.

"What—what is it?" The girl stumbled to her feet.

"I'm going away—anywhere. To those mountains, I think. I'm leaving now!"

"But—you wish to die, then?"

"Better the real thing than a living death like this," he said. "At least I'll have a little more excitement first."

"But, what of your food? There's nothing to keep you alive, even if you escape the greater dangers. Why, you'll dare not even lie down on the grass at night—it would eat you alive! You have no chance at all to live if you leave this grove—and me."

"If I must die, I shall," he said. "I've been thinking it over, and I've made up my mind. I could explore the Temple and so come on *it* and die. But do *something* I must, and it seems to me my best chance is in trying to reach some country where food grows before I starve. It's worth trying. I can't go on like this."

She looked at him miserably, tears brimming her sherry eyes. He opened his mouth to speak, but before he could say a word her eyes strayed beyond his shoulder and suddenly she smiled, a dreadful, frozen little smile.

"You will not go," she said. "Death has come for us now."

She said it so calmly, so unafraid that he did not understand until she pointed beyond him. He turned.

The air between them and the shrine was curiously agitated. As he watched, it began to resolve itself into a nebulous blue mist that thickened and darkened . . . blurry tinges of violet and green began to blow through it vaguely, and then by imperceptible degrees a flush of rose appeared in the mist—deepened, thickened, contracted into burning scarlet that seared his eyes, pulsed alively—and he knew that it had come.

An aura of menace seemed to radiate from it, strengthening as the mist strengthened, reaching out in hunger toward his mind. He felt it as tangibly as he saw it—cloudy danger reaching out avidly for them both.

The girl was not afriad. Somehow he knew this, though he dared not turn, dared not wrench his eyes from that hypnotically pulsing scarlet. . . . She whispered very softly from behind him.

"So I die with you, I am content." And the sound of her voice freed him from the snare of the crimson pulse.

He barked a wolfish laugh, abruptly—welcoming even this diversion from the eternal idyl he had been living—and the gun leaping to his hand spurted a long blue flame so instantly that the girl behind him caught her breath. The steel-blue dazzle illumined the gathering mist lividly, passed through it without obstruction and charred the ground beyond. Smith set his teeth and swung a figure-eight pattern of flame through and through the mist, lacing it with blue heat. And when that finger of fire crossed the scarlet pulse the impact jarred the whole nebulous cloud violently, so that its outlines wavered and shrank, and the pulse of crimson sizzled under the heat—shriveled—began to fade in desperate haste.

Smith swept the ray back and forth along the redness, tracing its pattern with destruction, but it faded too swiftly for him. In little more than an instant it had pale and disembodied and vanished save for a fading flush of rose, and the blue-hot blade of his flame sizzled harmlessly through the disappearing mist to sear the ground beyond. He switched off the heat, then, and stood breathing a little unevenly as the death-cloud thinned and paled and vanished before his eyes, until no trace of it was left and the air glowed lucid and transparent once more.

The unmistakable odor of burning flesh caught at his nostrils, and he wondered for a moment if the Thing had indeed materialized a nucleus of matter, and then he saw that the smell came from the seared grass his flame had struck. The tiny, furry blades were all writhing away from the burnt spot, straining at their roots as if a wind blew them back and from the blackened area a thick smoke rose, reeking with the odor of burnt meat. Smith, remembering their vampire habits, turned away, half nauseated.

The girl had sunk to the sand behind him, trembling violently now that the danger was gone.

"Is—it dead?" she breathed, when she could master her quivering mouth.

"I don't know. No way of telling. Probably not."

"What will—will you do now?"

He slid the heat-gun back into its holster and settled the belt purposefully.

"What I started out to do."

The girl scrambled up in desperate haste.

"Wait!" she gasped, "wait!" and clutched at his arm to steady herself. And he waited until the trembling had passed. Then she went on, "Come up to the Temple once more before you go."

"All right. Not a bad idea. It may be a long time before my next—meal."

And so again they crossed the fur-soft grass that bore down upon them in long ripples from every part of the meadow.

The Temple rose dim and unreal before them, and as they entered blue twilight folded them dreamily about. Smith turned by habit toward the gallery of the drinkers, but the girl laid upon his arms a hand that shook a little, and murmured, "Come this way."

He followed in growing surprise down the hallway through the drifting mists and away from the gallery he knew so well. It seemed to him that the mist thickened as they advanced, and in the uncertain light he could never be sure that the walls did not waver as nebulously as the blurring air. He felt a curious impulse to step through their intangible barriers and out of the hall into—what?

Presently steps rose under his feet, almost imperceptibly, and after a while the pressure on his arm drew him aside. They went in under a low, heavy arch of stone and entered the strangest room he had ever seen. It appeared to be seven-sided, as nearly as he could judge through the drifting mist, and curious, converging lines were graven deep in the floor.

It seemed to him that forces outside his comprehension were beating violently against the seven walls, circling like hurricanes through the dimness until the whole room was a maelstrom of invisible tumult.

When he lifted his eyes to the wall, he knew where he was. Blazoned on the dim stone, burning through the twilight like some other-dimensional fire, the scarlet pattern writhed across the wall.

The sight of it, somehow, set up a commotion in his brain, and it was with whirling head and stumbling feet that he answered to the pressure on his arm. Dimly he realized that he stood at the very center of those strange, converging lines, feeling forces beyond reason coursing through him along paths outside any knowledge he possessed.

Then for one moment arms clasped his neck and a warm, fragrant body pressed against him, and a voice sobbed in his ear.

"If you must leave me, then go back through the Door, beloved—life without you—more dreadful even than a death like this. . . ." A kiss that stung of blood clung to his lips for an instant; then the clasp loosened and he stood alone.

Through the twilight he saw her dimly outlined against the Word. And he thought, as she stood there, that it was as if the invisible current beat bodily against her, so that she swayed and wavered before him, her outlines blurring and forming again as the forces from which he was so mystically protected buffeted her mercilessly.

And he saw knowledge dawning terribly upon her face, as

the meaning of the Word seeped slowly into her mind. The sweet brown face twisted hideously, the blood-red lips writhed apart to shriek a Word—in a moment of clarity he actually saw her tongue twisting incredibly to form the syllables of the unspeakable thing never meant for human lips to frame. Her mouth opened into an impossible shape . . . she gasped in the blurry mist and shrieked aloud. . . .

IV

Smith was walking along a twisting path so scarlet that he could not bear to look down, a path that wound and unwound and shook itself under his feet so that he stumbled at every step. He was groping through a blinding mist clouded with violet and green, and in his ears a dreadful whisper rang—the first syllable of an unutterable Word. . . . Whenever he neared the end of the path it shook itself under him and doubled back, and weariness like a drug was sinking into his brain, and the sleepy twilight colors of the mist lulled him, and—

"He's waking up!" said an exultant voice in his ear.

Smith lifted heavy eyelids upon a room without walls—a room wherein multiple figures extending into infinity moved to and fro in countless hosts. . . .

"Smith! N.W.! Wake up!" urged that familiar voice from somewhere near.

He blinked. The myriad diminishing figures resolved themselves into the reflections of two men in a steel-walled room, bending over him. The friendly, anxious face of his partner, Yarol the Venusian, leaned above the bed.

"By Pharol, N.W.," said the well-remembered, ribald voice, "you've been asleep for a week! We thought you'd never come out of it—must have been an awful brand of whisky!"

Smith managed a feeble grin—amazing how weak he felt—and turned an inquiring gaze upon the other figure.

"I'm a doctor," said that individual, meeting the questing

stare. "Your friend called me in three days ago and I've been working on you ever since. It must have been all of five or six days since you fell into this coma—have you any idea what caused it?"

Smith's pale eyes roved the room. He did not find what he sought, and though his weak murmur answered the doctor's question, the man was never to know it.

"Shawl?"

"I threw the damned thing away," confessed Yarol. "Stood it for three days and then gave up. That red pattern gave me the worst headache I've had since we found that case of black wine on the asteroid. Remember?"

"Where—?"

"Gave it to a space-rat checking out for Venus. Sorry. Did you really want it? I'll buy you another."

Smith did not answer, the weakness was rushing up about him in gray waves. He closed his eyes, hearing the echoes of that first dreadful syllable whispering through his head . . . whisper from a dream. . . . Yarol heard him murmur softly,

"And—I never even knew—her name. . . ."

DUST OF GODS

"Pass the whisky, N.W.," said Yarol the Venusian persuasively.

Northwest Smith shook the black bottle of Venusian *segir*-whisky tentatively, evoked a slight gurgle, and reached for his friend's glass. Under the Venusian's jealous dark gaze he measured out exactly half of the red liquid. It was not very much.

Yarol regarded his share of the drink disconsolately.

"Broke again," he murmured. "And me so thirsty." His glance of cherubic innocence flashed along the temptingly laden counters of the Martian saloon wherein they sat. His face with its look of holy innocence turned to Smith's, the wise black gaze meeting the Earthman's pale-steel look questioningly. Yarol lifted an arched brow.

"How about it?" he suggested delicately. "Mars owes us a drink anyhow, and I just had my heat-gun recharged this morning. I think we could get away with it."

Under the table he laid a hopeful hand on his gun. Smith grinned and shook his head.

"Too many customers," he said. "And you ought to know better than to start anything here. It isn't healthful."

Yarol shrugged resigned shoulders and drained his glass with a gulp.

"Now what?" he demanded.

"Well, look around. See anyone here you know? We're open for business—any kind."

Yarol twirled his glass wistfully and studied the crowded room from under his lashes. With those lashes lowered he might have passed for a choir boy in any of Earth's cathedrals. But too dark a knowledge looked out when they rose for that illusion to continue long.

It was a motley crowd the weary black gaze scrutinized—hard-faced Earthmen in space-sailors' leather, sleek Venusians with their sidelong, dangerous eyes, Martian drylanders muttering the blasphemous gutturals of their language, a sprinkling of outlanders and half-brutes from the wide-flung borders of civilization. Yarol's eyes returned to the dark, scarred face across the tble. He met the pallor of Smith's no-colored gaze and shrugged.

"No one who'd buy us a drink," he sighed. "I've seen one or two of 'em before, though. Take those two space-rats at the next table: the little red-faced Earthman—the one looking over his shoulder—and the drylander with an eye gone. See? I've heard they're hunters."

"What for?"

Yarol lifted his shoulders in the expressive Venusian shrug. His brows rose too, quizzically.

"No one knows what they hunt—but they run together."

"Hm-m." Smith turned a speculative stare toward the neighboring table. "They look more hunted than hunting, if you ask me."

Yarol nodded. The two seemed to share one fear between them, if over-the shoulder glances and restless eyes spoke truly. They huddled together above their *segir* glasses, and though they had the faces of hard men, inured to the spaceway dangers, the look on those faces was curiously compounded of many unpleasant things underlying a frank, unreasoning alarm. It was a look Smith could not quite fathom—a haunted, uneasy dread with nameless things behind it.

"They do look as if Black Pharol were one jump behind," said Yarol. "Funny, too. I've always heard they were pretty tough, both of 'em. You have to be in their profession."

Said a husky half-whisper in their very ears,

"Perhaps they found what they were hunting."

It produced an electric stillness. Smith moved almost imperceptibly sidewise in his chair, the better to clear his gun, and Yarol's slim fingers hovered above his hip. They turned expressionless faces toward the speaker.

A little man sitting alone at the next table had bent forward to fix them with a particularly bright stare. They met it in silence, hostile and waiting, until the husky half-whisper spoke again.

"May I join you? I couldn't help overhearing that—that you were open for business."

Without expression Smith's colorless eyes summed up the speaker, and a puzzlement clouded their paleness as he looked. Rarely does one meet a man whose origin and race are not apparent even upon close scrutiny. Yet here was one whom he could not classify. Under the deep burn of the man's skin might be concealed a fair Venusian pallor or an Earthman bronze, canal-Martian rosiness or even a leathery dryland hide. His dark eyes could have belonged to any race, and his husky whisper, fluent in the jargon of the spaceman, effectively disguised its origin. Little and unobtrusive, he might have passed for native on any of the three planets.

Smith's scarred, impassive face did not change as he looked, but after a long moment of scrutiny he said, "Pull up," and then bit off the words as if he had said too much.

The brevity must have pleased the little man, for he smiled as he complied, meeting the passively hostile stare of the two without embarrassment. He folded his arms on the table and leaned forward. The husky voice began without preamble,

"I can offer you employment—if you're not afraid. It's dangerous work, but the pay's good enough to make up for it—if you're not afraid."

"What is it?"

"Work they—those two—failed at. They were—hunters—until they found what they hunted. Look at them now."

Smith's no-colored eyes did not swerve from the speaker's face, but he nodded. No need to look again upon the fear-ridden faces of the neighboring pair. He understood.

"What's the job?" he asked.

The little man hitched his chair closer and sent a glance round the room from under lowered lids. He scanned the faces of his two companions half doubtfully. He said, "There have been many gods since time's beginning," then paused and peered dubiously into Smith's face.

Northwest nodded briefly. "Go on," he said.

Reassured, the little man took up his tale, and before he had gone far enthusiasm drowned out the doubtfulness in his husky voice, and a tinge of fanaticism crept in.

"There were gods who were old when Mars was a green planet, and a verdant moon circled an Earth blue with steaming seas, and Venus, molten-hot, swung round a younger sun. Another world circled in space then, between Mars and Jupiter where its fragments, the planetoids, now are. You will have heard rumors of it—they persist in the legends of every planet. It was a mighty world, rich and beautiful, peopled by the ancestors in mankind. And on that world dwelt a mighty Three in a temple of crystal, served by strange slaves and worshipped by a world. They were not wholly abstract, as most modern gods have become. Some say they were from beyond, and real, in their way, as flesh and blood.

"Those three gods were the origin and beginning of all other gods that mankind has known. All modern gods are echoes of them, in a world that has forgotten the very name of the Lost Planet. Säig they called one, and Lsa was the second. You will never have heard of them—they died before your world's hot seas had cooled. No man knows how they vanished, or why, and no trace of them is left anywhere in the universe we know. But there was a Third—a mighty Third set above these two and ruling the Lost Planet; so mighty a Third that even today, unthinkably long afterward, his name has not died from the lips of man. It has become a byword now—his name, that once no living man dared utter! I heard you call upon him not ten minutes past—Black Pharol!''

His husky voice sank to a quiver as it spoke the hackneyed name. Yarol gave a sudden snort of laughter, quickly hushed, and said, ''Pharol! Why—''

''Yes, I know. Pharol, today, means unmentionable rites to an ancient no-god of utter darkness. Pharol has sunk so low that his very name denotes nothingness. But in other days—ah, in other days! Black Pharol has not always been a blur of dark worshipped with obscenity. In other days men knew what things that darkness hid, nor dared pronounce the name you laugh at, lest unwittingly they stumble upon that secret twist of its inflection which opens the door upon the dark that is Pharol. Men have been engulfed before now in that utter blackness of the god, and in that dark have seen fearful things. I know''—the raw voice trailed away into a murmur—''such fearful things that a man might scream his throat hoarse and never speak again above a whisper. . . .''

Smith's eyes flicked Yarol's. The husky murmur went on after a moment.

''So you see the old gods have not died utterly. They can never die as we know death: they come from too far Beyond to know either death or life as we do. They came from so very far that to touch us at all they had to take a visible form among mankind—to incarnate themselves in a material body through which, as through a door, they might reach out and touch the bodies and minds of men. The form they chose does not matter now—I do not know it. It was a material thing, and it has gone to dust so long ago that the very memory of its shape has vanished from the minds of men. But that dust still exists. Do you hear me? That dust which was once the first and the greatest of all gods, still exists! It was that which those men hunted. It was that they found, and fled in deadly terror of what they saw there. You look to be made of firmer stuff. Will you take up the search where they left it?''

Smith's pale stare met Yarol's black one across the table. Silence hung between them for a moment. Then Smith said,

''Any objection to us having a little talk with those two over there?''

''None at all,'' answered the hoarse whisper promptly. ''Go now, if you like.''

Smith rose without further words. Yarol pushed back his chair noiselessly and followed him. They crossed the floor with the spaceman's peculiar, shifting walk and slid into opposite chairs between the huddling two.

The effect was startling. The Earthman jerked convulsively and turned a pasty face, eloquent with alarm, toward the interruption. The drylander stared from Smith's face to Yarol's in dumb terror. Neither spoke.

''Know that fellow over there?'' inquired Smith abruptly, jerking his head toward the table they had quitted.

After a moment's hesitation the two heads turned as one. When they faced around again the terror on the Earthman's face was giving way to a dawning comprehension. He said from a dry throat, ''He—he's hiring you, eh?''

Smith nodded. The Earthman's face crumpled into terror again and he cried,

''Don't do it. For God's sake, you don't know!''

''Know what?''

The man glanced furtively round the room and licked his lips uncertainly. A curious play of conflicting emotions flickered across his face.

''Dangerous—'' he mumbled. ''Better leave well enough alone. We found that out.''

''What happened?''

The Earthman stretched out a shaking hand for the *segir* bottle and poured a brimming glass. He drained it before he spoke, and the incoherence of his speech may have been due to the glasses that had preceded it.

"We went up toward the polar mountains, where he said. Weeks . . . it was cold. The nights get dark up there . . . dark. Went into the cave that goes through the mountain—a long way. . . . Then our lights went out—full-charged batteries in new super-Tomlinson tubes, but they went out like candles, and in the dark—in the dark the white thing came. . . ."

A shudder went over him strongly. He reached out shaking hands for the *segir* bottle and poured another glass, the rim clicking against his teeth as he drank. Then he set down the glass hard and said violently,

"That's all. We left. Don't remember a thing about getting out—or much more than starving and freezing in the saltlands for a long time. Our supplies ran low—hadn't been for him"—nodding across the table—"we'd both have died. Don't know how we did get out finally—but we're out, understand? Out! Nothing could hire us to go back—we've seen enough. There's something about it that—that makes your head ache—we saw . . . never mind. But—"

He beckoned Smith closer and sank his voice to a whisper. His eyes rolled fearfully.

"It's after us. Don't ask me what . . . I don't know. But—feel it in the dark, watching—watching in the dark. . . ."

The voice sank to a mumble and he reached again for the *segir* bottle.

"It's here now—waiting—if the lights go out—watching—mustn't let the lights go out—more *segir*. . . ."

The bottle clinked on the glass-rim, the voice trailed away into drunken mutterings.

Smith pushed back his chair and nodded to Yarol. The two at the table did not seem to notice their departure. The drylander was clutching the *segir* bottle in turn and pouring out red liquid without watching the glass—an apprehensive one-eyed stare turned across his shoulder.

Smith laid a hand on his companion's shoulder and drew him across the room toward the bar. Yarol scowled at the approaching bartender and suggested,

"Suppose we get an advance for drinks, anyhow."

"Are we taking it?"

"Well, what d'you think?"

"It's dangerous. You know, there's something worse than whisky wrong with those two. Did you notice the Earthman's eyes?"

"Whites showed all around," nodded Yarol. "I've seen madmen look like that."

"I thought of that, too. He was drunk, of course, and probably wouldn't be so wild-sounding, sober—but from the looks of him he'll never be sober again till he dies. No use trying to find out anything more from him. And the other—well, did you ever try to find out anything from a drylander? Even a sober one?"

Yarol lifted expressive shoulders. "I know. If we go into this, we go blind. Never dig any more out of those drunks. But something certainly scared them."

"And yet," said Smith, "I'd like to know more about this. Dust of the gods—and all that. Interesting. Just what does he want with this dust, anyhow?"

"Did you believe that yarn?"

"Don't know—I've come across some pretty funny things here and there. He does act half-cracked, of course, but—well, those fellows back there certainly found *something* out of the ordinary, and they didn't go all the way at that."

"Well, if he'll buy us a drink I say let's take the job," said Yarol. "I'd as soon be scared to death later as die of thirst now. What do you say?"

"Good enough," shrugged Smith. "I'm thirsty, too."

The little man looked up hopefully as they reseated themselves at the table.

"If we can come to terms," said Smith, "we'll take it. And if you can give us some idea of what we're looking for, and why."

"The dust of Pharol," said the husky voice impatiently. "I told you that."

"What d'you want with it?"

The little bright eyes stared suspiciously across the table into Smith's calm gaze.

"What business is it of yours?"

"We're risking our necks for it, aren't we?"

Again the bright, small eyes bored into the Earthman's. The husky voice fell lower, to the very echo of a whisper, and he said, secretly.

"I'll tell you, then. After all, why not? You don't know how to use it—it's of no value to anyone but me. Listen, then—I told you that the Three incarnated themselves into a material form to use as a door through which they could reach humanity. They had to do it, but it was a door that opened both ways—through it, if one dared, man could reach the Three. No one dared in those days—the power beyond was too terrible. It would have been like walking straight through a gateway into hell. But time has passed since then. The gods have drawn away from humanity into farther realms. The terror that was Pharol is only an echo in a forgetful world. The spirit of the god has gone—but not wholly. While any remnant of that shape which was once incarnate Pharol exists, Pharol can be reached. For the man who could lay hands on that dusk, knowing the requisite rites and formulae, all knowledge, all power would lie open like a book. To enslave a god!"

The raw whisper rasped to a crescendo; fanatic lights flared in the small, bright eyes. He had forgotten them entirely—his piercing stare fixed on some shining future, and his hands on the table clenched into white-knuckled fists.

Smith and Yarol exchanged dubious glances. Obviously the man was mad. . . .

"Fifty thousand dollars to your account in any bank you choose," the hoarse voice, eminently sane, broke in abruptly upon their dubiety. "All expenses, of course, will be paid. I'll give you charts and tell you all I know about how to get there. When can you start?"

Smith grinned. Touched the man might be, but just then

Smith would have stormed the gates of hell, at any madman's request, for fifty thousand Earth dollars.

"Right now," he said laconically. "Let's go."

II

Northward over the great curve of Mars, red slag and red dust and the reddish, low-lying dryland vegetation gave way to the saltlands around the Pole. Scrub grows there, and sparse, coarse grass, and the snow that falls by night lies all the cold, thin day among the tough grass-roots and in the hillocks of the dry salt soil.

"Of all the God-forsaken countries," said Northwest Smith, looking down from his pilot seat at the gray lands slipping past under the speed of their plane, "this must be the worst. I'd sooner live on Luna or one of the asteroids."

Yarol tilted the *segir* bottle to his lips and evoked an eloquent gurgle from its depths.

"Five days of flying over this scenery would give anyone the jitters," he pronounced. "I'd never have thought I'd be glad to see a mountain range as ugly as that, but it looks like Paradise now," and he nodded toward the black, jagged slopes of the polar mountains that marked their journey's end so far as flying was concerned; for despite their great antiquity the peaks were jagged and rough as mountains new-wrenched from a heaving world.

Smith brought the plane down at the foot of the rising black slopes. There was a triangular gap there with a streak of white down its side, a landmark he had been watching for, and the plane slid quietly into the shelter to lie protected under the shelving rock. From here progress must be made afoot and painfully through the mountains. There was no landing-place any nearer their goal than this. Yet in measure of distance they had not far to go.

The two climbed stiffly out. Smith stretched his long legs and sniffed the air. It was bitterly cold, and tinged with that nameless, dry salt smell of eon-dead seas which is encountered nowhere in the known universe save in the northern saltlands of Mars. He faced the mountains doubtfully. From their beginnings here, he knew, they rolled away, jagged and black and deadly, to the very Pole. Snow lay thickly upon them in the brief Martian winter, unmarked by any track until it melted for the canals, carving deeper runnels into the already jig-sawed peaks.

Once in the very long-past days, so the little whispering fanatic had said, Mars was a green world. Seas had spread here, lapping the feet of gentler mountains, and in the slopes of those hills a mighty city once lay—a nameless city, so far as the present generations of man remembered, and a nameless star shone down upon it from a spot in the heavens now empty—the Lost Planet, shining on a lost city. The dwellers there must have seen the catastrophe which blasted that sister planet from the face of the sky. And if the little man were right, the gods of that Lost Planet had been saved from the wreckage and spirited across the void to a dwelling-place in this greatly honored city of the mountains that is not even a memory today.

And time passed, so the story went. The city aged—the gods aged—the planet aged. At last, in some terrible catastrophe, the planet heaved under the city's foundations, the mountains shook it into ruins and folded themselves into new and dreadful shapes. The seas receded, the fertile soil sluffed away from the rocks and time swallowed up the very memory of that city which once had been the dwelling-place of gods—which was still, so the hoarse whisper had told them, the dwelling-place of gods.

"Must have been right around here somewhere," said Smith, "that those two found the cave."

"Out around the slope to the left," agreed Yarol. "Let's go." He squinted up at the feeble sun. "Not very long past dawn. We ought to be back again by dark if things go right."

They left the ship in its shelter and struck out across the salt drylands, the harsh scrub brushing about their knees and their breath clouding the thin air as they advanced. The slope curved away to the left, rising in rapid ascent to black peaks that were unscalable and forbidding. The only hope of penetrating that wall lay in finding the cavern that their predecessors had fled . . . and in that cavern—Smith loosened the heat-gun in its holster at his side.

They had plodded for fifteen minutes through the scrub, dry snow rising under their feet and the harsh salt air frosting their breath, before the mouth of the cave they were hunting appeared darkly under the overhanging rock they had been told of.

The two peered in doubtfully. That jagged floor might never have known the tread of human feet, so far as one might know by the look of it. Powdered snow lay undisturbed in the deep crannies, and daylight did not penetrate very far into the forbidding dark beyond. Smith drew his gun, took a deep breath and plunged into the blackness and the cold, with Yarol at his heels.

It was like leaving everything human and alive for some frosty limbo that had never known life. The cold struck sharply through their leather garments. They took out their Tomlinson tubes before they had gone more than twenty paces, and the twin beams illumined a scene of utter desolation, more dead than death, for it seemed never to have known life.

For perhaps fifteen minutes they stumbled through the cold dark. Smith kept his beam focused on the floor beneath them; Yarol's roved the walls and pierced the blackness ahead. Rough walls and ragged ceiling and teeth of broken stone projecting from the floor to slash at their boots—no sound but their footsteps, nothing but the dark and the frost and the silence. Then Yarol said, "It's foggy in here," and something clouded the clear beams of the lights for an instant; then darkness folded round them as suddenly and completely as the folds of a cloak.

Smith stopped dead-still, tense and listening. No sound. He felt the lens of his light-tube and knew that it still burned—it was warm, and the faint vibration under the glass told him that the tubes still functioned. But something intangible and strange blotted it out at the source . . . a thick, stifling blackness that seemed to muffle their senses. It was like a bandage over the eyes—Smith, holding the burning lightlens to his eyes, could not detect even its outline in that all-cloaking dark.

For perhaps five minutes that dead blackness held them. Vaguely they knew what to expect, but when it came, the shock of it took their breath away. There was no sound, but quite suddenly around a bend of the cavern came a figure of utter whiteness, seen at first fragmentarily through a screen of rock-toothed jags, then floating full into view against the background of the dark. Smith thought he had never seen whiteness before until his incredulous eyes beheld this creature—if creature it could be. Somehow he thought it must be partly below the level of the floor along which it moved; for though in that blind black he had no way of gauging elevation, it seemed to him that the apparition, moving with an effortless glide, advanced unopposed through the solid rock of the floor. And it was whiter than anything living or dead had ever been before—so white that it sickened him, somehow, and the flesh crept along his spine. Like a cut-out figure of paper, it blazed against the flat black beyond. The dark did not affect it, no shadows lay upon its surface; in two arbitrary dimensions only, blind white superimposed upon blind dark, it floated toward them. And it was tall, and somehow man-formed, but of no shape that words could describe.

Smith heard Yarol catch his breath in a gasp behind him. He heard no other sound, though the whiteness floated swiftly forward *through* the rocky floor. He was sure of that now—a part of it extended farther down than his feet, and they were planted upon solid rock. And though his skin crawled with unreasoning terror, and the hair on his neck prickled with the weird, impossible approach of the impossible thing, he kept his head enough to see that it was apparently solid, yet somehow milkily translucent; that it had form and depth, though no shadows of that darkness lay upon it; that from where no face should have been a blind, eyeless visage fronted him impassively. It was very close now, and though the extremities of it trailed below the floor line, its height lifted far above his head.

And a nameless, blind force beat out from it and assailed him, a force that somehow seemed to be driving him into unnamable things—an urge to madness, beating at his brain with the reasonless buffeting of insanity, but a wilder, more incomprehensible insanity than the sane mind could understand.

Something frantic within him clamored for instant, headlong flight—he heard Yarol's breathing panicky behind him and knew that he too wavered on the verge of bolting—but something insistent at the roots of his brain held him firm before the whiteness bearing down in its aura of madness—something that denied the peril, that hinted at solution. . . .

Scarcely realizing that he had moved, he found the heatgun in his hand, and on a sudden impulse jerked his arm up and sent a long, blue-hot streamer of flame straight at the advancing apparition. For the briefest of instants the blue dazzle flashed a light-blade through the dark. It struck the floating whiteness full—vanished—Smith heard a faint crackle of sparks on the invisible floor beyond and knew that it had passed through the creature without meeting resistance. And in that flashing second while the blue gaze split the thickness of the dark he saw it shine luridly upon a splinter of rock in its path, but not upon the white figure. No blaze of blueness affected the deathly pallor of it—he had a sudden conviction that though a galaxy of colored lights were played upon it no faintest hint of color could ever tinge it with any of man's hues. Fighting the waves of madness that buffeted at his brain, he realized painfully that it must be beyond the reach of men—and therefore—

He laughed unsteadily and holstered his gun.

"Come on," he yelled to Yarol, reaching out blindly to grasp his comrade's arm, and—suppressing a tingle of terror—plunged straight through that towering horror.

There was an instant of blaze and blinding whiteness, a moment of turmoil while dizziness swirled round him and the floor rocked under his feet and a maelstrom of mad impulses battered through his brain; then everything was black again and he was plunging recklessly ahead through the dark, dragging a limply acquiescent Yarol behind him.

After a while of stumbling progress, punctuated with falls, while the white horror dropped away behind them, not following, though the muffling dark still sealed their eyes—the almost forgotten light in Smith's hand suddenly blazed forth again. In its light he faced Yarol, blinking at the abrupt illumination. The Venusian's face was a mask of question, his black eyes bright with inquiry.

"What happened? What was it? How did you—how could we—"

"It can't have been real," said Smith with a shaky grin. "I mean, not material in the sense that we know. Looked awful enough, but—well, there were too many things about it that didn't hitch up. Notice how it seemed to trail through the solid floor? And neither light nor dark affected it—it had no shadows, even in that blackness, and the flash of my gun didn't even give it a blue tinge. Then I remembered what that little fellow had told us about his three gods: that, though they had real existence, it was on such a widely different plane from ours that they couldn't touch us except by providing themselves with a material body. I think his thing was like that also: visible, but too other-dimensional to reach us except through sight. And when I saw that the floor didn't offer any resistance to it I thought that maybe, conversely, it wouldn't affect us either. And it didn't. We're through."

Yarol drew a deep breath.

"The master-mind," he gibed affectionately. "Wonder if anyone else ever figured that out, or are we the first to get through?"

"Don't know. Don't get the idea it was just a scarecrow, though. I think we moved none too soon. A minute or two longer and—and—I felt as if someone were stirring my brains with a stick. Nothing seemed—right. I think I know now what was wrong with those other two—they waited too long before they ran. Good thing we moved when we did."

"But what about that darkness?"

"I suppose we'll never really know. Must have had some relation to the other—the white thing, possibly some force or element out of that other dimension; because just as dark couldn't touch the whiteness of that thing, so light had no effect on the dark. I got the impression, somehow, that the dark space is a fixed area there, as if a section out of the other world has been set down in the cave, for the white thing to roam about in—a barrier of blackness across the way. And I don't suppose that it can move outside the darkness. But I may be wrong—let's go!"

"Right behind you!" said Yarol. "Get along."

The cave extended for another fifteen-minute walk, cold and silent and viciously rough underfoot, but no further mishap broke the journey. Tomlinson-lights gleaming, they traversed it, and the glow of cold day at the far end looked like the gleam of paradise after that journey through the heart of the dead rock.

They looked out upon the ruins of that city where once the gods had dwelt—ragged rock, great splintered teeth of stone upflung, the bare black mountainside folded and tortured into wild shapes of desolation. Here and there, buried in the debris of ages, lay huge six-foot blocks of hewn stone, the only reminder that here had stood Mars' holiest city, once, very long ago.

After five minutes of search Smith's eyes finally located the outline of what might, millions of years ago, have been a street. It led strait away from the slope at the cave-mouth, and the blocks of hewn stone, the crevices and folded ruins of earthquake choked it, but the course it once had run was not entirely obliterated even yet. Palaces and temples must have lined it once. There was no trace of them now save in the blocks of marble lying shattered among the broken stones.

Time had erased the city from the face of Mars almost as completely as from the memories of man. Yet the trace of this one street was all they needed now to guide them.

The going was rough. Once down among the ruins it was difficult to keep in the track, and for almost an hour they clambered over broken rock and jagged spikes of stone, leaping the crevices, skirting great mounds of ruin. Both were scratched and breathless by the time they came to the first landmark they recognized—a black, leaning needle of stone, half buried in fragments of broken marble. Just beyond it lay two blocks of stone, one upon the other, perhaps the only two in the whole vast ruin which still stood as the hands of man had laid them hundreds of centuries ago.

Smith paused beside them and looked at Yarol, breathing a little heavily from exertion.

"Here it is," he said. "The old boy was telling the truth after all."

"So far," amended Yarol dubiously, drawing his heat-gun. "Well, we'll see."

The blue pencil of flame hissed from the gun's muzzle to splatter along the crack between the stones. Very slowly Yarol traced that line, and in spite of himself excitement quickened within him. Two-thirds of the way along the line the flame suddenly ceased to spatter and bit deep. A blackening hole appeared in the stone. It widened swiftly, and smoke rose, and there came a sound of protesting rock wrenched from its bed of eons as the upper stone slowly ground half around on the lower, tottered a moment and then fell.

The lower stone was hollow. The two bent over curiously, peering down. A tiny breath of unutterable antiquity rose in their faces out of that darkness, a little breeze from a million years ago. Smith flashed his light-tube downward and saw level stone a dozen feet below. The breeze was stronger now, and dust danced up the shaft from the mysterious depths—dust that had lain there undisturbed for unthinkably long ages.

"We'll give it a while to air out," said Smith, switching

off his light. "Must be plenty of ventilation, to judge from that breeze, and the dust will probably blow away before long. We can be rigging up some sort of ladder while we wait."

By the time a knotted rope had been prepared and anchored about a near-by needle of rock the little wind was blowing cleanly up the shaft, still laden with that indefinable odor of ages, but breathable. Smith swung over first, lowering himself cautiously until his feet touched the stone. Yarol, when he came down, found him swinging the Tomlinson-beam about a scene of utter lifelessness. A passageway stretched before them, smoothly polished as to walls and ceiling, with curious, unheard-of-frescoes limned in dim colors under the glaze. Antiquity hung almost tangibly in the air. The little breeze that brushed past their faces seemed sacrilegiously alive in this tomb of dead dynasties.

That glazed and patterned passageway led downward into the dark. They followed it dubiously, feet stirring in the dust of a dead race, light-beams violating the million-years night of the underground. Before they had gone very far the circle of light from the shaft disappeared from sight beyond the up-sloping floor behind them, and they walked through antiquity with nothing but the tiny, constant breeze upon their faces to remind them of the world above.

They walked a very long way. There was no subterfuge about the passage, no attempt to confuse the traveler. No other halls opened from it—it led straight forward and down through the stillness, the dark, the odor of very ancient death. And when at long last they reached the end, they had passed no other corridor-mouth, no other openings at all save the tiny ventilation holes at intervals along the ceiling.

At the end of that passage a curving wall of rough, unworked stone bulged like the segment of a sphere, closing the corridor. It was a different stone entirely from that under the patterned glaze of the way along which they had come. In the light of their Tomlinson-tubes they saw a stone door set flush with the slightly bulging wall that held it. And in the door's very center a symbol was cut deep and vehement and black against the gray background. Yarol, seeing it, caught his breath.

"Do you know that sign?" he said softly, his voice reverberating in the stillness of the underground, and echoes whispered behind him down the darkness, "*–know that sign . . . know that sign?*"

"I can guess," murmured Smith, playing his light on the black outline of it.

"The symbol of Pharol," said the Venusian in a near-whisper, but the echoes caught it and rolled back along the passage in diminishing undertones, "*–Pharol . . . Pharol . . . Pharol!*"

"I saw it once carved in the rock of an asteroid," whispered Yarol. "Just a bare little fragment of dead stone whirling around and around through space. There was one smooth surface on it, and this same sign was cut there. The Lost Planet must really have existed, N.W., and that must have been a part of it once, with the god's name cut so deep that even the explosion of a world couldn't wipe it out."

Smith drew his gun. "We'll soon know," he said. "This will probably fall, so stand back."

The blue pencil of heat traced the door's edges, spattering against the stone as Yarol's had in the city above. And as before, in its course it encountered the weak place in the molding and the fire bit deep. The door trembled as Smith held the beam steady; it uttered an ominous creaking and began slowly to tilt outward at the top. Smith snapped off his gun and leaped backward, as the great stone slab tottered outward and fell. The mighty crash of it reverberated through the dark, and the concussion of its fall shook the solid floor and flung both men staggering against the wall.

They reeled to their feet again, shielding blinded eyes from the torrent of radiance that poured forth out of the doorway. It was a rich, golden light, somehow thick, yet clear, and they saw almost immediately, as their eyes became accustomed to the sudden change from darkness, that it was like no light they had ever known before. Tangibly it poured past them down the corridor in hurrying waves that lapped one another and piled up and flowed as a gas might have done. It was light which had an unnamable body to it, a physical, palpable body which yet did not affect the air they breathed.

They walked forward into a sea of radiance, and that curious light actually eddied about their feet, rippling away from the forward motion of their bodies as water might have done. Widening circles spread away through the air as they advanced, breaking soundlessly against the wall, and behind them a trail of bright streaks steamed away like the wake of a ship in water.

Through the deeps of that rippling light they walked a passage hewn from ragged stone, a different stone from that of the outer corridor, and somehow older. Tiny speckles of brightness glinted now and again on the rough walls, and neither could remember ever having seen just such mottled, bright-flecked rock before.

"Do you know what I think this is?" demanded Smith suddenly, after a few minutes of silent progress over the uneven floor. "An asteroid! That rough wall bulging into the corridor outside was the outer part of it. Remember, the three gods were supposed to have been carried away from the catastrophe on the other world and brought here. Well, I'll bet that's how it was managed—a fragment of that planet, enclosing a room, possibly, where the gods' images stood, was somehow detached from the Lost Planet and hurled across space to Mars. Must have buried itself in the ground here, and the people of this city tunneled in to it and built a temple over the spot. No other way, you see, to account for that protruding wall and the peculiar formation of this rock. It must have come from the lost world—never saw anything like it anywhere, myself."

"Sounds logical," admitted Yarol, swinging his foot to start an eddy of light toward the wall. "And what do you make of this funny light?"

"Whatever other-dimensional place those gods came

from, we can be pretty sure that light plays funny tricks there. It must be nearly material—physical. You saw it in that white thing in the cave, and in the dark that smothered our tubes. It's as tangible as water, almost. You saw how it flowed out into the passage when the door fell, not as real light does, but in succeeding waves, like heavy gas. Yet I don't notice any difference in the air. I don't believe—say! Look at that!"

He stopped so suddenly that Yarol bumped into him from behind and muttered a mild Venusian oath. Then across Smith's shoulder he saw it too, and his hand swept downward to his gun. Something like an oddly shape hole opening onto utter dark had appeared around the curve of the passage. And as they stared, it moved. It was a Something blacker than anything in human experience could ever have been before—as black as the guardian of the cave had been white—so black that the eye refused to compass it save as a negative quality, an emptiness. Smith, remembering the legends of Pharol the No-God of utter nothingness, gripped his gun more firmly and wondered if he stood face to face with one of the elder gods.

The Thing had shifted is shape, flowing to a stabler outline and standing higher from the floor. Smith felt that it must have form and thickness—at least three dimensions and probably more—but try though he would, his eyes could not discern it save as a flat outline of nothingness against the golden light.

And as from the white dweller in darkness, so from this black denizen of the light there flowed a force that goaded the brain to madness. Smith felt it battering in blind waves at the foundations of his mind—but he felt more than the reasonless urge in this force assailing him. He sensed a struggle of some sort, as if the black guardian were turning only a part of its attention to him—as if it fought against something unseen and powerful. Feeling this, he began to see signs of that combat in the black outlines of the thing. It rippled and flowed, its shape shifted fluidly, it writhed in protest against something he could not comprehend. Definitely now he felt that it fought a desperate battle with some unseen enemy, and a little shudder crawled down his back as he watched.

Quite suddenly it dawned upon him what was happening. Slowly, relentlessly, the black nothingness was being drawn down the passage. And it was—it must be—the flow of the golden radiance that drew it, as a fish might be carried forward down a stream. Somehow the opening of the door must have freed the pent-up lake of light, and it was flowing slowly out down the passage as water flows, draining the asteroid, if asteroid it was. He could see now that though they had halted the wake of rippling illumination behind them did not cease. Past them in a bright tide streamed the light. And on that outflowing torrent the black guardian floated, struggling but helpless.

It was closer now, and the beat of insistent impulses against Smith's brain was stronger, but he was not greatly alarmed by it. The panic of the thing must be deep, and the waves of force that washed about him were dizzying but not deep-reaching. Because of this increasing dizziness, as the thing approached, he was never sure afterward just what had happened. Rapidly it drew nearer, until he could have put out his hand and touched it—though instinctively he felt that, near as it seemed, it was too far away across dimensional gulfs for him ever to lay hand upon it. The blackness of it, at close range, was stupefying, a blackness that the eye refused to comprehend—that could not be, and was.

With the nearness of it his brain seemed to leave its moorings and plunge in mad, impossible curves through a suddenly opened space wherein the walls of the passage were shadows dimly seen and his own body no more than a pillar of mist in a howling void. The black thing must have rolled over him in passing, and engulfed him in its reasonless and incredible dark. He never knew. When his plunging brain finally ceased its lunges through the void and returned reluctantly to his body, the horror of nothingness had receded past them down the corridor, still struggling, and the waves of its blinding force weakened with the distance.

Yarol was leaning against the wall, wide-eyed and gasping. "Did it get you, too?" he managed to articulate after several attempts to control his hurrying breath.

Smith found his own lungs laboring. He nodded breathless.

"I wonder," he said when he had recovered a measure of normality, "if that thing would look as white in the dark as it did in the light? I'll bet it would. And do you suppose it can't exist outside the light? Reminded me of a jelly-fish caught in a mill-race. Say, if the light's flowing out that fast, d'you think it may go entirely? We'd better be moving."

Under their feet the passage sloped downward still. And when they reached the end of their quest, it came very suddenly. The curve of the passage sharpened to an angle, and round the bend the corridor ended abruptly at the threshold of a great cavity in the heart of the asteroid.

In the rich golden light it glittered like the center of a many-faceted diamond—that vast crystal room. The light brimmed it from wall to wall, from floor to ceiling. And it was strange that in that mellow flood of radiance the boundaries of the room seemed hard to define—somehow it looked limitless, though the walls were clear to be seen.

All this, though, they were realizing only subconsciously. Their eyes met the throne in the center of the crystal vault and clung there, fascinated. It was a crystal throne, and it had been fashioned for no human occupant. On this the mighty Three of measureless antiquity had sat. It was not an altar—it was a throne where incarnate godhood reigned once, too long ago for the mind to comprehend. Roughly triform, it glittered under the great arch of the ceiling. There was no knowing from the shape of it now, what form the Three had worn who sat upon it. But the forms must have been outside modern comprehension—nothing the two explorers had ever seen in all their wanderings could have occupied it.

Two of the pedestals were empty. Saig and Lsa had vanished as completely as their names from man's memory. On the third—the center and the highest . . . Smith's breath caught in his throat suddenly. Here then, on the great throne before them, lay all that was left of a god—the greatest of antiquity's deities. This mound of gray dust. The oldest thing upon three worlds—older than the mountains that held it, older than the very old beginnings of the mighty race of man. Great Pharol—dust upon a throne.

"Say, listen," broke in Yarol's matter-of-fact voice. "Why did the image turn to dust when the room and the throne didn't? The whole room must have come from that crystal temple on the other world. You'd think—"

"The image must have been very old long before the temple was built," said Smith softly. He was thinking how dead it looked, lying there in a soft gray mound on the crystal. How dead! how immeasurably old!—yet if the little man spoke truly, life still dwelt in these ashes of forgotten deity. Could he indeed forge from the gray dust a cable that would reach out irresistibly across the gulfs of time and space, into dimensions beyond man's understanding, and draw back the vanished entity which had once been Great Pharol? Could he? And if he could—suddenly doubt rose up in Smith's mind. What man, with a god to do his bidding, would stop short of domination over the worlds of space—perhaps of godhood for himself? And if that man were half mad? . . .

He followed Yarol across the shining floor in silence. It took them longer to reach the throne than they had expected—there was something deceptive about the crystal of that room, and the clarity of the brimming golden light. The translucent heights of the triumvirate structure that had enthroned gods towered high over their heads. Smith looked upward toward that central pedestal bearing its eon-old burden, wondering what men had stood here before him at the foot of the throne, what men of nameless races and forgotten worlds, worshipping the black divinity that was Pharol. On this crystal floor the feet of—

A scrambling sound interrupted his wondering. The irreverent Yarol, his eyes on the gray dust above them, was climbing the crystal throne. It was slippery, and never meant for mounting, and his heavy boots slid over the smoothness of it. Smith stood watching with a half-smile. For long ages no living man had dared approach this place save in reverence, on his knees, not venturing so much as to lift his eyes to that holy of holies where sat incarnate godhood. Now—Yarol's foot slipped on the last step of the ascent and he muttered under his breath, reaching out to clutch the pedestal where Great Pharol, first of the living gods, had ruled a mightier world than any men inhabit now.

At the summit he paused, looking down from an eminence whence no eyes save those of gods had ever looked before. And he frowned in a puzzled way as he looked.

"Something wrong here, N.W.," he said. "Look up. What's going on around the ceiling?"

Smith's pale gaze rose. For a moment he stared in utter bewilderment. For the third time that day his eyes were beholding something so impossible that they refused to register the fact upon an outraged brain. Something dark and yet not dark was closing down upon them. The roof seemed to lower—and panic stirred within him briefly. The ceiling, coming down to crush them? Some further guardian of the gods descending like a blanket over their heads? What?

And then understanding broke upon him, and his laugh of sheer relief echoed almost blasphemously in the silence of the place.

"The light's running out," he said. "Like water, just draining away. That's all."

And the incredible thing was true. That shining lake of light which brimmed the crystal hollow was ebbing, pouring through the door, down the passage, out into the upper air, and darkness, literally, was flowing in behind it. And it was flowing fast.

"Well," said Yarol, casting an imperturbable glance upward, "we'd better be moving before it all runs out. Hand me up the box, will you?"

Hesitantly, Smith unslung the little lacquered steel box they had been given. Suppose they brought him back the dust to weld it from—what then? Such limitless power even in the hands of an eminently wise, eminently sane and balanced man would surely be dangerous. And in the hands of the little whispering fanatic—

Yarol, looking down from his height, met the troubled eyes and was silent for a moment. Then he whistled softly and said, though Smith had not spoken,

"I never thought of that. . . . D'you suppose it really could be done? Why, the man's half crazy!"

"I don't know," said Smith. "Maybe he couldn't—but he told us the way here, didn't he? He knew this much—I don't think we'd better risk his not knowing any more. And suppose he did succeed, Yarol—suppose he found some way to bring this—this monster of the dark—through into our dimension—turned it loose on our worlds. Do you think he could hold it? He talked about enslaving a god, but could he? I haven't much doubt that he knows some way of opening a door between dimensions to admit the thing that used to be Pharol—it can be done. It has been done. But once he gets it opened, can he close it? Could he keep the thing under control? You know he couldn't! You know it'd break loose, and—well, anything could happen then."

"I hadn't thought of that," said Yarol again. "Gods! Suppose—"

He broke off, staring in fascination at the gray dust that held such terrible potentialities. And there was silence for a while in the crystal place.

Smith, looking upward at the throne and his friend, saw that the dark was flowing in faster and faster. And the light thinned about them, and long streaks of brilliance wavered out behind him as the light ebbed by a racing torrent.

"Suppose we don't take it back, then," said Yarol suddenly. "Say we couldn't find the place—or that it was buried under debris or something. Suppose we—gods, but it's getting dark in here!"

The line of light was far down the walls now. Above them the black night of the underground brimmed in relentlessly.

They watched in half-incredulous wonder as the tidemark of radiance ebbed down and down along the crystal. Now it touched the level of the throne, and Yarol gasped as he was plunged head and shoulders into blackness, starring down as into a sea of light in which his own lower limbs moved shimmeringly, sending long ripples outward as they stirred.

Very swiftly the tide-race ran. Fascinated, they watched it ebb away, down Yarol's legs, down beyond him entirely, so that he perched in darkness above the outrunning tide, down the heights of the throne, down to touch Smith's tall head with blackness. Uncannily he stood in the midst of a receding sea, shoulder-deep—waist-deep—knee-deep . . .

The light that so short a time before—for so many countless ages before—had brimmed this chamber lay in a shallow, gleaming sea ankle-deep on the floor. For the first time in eons the throne of the Three stood in darkness.

Not until the last dregs of illumination were snaking along a black floor in rivulets that ran swiftly, like fiery snakes, toward the door, did the two men awake from their wonder. The last of the radiance that must have been lighted on a lost world millions of years ago, perhaps by the hands of the first gods—ebbed doorward. Smith drew a deep breath and turned in the blackness toward the spot where the throne must be standing in the first dark it had known for countless ages. Those snakes of light along the floor did not seem to give out any radiance—the place was blacker than any night above ground. Yarol's light-tube suddenly stabbed downward, and Yarol's voice said from the dark,

"Whew! Should have bottled some of that to take home. Well, what d'you say, N.W.? Do we leave with the dust or without it?"

"Without it," said Smith slowly. "I'm sure of that much, anyhow. But we can't leave it here. The man would simply send others, you know. With blasting material, maybe, if we said the place was buried. But he'd get it."

Yarol's beam shifted, a white blade in the dark, to the gray, enigmatic mound beside him. In the glare of the

Tomlinson-tube it lay inscrutably, just as it had lain for all the eons since the god forsook it—waiting, perhaps, for this moment. And Yarol drew his gun.

"Don't know what that image was made of," he said, "but rock or metal or anything else will melt into nothing in the full-power heat of a gun."

And in a listening silence he flicked the catch. Bluewhite and singing, the flame leaped irresistibly from is muzzle—struck full in an intolerable violence of heat upon that gray mound which had been a god. Rocks would have melted under the blast. Rocket-tube steel would have glowed molten. Nothing that the hands of man can fashion could have resisted the heat-blast of a ray-gun at full strength. But in its full blue glare the mound of dust lay motionless.

Above the hissing of the flame Smith heard Yarol's muttered "*Shar!*" of amazement. The gun muzzle thrust closer into the gray heap, until the crystal began to glow in the reflected heat and blue sparks spattered through the darkness. And very slowly the edges of the mound began to turn red and sullen. The redness spread. A little blue flame licked up; another.

Yarol flipped off the gun-catch and sat watching as the dust began to blaze. Presently, as the brilliance of it grew stronger, he slid down from his pedestal and made his precarious way along the slippery crystal to the floor. Smith scarcely realized that he had come. His eyes were riveted on the clear, burning flame that was once a god. It burned with a fierce, pale light flickering with nameless evanescent colors—the dust that had been Pharol of the utter darkness burning slowly away in a flame of utter light.

And as the minutes passed and the flame grew stronger, the reflections of it began to dance eerily in the crystal walls and ceiling, sending long wavers downward until the floor was carpeted with dazzles of flame. An odor of unnamable things very faintly spread upon the air—smoke of dead gods. . . . It went to Smith's head dizzily, and the reflections wavered and ran together until he seemed to be suspended in a space while all about him pictures of flame went writhing through the dark—pictures of flame—nebulous, unreal pictures waving across the walls and vanishing—flashing by uncertainly overhead, running under his feet, circling him round from wall to wall in reeling patterns, as if reflections made eons ago on another world had buried deep in the crystal were waking to life at the magic touch of the burning god.

With the smoke eddying dizzily in his nostrils he watched—and all about him, overhead, underfoot, the strange, wild pictures ran blurrily through the crystal and vanished. He thought he saw mighty landscapes ringed by such mountains as none of today's world know . . . he thought he saw a whiter sun than has shone for eons, lighting a land where rivers thundered between green banks . . . thought he saw many moons parading across a purple night wherein shone constellations that haunted him with familiarity in the midst of their strangeness . . . saw a green star where red Mars should be, and a far pin-prick of white where the green point that is Earth hangs. Cities reeled past across the crystal darkness in shapes stranger than any that history records. Peaks and spires and angled domes towered high and shining under the hot white sun—strange ships riding the airways. . . . He saw battles—weapons that have no names today blasting the tall towers into ruins, wiping great smears of blood across the crystal—saw triumphant marches where creatures that might have been the forerunners of men paraded in a blaze of color through shining streets . . . strange, sinuous creatures, half seen, that were men, yet not men. . . . Nebulously the history of a dead and forgotten world flared by him in the dark.

He saw the man-things in their great shining cities bowing down before a—something—of darkness that spread monstrously across the white-lit heavens . . . saw the beginnings of Great Pharol . . . saw the crystal throne in a room of crystal where the sinuous, man-formed beings lay face down in worshipping windrows about a great triple pedestal toward which, for the dazzle and the darkness of it, he could not turn his eyes. And then without warning, in a mighty blast of violence, all the wild pictures in the flickering flamelight ran together and shivered before his dizzied eyes, and a great burst of blinding light leaped across the walls until the whole great chamber once more for an instant blazed with radiance—but a radiance so searing that it did not illuminate but stunned, blinded, exploded in the very brains of the two men who watched. . . .

In the flash of an instant before oblivion overtook him, Smith knew they had looked upon the death of a world. Then, with blinded eyes and reeling brain, he stumbled and sank into darkness.

Blackness was all about them when they opened their eyes again. The fire on the throne had burnt away into eternal darkness. Stumblingly they followed the white guidance of their tube-lights down the long passage and out into the upper air. The pale Martian day was darkening over the mountains.

LOST PARADISE

Across the table-top Yarol the Venusian reached a swift hand that closed on Northwest Smith's wrist heavily. "Look!" he said in a low voice.

Smith's no-colored eyes turned leisurely in the direction of the little Venusian's almost imperceptible nod.

The panorama that stretched out under his casual gaze would have caught at a newcomer's breath with its very magnitude, but to Smith the sight was an old story. Their table was one of many ranged behind a rail along the edge of a parapet below which the dizzy gulf of New York's steel terraces dropped away in a thousand-foot sweep to the far earth. Lacing that swooning gulf of emptiness the steel spans of the traffic bridges arched from building to building, a swarm with New York's countless hordes. Men from the three planets, wanderers and space-rangers and queer, brutish things that were not wholly human mingled with the throngs of Earth as they streamed endlessly over the great steel bridges spanning the gulfs of New York. From the high parapet table where Smith and Yarol sat one could watch the solar system go by, world upon world, over the arches that descended by tiers and terraces into the perpetual darkness and twinkling, far-off lights of the deeps where solid earth lay hidden. In mighty swoops and arcs they latticed the void yawning below the parapet on which Yarol leaned a negligent elbow and stared.

Smith's pale eyes, following that stare, saw only the usual crowd of pedestrians swarming across the steel span of the bridge a story below.

"See?" murmured Yarol. "That little fellow in the red leather coat. The white-haired one, walking slow at the edge of the rail. See?"

"Um-m." Smith made a non-commital noise in his throat as he found the object of Yarol's interest. It was an odd-looking specimen of humanity that loitered slowly along in the outer edges of the crowd surging across the bridge. His red coat was belted about a body whose extreme fragility was apparent even at this elevation; though from what Smith could see of his foreshortened figure he did not seem like one in ill health. On his uncovered head the hair grew silky and silvery, and under one arm he clutched a squarish package which he was careful, Smith noticed, to keep on the railing side, away from the passing crowd.

"I'll bet you the next drinks," murmured Yarol, his wise black eyes twinkling under long lashes, "that you can't guess what race that little fellow's from, or where it originated."

"The next drinks are on me anyhow," grinned Smith. "No I can't guess. Does it matter?"

"Oh—curious, that's all. I've seen a member of that race only once before in my life, and I'll bet you never saw one. And yet it's an Earth race, perhaps the very oldest. Did you ever hear of the Seles?"

Smith shook his head silently, his eyes on the little figure below, which was slowly drawing out of sight beneath the overhang of the terrace on which they sat.

"They live somewhere in the remotest part of Asia, no one knows exactly where. But they're not Mongolian. It's a pure race, and one that has no counterpart anywhere in the solar system that I ever heard of. I think even among themselves their origin has been forgotten, though their legends go back so far it makes you dizzy to think of it. They're queer-looking, all white-haired and fragile as glass. Keep very much to themselves, of course. When one ventures out into the world you can be sure it's for some tremendously important reason. Wonder why that fellow—oh well, not that it matters. Only seeing him reminded me of the queer story that's told about them. They have a Secret. No, don't laugh; it's supposed to be something very strange and wonderful, which their race life is dedicated to keeping quiet. I'd give a lot to know what it is, just for curiosity's sake."

"None of your business, my boy," said Smith sleepily. "Like as not it's better for you that you don't know. These secrets have a way of being uncomfortable things to know."

"No such luck," Yarol shrugged. "Let's have another drink—on you, remember—and forget it."

He lifted a finger to summon the hurrying waiter.

But the summons was never given. For just then, around the corner of the railing which separated the little enclosure of tables from the street running along the edge of the terrace came a flash of red that caught Yarol's eye abruptly. It was the little white-haired man, hugging his squarish parcel and walking timorously, as if he were not accustomed to thronged streets and terraces a thousand feet high in steel-shimmering air.

And at the moment Yarol's eye caught him, something happened. A man in a dirty brown uniform, whose defaced insignia was indecipherable pushed forward and jostled the red-coated stroller roughly. The little man gave a squeak of alarm and clutched frantically at his parcel, but too late. The jostling had knocked it almost out from under his arm, and before he could recover his grip the burly assailant had seized it and shouldered quickly away through the crowd.

Stark terror was livid on the little man's face as he stared wildly around. And in the first desperate glance his eyes encountered the two men at the table watching him with absorbing interest. Across the rail his gaze met theirs in a passion of entreaty. There was something about the attitude of them, their worn spaceman's leather and faces stamped with the indefinable seal of lives lived dangerously, which must have told him in that desperate glimpse that perhaps help lay here. He gripped the rail, white-knuckled, and gasped across it,

"Follow him! Get it back—reward—oh, hurry!"

"How much of a reward?" demanded Yarol with sudden purpose in his voice.

"Anything—your own price—only hurry!"

"You swear that?"

The little man's face was suffusing with anguished scarlet. "I swear it—of course I swear it! But hurry! Hurry, or you'll—"

"Do you swear it by—" Yarol hesitated and cast a curiously guilty glance over his shoulder at Smith. Then he rose and leaned across the rail, whispering something in the stranger's ear. Smith saw a look of intense terror sweep across the flushed face. In its wake the crimson drained slowly away, leaving the man's moon-white features blank with an emotion to which Smith could put no name. But he nodded frantically. In a voice that had strained itself to a hoarse and gasping whisper he said,

"Yes, I swear. Now go!"

With no further words Yarol vaulted the rail and plunged into the crowd in the wake of the vanishing thief. The little man stared after him for an instant, then came slowly around to the gate in the railing and threaded the empty tables to Smith's. He sank into the chair Yarol had left and buried his silkily silver head in hands that shook.

Smith regarded him impassively. He was somewhat surprised to see that it was not an old man who sat here opposite him. The mark of no more than middle years lay upon the anxiety-ravaged face, and the hands which were clenched above the bowed head were strong and firm, with a queerly fragile slenderness that somehow did not belie the sense of indwelling strength which he had noticed in his first glance. It was not, thought Smith, an individual slenderness, but, as Yarol had said, a racial trait that made the man look as if a blow would break him into fragments. And the race, had he not known better, he would have sworn dwelt upon some smaller planet than Earth, some world of lesser gravity where such delicate bone-structure as this would have purpose.

After a while the stranger's head rose slowly and he stared at Smith with haggard eyes. They were a queer color, those eyes—dark, soft, veiled in a sort of filmed translucency so that they seemed never to dwell directly upon anything. They gave the whole face a look of withdrawn, introspective peace wildly at odds now with the anguish of unrest upon the delicate features of the man.

He was scrutinizing Smith, the depseration in his eyes robbing the long stare of any impertinence. With averted eyes Smith let him look. Twice he was aware that the other's lips had parted and his breath caught as if for speech; but he must have seen something in that dark, impassive face across the table, scarred with the tale of many battles, cold-eyes, emotionless, which made him think better of attempting questions. So he sat there silently, hands twisting on the table, naked anguish in his eyes, waiting.

The minutes went by slowly. It must have been all of a quarter of an hour before Smith heard a step behind him and knew by the light which dazzled across the face of the man opposite that Yarol had returned. The little Venusian pulled up a chair and sank into it silently, grinning and laying on the table a flat, squarish package.

The stranger pounced upon it with a little, inarticulate cry, running anxious hands over the brown paper in which it was wrapped, testing the brown seals which splotched the side where the edges of the covering came together. Satisfied then, he turned to Yarol. The wild desperation had died upon his face now, magically allowing it to fall into lines of a vast tranquility. Smith thought he had never seen a face so suddenly and serenely at peace. And yet there was in its peacefulness a queer sort of resignation, as if something lay ahead of him which he accepted without a struggle; as if, perhaps, he was prepared to pay whatever tremendous price Yarol asked, and knew it would be high.

"What is it," he asked Yarol in a gentle voice, "that you wish as your reward?"

"Tell me the Secret," said Yarol boldly. He was grinning as he said it. The rescue of the package had not been a task of any great difficulty for a man of his knowledge and character. How he had accomplished it not even Smith knew—the ways of Venusians are strange—but he had had no doubt that Yarol would succeed. He was not looking now at the Venusian's fair, cherubic face with its wise black eyes dancing. He was watching the stranger, and he saw no surprise upon the man's delicate features, only a little flash of quickly darkened brightness behind the veiled eyes, a little spasm of pain and acknowledgment twisting his face for a moment.

"I might have known that," he said quietly, in his soft, low voice that held a taint of some alien inflection of speech beneath its careful English. "Have you any conception of what it is you ask?"

"A little." Yarol's voice was sobering under the graveness of the other's tones. "I—I knew one of your race once—one of the Seles—and learned just enough to make me want very badly the whole Secret."

"You learned—a name, too," said the little man gently. "And I swore by it to give you what you asked. I shall give it to you. But you must understand that I would never have given that oath had even so vital a thing as my own life depended upon it. I, or any of the Seles, would die before swearing by that name in a cause less great than—than the one for which I swore. By that"—he smiled faintly—"you may guess how precious a thing this package is. Are you sure, are you very sure you wish to know our secret?"

Smith recognized the stubbornness that was beginning to shadow Yarol's finely featured face.

"I am," said the Venusian firmly. "And you promised it

to me in the name of—" he broke off, faintly mouthing syllables he did not utter. The little man smiled at him with a queer hint of pity on his face.

"You are invoking powers," he said, "which you very clearly know nothing of. A dangerous thing to do. But—yes, I have sworn, and I will tell you. I must tell you now, even if you did not wish to know; for a promise made in that name *must* be fulfilled, whatever it cost either promiser or promised, I am sorry—but now you *must* know."

"Tell us, then," urged Yarol, leaning forward across the table.

The little man turned to Smith, his face serene with a peace that vaguely roused unease in the Earthman's mind.

"Do you, too, wish to know?" he asked.

Smith hesitated for an instant, weighing that nameless unease against his own curiosity. Despite himself he felt curiously impelled to know the answer to Yarol's question, though he sensed more surely as he thought it over a queer, quiet threat behind the little stranger's calmness. He nodded shortly and scowled at Yarol.

Without further ado the man crossed his arms on the table over his precious parcel, leaned forward and began to speak in his soft, slow voice. And as he talked, it seemed to Smith that a greater serenity even than before was coming into his eyes, something as vast and calm as death itself. He seemed to be leaving life behind as he spoke, with every word sinking deeper and deeper into a peace that nothing in life could trouble. And Smith knew that the preciously guarded secret must not be thus on the verge of betrayal, and its betrayer so deathly calm, unless a peril as great as death itself lay behind the revelation. He caught his breath to check the disclosures, but a compulsion seemed to be on him now that he could not break. Almost apathetically he listened.

"You must imagine," the little man was saying quietly, "the analogy of—well, for example, of a race of people driven by necessity into pitch-black caverns where their children and grandchildren are reared without ever once having seen light or made any use of their eyes. As the generations passed a legend would grow up around the ineffable beauty and mystery of Sight. It would become a religion, perhaps, the tale of a greater glory than words could describe—for how can one describe sight to the blind?—which their forebears had known and which they still possessed the organs for perceiving, if conditions were such as to permit it.

"Our race has such a legend. There is a faculty—a sense—that we have lost through the countless eons since at our peak and origin we possessed it. With us 'peak' and 'origin' are synonymous; for, like no other race in existence, our most ancient legends begin in a golden age of the infinitely long past. Beyond that they do not go. We have no stories among us of any crude beginnings, like other races. Our origin is lost to us, though the legends of our people go farther back than I could make you believe. But so far as history tells us, we sprange full-fledged from some remote, unlegended birth into highly civilized, perfectly cultured being. And in that state of perfection we possessed the lost sense which exists only in veiled tradition today.

"In the wilderness of Tibet the remnants of our once mighty race dwell. Since Earth's beginnings we have dwelt there, while in the outside world mankind struggled slowly up out of savagery. And by infinite degrees we have declined, until to the majority of us the Secret is lost. Yet our past is too splendid to forget, and we disdain even now to mingle with the young civilizations that have risen. For our glorious Secret is not wholly gone. Our priests know it, and guard it with dreadful magics, and though it is not meet that even the whole of our own race should share the mystery, yet the meanest of us would scorn even so much as the crown of your greatest empire, because we, who inherited the Secret, are so far greater than kings."

He paused, and the withdrawn look in his queer, translucent eyes deepened. Yarol said urgently, as if to call him back into the present again.

"Yes, but what is it? What is the Secret?"

The soft eyes turned to him compassionately.

"Yes—you must be told. There is no escape for you now. How you learned that name by which you invoked me I cannot guess, but I know that you did not learn much more, or you would never have used the power of it to ask me this question. It is—unfortunate—for us all that I can answer you—that I am one of the few who know. None but we priests ever venture outside our mountain retreat. So you have asked your question of one of the little number who could answer—and that is a misfortune for you as well as for me."

Again he paused, and Smith saw that vast tranquility deepening upon his serene features. So might a man look who gazes, without protest, into the face of death.

"Go on," urged Yarol impatiently. "Tell us. Tell us the Secret."

"I can't," the little man's white head shook. He smiled faintly. "There are no words. But I will show you. Look."

He reached out one fragile hand and tilted the glass that stood at Smith's elbow so that the red dregs of the *segir*-whisky spilled in a tiny pool on the table.

"Look," he said again.

Smith's eyes sought the shining redness of the spilled liquid. There was a darkness in it through which pale shadows moved so strangely that he bent closer to see, for nothing near them could possibly have cast such reflections. He was conscious that Yarol too was leaning to look, but after that he was conscious of nothing but the red darkness of the pool stirred with pale flickerings, and his eyes were plunging so deeply into its secretness that he could not stir a muscle, and the table and the terrace and the whole great teeming city of steel about him was a mist that faded into oblivion.

From a great way off he heard that soft, slow voice, full of infinite resignation, infinite calm, and a vast, transcendent pity.

"Do not struggle," it said gently. "Surrender your minds

to mine and I will show you, poor foolish children, what you ask. I must, by virtue of the name. And it may be that the knowledge you gain will be worth even the price it costs us all—for we three must die when the secret is revealed. You understand that, surely? Our whole race-life, from ages immemorial, is dedicated to the Secret's keeping, and any outside the circle of our priesthood who learn it must die that the knowledge be not betrayed. And I, who in my foolishness swore by the name, must tell you what you ask, and see that you die before I pay the price of my own weakness—with my own death.

"Well, this was ordained. Do not struggle against it—it is the pattern into which our lives are woven, and from our births we three moved forward to this moment around a table, together. Now watch, and listen—and learn.

"In the fourth dimension, which is time, man can travel only with the flow of its stream. In the other three he can move freely at will, but in time he must submit to the forward motion which is all he knows. Incidentally, only this dimension of the four affects him physically. As he moves along the fourth dimension he ages. Now once we knew the secret of moving as freely through time as through space, and in a way that did not affect our bodies any more than the motion of stepping forward or back, up or down. That secret involved the use of a special sense which I believe all men possess, though through ages of disuse it has atrophied almost to non-existence. Only among the Seles does even a memory of it exist, and only among our priesthood have we those who possess that ancient sense in its full power.

"It is not physically that even we can move at will through time. Nor can we in any way affect what has gone before or is to come after, save in the knowledge of past and future which we gain in our journeyings. For our motion in time is confined strictly to what you may call memory. Through that all but lost sense we can look back into the lives of those who went before, or forward through the still unbodied but definitely existent 'memories' of those who come after us. For as I have said, all life is woven into a finished pattern, in which future and past are irrevocably limned.

"There is danger, even in this way of traveling. Just what it is no one knows, for none who meet the danger return. Perhaps the voyager chances into the memories of a man dying, and cannot escape. Or perhaps—I do not know. But sometimes the mind does not return—snaps out. . . .

"Though there are no limits to any of these four dimensions so far as mankind is concerned, yet the distance which we may venture along any one of them is limited to the capacity of the mind that journeys. No mind, however powerful, could trace life back to its origin. For that reason we have no knowledge of our own beginnings, before that golden age I spoke of. But we do know that we are exiles from a place too lovely to have lasted, a land more exquisite than anything Earth can show. From a world like a jewel we came, and our cities were so fair that even now children sing songs of Baloise the Beautiful, and ivory-walled Ingala and Nial of the white roofs.

"A catastrophe drove us out of that land—a catastrophe that no one understands. Legend says that our gods were angered and forsook us. What actually happened no one seems to know. But we mourn still for the lovely world of Seles where we were born. It was—but look, you shall see."

The voice had been a low rising and falling of undernotes upon a sea of darkness; but now Smith, all his consciousness still centered upon the reflecting pool of hypnotic red, was aware of a stirring and subtle motion deep down in its darkness. Things were moving, rising, dizzily so that his head swam and the void trembled about him.

Out of that shaking darkness a light began to glow. Reality was taking shape about him, a new substance and a new scene, and as the light and the landscape formed out of darkness, so his own mind clothed itself in flesh again, taking on reality by slow degrees.

Presently he was standing on the slope of a low hill, velvet with dark grass in the twilight. Below him in that lovely half-translucency of dusk Baloise the Beautiful lay outspread, ivory-white, glimmering through the dimness like a pearl half drowned in dark wine. Somehow he knew the city for what it was, knew its name and loved every pale spire and dome and archway spread out in the dusk below him. Baloise the Beautiful, his lovely city.

He had no time to wonder at this sudden, aching familiarity; for beyond the ivory roofs a great moony shimmer was beginning to lighten the dim sky, such a vast and far-spreading glow that he caught his breath as he stood watching; for surely no moon that ever rose on Earth gave forth so mighty an illumination. It spread behind the stretch of Baloise's ivory roof-tops in a great halo that turned the whole night breathless with coming miracle. Then beyond the city he saw the crest of a vast silver circle glimmering through a wash of ground vapor, and suddenly he understood.

Slowly, slowly it rose. The ivory roof-tops of Baloise the Beautiful took that great soft glimmering light and turned it into pearly gleaming, and the whole night was miraculous with the wonder of rising Earth.

On the hillside Smith was motionless while the vast bright globe swung clear of the roofs and floated free at last in the pale light of the Moon. He had seen this sight before, from a dead and barren satellite, but never the exquisite luminance of Earth through the vapors of Moon-air that veiled the vast globe in a shimmer of enchantment as it swung mistily through the dusk, all its silvery continents faintly flushed with green, the translucent wonder of its seas shining jewel-clear, jewel-pale, colored like opals in the lucid tranquility of the Earth-bright dark.

It was almost too lovely a sight for man to gaze on unprepared. His mind was an ache of beauty too vivid for eyes to dwell on long as he found himself moving slowly down the hill. Not until then did he realize that this was not his own body through whose eyes he looked. He had no control over it; he had simply borrowed it to convey him through the moony dusk down the hillside, that he might perceive by its perceptions the immeasurably long-ago time which he was beholding now. This, then, was the "sense" the little stranger had spoken of. In some eons-dead moon-dweller's memory the sight of rising Earth, marvelous over the spires of the forgotten city, had been graven so deeply that the wash of countless ages could not blot it away. He was seeing now, feeling now what this unknown man had known on a hillside on the Moon a million years ago.

Through the magic of that lost "sense" he walked the Moon's verdant surface toward that exquisite city which was lost to everything but dreams so many eons ago. Well, he might have guessed from the little priest's extreme fragility alone that his race was not a native of Earth. The lesser gravity of the Moon would have bred a race of bird-like delicacy. Curious that they had moon-silver hair and eyes as translucent and remote as the light of the dead Moon. A queer, illogical link with their lost homeland.

But there was little time for wonder and speculation now. He was watching the loveliness of Baloise floating nearer and nearer through the dusk that seemed aswim with a radiance so softly real that it was like walking through darkly shining water. He was testing just how much latitude this new experience allowed him. He could see what his host saw, and he began to realize now that the man's other senses were open to his perception too. He could even share in his emotions, for he had known a moment of passionate longing for the whole white city of Baloise as he looked down from the hill, longing and love such as an exile might feel for his native city.

Gradually, too, he became aware that the man was afraid. A queer, dark, miasmic terror lurked just below the surface of his conscious thoughts, something whose origin he could not fathom. It gave the loveliness he looked on a poignancy almost as sharp as pain, etching every white spire and gleaming dome of Baloise deep into his remembering mind.

Slowly, moving in the shadow of his own dark terror, the man went down the hill. The ivory wall that circled Baloise rose over him, a low wall with a crest fretted into a band of lacy carving upon whose convolutions the lucent Earthlight lay like silver. Under a pointed arch he walked, still moving with that slow resolute step as if he approached something dreadful from which there was no escape. And strongly and more strongly Smith was aware of the fear that drowned the man's unformulated thoughts, washing in a dark tide beneath the consciousness of everything he did. And stronger still the poignant love for Baloise ached in him and his eyes lingered like slow caresses on the pale roofs and Earth-washed walls and the pearly dimness that lay shadowily between, where the light of rising Earth was only a reflection. He was memorizing the loveliness of Baloise, as an exile might do. He was lingering upon the sight of it with a yearning so deep that it seemed as if even unto death he must carry behind his eyes the Earth-lit loveliness on which he gazed.

Pale walls and translucent domes and arches rose about him as he walked slowly along a street paved in white seasand, so that his feet fell soundlessly upon its surface and he might have been walking in a translucent dream. Now Earth had swum higher above the reflecting roofs, and the great shining globe of it floated free overhead, veiled and opalescent with the rainbow seas of its atmosphere. Smith, looking up through the eyes of this unknown stranger, could scarcely recognize the configuration of the great green continents spread out beneath their veils of quivering air, and the shapes of the shining seas were strange to him. He looked into a past so remote that little upon his native planet was familiar to him.

Now his strange host was turning aside from the broad, sandy street. He went down a little paved alley, dim in the swimming light of Earth, and pushed open the gate of grillework that closed its end. Under the opened arch he walked into a garden, beyond whose Earth-bright loveliness a low white house rose pale as ivory against dark trees.

There was a pool in the garden's center, Earth swam like a great glimmering opal in its darkness, brimming the water with a greater glory than ever shone into earthly pool. And bending over that basin of spilled Earthlight was a woman.

The silvery cascade of her hair swung forward about a face paler than the pallor of rising Earth, and lovely with a delicacy more exquisite than ever shaped an Earthwoman's features into beauty. Her moon-born slimness as she bent above the pool was the slimness of some airy immortal; for no Earthly woman ever walked whose delicacy was half so sweet and fragile.

She lifted her head as the grille-gate opened, and swayed to her feet in a motion so unearthly light that she scarcely seemed to touch the grass as she moved forward, a creature of pale enchantment in an enchanted Moon-garden. The man crossed the grass to her reluctantly, and Smith was aware in him of a dread and a soul-deep aching that choked up in his throat until he could scarcely speak. The woman lifted her face, clear now in the Earthlight and so delicately modeled that it was more like some exquisite jewel-carving than a face of bone and Moon-white flesh. Her eyes were great and dark with an unnamed dread. She breathed in the lightest echo of a voice.

"It has come?" . . . and the tongue she spoke rippled like running water, in strange, light, breathing cadences that Smith understood only through the mind of the man whose memory he shared.

His host said in a voice that was a little too loud in its resolution not to quiver.

"Yes—it has come."

At that the woman's eyes closed involuntarily, her whole exquisite face crumpling into sudden, stricken grief so heavy that it seemed those fragile creatures must be crushed under the weight of it, the whole delicate body sink overburdened to the grass. But she did not fall. She stood swaying for an instant, and then the man's arms were about her, holding her close in a desperate embrace. And through the memory of the long-dead man who held her, Smith could feel the delicacy of the eons-dead woman, the warm softness of her flesh, the tiny bones, like a bird's. Again he felt futilely that she was too fragile a creature to know such sorrow as racked her now, and a helpless anger rose in him against whatever unnamed thing it was that kindled such terror and heartbreak in them both.

For a long moment the man held her close, feeling the soft fragility of her body warm against him, the rack of silent sobs that must surely tear her very bones apart, so delicate were they, so desperate her soundless agony. And in his own throat the tightness of sorrow was choking, and his own eyes burned with unshed tears. The dark miasma of terror had strengthened until the Earth-lit garden was blotted out behind it, and nothing remained but the black weight of his fear, the pain of his hopeless grief.

At last he loosed the girl in his arms a little and murmured against her silvery hair,

"Hush, hush, my darling. Do not sorrow so—we knew that this must come some day. It comes to everyone alive—it has come to us too. Do not weep so. . . ."

She sobbed once more, a deep ache of pure pain, and then stood back in his arms and nodded, shaking back the silver hair.

"I know," she said. "I know." She lifted her head and looked up toward Earth's great haloed mystery swimming through veils of colored enchantment above them. The light of it glistened in the tears on her face. "Almost," she said, I wish we two had gone—there."

He shook her a little in his arms.

"No—life in the colonies, with only Seles' little glimmer of green light shining down on us to tear our hearts with memories of home—no, my dear. That would have been a lifetime of longing and yearning to return. We have lived in happiness here, knowing only this moment of pain at the end. It is better."

She bent her head and laid her forehead against his shoulder, shutting out the sight of risen Earth.

"Is it?" she asked him thickly, her voice indistinct with tears. "Is a lifetime of nostalgia and grieving, with you, not better than paradise without you? Well, the choice is made now. I am happy only in this—that you have been summoned first and need not know this—this dreadfulness—of facing life alone. You must go now—quickly, or I shall never let you. Yes—we knew it must end—that the summons must come. Good-bye—my very dear."

She lifted her wet face and closed her eyes.

Smith would have looked away then if it had been possible for him. But he could not detach himself even in emotion from the host whose memory he shared, and the unbearable instant stabbed as deeply at his own heart as it did at the man whose memory he shared. He took her gently again into his arms and kissed the quivering mouth, salt with the taste of her tears. And then without a backward glance he turned toward the open gate and walked slowly out under its arch, moving as a man moves to his doom.

He went down the narrow way into the open street again, under the glory of risen Earth. The beauty of the eons-dead Baloise he walked through ached like a dull pain in his heart beneath the sharper anguish of that farewell. The salt of the girl's tears was still on his lips, and it seemed to him that not even the death he went to could give him ease from the pain of the moments he had just passed through. He went on resolutely.

Smith realized that they were turning now toward the center of Baloise the Beautiful. Great open squares here and there broke the ivory ranks of the buildings, and there were men and women moving infrequently through the streets, fragile as birds in their Moon-born delicacy, silvery pale under the immense pale disk of high-swinging Earth that dominated that scene until nothing seemed real but its vast marvel hanging overhead. The buildings were larger here, and though they lost none of their enchanted beauty they were more clearly places of industry than had been those domed and grille-fretted dwellings on the outskirts of the city.

Once they skirted a great square in whose center bulked a vast sphere of silvery sheen that reflected the brightness of the sky-filled Earth. It was a ship—a space-ship. Smith's eyes would have told him that even if the knowledge that floated through his mind from the mind of the Moon-dweller had not made it clear. It was a space-ship loaded with men and machinery and supplies for the colonies struggling against the ravening jungles upon steamy, prehistoric Earth.

They watched the last passengers filing up the ramps that led to orifices in its lower curve, Moon-white people moving silently as people in a dream under the vast pale glowing of the Moon-high Earth. It was queer how silent they were. The whole great square and the immense sphere that filled it and the throngs moving up and down the ramps might have been figures in a dream. It was hard to realize that they were not—that they had existed, flesh and blood, stone and steel, under the light of a vast, heaven-filling globe haloed in its rainbowy haze of atmosphere, once, milleniums ago.

As they neared the farther side of the square, Smith saw through his host's scarcely observing eyes the ramps lower and the orifices close in the huge bubble-ship. The Moonman was too wrapped in his agony and heartbreak and despair to pay much heed to what was taking place there in the square, so that Smith caught only abstract glimpses of the great ship floating bubble-light up from the pavement, silently, effortlessly, with no such bursts of thunderous noise and great washes of flame as attend the launching of modern space-ships. Curiosity rode him hard, but he could do nothing. His only glimpses of this ages-past scene must be taken through the eyes of his host's memory. They went on out of the square.

A great dark building loomed up above the pale-roofed houses. It was the only dark thing he had seen in Baloise, and the sight of it woke into sudden life the terror that had been dwelling formlessly and deep in the mind of his host. But he went on unhesitatingly. The broad street led straight up to the archway that opened in the dark wall's façade, a portal as cavernous and blackly threatening as the portals of death itself.

Under the shadow of it the man paused. He looked back lingeringly upon the pearly pallor of Baloise. Over the domed and pinnacled roofs the great pale light of Earth brooded. Earth itself, swimming in seas of opalescent atmosphere, all its continents silver-green, all its seas colored like veiled jewels, glowed down upon him for the last time. The full tide of his love for Baloise, of his love for the lost girl in the garden, of his love for the whole green, sweet satellite he lived on came choking up in his throat, and his heart was near bursting with the sweet fullness of the life he must leave.

Then he turned resolutely and went in under the dark archway. Through his set eyes Smith could see nothing within but a gloom like moonlight shining through mist, so that the space inside was full of a grayness faintly translucent, faintly luminous. And the terror that clogged the man's mind was laying hold on his own as they went steadily forward, in sick fright, through the gloom.

The dimness brightened as they advanced. More and more inexplicable in Smith's mind grew the wonder that, though fear was turning the Moon-dweller's very brain icy with dread, yet he went unhesitatingly forward, no compulsion driving him but his own will. It was death he went to—there was no doubt about that now, from the glimpses he had of his host's mind—a death from which by instinct he shrank with every fiber of his being. But he went on.

Now walls were becoming visible through the dim fog of the darkness. They were smooth walls, black, unfeatured. The interior of this great dark building was appalling in its very simplicity. Nothing but a wide black corridor whose walls rose into invisibility overhead. Contrasting with the ornateness of every other man-made surface in Baloise, the stark severity of the building struck a note of added terror into the numbed brain of the man who walked here.

The darkness paled and brightened. The corridor was widening. Presently its walls had fallen back outside range of sight; and over a black, unlustered floor, through misty brightness the Moon-man walked forward to his death.

The room into which the hall had widened was immense. Smith thought it must comprise the whole interior of the great dark building; for many minutes passed while his host paced steadily, slowly forward over the darkness of the floor.

Gradually through that queer bright dimness a flame began to glow. It danced in the mist like the light of a windblown fire, brightening, dimming, flaring up again so that the mist pulsed with its brilliance. There was the regularity of life in that pulsing.

It was a wall of pale flame, stretching through the misty dimness as far as the eye could reach on either side. The man paused before it, with bowed head, and he tried to speak. Terror thickened his voice so that it was only on the third attempt that he managed to articulate, very low, in a choked voice, "Hear me, O Mighty. I am come."

In the silence after his voice ceased, the wall of beating flame flickered once again, like a heart's beat, and then rolled back on both sides like curtains. Beyond the back-drawn flame a high-roofed hollow in the mist loomed dimly. It had no more tangibility than the mist itself, the inside of a sphere of dim clarity. And in that mist-walled hollow three gods sat. Sat? They crouched, dreadfully, hungrily, with such a bestial ravening in their poise that only gods could maintain the awful dignity which veiled them with terror despite the ugly humped hunger of their posture.

This one glimpse through glazing eyes Smith caught as the Moonman flung himself face down on the black floor, the breath stopping in his throat, choking against unbearable terror as a drowning man chokes against sea-water. But as the eyes through which he looked lost sight of the three ravenous figures, Smith had an instant's glimpse of the shadow behind them, monstrous on the curved mist-wall that hollowed them in, cast waveringly by the back-drawn flame. And it was a single shadow. These three were One.

And the One spoke. In a voice like the lick of flames, tenuous as the mist that reflected it, terrible as the voice of death itself, the One said:

"What mortal dares enter our immortal Presence?"

"One whose god-appointed cycle is complete," gasped the prostrate man, his voice coming in little puffs as if he had been running hard. "One who fulfills his share of his race's debt to the Three who are One."

The voice of the One had been a voice full, complete, an individual speaking. Now out of the dim hollow where the three crouched a thin, flickering voice, like hot flame, less than full, less than complete, came quavering.

"Be it remembered," said the thin, hot little voice, "that all the world of Seles owes it existence to ourselves, who by our might hold fire and air and water around its globe. Be it remembered that only through ourselves does the flesh of life clothe this little world's bare bones. Be it remembered!"

The man on the floor shuddered in one long quiver of acquiescence. And Smith, his mind aware as that other mind was aware, knew that it was true. The Moon's gravity was too weak, even in this long-vanished era, to hold its cloak of life-supporting air without the aid of some other force than its own. Why these Three furnished that power he did not know, but he was beginning to guess.

A second little voice, hungry as flame, took up the ritual chant as the first died away.

"Be it remembered that only for a price do we wrap the robe of life about Seles' bones. Be that bargain remembered that the progenitors of the race of Seles made with the Three who are One, in the very long ago when even the gods were young. Let the price be not forgotten that every man must pay at the end of his appointed cycle. Be it remembered that only through our divine hunger can mankind reach us to pay his vow. All who live owe us the debt of their living, and by the age-old pact of their forefathers must return when we summon them into the shadow that gives their loved world life."

Again the prostrate man shuddered, deep and coldly, acknowledging the ritual truth. And a third voice quavered out of that misty hollow with a flame's flickering hunger in its sound.

"Be it remembered that all who come to pay the race's debt and buy anew our favor that their world may live, must come to us willingly, with no resistance against our divine hunger—must surrender without struggle. And be it remembered that if so much as one man alone dares resist our will, then in that instant is our power withdrawn, and all our anger called down upon the world of Seles. Let one man struggle against our desire, and the world of Seles goes bare to the void, all life upon it ceasing in a breath. Be that remembered!"

On the floor the Moonman's body shivered again. Through his mind ran one last ache of love and longing for the beautiful world whose greenness and Earth-lit wonder his death was to preserve. Death was a little thing, if by it Seles lived.

In one full, round thunder the One said terribly,

"Come you willingly into our Presence?"

From the prone man's hidden face a voice choked,

"Willingly—that Seles may live."

And the voice of the One pulsed through the flamewashed dimness so deeply that the ears did not hear, and only the beat of the Moonman's heart, the throbbing of his blood, caught the low thunder of the gods' command.

"Then come!"

He stirred. Very slowly he got to his feet. He faced the three. And for the first time Smith knew a quickened fear for his own safety. Heretofore the awe and terror he had shared with the Moon-host had been solely for the man himself. But now—was death not reaching out for him no less than for his host? For he knew of no way to dissociate his own spectator mind from the mind with which it was united that it might be aware of this fragment of the measureless past. And when the Moonman went forward into oblivion, must not oblivion engulf his own mind too? This, then, was what the little priest had meant when he told them that some, adventuring backward through the minds of their forebears, never returned. Death in one guise or another must have swallowed them up with the minds they looked through. Death yawned for himself, now, if he could not escape. For the first time he struggled, testing his independence. And it was futile. He could not break away.

With bowed head the Moonman stepped forward through the curtain of flame. It hissed hotly on either side, and then it was behind and he was close to that dim hell where the three gods sat, their shadow hovering terribly behind them on the mist. And it looked in that uncertain light, as if the three strained forward eagerly, hunger ravenous in every dreadful line of them, and the shadow behind spread itself like a waiting mouth.

Then with a swishing roar the flame-curtains swept to behind him, and darkness like the dark of death itself fell blindingly upon the hollow of the Three. Smith knew naked terror as he felt the mind he had hidden thus far falter as a horse falters beneath its rider—fail as a mount fails—and he was falling, falling into gulfs of vertiginous terror, emptier than the space between the worlds, a blind and empty hungriness that outravened vacuum itself.

He did not fight it. He could not. It was too tremendous. But he did not yield. One small conscious entity in an infinity of pure hunger, while sucking emptiness raved around him, he was stubborn and unwavering. The hunger of the Three must never before have known anything but acquiescence to the debt man owed them, and now fury roared through the vacuum of their hunger more terribly than any mortal mind could combat. In the midst of it, Smith clung stubbornly to his flicker of consciousness, incapable of doing anything more than resist feebly the ravenous desire that sucked at his life.

Dimly he realized what he was doing. It was the death of a world he compassed, if resistance to the hunger of the Three meant what they had threatened. It meant the death of every living thing on the satellite—of the girl in the Earth-bright garden, of all who walked Baloise's streets, of Baloise herself in the grinding eons, unprotected from the bombarding meteors that would turn this sweet green world into a pitted skull.

But the urge to live was blind in him. He could not have relinquished it if he would, so deeply rooted is the life-desire in us all, the raw, animal desperation against extinction. He would not die—he would not surrender, let the price be what it might. He could not fight that blind ravening that typhooned about him, but he would not submit. He was simply a passive stubbornness against the hunger of the Three, while eons swirled about him and time ceased and nothing had existence but himself, his living, desperate self, rebellious against death.

Others, adventuring through the past, must too have met this peril, must have succumbed to it in the weakness of their inborn love for the green Moon-world. But he had no such weakness. Nothing was so important as life—his own life, here and now. He would not surrender. Deep down under the veneer of his civilized self lay a bed-rock of pure savage power that nothing on any world he knew had ever tested beyond its strength. It supported him now against the anger of divinity, the unshakable foundation of his resolution not to yield.

And slowly, slowly the ravening hunger abated its fury about him. It could not absorb what refused to surrender, and all its fury could not terrorize him into acquiescence. This, then, was why the Three had demanded and reiterated the necessity for submission to their hunger. They had not the power to overcome that unshakable life-urge if it were not willingly put aside, and they dared not let the world they terrorized know this weakness in their strength. For a flashing moment he visioned the vampire Three, battening on a race that dared not defy them for love of the beautiful cities, the soft gold days and Earth-bright miracles of nights that counted more to mankind than its own life counted. But it was ended now.

One last furnace-blast of white-hot hunger raved around Smith's stubbornness. But whatever vampiric things they were, spawned in what unknown, eons-forgotten place, the Three who were One had not the power to break down that last rock-steady savagery in which all that was Smith rooted deep. And at last, in one final burst of typhoon-fury, which roared about him in tornado-blasts of hunger and defeat, the vacuum ceased to be.

For one blinding instant sight flashed unbearably through his brain. He saw sleeping Seles, the green Moonworld that time itself was to forget, pearl-pale under the glory of risen Earth, washed with the splendor of a brighter night than man was to know again, the mighty globe swimming through seas of floating atmosphere, veiled in it, glorious for one last brief instant in the wonder of its misty continents, its pearly seas. Baloise the Beautiful slept under the luminance of high-riding Earth. For one last radiant moment the exquisite Moon-world floated through its dreampale darkness that no world in space was ever to equal again, nor any descendant of the race that knew it ever wholly forget.

And then—disaster. In a stunned, remote way Smith was aware of a high, ear-splitting wail that grew louder, louder—intolerably louder until his very brain could no longer endure the agony of its sound. And over Baloise, over Seles and all who dwelt thereon, a darkness began to fall. High-swimming Earth shimmered through gathering dark, and from the rolling green hills and verdant meadows and silver sea of Seles the atmosphere ripped away. In long, opalescent streamers, bright under the light of Earth, the air of Seles was forsaking the world it cloaked. Not in gradual dissipation, but in abrupt angry destruction as if the invisible hands of the Three were tearing it in long bright ribbons from the globe of Seles—so the atmosphere fell away.

That was the last Smith saw of it as darkness closed him in—Seles, lovely even in its destruction, a little green jewel shimmering with color and brightness, unrolling from its cloak of life as the long, streaming ribbons of rainbowy translucency tore themselves away and trailed in the void behind, slowly paling into the blackness of space.

Then darkness closed in about him, and oblivion rolled over him and nothing—nothing. . . .

He opened his eyes, and startlingly, New York's steel towers were all about him, the hum of traffic in his ears. Irresistibly his eyes sought the sky, where a moment before, so it seemed to him, the great bright globe of pearly Earth hung luminous. And then, realization coming back slowly, he lowered his eyes and met across the table the wide, haunted stare of the little priest of the Moon-people. The face he saw shocked him. It had aged ten years in the incalculable interval of his journey back into the past. Anguish, deeper than any personal anguish could strike, had graven sharp lines into his unearthly pallor, and the great strange eyes were nightmare-haunted.

"It was through me, then," he was whispering, as if to himself. "Of all my race I was the one by whose hand Seles died. Oh, gods—"

"I did it!" Smith broke in harshly, driven out of his habit of silence in a blind effort to alleviate something of that unbearable anguish. "I was the one!"

"No—you were the instrument, I the wielder. I sent you back. I am the destroyer of Baloise and Nial and ivory-white Ingala, and all the green loveliness of our lost world. How can I ever look up again by night upon the bare white skull of the world I slew? It was I—I!"

"What the devil are you two talking about?" demanded Yarol across the table. "I didn't see a thing, except a lot of darkness and lights, and a sort of moon. . . ."

"And yet"—that haunted whisper went on, obliviously—"yet I have seen the Three in their temple. No other of all my race ever saw them before, for no living memory ever returned out of that temple save the memory that broke them. Of all my race only I know the secret of the Disaster. Our legends tell of what the exiles saw, looking up that night in terror through the thick air of Earth—but I *know!* And no man of flesh and blood can bear that knowledge long—who murdered a world by his blundering. Oh gods of Seles—help me!"

His Moon-white hands groped blindly over the table, found the square package that had cost him so dear a price. He stumbled to his feet. Smith rose too, actuated by some inarticulate emotion he could not have named. But the Moonpriest shook his head.

"No," he said, as if in answer to some question of his own mind, "you are not to blame for what happened so many eons ago—and yet in the last few minutes. This tangle of time and space, and the disaster that a living man can bring to something dead millenniums ago—it is far beyond our narrow grasp of understanding. I was chosen to be the vessel of that disaster—yet not I alone am responsible, for this was ordained from time's beginning. I could not have changed it had I known at the beginning what the end must be. It is not for what you did, but for what you know now—that you must die!"

The words had not wholly left his lips before he was swinging up his square parcel like a deadly weapon. Close against Smith's face he held it, and the shadow of death was in his Moon-pale eyes and dark upon his anguished white face. For the flash of an instant it seemed to Smith that a blaze of intolerable light was bursting out all around the square of the package, though actually he could see nothing but the commonplace outlines of it in the priest's white hands.

For the breath of an instant almost too brief to register on his brain, death brushed him hungrily. But in that instant as the threatening hands swung up there was a burst of blue-white flame behind the priest's back, the familiar crackle of a gun. The little man's face turned livid with pain for an instant, and then peace in a great gush of calmness washed across it, blanking the anguished dark eyes. He slumped sidewise, the square box falling.

Across the huddle of his body on the floor Yarol's crouched figure loomed, slipping the heat-gun back into its holster as he glanced across his shoulder.

"Come on—come on!" he whispered urgently. "Let's get out of here!"

There was a shout from behind Smith, the beat of running

feet. He cast one covetous glance at the fallen square of that mysterious package, but it was a fleeting one as he cleared the body in a leap and on Yarol's flying heels made for the lower ramp to the crowded level beneath. He would never know.

JULHI

The tale of Smith's scars would make a saga. From head to foot his brown and sunburnt hide was scored with the marks of battle. The eye of a connoisseur would recognize the distinctive tracks of knife and talon and rayburn, the slash of the Martian drylander *cring*, the clean, thin stab of the Venusian stiletto, the crisscross lacing of Earth's penal whip. But one or two scars that he carried would have baffled the most discerning eye. That curious, convoluted red circlet, for instance, like some bloody rose on the left side of his chest just where the beating of his heart stirred the sun-darkened flesh. . . .

In the starless dark of the thick Venusian night Northwest Smith's pale steel eyes were keen and wary. Save for those restless eyes he did not stir. He crouched against a wall that his searching fingers had told him was stone, and cold; but he could see nothing and he had no faintest idea of where he was or how he had come there. Upon this dark five minutes ago he had opened puzzled eyes, and he was still puzzled. The dark-piercing pallor of his gaze flickered restlessly through the blackness, searching in vain for some point of familiarity. He could find nothing. The dark was blurred and formless around him, and though his keen senses spoke to him of enclosed spaces, yet there was a contradiction even in that, for the air was fresh and blowing.

He crouched motionless in the windy dark, smelling earth and cold stone, and faintly—very faintly—a whiff of something unfamiliar that made him gather his feet under him noiselessly and poise with one hand against the chill stone wall, tense as a steel spring. There was motion in the dark. He could see nothing, hear nothing, but he felt that stirring come cautiously nearer. He stretched out exploring toes, found the ground firm underfoot, and stepped aside a soundless pace or two, holding his breath. Against the stone where he had been leaning an instant before he heard the soft sound of hands fumbling, with a queer, sucking noise, as if they were sticky. Something exhaled with a small, impatient sound. In a lull of the wind he heard quite distinctly the slither over stone of something that was neither feet nor paws nor serpent-coils, but akin to all three.

Smith's hand sought his hip by instinct, and came away empty. Where he was and how he came there he did not know, but his weapons were gone and he knew that their absence was not accidental. The something that was pursuing him sighed again, queerly, and the shuffling sound over the stones moved with sudden, appalling swiftness, and something touched him that stung like an electric shock. There were hands upon him, but he scarcely realized it, or that they were no human hands, before the darkness spun around him and the queer, thrilling shock sent him reeling into a blurred oblivion.

When he opened his eyes again he lay once more upon cold stone in the unfathomable dark to which he had awakened before. He lay as he must have fallen when the searcher dropped him, and he was unhurt. He waited, tense and listening, until his ears ached with the strain and the silence. So far as his blade-keen senses could tell him, he was quite alone. No sound broke the utter stillness, no sensation of movement, no whiff of scent. Very cautiously he rose once more, supporting himself against the unseen stones and flexing his limbs to be sure that he was unhurt.

The floor was uneven underfoot. He had the idea now that he must be in some ancient ruins, for the smell of stone and chill and desolation was clear to him, and the breeze moaned a little through unseen openings. He felt his way along the broken wall, stumbling over fallen blocks and straining his senses against the blanketing gloom around him. He was trying vainly to recall how he had come here, and succeeding in recapturing only vague memories of much red *segir* whisky in a nameless dive, and confusion and muffled voices thereafter, and wide spaces of utter blank—and then awakening here in the dark. The whisky must have been drugged, he told himself defensively, and a slow anger began to smolder within him at the temerity of whoever it was who had dared lay hands upon Northwest Smith.

Then he froze into stony quiet, rigid in mid-step, at the all but soundless stirring of something in the dark near by. Blurred visions of the unseen thing that had seized him ran through his head—some monster whose gait was a pattering glide and whose hands were armed with the stunning shock of an unknown force. He stood frozen, wondering if it could see him in the dark.

Feet whispered over the stone very near him, and something breathed pantingly, and a hand brushed his face. There was a quick suck of indrawn breath, and then Smith's arms leaped out to grapple the invisible thing to him. The surprise of that instant took his breath, and then he laughed deep in his throat and swung the girl round to face him in the dark.

He could not see her, but he knew from the firm curves of her under his hands that she was young and feminine, and from the sound of her breath that she was near to fainting with fright.

"Sh-h-h," he whispered urgently, his lips at her ear and her hair brushing his cheek fragrantly. "Don't be afraid.

Where are we?"

It might have been reaction from her terror that relaxed the tense body he held, so that she went limp in his arms and the sound of her breathing almost ceased. He lifted her clear of the ground—she was light and fragrant and he felt the brush of velvet garments against his bare arms as unseen robes swept him—and carried her across to the wall. He felt better with something solid at his back. He laid her down there in the angle of the stones and crouched beside her, listening, while she slowly regained control of herself.

When her breathing was normal again, save for the faint hurrying of excitement and alarm, he heard the sound of her sitting up against the wall, and bent closer to catch her whisper.

"Who are you?" she demanded.

"Northwest Smith," he said under his breath, and grinned at her softly murmured "Oh-h!" of recognition. Whoever she was, she had heard that name before. Then,

"There has been a mistake," she breathed, half to herself. "They never take any but the—space-rats and the scum of the ports for Julhi to—I mean, to bring here. They must not have known you, and they will pay for that mistake. No man is brought here who might be searched for—afterward."

Smith was silent for a moment. He had thought her lost like himself, and her fright had been too genuine for pretense. Yet she seemed to know the secrets of this curious, unlit place. He must go warily.

"Who are you?" he murmured. "Why were you so frightened? Where are we?"

In the dark her breath caught in a little gasp, and went on unevenly.

"We are in the ruins of Vonng," she whispered. "I am Apri, and I am condemned to death. I thought you were death coming for me, as it will come at any instant now." Her voice failed on the last syllables, so that she spoke in a fading gasp as if terror had her by the throat and would not let her breathe. He felt her trembling against his arm.

Many questions crowded up to his lips, but the most urgent found utterance.

"What will come?" he demanded. "What is the danger?"

"The haunters of Vonng," she whispered fearfully. "It is to feed them that Julhi's slaves bring men here. And those among us who are disobedient must feed the haunters too. I have suffered her displeasure—and I must die."

"The haunters—what are they? Something with a touch like a live wire had me awhile ago, but it let me loose again. Could that have been—"

"Yes, one of them. My coming must have disturbed it. But as to what they are, I don't know. They come in the darkness. They are of Julhi's race, I think, but not flesh and blood, like her. I—I can't explain."

"And Julhi—?"

"Is—well, simply Julhi. You don't know?"

"A woman? Some queen, perhaps? You must remember I don't even know where I am."

"No, not a woman. At least, not as I am. And much more than queen. A great sorceress, I have thought, or perhaps a goddess. I don't know. It makes me ill to think, here in Vonng. It makes me ill to—to—oh, I couldn't bear it! I think I was going mad! It's better to die than go mad, isn't it? But I'm so afraid—"

Her voice trailed away incoherently, and she cowered shivering against him in the dark.

Smith had been listening above her shuddering whispers for any tiniest sound in the night. Now he turned his mind more fully to what she had been saying, though with an ear still alert for any noises about them.

"What do you mean? What was it you did?"

"There is a—a light," murmured Apri vaguely. "I've always seen it, even from babyhood, whenever I closed my eyes and tried to make it come. A light, and queer shapes and shadows moving through it, like reflections from somewhere I never saw before. But somehow it got out of control, and then I began to catch the strangest thought-waves beating through, and after a while Julhi came—through the light. I don't know—I can't understand. But she makes me summon up the light for her now, and then queer things happen inside my head, and I'm ill and dizzy, and—and I think I'm going mad. But she makes me do it. And it grows worse, you know, each time worse, until I can't bear it. Then she's angry, and that dreadful still look comes over her face—and this time she sent me here. The haunters will come, now—"

Smith tightened his arm comfortingly about her, thinking that she was perhaps a little mad already.

"How can we get out of here?" he demanded, shaking her gently to call back her wandering mind. "Where are we?"

"In Vonng. Don't you understand? On the island where Vonng's ruins are."

He remembered then. He had heard of Vonng, somewhere. The ruins of an old city lost in the tangle of vines upon a small island a few hours off the coast of Shann. There were legends that it had been a great city once, and a strange one. A king with curious powers had built it, a king in league with beings better left unnamed, so the whispers ran. The stone had been quarried with unnamable rites, and the buildings were very queerly shaped, for mysterious purposes. Some of its lines ran counterwise to the understanding even of the men who laid them out, and at intervals in the streets, following a pattern certainly not of their own world, medallions had been set, for reasons known to none but the king. Smih remembered what he had heard of the strangeness of fabulous Vonng, and of the rites that attended its building, and that at last some strange plague had overrun it, driving men mad . . . something about ghosts that flickered through the streets at mid-day; so that at last the dwellers there had deserted it, and for centuries it had stood here, slowly crumbling into decay. No one ever visited the place now, for civilization had moved inland since the days of Vonng's glory, and uneasy tales still ran through men's minds about the queer things that had happened here once.

"Julhi lives in these ruins?" he demanded.

"Julhi lives here but not in a ruined Vonng. Her Vonng is a splendid city. I have seen it, but I could never enter."

"Quite mad," thought Smith compassionately. And aloud, "Are there no boats here? No way to escape at all?"

Almost before the last words had left his lips he heard something like the humming of countless bees begin to ring in his ears. It grew and deepened and swelled until his head was filled with sound, and the cadences of that sound said,

"No. No way. Julhi forbids it."

In Smith's arms the girl startled and clung to him convulsively.

"It is Julhi!" she gasped. "Do you feel her, singing in your brain? Julhi!"

Smith heard the voice swelling louder, until it seemed to fill the whole night, humming with intolerable volume.

"Yes, my little Apri. It is I. Do you repent your disobedience, my Apri?"

Smith felt the girl trembling against him. He could hear her heart pounding, and the breath rushed chokingly through her lips.

"No—no, I do not," he heard her murmur, very softly. "Let me die, Julhi."

The voice hummed with a purring sweetness.

"Die, my pretty? Julhi could not be so cruel. Oh no, little Apri, I but frightened you for punishment. You are forgiven now. You may return to me and serve me again, my Apri. I would not let you die." The voice was cloyingly sweet.

Apri's voice crescendoed into hysterical rebellion.

"No, no! I will not serve you! Not again, Julhi! Let me die!"

"Peace, peace my little one." That humming was hypnotic in its soothing lilt. "You will serve me. Yes, you will obey me as before, my pretty. You have found man there, haven't you, little one? Bring him with you, and come."

Apri's unseen hands clawed frantically at Smith's shoulders, tearing herself free, pushing him away.

"Run, run!" she gasped. "Climb this wall and run! You

can throw yourself over the cliff and be free. Run, I say, before it's too late. Oh, *Shar, Shar,* if I were free to die!"

Smith prisoned the clawing hands in one of his and shook her with the other.

"Be still!" he snapped. "You're hysterical. Be still!"

He felt the shuddering slacken. The straining hands fell quiet. By degrees her panting breath evened.

"Come," she said at last, and in quite a different voice. "Julhi commands it. Come."

Her fingers twined firmly in his, and she stepped forward without hesitation into the dark. He followed, stumbling over debris, bruising himself against the broken walls. How far they went he did not know, but the way turned and twisted and doubled back upon itself, and he had, somehow, the curious idea that she was not following a course through corridors and passages which she knew well enough not to hesitate over, but somehow, under the influence of Juhli's sorcery, treading a symbolic pattern among the stones, tracing it out with unerring feet—a witch-pattern that, when it was completed, would open a door for them which no eyes could see, no hands unlock.

It may have been Julhi who put that certainty in his mind, but he was quite sure of it as the girl walked on along her intricate path, threading silently in and out among the unseen ruins, nor was he surprised when without warning the floor became smooth underfoot and the walls seemed to fall away from about him, the smell of cold stone vanished from the air. Now he walked in darkness over a thick carpet, through sweetly scented air, warm and gently moving with invisible currents. In that dark he was somehow aware of eyes upon him. Not physical eyes, but a more all-pervading inspection. Presently the humming began again, swelling through the air and beating in his ears in sweetly pitched cadences.

"Hm-m-m . . . have you brought me a man from Earth, my Apri? Yes, an Earthman, and a fine one. I am pleased with you, Apri for saving me this man. I shall call him to me presently. Until then let him wander, for he can not escape."

The air fell quiet again, and about him Smith gradually became aware of a dawning light. It swelled from no visible source, but it paled the utter dark to a twilight through which he could see tapestries and richly glowing columns about him, and the outlines of the girl Apri standing at his side. The twilight paled in turn, and the light grew strong, and presently he stood in full day among the queer, rich furnishings of the place into which he had come.

He stared round in vain for signs of the way they had entered. The room was a small cleared space in the midst of a forest of shining pillars of polished stone. Tapestries were stretched between some of them, swinging down in luxuriant folds. But as far as he could see in all directions the columns reached away in diminishing aisles, and he was quite sure that they had not made their way to this place through the clustering pillars. He would have been aware of them. No, he had stepped straight from Vonng's stonestrewn ruins upon this rug which carpeted the little clear space, through some door invisible to him.

He turned to the girl. She had sunk upon one of the divans which stood between the columns around the edge of the circular space. She was paler than the marble, and very lovely, as he had known she would be. She had the true Venusian's soft, dark, sidelong eyes, and her mouth was painted coral, and her hair swept in black, shining clouds over her shoulders. The tight-swathed Venusian robe clung to her in folds of rose-red velvet, looped to leave one shoulder bare, and slit, as all Venusian's women's garments are, to let one leg flash free with every other step. It is the most flattering dress imaginable for any woman to wear, but Apri needed no flattery to make her beautiful. Smith's pale eyes were appreciative as he stared.

She met his gaze apathetically. All rebellion seemed to have gone out of her, and a strange exhaustion had drained the color from her face.

"Where are we now?" demanded Smith.

She gave him an oblique glance.

"This is the place Julhi uses for a prison," she murmured, almost indifferently. "Around us I suppose her slaves are moving, and the halls of her palace stretch. I can't explain it to you, but at Julhi's command anything can happen. We could be in the midst of her palace and never suspect it, for there is no escape from here. We can do nothing but wait."

"Why?" Smith nodded toward the columned vistas stretching away all around them. "What's beyond that?"

"Nothing. It simply extends like that until—until you find yourself back here again."

Smith glanced at her swiftly under lowered lids, wondering just how mad she really was. Her white, exhausted face told him nothing.

"Come along," he said at last. "I'm going to try anyhow."

She shook her head.

"No use. Julhi can find you when she is ready. There is no escape from Julhi."

"I'm going to try," he said again, stubbornly. "Are you coming?"

"No. I'm—tired. I'll wait here. You'll come back."

He turned without further words and plunged at random into the wilderness of pillars surrounding the little carpeted room. The floor was slippery under his boots, and dully shining. The pillars, too, shone along all their polished surfaces, and in the queer light diffused throughout the place no shadows fell; so that a dimension seemed to be lacking and a curious flatness lay over all the shining forest. He went on resolutely, looking back now and again to keep his course straight away from the little clear space he had left. He watched it dwindle behind him and lose itself among the columns and vanish, and he wandered on through endless wilderness, to the sound of his own echoing footsteps, with nothing to break the monotony of the shining pillars until he thought he glimpsed a cluster of tapestries far ahead through the unshadowed vistas and began to hurry, hoping against hope that he had found at least a way out of the forest. He reached the place at last, and pulled aside the tapestry, and met Apri's wearily smiling eyes. The way somehow had doubled back upon him.

He snorted disgustedly at himself and turned again to plunge into the columns. This time he had wandered for no more than ten minutes before he found himself coming back once more into the clearing. He tried a third time, and it seemed had taken no more than a dozen steps before the way twisted under his feet and catapulted him back again into the room he had just left. Apri smiled as he flung himself upon one of the divans and regarded her palely from under knit brows.

"There is no escape," she repeated. "I think this place is built upon some different plan from any we know, with all its lines running in a circle whose center is this room. For only a circle has boundaries, yet no end, like this wilderness around us."

"Who is Julhi?" asked Smith abruptly. "*What* is she?"

"She is—a goddess, perhaps. Or a devil from hell. Or both. And she comes from the place beyond the light—I can't explain it to you. It was I who opened the door for her, I think, and through me she looks back into the light that I must call up for her when she commands me. And I shall go mad—mad!"

Desperation flamed from her eyes suddenly and faded again, leaving her face whiter than before. Her hands rose in a small, futile gesture and dropped to her lap again. She shook her head.

"No—not wholly mad. She would never permit me even that escape, for then I could not summon up the light and so open the window for her to look backward into that land from which she came. That land—"

"Look!" broke in Smith. "The light—"

Apri glanced up and nodded almost indifferently.

"Yes. It's darkening again. Julhi will summon you now, I think."

Rapidly the illumination was failing all about them, and

the columned forests melted into dimness, and dark veiled the long vistas, and presently everything clouded together and black night fell once more. This time they did not move, but Smith was aware, remotely, of a movement all about them, subtle and indescribable, as if the scenes were being shifted behind the curtain of the dark. The air quivered with motion and change. Even under his feet the floor was shifting, not tangibly but with an inner metamorphosis he could put no name to.

And then the dark began to lift again. Light diffused slowly through it, paling the black, until he stood in a translucent twilight through whose veil he could see that the whole scene had changed about him. He saw Apri from the corner of his eye, heard her quickened breathing beside him, but he did not turn his head. Those columned vistas were gone. The limitless aisles down which he had wandered were closed now by great walls uplifting all around.

His eyes rose to seek the ceiling, and as the dusk lightened into day once more he became aware of a miraculous quality about those walls. A curious wavy pattern ran around them in broad bands, and as he stared he realized that the bands were not painted upon the surface, but were integrally part of the walls themselves, and that each successive band lessened in density. Those along the base of the walls were heavily dark, but the rising patterns paled and became less solid as they rose, until at half-way up the wall they were like layers of patterned smoke, and farther up still bands of scarcely discernible substance more tenuous than mist. Around the heights they seemed to melt into pure light, to which he could not lift his eyes for the dazzling brilliance of it.

In the center of the room rose a low black couch, and upon it—Julhi. He knew that instinctively the moment he saw her, and in that first moment he realized nothing but her beauty. He caught his breath at the sleek and shining loveliness of her, lying on her black couch and facing him with a level, unwinking stare. Then he realized her unhumanity, and a tiny prickling ran down his back—for she was one of that very ancient race of one-eyed beings about which whispers persist so unescapably in folklore and legend, though history has forgotten them for ages. One-eyed. A clear eye, uncolored, centered in the midst of a fair, broad forehead. Her features were arranged in a diamond-shaped pattern instead of humanity's triangle, for the slanting nostrils of her low-bridged nose were set so far apart that they might have been separate features, tilting and exquisitely modeled. Her mouth was perhaps the queerest feature of her strange yet somehow lovely face. It was perfectly heartshaped, in an exaggerated cupid's-bow, but it was not a human mouth. It did not close, ever. It was a beautifully arched orifice, the red lip that rimmed it compellingly crimson, but fixed and moveless in an unhinged jaw. Behind the bowed opening he could see the red, fluted tissue of flesh within.

Above that single, clear, deep-lashed eye something sprang backward from her brow in a splendid sweep, something remotely feather-like, yet no such feather as was ever fledged upon any bird alive. It was exquisitely iridescent, and its fronds shivered with blowing color at the slight motion of her breathing.

For the rest—well, as the lines of a lap-dog travesty the clean, lean grace of a racing greyhound, so humanity's shape travestied the serpentine loveliness of her body. And it was definitely humanity that aped her form, not herself aping humanity. Somehow she was so *right* in every flowing, curving line, so unerringly fashioned toward some end he could not guess, yet to which instinctively he conceded her perfect fitness.

There was a fluidity about her, a litheness that partook more of the serpent's rippling flow than of any warm-blooded creature's motion, but her body was not like any being, warm-blooded or cold, that he had ever seen before. From the waist up she was human, but below all resemblance ended. And yet she was so breath-takingly lovely. Any attempt to describe the alien beauty of her lower limbs would sound grotesque, and she was not grotesque even in her unnamable shape, even in the utter weirdness of her face.

That clear, unwinking eye turned its gaze upon Smith. She lay there luxuriously upon her black couch, ivory-pale against the darkness of it, the indescribable strangeness of her body lolling with a serpent's grace upon the cushions. He felt the gaze of that eye go through him, searching out all the hidden places in his brain and flickering casually over the lifetime that lay behind him. The feathery crest quivered very gently above her head.

He met the gaze steadily. There was no expression upon that changeless face, for she could not smile, and the look in her single eye was meaningless to him. He had no way of guessing what emotions were stirring behind the alien mask. He had never realized before how essential is the mobility of the mouth in expressing moods, and hers was fixed, immobile, for ever stretched into its heart-shaped arch—like a lyre-frame, he thought, but irrevocably dumb, surely, for such a mouth as hers, in its immovable unhinged jaw, could never utter human speech.

And then she spoke. The shock of it made him blink, and it was a moment before he realized just how she was accomplishing the impossible. The fluted tissue within the arched opening of her mouth had begun to vibrate like harp-strings, and the humming he had heard before went thrilling through the air. Beside him he was aware of Apri shuddering uncontrollably as the humming strengthened and swelled, but he was listening too closely to realize her save subconsciously; for there was in that humming something that—that, yes, it was rounding into the most queerly uttered phrases, in a sort of high, unutterably sweet singing note, like the sound of a violin. With her moveless lips she could not articulate, and her only enunciation came from the varied intensities of that musical tone. Many languages could not be spoken so, but the High Venusian's lilt is largely that of pitch, every word-sound bearing as many meanings as it has degrees of intensity, so that the exquisitely modulated notes which came rippling from her harp-like mouth bore as clear a meaning as if she were enunciating separate words.

And it was more eloquent than speech. Somehow those singing phrases played upon other senses than the aural. From the first lilted note he recognized the danger of that voice. It vibrated, it thrilled, it caressed. It rippled up and down his answering nerves like fingers over harp-strings.

"Who are you, Earthman?" that lazy, nerve-strumming voice demanded. He felt, as he answered, that she knew not only his name but much more about him than he himself knew. Knowledge was in her eye, serene and all-inclusive.

"Northwest Smith," he said, a little sullenly. "Why have you brought me here?"

"A dangerous man." There was an undernote of mockery in the music. "You were brought to feed the dwellers of Vonng with human blood, but I think—yes, I think I shall keep you for myself. You have known much of emotions that are alien to me, and I would share them fully, as one with your own strong, hot-blooded body, Northwest Smith. *Aie-e-e"*—the humming wailed along an ecstatic upward note that sent shivers down the man's spine—"and how sweet and hot your blood will be, my Earthman! You shall share my ecstasy as I drink it! You shall—but wait. First you must understand. Listen, Earthman."

The humming swelled to an inarticulate roaring in his ears, and somehow his mind relaxed under that sound, smoothed out, pliantly as wax for the recording of her voice. In that queer, submissive mood he heard her singing,

"Life dwells in so many overlapping planes, my Earthman, that even I can comprehend but a fraction of them. My plane is very closely akin to your own, and at some places they overlap in so intimate a way that it takes little effort to break through, if one can find a weak spot. This city of Vonng is one of the spots, a place which exists simultaneously in both planes. Can you understand that? It was laid out along certain obscure patterns in a way and for a purpose which are stories in themselves; so that in my own plane as well as here in yours Vonng's walls and streets and buildings are tangible. But time is different in our two worlds. It moves faster here. The strange alliance between your plane and mine, through two sorcerers of our alien worlds, was brought about very curiously. Vonng was built by men of your own plane, laboriously, stone by stone. But to us it seemed that through the magic of that sorcerer of ours a city suddenly appeared at his command, empty and complete. For your time moves so much faster than ours.

"And though through the magic of those strangely matched conspirators the stone which built Vonng existed in both planes at once, no power could make the men who dwelt in Vonng accessible to use. Two races simultaneously inhabited the city. To mankind it seemed haunted by nebulous, imponderable presences. That race was ourselves. To us you were tantalizingly perceptible in flashes, but we could not break through. And we wanted to very badly. Mentally, sometimes we could reach you, but physically never.

"And so it went on. But because time moved faster here, your Vonng fell into ruins and has been deserted for ages, while to our perceptions it is still a great and thronging city. I shall show you presently.

"To understand why I am here you must understand something of our lives. The goal of your own race is the pursuit of happiness, is it not so? But our lives are spent wholly in the experiencing and enjoyment of sensation. To us that is food and drink and happiness. Without it we starve. To nourish our bodies we must drink the blood of living creatures, but that is a small matter beside the ravenous hunger we know for the sensations and the emotions of the flesh. We are infinitely more capable of experiencing them than you, both physically and mentally. Our range of sensation is vast beyond your comprehension, but to us it is an old story, and always we seek new sensations, other alien emotions. We have raided many worlds, many planes, many dimensions, in search of something new. It was only a short while ago that we succeeded in breaking into yours, through the help of Apri here.

"You must understand that we could not have come had there not been a doorway. Ever since the building of Vonng we have been mentally capable of entering, but to experience the emotions we crave we must have physical contact, a temporary physical union through the drinking of blood. And there has never been a way to enter until we found Apri. You see, we have long known that some are born with a wider range of perceptions than their comrades can understand. Sometimes they are called mad. Sometimes in their madness they are more dangerous than they realize. For Apri was born with the ability to gaze in upon our world, and though she did not know this, or understand what the light was which she could summon up at will, she unwittingly opened the door for us to enter here.

"It was through her aid that I came, and with her aid that I maintain myself here and bring others through in the dark of the night to feed upon the blood of mankind. Our position is precarious in your world, and we have not yet dared make ourselves known. So we have begun upon the lowest types of man, to accustom ourselves to the fare and to strengthen our hold upon humanity, so that when we are ready to go forth openly we shall have sufficient power to withstand your resistance. But soon now we shall come."

The long, lovely, indescribable body upon the couch writhed round to front him more fully, the motion rippling along her limbs like a wavelet over water. The deep, steady gaze of the eye bored into his, the voice pulsed with intensity.

"Great things are waiting for you, Earthman—before you die. We shall become one, for a while. I shall savor all your perceptions, suck up the sensations you have known. I shall open new fields to you, and see them through your senses with a new flavor, and you shall share my delight in the taste of your newness. And as your blood flows you shall know all beauty, and all horror, and all delight and pain, and all the other emotions and sensations, nameless to you, that I have known."

The humming music of her voice spun through Smith's brain soothingly. Somehow what she said held no urgency for him. It was like a legend of something which had happened long ago to another man. He waited gravely as the voice went on again, dreamily, gloatingly.

"You have known much of danger, O wanderer. You have looked upon strange things, and life has been full for you, and death an old comrade, and love—and love—those arms have held many women, is it not so? . . . Is it not so?"

Unbearably sweet, the voice lingered murmurously over the vibrant query, something compelling and irresistible in the question, in the pitch and the queer, ringing tone of it. And quite involuntarily memories flashed back across the surface of his mind. He was quiet, remembering.

The milk-white girls of Venus are so lovely, with their sidelong eyes and their warm mouths and their voices pitched to the very tone of love. And the canal-women of Mars—coral pink, sweet as honey, murmurous under the moving moons. And Earth's girls are vibrant as swordblades, and heady with kisses and laughter. There were others, too. He remembered a sweet brown savage on a lost asteroid, and one brief, perfume-dizzied night under the reeling stars. And there had been a space-pirate's wench in stolen jewels, flame-gun belted, who came to him in a camptown on the edge of Martian civilization, where the drylands begin. There was that rosy Martian girl in the garden palace by the canal, where the moons went wheeling through the sky. . . . And once, very long ago, in a garden upon Earth—he closed his eyes and saw again the moonlight of home silvering a fair, high head, and level eyes looking into his and a mouth that quivered, saying—

He drew a long, unsteady breath and opened his eyes again. The pale steel stare of them was expressionless, but that last, deep-buried memory had burnt like a heat-ray, and he knew she had tasted the pain of it, and was exulting. The feathery crest that swept backward from her forehead was trembling rhythmically, and the colors blowing through it had deepened in intensity and were changing with bewildering swiftness. But her still face had not changed, although he thought there was a softening in the brilliance of her eyes, as if she were remembering too.

When she spoke, the sustained, fluting note of her voice was breathless as a whisper, and he realized anew how infinitely more eloquent it was than a voice which spoke in words. She could infuse into the vibrant lilt blood-stirring intensities and soft, rich purrs that went sweeping along his nerves like velvet. His whole body was responding to the pitch of her voice. She was playing upon him as upon a harp, evoking chords of memory and sending burring thrills down his back and setting the blood athrob in his pulses by the very richness and deepness of her tone. And it strummed not only upon the responses of his body but also upon the chords of his very mind, waking thoughts to match her own, compelling him into the channels she desired. Her voice was purest magic, and he had not even the desire to resist it.

"They are sweet memories—sweet?" she purred caressingly. "The women of the worlds you know—the women who have lain in those arms of yours—whose mouths have clung to yours—do you remember?"

There was the most flagrant mesmerism in her voice as it ran on vibrantly over him—again he thought of fingers upon harp-strings—evoking the melodies she desired, strumming at his memories with words like hot, sweet flames. The room misted before his eyes, and that singing voice was a lilt through timeless space, no longer speaking in phrases but in a throbbingly inarticulate purr, and his body was no more than a sounding-board for the melodies she played.

Presently the mesmerism of her tone took on a different pitch. The humming resolved itself into words again, thrilling through him now more clearly than spoken phrases.

"And in all these remembered women"—it sang—"in all these you remember me. . . . For it was I in each of them whom you remember—that little spark that was myself—and I am all women who love and are loved—my arms held you—do you not remember?"

In the midst of that hypnotic murmuring he did remember, and recognized dimly through the reeling tumult of his blood some great, veiled truth he could not understand.

The crest above her forehead trembled in slow, languorous rhythm, and rich colors flowed through it in tints that caressed the eyes—velvety purples, red like embers, flame colors and sunset shades. When she rose upon her couch with an unnamed gliding movement and held out her arms he had no recollection of moving forward, but somehow he was clasping her and the outstretched arms had coiled like serpents about him, and very briefly the heart-shaped orifice which was her mouth brushed against his lips.

Something icy happened then. The touch was light and fluttering, as if the membrane that lined that bowed and rigid opening had vibrated delicately against his mouth as swiftly and lightly as the brush of humming-birds' wings. It was not a shock, but somehow with the touch all the hammering tumult within him died. He was scarcely aware that he possessed a body. He was kneeling upon the edge of Julhi's couch, her arms like snakes about him, her weird, lovely face upturned to his. Some half-formed nucleus of rebellion in his mind dissipated in a breath, for her single eye was a magnet to draw his gaze, and once his pale stare was fixed upon it there was no possibility of escape.

And yet the eye did not seem to see him. It was fixed and glowing upon something immeasurably distant, far in the past, so intently that there was no consciousness in it of the walls about them, nor of himself so near, staring into the lucid depths wherein vague, cloudy reflections were stirring, queer shapes and shadows which were the images of nothing he had ever seen before.

He bent there, tense, his gaze riveted upon the moving

shadows in her eyes. A thin, high humming fluted from her mouth in a monotone which compelled all his consciousness into one straight channel, and that channel the clouded deeps of her remembering eye. Now the past was moving more clearly through it, and he could see the shapes of things he had no name for stirring sluggishly across a background of dimness veiling still deeper pasts.

Then all the shapes and shadows ran together in a blackness like a vacuum, and the eye was no longer clear and lucid, but darker than sunless space, and far deeper . . . a dizzy deep that made his senses whirl. Vertigo came upon him overwhelmingly, and he reeled and somehow lost all hold upon reality, and was plunging, falling, whirling through the immeasurable, bottomless abysses of that dark.

Stars reeled all about him, streaks of light against a velvet black almost tangible in its utter dark. Slowly the lights steadied. His giddiness ceased, though the rush of his motion did not. He was being borne more swiftly than the wind through a dark ablaze with fixed points of brilliance, starry and unwinking. Gradually he became aware of himself, and knew without surprise that he was no longer of flesh and blood, a tangible human creature, but something nebulous and diffused and yet of definite dimensions, freer and lither than the human form and light as smoke.

He was riding through the starry dark a something all but invisible even to his keen new eyes. That dark did not muffle him as it would have blinded a human being. He could see quite clearly, his eyes utilizing something other than light in their perception. But this dim thing he rode was no more than a blur even to the keenness of his dark-defying gaze.

The vague outlines of it which were all he could catch as they flashed and faded and formed again, were now of one shape and now of another, but most often that of some fabulous monster with heaven-spanning wings and a sinuous body trailing out to incredible length. Yet somehow he knew that it was not in reality any such thing. Somehow he knew it for the half-visible manifestation of a force without name, a force which streamed through this starry dark in long, writhing waves and tides, taking fantastic shapes as it flowed. And those shapes were controlled in a measure by the brain of the observer, so that he saw what he expected to see in the nebulous outlines of the dark.

The force buoyed him up with a heady exhilaration more intoxicating than wine. In long arcs and plunges he swept on through the spangled night, finding that he could control his course in some dim way he managed without understanding. It was as if he had wings spread out upon conflicting currents, and by the poise and beat of them rode the air more easily than a bird—yet he knew that his strange new body bore no wings.

For a long while he swept and curved and volplaned upon those forces which flowed invisibly through the dark, giddy with the intoxicating joy of flight. He was aware of neither up nor down in this starry void. He was weightless, disembodied, a joyous ghost breasting the air-currents upon unreal wings. Those points of light which flecked the blackness lay strewn in clusters and long winnowed swaths and strange constellations. They were not distant, like real stars, for sometimes he plunged through a swarm of them and emerged with the breathless sensation of one who has dived into a smother of foaming seas and risen again, yet the lights were intangible to him. That refreshing sensation was not a physical one, nor were the starry points real. He could see them, but that was all. They were like the reflections of something far away in some distant dimension, and though he swung his course straight through a clustering galaxy he did not disarrange a single star. It was his own body which diffused itself through them like smoke, and passed on gasping and refreshed.

As he swept on through the dark he began to find a tantalizing familiarity in the arrangement of some of those starry groups. There were constellations he knew . . . surely that was Orion, striding across the sky. He saw Beteleguese's redly glowing eye, and Rigel's cold blue blaze. And beyond, across gulfs of darkness, twin Sirius was spinning, blue-white against the black. The red glimmer in the midst of that wide swath of spangles must be Antares, and the great clustering galaxy that engulfed it—surely the Milky Way! He swerved upon the currents that bore him up, tilted wide, invisible pinions and plunged through its sparkling froth of stars, intoxicated with the space-devouring range of his flight. He spanned a billion light-years with one swoop, volplaned in a long steep curve across a universe. He looked for the tiny sun round which his native planets spun, and could not find it in the wilderness of splendor through which he was plunging. It was a giddy and joyous thing to know that his body dwelt upon some light-point too small to be seen, while here in the limitless dark he soared heedlessly through a welter of constellations, defying time and space and matter itself. He must be swooping through some airy plane where distance and size were not measured in the terms he knew, yet upon whose darkness the reflections of familiar galaxies fell.

Then in his soaring course he swept on beyond the familiar stars, across an intervening gulf of dark, and into another spangled universe whose constellations traced strange and shining patterns across the sky. Presently he became aware that he was not alone. Outlined like wraiths against the blackness, other forms went plunging down the spaceways, sweeping in long curves upon currents of flowing force, plunging into smothers of starry brilliance and bursting through a-sparkle with it to go swinging on again down swooping arcs of darkness.

And then reluctantly he felt the exhilaration begin to fade. He fought against the force that was drawing him backward, clinging stubbornly to this new and intoxicating pleasure, but despite himself the vision was paling, the constellations fading. The dark rolled suddenly away, curtainwise, and with a jerk he was back again in Julhi's queerly walled room, solid and human once more, and Julhi's lovely and incredible body was pressing close to his, her magical voice humming again through his head.

It was a wordless humming she sang now, but it chose its

pitch unerringly to play upon the nerves she sought, and his heart began to hammer and his breath came fast, and the noise of war was roaring in his ears. That singing was a Valkyrie battle-chant, and he heard the crash of conflict and the shouts of struggling men, smelled burnt flesh and felt the kick of the ray-gun's butt against his gripping hand. All the sensations of battle poured over him in unrelated disarray. He was aware of smoke and dust and the smell of blood, felt the pain of ray-burns and the bite of blades, tasted sweat and salt blood, knew again the feel of his fists crashing into alien faces, the heady surge of power through his long, strong body. The wild exhilaration of battle flamed through him in deepening waves to the sorcery of Julhi's song.

It grew stronger then, and more intense, until the physical sensation faded wholly and nothing was left but that soul-consuming ecstasy, and that in turn intensified until he no longer stood upon solid ground, but floated free through void again, pure emotion divorced from all hint of flesh. Then the void took nebulous shape around him, as he passed upward by the very intensity of his ecstasy into some higher land beyond the reach of any sense he possessed. For a while he floated through cloudy shapes of alien form and meaning. Little thrills of perception tingled through the calm of his exultation as he brushed by the misty things that peopled the cloudland to which he had penetrated. They came swifter, until that calm was rippled across and across with conflicting thrills and ecstasies that ran at cross-currents and tossed up little wavelets, and clashed together, and—

Everything spun dizzily and with breath-taking abruptness he leaned once more in Julhi's embrace. Her voice lilted through his brain.

"That was new! I've never gone so high before, or even suspected that such a place existed. But you could not have endured that pitch of ecstasy longer, and I am not ready yet for you to die. Let us sing now of terror. . . ."

And as the tones that went humming over him shivered through his brain, dim horrors stirred in their sleep and lifted ghastly heads in the lowest depths of his consciousness to the awakening call of the music, and terror rippled along his nerves until the air dimmed about him again and he was fleeing unnamable things down endless vistas of insanity, with that humming to hound him along.

So it went. He ran the gamut of emotion over and over again. He shared the strange sensations of beings he had never dreamed existed. Some he recognized, but more he could not even guess at, nor from what far worlds their emotions had been pilfered, to lie hoarded in Julhi's mind until she evoked them again.

Faster they came, and faster. They blew over him in dizzy succession, unknown emotions, familiar ones, strange ones, freezingly alien ones, all hurrying through his brain in a blurred confusion, so that one merged into another and they two into a third before the first had done more than brush the surface of his consciousness. Faster still, until at last the whole insane tumult blended into a pitch of wild intensity which must have been too great for his human fiber to endure; for as the turmoil went on he felt himself losing all grasp upon reality, and catapulting upon the forces that ravaged him into a vast and soothing blankness which swallowed up all unrest in the nirvana of its dark.

After an immeasurable while he felt himself wakening, and fought against it weakly. No use. A light was broadening through that healing night which all his stubbornness could not resist. He had no sensation of physical awakening, but without opening his eyes he saw the room more clearly than he had ever seen it before, so that there were tiny rainbows of light around all the queer objects there, and Apri—

He had forgotten her until now, but with this strange awareness that was not of the eyes alone he saw her standing before the couch upon which he leaned in Julhi's arms. She stood rigid, rebellion making a hopeless mask of her face, and there was agony in her eyes. All about her like a bright nimbus the light rayed out. She was incandescent, a torch whose brilliance strengthened until the light radiating from her was almost palpable.

He sensed in Julhi's body, clinging to his, a deep-stirring exultation as the light swelled about her. She luxuriated in it, drank it in like wine. He felt that for her it was indeed tangible, and that he looked upon it now, in this queer new way, through senses that saw it as she did. Somehow he was sure that with normal eyes it would not have been visible.

Dimly he was remembering what had been said about the light which opened a door into Julhi's alien world. And he felt no surprise when it became clear to him that the couch no longer supported his body—that he had no body—that he was suspended weightlessly in midair, Julhi's arms still clapsing him in a queer, unphysical grip, while the strangely banded walls moved downward all about him. He had no sensation of motion himself; yet the walls seemed to fall away below and he was floating freely past the mounting bands of mist that paled and brightened swiftly until he was bathed in the blinding light that ringed the top.

There was no ceiling. The light was a blaze of splendor all about him, and out of that blaze, very slowly, very nebulously, the streets of Vonng took shape, it was not that Vonng which had stood once upon the little Venusian island. The buildings were the same as those which must once have risen where their ruins now stood, but there was a subtle distortion of perspective which would have made it clear to him, even had he not known, that this city stood in another plane of existence than his own. Sometimes amidst the splendor he thought he caught glimpses of vine-tangled ruins. A wall would shimmer before his eyes for an instant and crumble into broken blocks, and the pavement would be debris-strewn and mossy. Then the vision faded and the wall stood up unbroken again. But he knew he was looking through the veil which parted the two worlds so narrowly, upon the ruins which were all that remained of Vonng in his own plane.

It was the Vonng which had been shaped for the needs of two worlds simultaneously. He could see, without really understanding, how some of the queerly angled buildings and twisted streets which could have no meaning to the eyes of a man were patterned for the use of these gliding people. He saw in the pavement the curious medallions set by the long-dead sorcerers to pin two planes together at this point of intersection.

In these shimmering unstable streets he saw for the first time in full light shapes which must be like that of the creature which had seized him in the dark. They were of Julhi's race, unmistakably, but he saw now that in her metamorphosis into a denizen of his own world she had perforce taken on a more human aspect than was normally her own. The beings that glided through Vonng's strangely altered streets could never have been mistaken, even at the first glance, as human. Yet they gave even more strongly than had Julhi the queer impression of being exquisitely fitted for some lofty purpose he could not guess at, their shapes of a perfect proportion toward which mankind might have aimed and missed. For the hint of humanity was there, as in man there is a hint of the beast. Julhi in her explanation had made them seem no more than sensation-eaters, intent only upon the gratification of hunger. But, looking upon their perfect, indescribable bodies, he could not believe that the goal for which they were so beautifully fashioned could be no more than that. He was never to know what that ultimate goal was, but he could not believe it only the satisfaction of the senses.

The shining crowds poured past him down the streets, the whole scene so unstable that great rifts opened in it now and again to let the ruins of that other Vonng show through. And against this background of beauty and uncertainty he was sometimes aware of Apri, rigid and agonized, a living torch to light him on his way. She was not in the Vonng of the alien plane nor in that of the ruins, but somehow hung suspended between the two in a dimension of her own. And whether he moved or not, she was always there, dimly present, radiant and rebellious, the shadow of a queer, reluctant madness behind her tortured eyes.

In the strangeness of what lay before him he scarcely

heeded her, and he found that when he was not thinking directly of the girl she appeared only as a vague blur somewhere in the back of his consciousness. It was a brain-twisting sensation, this awareness of overlapping planes. Sometimes in flashes his mind refused to encompass it and everything shimmered meaninglessly for an instant before he could get control again.

Julhi was beside him. He could see her without turning. He could see a great many strange things here in a great many queer, incomprehensible ways. And though he felt himself more unreal than a dream, she was firm and stable with a different sort of substance from that she had worn in the other Vonng. Her shape was changed too. Like those others she was less human, less describable, more beautiful even than before. Her clear, unfathomable eye turned to him limpidly. She said,

"This is my Vonng," and it seemed to him that though her humming thrilled compellingly through the smoky immaterialism which was himself, her words, in some new way, had gone directly from brain to brain with no need of that pseudo-speech to convey them. He realized then that her voice was primarily not for communication, but for hypnosis—a weapon more potent than steel or flame.

She turned now and moved away over the tiled street, her gait a liquidly graceful gliding upon those amazing lower limbs. Smith found himself drawn after her with a power he could not resist. He was smokily impalpable and without any independent means of locomotion, and he followed her as helplessly as her shadow followed.

At a corner ahead of them a group of the nameless beings had paused in the onward sweep which was carrying so many of Vonng's denizens along toward some yet unseen goal. They turned as Julhi approached, their expressionless eyes fixed on the shadow-wraith behind her which was Smith. No sound passed between them, but he felt in his increasingly receptive brain faint echoes of thoughts that were flashing through the air. It puzzled him until he saw how they were communicating—by those exquisitely feathery crests which swept backward above their foreheads.

It was a speech of colors. The crests quivered unceasingly, and colors far beyond the spectrum his earthly eyes could see blew through them in bewildering sequence. There was a rhythm about it that he gradually perceived, though he could not follow it. By the vagrant echoes of their thoughts which he could catch he realized that the harmony of the colors reflected in a measure the harmony of the two minds which produced them. He saw Julhi's crest quiver with a flush of gold, and those of the rest were royally purple. Green flowed through the gold, and a lusciously rosy tinge melted through the purple of the rest. But all this took place faster than he could follow, and before he was aware of what was happening a discord in the thoughts that sounded in his mind arose, and while Julhi's crest glowed orange those of the rest were angrily scarlet.

Violence had sprung up between them, whose origin he could not quite grasp though fragments of their quarrel flashed through his brain from each of the speakers, and wildly conflicting colors rippled through the plumes. Julhi's ran the gamut of a dozen spectra in tints that were eloquent of fury. The air quivered as she turned away, drawing him after her. He was at a loss to understand the suddenness of the rage which had swept over her so consumingly, but he could catch echoes of it vibrating through his mind from her own hot anger. She flashed on down the street with blurring swiftness, her crest trembling in swift, staccato shivers.

She must have been too furious to notice where she went, for she had plunged now straight into that streaming crowd which poured through the streets, and before she could win free again the force of it had swallowed her up. She had no desire to join the torrent, and Smith could feel her struggling violently against it, the fury rising as her efforts to be free were vain. Colors like curses raved through her trembling crest.

But the tide was too strong for her. They were carried

along irresistibly past the strangely angled buildings, over the patterned pavements, toward an open space which Smith began to catch glimpses of through the houses ahead of them. When they reached the square it was already nearly filled. Ranks of crested, gliding creatures thronged it, their one-eyed faces, heart-mouths immobile, were lifted toward a figure on a dais in the center. He sensed in Julhi a quivering of hatred as he faced that figure, but in it he thought he saw a serenity and a majesty of bearing which even Julhi's indescribable and lovely presence did not have. The rest waited in packed hundreds, eyes fixed, crests vibrating.

When the square was filled he watched the being on the dais lift undulant arms for quiet, and over the crowd a rigid stillness swept. The feathery crests poised motionless above intent heads. Then the plume of the leader began to vibrate with a curious rhythm, and over all the crowd the antennae-like plumes quivered in unison. Every ripple of that fronded crest was echoed to the last shiver by the crowd. There was something infinitely stirring in the rhythm. Obscurely it was like the beat of marching feet, the perfect timing of a dance. They were moving faster now, and the colors that swept through the leader's crest were echoed in those of the crowd. There was no opposition of contrast or complement here; the ranks followed their leader's harmonies in perfect exactitude. His thoughts were theirs.

Smith watched an exquisitely tender rose shiver through that central crest, darken to crimson, sweep on through richness of deepening tones to infra-red and mount in an eloquence of sheer color that stirred his being, even though he could not understand. He realized the intense and rising emotion which swept the crowd as the eloquence of the leader went vibrating through their senses.

He could not have shared that emotion, or understood a fraction of what was taking place, but as he watched, something gradually became clear to him. There was a glory about them. These beings were not innately the sensation-hungry vampires Julhi had told him of. His instinct had been right.

No one could watch them in their concerted harmony of emotion and miss wholly the lofty ardor which stirred them now. Julhi must be a degenerate among them. She and her followers might represent one side of these incomprehensible people, but it was a baser side, and not one that could gain strength among the majority. For he sensed sublimity among them. It thrilled through his dazzled brain from that intent, worshipping crowd about him.

And knowing this, rebellion suddenly surged up within him, and he strained in awakening anger at the mistiness which held him impotent. Julhi felt the pull. He saw her turn, anger still blazing in her crest and her single eye glowing with a tinge of red. From her rigid lips came a furious hissing, and colors he could not name rippled through the plume in surges eloquent of an anger that burned like a heatgun's blast. Something in the single-minded ardor of the crowd, the message of the orator, must have fanned the flame of her for at the first hint of rebellion in her captive she turned suddenly upon the crowd which hemmed her in and began to shoulder her way free.

They did not seem to realize her presence or feel the force of her pushing them aside. Devoutly all eyes were riveted upon the leader, all the feathery crests vibrated in perfect unison with his own. They were welded into an oblivious whole by the power of his eloquence. Julhi made her way out of the thronged square without distracting a single eye.

Smith followed like a shadow behind her, rebellious but impotent. She swept down the angled streets like a wind of fury. He was at a loss to understand the consuming anger which blazed higher with every passing moment, though they were vague suspicions in his mind that he must have guessed rightly as he watched the crested orator's effect upon the throng—that she was indeed degenerate, at odds with the rest, and hated them the more fiercely for it.

She swept him on along deserted streets whose walls shimmered now and again into green-wreathed ruins, and took shape again. The ruins themselves seemed to flicker curiously with dark and light that swept over them in successive waves, and suddenly he realized that time was passing more slowly here than in his own plane. He was watching night and day go by over the ruins of that elder Vonng.

They were coming now into a courtyard of strange, angular shape. As they entered, the half-forgotten blur at the back of his mind which was Apri glowed into swift brilliance, and he saw that the light which streamed from her was bathing the court in radiance, stronger than the light outside. He could see her vaguely, hovering over the exact center of the courtyard in that curious dimension of her own, staring with mad, tortured eyes through the veils of the planes between. About the enclosure shapes like Julhi's moved sluggishly, the colors dull on their crests, their eyes filmed. And he saw, now that a suspicion of the truth had entered his mind, that Julhi herself did not have quite the clear and shining beauty of those who had thronged the square. There was an indescribable dullness over her.

When she and her shadowy captive entered the court those aimlessly moving creatures quickened into sudden life. A scarlet the color of fresh blood flowed through Julhi's crest, and the others echoed it with eager quiverings of their plumes which were somehow obscene and avid. And for the first time Smith's dulled consciousness awoke into fear, and he writhed helplessly in the recesses of his mind away from the hungry shapes around him. The crowd was rushing forward now with quivering plumes and fluttering, wide-arched mouths that had flushed a deeper crimson as if in anticipation. For all their strangeness, their writhing shapes and weird, alien faces, they were like wolves bearing down hungrily upon their quarry.

But before they reached him something happened. Somehow Julhi had moved with lightning swiftness, and vertigo seized Smith blindingly. The walls around them shimmered and vanished. Apri vanished, the light blazed into a dazzle and he felt the world shifting imponderably about him. Scenes he recognized flashed and faded—the black ruins he had awakened in, Julhi's cloud-walled room, the wilderness of pillars, this curiously shaped courtyard itself, all melted together and blurred and faded. In the instant before it vanished he felt, as from far away, the touch upon the mistiness of his bodiless self of hands that were not human, hands that stung with the shock of lightning.

Somehow in the timeless instant while this took place he realized that he had been snatched away from the pack for some obscure purpose. Somehow, too, he knew that what Apri had told him had been true, though he had thought her mad at the time. In some vague way all these scenes were the same. They occupied the same place, at the same time—ruined Vonng, the Vonng that Julhi knew, all those places he had known since he met Apri in the dark—they were overlapping planes through which, as through open doors, Julhi had drawn him.

He was aware of an unnamable sensation then, within himself, and the mistiness which had prisoned him gave way before the returning strength of his flesh-and-blood body. He opened his eyes. Something was clinging to him in heavy coils, and a pain gnawed at his heart, but he was too stunned at what surrounded him to heed it just then.

He stood among the ruins of a court which must once, long ago, have been the court he had just left—or had he? For he saw now that it too surrounded him, flickering through the ruins in glimpses of vanished splendor. He stared round wildly. Yes, shining through the crumbled walls and the standing walls that were one and the same, he could catch glimpses of that columned wilderness through which he had wandered. And rising above this, one with it, the misty-walled chamber where he had met Julhi. They were all here, occupying the same space, at the same time. The world was a chaos of conflicting planes all about him. There were other scenes too, intermingling with these, places he had never seen before. And Apri, incandescent and agonized, peered with mad eyes through the bewildering tangle of worlds. His brain lurched sickeningly with the incredible things it could not comprehend.

Around him through the chaotic jumbling of a score of

planes prowled strange forms. They were like Julhi—yet unlike her. They were like those figures which had rushed upon him in that other Vonng—but not wholly. They had bestialized in the metamorphosis. The shining beauty was dulled. The incomparable grace of them had thickened into animal gropings. Their plumes burned with an ugly crimson and the clarity of their eyes was clouded now with a blind and avid hunger. They circled him with a baffled gliding.

All this he was aware of in the flashing instant when his eyes opened. Now he looked down, for the first time consciously aware of that pain which gnawed at his heart, of the clinging arms. And suddenly that pain stabbed like a heatray, and he went sick with the shock of what he saw. For Julhi clung to him, relaxed in avid coils. Her eyes were closed, and her mouth was fastened tightly against the flesh of his left breast, just over the heart. The plume above her head quivered from base to tip with long, voluptuous shudders, and all the shades of crimson and scarlet and bloody rose that any spectrum ever held went blowing through it.

Smith choked on a word half-way between oath and prayer, and with shaking hands ripped her arms away, thrust against her shoulders blindly to tear loose that clinging, agonizing mouth. The blood spurted as it came free. The great eye opened and looked up into his with a dull, glazed stare. Swiftly the glaze faded, the dullness brightened into a glare behind which hell-fires flamed scorchingly, to light up the nameless hells within. Her plume whipped erect and blazed into angry red. From the arched mouth, wet now, and crimson, a high, thin, nerve-twanging hum shrilled agonizingly.

That sound was like the flick of a wire whip on raw flesh. It bit into his brain-centers, sawed at his quivering nerves excruciatingly, unbearably. Under the lash of that voice Smith wrenched away from her clinging arms, stumbling over the stones, blundering anywhere away from the punishing shrill of that hum. The chaos spun about him, scenes shifting and melting together maddeningly. The blood ran down his breast.

Through his blind agony, as the world dissolved into shrilling pain, one thing alone was clear. That burning light. That steady flame. Apri. He was blundering unimpeded through solid walls and columns and buildings in their jumble of cross-angled planes, but when he came to her at last she was tangible, she was real. And with the feel of her firm flesh under his hands a fragment of sanity rose out of that piercing anguish which shivered along his nerves. Dully he knew that through Apri all this was possible. Apri the light-maker, the doorway between worlds . . . His fingers closed on her throat.

Blessedly, blessedly that excruciating song was fading. He knew no more than that. He scarcely realized that his fingers were sunk yet in the softness of a woman's throat. The chaos was fading around him, the crazy planes righting themselves, paling, receding backward into infinity. Through their fragments the solid rocks of Vonng loomed up in crumbling ruins. The agony of Julhi's song was a faint shrilling from far away. And about him in the air he sensed a frenzied tugging, as if impalpable hands were clutching at his, ghostly arms pulling ineffectually upon him. He looked up, dazed and uncertain.

Where Julhi had stood among the tumbling planes an expanding cloudy image hovered now, bearing still the lovely outlines that had been hers, but foggy, spreading and dissipating like mist as the doorway closed between planes. She was scarcely more than a shadow, and fading with every breath, but she wrenched at him yet with futile, cloudy hands, striving to the last to preserve her gate into the world she hungered for. But as she clawed she was vanishing. Her outlines blurred and melted as smoke fades. She was no more than a darkening upon the air now, tenuous, indistinguishable. Then the fog that had been lovely Julhi had expanded into nothingness—the air was clear.

Smith looked down, shook his dulled head a little, bent to what he still gripped between his hands. It needed no more than a glance, but he made sure before he released his grasp. Pity clouded his eyes for an instant—Apri was free now, in the freedom she had longed for, the madness gone, the terrible danger that was herself banished. Never again through that gate would Julhi and her followers enter. The door was closed.

THE COLD GRAY GOD

Snow fell over Righa, pole city of Mars. Bitter snow, whirling in ice-hard particles on the thin, keen wind that always seems to blow through Righa's streets. These cobblestoned ways were nearly empty today. Squat stone houses crouched low under the assaults of that storm-laden wind, and the dry snow eddied in long gusts down the reaches of the Lakklan, Righa's central street. The few pedestrians along the Lakklan huddled collars high about their ears and hurried over the cobbles.

But there was one figure in the street that did not hurry. It was a woman's figure, and by the swing of her gait and the high poise of her head one might guess that she was young, but it would be no more than a guess, for the fur cloak she clutched about her muffled every line of her body and the peaked hood of it hid her face. That fur was the sleek white hide of the almost extinct saltland snow-cat, so that one might presuppose her wealth. She walked with a swinging grace rarely encountered in Righa's streets. For Righa is an outlaw city, and young women, wealthy and beautiful and unattended, are seldom seen upon the Lakklan.

She strolled slowly down the broad, uneven way, her long hooded cloak making a white enigma of her. But she was somehow alien to this bleak, bitter scene. That almost dancing litheness which attended her motion, eloquent even through the concealing folds of rich snow-cat fur, was not a characteristic of Martian women, even the pink beauties of the canals. Indefinably she was foreign—exotically foreign.

From the shadow of her hood an eager gaze roved the street, avidly scanning the few faces she passed. They were hard-featured faces for the most part, bleak and cold as the gray city about them. And the eyes that met hers boldly or slyly, according to the type of passer-by, were curiously alike in their furtiveness, their shadow of alert and hunted watching. For men came to Righa quietly, by devious ways, and dwelt in seclusion and departed without ostentation. And their eyes were always wary.

The girl's gaze flicked by them and went on. If they stared after her down the street she did not seem to know, or greatly to care. She paced unhurriedly on over the cobbles.

Ahead of her a broad, low door opened to a burst of noise and music, and warm light streamed briefly out into the gray day as a man stepped over the sill and swung the door shut behind him. Sidelong she watched the man as he belted his heavy coat of brown pole-deer hide and stepped briskly out into the street. He was tall, brown as leather, hard-featured under the pole-deer cap pulled low over his eyes. They were startling, those eyes, cold and steady, icily calm. Indefinably he was of Earth. His scarred dark face had a faintly piratical look, and he was wolfishly lean in his spaceman's leather as he walked lightly down the Lakklan, turning up the deer-hide collar about his ears with one hand. The other, his right, was hidden in the pocket of his coat.

The woman swerved when she saw him. He watched her subtly swaying approach without a flicker of expression on his face. But when she laid a milkily white hand upon his arm he gave a queer little start, involuntarily, like a shiver quickly suppressed. A ripple of annoyance crossed his face briefly and was gone, as if the muscular start had embarrassed him. He turned upon her an absolutely expressionless stare and waited.

"Who are you?" cooed a throatily velvet voice from the depths of the hood.

"Northwest Smith." He said it crisply, and his lips snapped shut again. He moved a little away from her, for her hand still lay upon his right arm, and his right hand was still hidden in the coat pocket. He moved far enough to free his arm, and stood waiting.

"Will you come with me?" Her voice throbbed like a pigeon's from the shadow of her hood.

For a quick instant his pale eyes appraised her, as caution and curiosity warred within him. Smith was a wary man, very wise in the dangers of the spaceways life. Not for a moment did he mistake her meaning. Here was no ordinary woman of the streets. A woman robed in snow-cat furs had no need to accost casual strangers along the Lakklan.

"What do you want?" he demanded. His voice was deep and harsh, and the words fairly clicked with a biting brevity.

"Come," she cooed, moving nearer again and slipping one hand inside his arm. "I will tell you that in my own house. It is so cold here."

Smith allowed himself to be pulled along down the Lakklan, too puzzled and surprised to resist. That simple act of hers had amazed him out of all proportion to its simplicity. He was revising his judgment of her as he walked along over the snow-dust cobbles at her side. For by that richly throaty voice that throbbed as colorfully as a dove's, and by the milky whiteness of her hand on his arm, and by the subtle swaying of her walk, he had been sure, quite sure, that she came from Venus. No other planet breeds such beauty, no other women are born with the instinct of seduction in their very bones. And he had thought, dimly, that he recognized her voice.

But no, if she were Venus-bred, and the woman he half suspected her of being, she would never have slid her arm through his with that little intimate gesture or striven to override his hesitation with the sheer strength of her own charm. His one small motion away from her hand on his arm would have warned a true Venusian not to attempt further intimacy. She would have known by the look in his still eyes, by the wolfish, scarred face, tight-mouthed, that his weakness did not lie along the lines she was mistress of. And if she were the woman he suspected, all this was doubly sure. No, she could not be Venus-bred, nor the woman her voice so recalled to him.

Because of this he allowed her to lead him down the Lakklan. Not often did he permit curiosity to override his native caution, or he would never have come unscathed through the stormy years that lay behind him. But there was something so subtly queer about this woman, so contradictory to his preconceived opinions. Very vital to Smith were his own quick appraisements, and when one went all awry from the lines he intuitively expected, he felt compelled to learn why. He went on at her side, shortening his strides to the gliding gait of the woman on his arm. He did not like the contact of her hand, although he could not have said why.

No further words passed between them until they had reached a low stone building ten minutes' walk on down the Lakklan. She rapped on the heavy door with a quick, measured beat, and it swung open upon dimness. Her bare white hand in the crook of Smith's arm pulled him inside.

A gliding servant took his coat and fur cap. Without ostentation, as he removed the coat he slipped out the gun which had lain in his right hand pocket and upon which his hand had rested all the while he was in the street. He tucked it inside his leather jacket and followed the still cloaked woman down a short hallway and through a low arch under which he had to stoop his head. The room they entered was immemorially ancient, changelessly Martian. Upon the dark stone floor, polished by the feet of countless generations, lay the furs of saltland beasts and the thick-pelted animals of the pole. The stone walls were incised with those inevitable, mysterious symbols which have become nothing more than queer designs now, though a million years ago they bore deep significance. No Martian house, old or new, lacks them, and no living Martian knows their meaning.

Remotely they must be bound up with the queer, cold darkness of that strange religion which once ruled Mars and which dwells still in the heart of every true Martian, though its shrines are secret now and its priests discredited. Perhaps if one could read those symbols they would tell the name of the cold god whom Mars worships still, in its heart of hearts, yet whose name is never spoken.

The whole room was fragrant and a little mysterious with the aromatic fumes of the braziers set at intervals about the irregularly shaped room, and the low ceiling pressed the perfume down so that it hung in smoky layers in the sweet, heavy air.

"Be seated," murmured the woman from the depths of her hood.

Smith glanced about in distaste. The room was furnished in the luxuriant Martian style so at odds with the harsh characteristics of the Martian people. He selected the least voluptuous-looking of the couches and sat down, regarding the woman obliquely as he did so.

She had turned a little away from him now and was slowly unfastening her furs. Then in one slow, graceful motion she flung back the cloak.

Smith caught his breath involuntarily, and a little shiver rippled over him, like the queer shock which had shaken his usually iron poise in the street. He could not be certain whether it were admiration or distaste he felt more strongly. And this despite her breath-taking beauty. Frankly he stared.

Yes, she was Venusian. Nowhere save upon that sunless, mist-drenched planet are such milk-white women bred. Voluptuously slim she was, in the paradoxical Venusian way, and the sweet, firm curves of her under velvet were more eloquent than a love-song. Her deeply crimson robe swathed her close in the traditional Venusian way, leaving one arm and rose-white shoulder bare and slit so that at every other step her milky thigh gleamed through. Heavy lids veiled her eyes from him as she turned. Unmistakably, exquisitely, she was Venusian, and from head to foot so lovely that despite himself Smith's pulses quickened.

He bent forward, eyes eager upon her face. It was flawlessly lovely, the long eyes subtly tilted, the planes of her cheekbones and the set of her chin eloquent of the beauty which dwelt in the very bones beneath her sweet white flesh, so that even her skull must be lovely. And with an odd little catch in his breath, Smith admitted to himself that she was indeed the woman he had guessed. He had not mistaken the throbbing richness of her voice. But—he looked closer, and wondered if he really did catch some hint of—wrongness—in that delicately tinted face, in the oddly averted eyes. For a moment his mind ran backward, remembering.

Judai of Venus had been the toast of three planets a few years past. Her heart-twisting beauty, her voice that throbbed like a dove's, the glowing charm of her had captured the hearts of every audience that heard her sing. Even the far outposts of civilization knew her. That colorful, throaty voice had sounded upon Jupiter's moons and sent the cadences of *Starless Night* ringing over the bare rocks of asteroids and through the darkness of space.

And then she vanished. Men wondered awhile, and there were searches and considerable scandal, but no one saw her again. All that was long past now. No one sang *Starless Night* any more, and it was the Earth-born Rose Robertson's voice which rang through the solar system in lilting praise of *The Green Hills of Earth*. Judai was years forgotten.

Smith knew her in the first glimpse he had of that high-cheeked, rose-tinted face. He had felt before he saw her that surely no two women of the same generation could speak in a voice so richly colored, so throbbingly sweet. And yet there was a hint of something alien in those gorgeously rich tones;

something indefinably wrong in her unforgettable face; something that sent a little shock of distaste through him in the first glimpse he had of her beauty.

Yes, his ears and his eyes told him that she was Judai, but that infallible animal instinct which had saved him so often in such subtly warning ways told him just as surely that she was not—could not be. Judai, of all women, to make such un-Venusian errors of intuition! Feeling a little dizzy, he sat back and waited.

She glided across the floor to his side. The subtly provocative sway of her body as she moved was innately Venusian, but she moved to the couch beside him and allowed her body to touch his in a brushing contact that sent a little thrill through him involuntarily, though he moved away. No, Judai would never have done that. She would have known better.

"You know me—yes?" she queried, richly murmurous.

"We haven't met before," he said non-committally.

"But you know Judai. You remember. I saw it in your eyes. You must keep my secret, Northwest Smith. Can I trust you?"

"That—depends." His voice was dry.

"I left, that night in New York, because something called which was stronger than I. No, it was not love. It was stronger than love, Northwest Smith. I could not resist it."

There was a subtle amusement in her voice, as if she told some secret jest that had meaning to none but her. Smith moved a little farther from her on the couch.

"I have been searching a long while," she went on in her low, rich voice, "for such a man as you—a man who can be entrusted with a dangerous task." She paused.

"What is it?"

"There is a man in Righa who has something I very much want. He lives on the Lakklan by that drinking-house they call The Spaceman's Rest."

Again she paused. Smith knew the place well, a dark, low-roofed den where the shadier and more scrupulously wary transients in Righa gathered. For the Spaceman's Rest was owned by a grim-jawed, leathery old drylander named Mhici, who was rumored to have great influence with the powers in Righa; so that a drink in The Spaceman's Rest was safely taken, without danger of interruption. He knew old Mhici well. He turned a mildly inquiring eye upon Judai, waiting for her to go on.

Her own eyes were lowered, but she seemed to feel his gaze, for she took up her story again instantly, without lifting her lashes.

"The man's name I do not know, but he is of Mars, from the canal-countries, and his face is deeply scarred across both cheeks. He hides what I want in a little ivory box of drylander carving. If you can bring that to me you may name your own reward."

Smith's pale eyes turned again, reluctantly, to the woman beside him. He wondered briefly why he disliked even to look at her, for she seemed lovelier each time his gaze rested upon that exquisitely tinted face. He saw that her eyes were still lowered, the feather lashes brushing her cheeks. She nodded without looking up as he echoed,

"Any price I ask?"

"Money or jewels or—what you will."

"Ten thousand gold dollars to my name in the Great Bank at Lakkjourna, confirmed by viziphone when I hand you the box."

If he expected a flicker of displeasure to cross her face at his matter-of-factness, he was disappointed. She rose in one long gliding motion and stood quietly before him. Smoothly, without lifting her eyes, she said,

"It is agreed, then. I will see you here tomorrow at this hour."

Her voice dropped with a note of finality and dismissal. Smith glanced up into her face, and at what he saw there started to his feet in an involuntary motion, staring undisguisedly. She was standing quite still, with downcast eyes, and all animation and allure were draining away from her face. Uncomprehending, he watched humanity fading as if some glowing inward tide ebbed away, leaving a husk of sweet, inanimate flesh where the radiant Judai had stood a moment before.

An unpleasant little coldness rippled down his back as he watched. Uncertainly he glanced toward the door, feeling more strongly than ever that inexplicable revulsion against some inner alienness he could not understand. As he hesitated, "Go, go!" came in an impatient voice from between her scarcely moving lips. And in almost ludicrous haste he made for the door. His last glance as it swung to of its own weight behind him revealed Judai standing motionless where he had left her, a still figure silhouetted white and scarlet against the immemorial pattern of the wall beyond. And he had a curious impression that a thin gray fog veiled her body in a lowly spreading nimbus that was inexplicably unpleasant.

Dusk was falling as he came out into the street again. A shadowy servant had given him his coat, and Smith departed so quickly that he was still struggling into the sleeves as he stepped out under the low arch of the door and drew a deep breath of the keen, icy air in conscious relief. He could not have explained, even to himself, the odd revulsion which Judai and her house had roused in him, but he was very glad to be free of them both and out in the open street again.

He shrugged himself deep into the warm fur coat and set off with long strides down the Lakklan. He was headed for The Spaceman's Rest. Old Mhici, if Smith found him in the right mood and approached him through the proper devious channels, might have information to give about the lovely lost singer and her strange house—and her credit at the Great Bank of Lakkjourna. Smith had small reason to doubt her wealth, but he took no needless chances.

The Spaceman's Rest was crowded. Smith made his way through the maze of tables toward the long bar at the end of the room, threading the crowd of hard-faced men whose wide diversity of races seemed to make little difference in the curious similarity of expression which dwelt upon every face. They were quiet and watchful-eyed and wore the indefinable air of those who live by their wits and their guns. The low-roofed place was thick with a pungent haze from the *nuari* which nearly all were smoking, and that in itself was evidence that in Mhici's place they considered themselves secure, for *nuari* is mildly opiate.

Old Mhici himself came forward to the voiceless summoning in Smith's single pale-eyed glance as it met his in the crowd about the bar. The Earthman ordered red *segir*-whisky, but he did not drink it immediately.

"I know no one here," he observed in the drylander idiom, which was a flagrant misstatement, but heavy with meaning. For the hospitable old saltlands' custom demands that the proprietor share a drink with any stranger who comes into his bar. It is a relic from the days when strangers were rare in the saltlands, and is very seldom recalled in populous cities like Righa, but Mhici understood. He said nothing, but he took the black Venusian bottle of *segir* by the neck and motioned Smith toward a corner table that stood empty.

When they were settled there and Mhici had poured himself a drink, Smith took one gulp of the red whisky and hummed the opening bars of *Starless Night*, watching the old drylander's pointed, leathery features. One of Mhici's eyebrows went up, which was the equivalent of a start of surprise in another man.

"Starless nights," he observed, "are full of danger, Smith."

"And of pleasure sometimes, eh?"

"Ur-r! Not this one."

"Oh?"

"No. And where I do not understand, I keep away."

"You're puzzled too, eh?"

"Deeply. What happened?"

Smith told him briefly. He knew that it is proverbial never to trust a drylander, but he felt that old Mhici was the exception. And by the old man's willingness to come to the point with a minimum of fencing and circumlocution he knew that he must be very perturbed by Judai's presence in Righa. Old Mhici missed little, and if he was puzzled by her presence Smith felt that his own queer reactions to the Venusian beauty had not been unjustified.

"I know the box she means," Mhici told him when he had finished. "There's the man, over there by the wall. See?"

Under his brows Smith studied a lean, tall canal-dweller with a deeply scarred face and an air of restless uneasiness. He was drinking some poisonously green concoction and smoking *nuari* so heavily that the clouds of it veiled his face. Smith grunted contemptuously.

"If the box is valuable he's not putting himself into any shape to guard it," he said. "He'll be dead asleep in half an hour if he keeps that up."

"Look again," murmured Mhici. And Smith, wondering a little at the dryness of the old man's voice, turned his head and studied the canal-dweller more carefully.

This time he saw what had escaped him before. The man was frightened, so frightened that the *nuari* pouring in and out of his lungs was having little effect. His restless eyes were hot with anxiety, and he had maneuvered his back to the wall so that he could command the whole room as he drank. That in itself, here in Mhici's place, was flagrant. Mhici's iron fist and ready gun had established order in The Spaceman's Rest long ago, and no man in years had dared break it. Mhici commanded not only physical but also moral respect, for his influence with the powers of Righa was exerted not only to furnish immunity to his guests but also to punish peace-breakers. The Spaceman's Rest was sanctuary. No, for a man to sit with his back to the wall here bespoke terror of something more deadly than guns.

"They're following him, you know," Mhici murmured over the rim of his glass. "He stole that box somewhere along the canals, and now he's afraid of his shadow. I don't know what's in the box, but it's damn valuable to someone and they're out to get it at any cost. Do you still want to relieve him of it?"

Smith squinted at the drylander through narrowed eyes. How old Mhici learned the secrets he knew, no one could guess, but he had never been caught in error. And Smith had little desire to call down upon himself the enmity of whatever perils it was which kindled the fear of death in the canal-dweller's eyes. Yet curiosity rode him still. The puzzle of Judai was a tantalizing mystery which he felt he must solve.

"Yes," he said slowly. "I've got to know."

"I'll get you the box," said Mhici suddenly. "I know where he hides it, and there's a way between here and the house next door that will let me at it in five minutes. Wait here."

"No," said Smith quickly. "That's not fair to you. I'll get it."

Mhici's wide mouth curved.

"I'm in little danger," he said. "Here in Righa no one would dare—and besides, that way is secret. Wait."

Smith shrugged. After all, Mhici knew how to take care of himself. He sat there gulping down *segir* as he waited, and watching the canal-dweller across the room. Terror played in changing patterns across the scarred face.

When Mhici reappeared he carried a small wooden crate labeled conspicuously in Venusian characters. Smith translated, "Six Pints Segir, Vanda Distilleries, Ednes, Venus."

"It's in this," murmured Mhici, setting down the box. "You'd better stay here tonight. You know, the back room that opens on the alley."

"Thanks," said Smith in some embarrassment. He was wondering why the old drylander had taken such pains in his behalf. He had expected no more than a few words of warning. "I'll split the money, you know."

Mhici shook his head.

"I don't think you'll get it," he said candidly. "And I don't think she really wants the box. Not half so much as she wants you, anyhow. There were any number of men who could have got the box for her. And you remember how she said she'd been looking a long time for someone like yourself. No, it's the man she wants, I think. And I can't figure out why."

Smith wrinkled his brows and traced a design on the tabletop in split *segir*.

"I've got to know," he said stubbornly.

"I've passed her in the street. I've felt that same revulsion, and I don't know why. I don't like this, Smith. But if you feel you have to go through with it, that's your affair. I'll help if I can. Let's drop it, eh? What are you doing tonight? I hear there's a new dancer at the Lakktal now."

Much later, in the shifting light of Mars' hurrying moons, Smith stumbled up the little alley behind The Spaceman's Rest and entered the door in the rear of the bar. His head was a bit light with much *segir*, and the music and the laughter and the sound of dancing feet in the Lakktal's halls made an echoing beat through his head. He undressed clumsily in the dark and stretched himself with a heavy sigh on the leather couch which is the Martian bed.

Just before sleep overtook him he found himself remembering Judai's queer little quirking smile when she said, "I left New York because something called—stronger than love. . . ." And he thought drowsily, "What is stronger than love? . . ." The answer came to him just as he sank into oblivion. "Death."

Smith slept late the next day. The tri-time steel watch on his wrist pointed to Martian noon when old Mhici himself pushed open the door and carried in a tray of breakfast.

"There's been excitement this morning," he observed as he set down his burden.

Smith sat up and stretched luxuriously.

"What?"

"The canal man shot himself."

Smith's pale eyes sought out the case labeled "Six Pints Segir" where it stood in the corner of the room. His brows went up in surprise.

"Is it so valuable as that?" he murmured. "Let's look at it."

Mhici shot the bolts on the two doors as Smith rose from the leather couch and dragged the box into the center of the floor. He pried up the thin board that Mhici had nailed down the night before over the twice-stolen box, and pulled out an object wrapped in brown canvas. With the old drylander bending over his shoulder he unwound the wrappings. For a full minute thereafter he squatted on his heels staring in perplexity at the thing in his hands. It was not large, this little ivory box, perhaps ten inches by four, and four deep. Its intricate drylander carving struck him as remotely familiar, but he had been staring at it for several seconds before it dawned upon him where he had seen those odd spirals and queer twisted characters before. Then he remembered. No wonder they looked familiar, for they had stared down upon him bafflingly from the walls of countless Martian dwellings. He lifted his eyes and saw a band of them circling the walls above him now. But they were large, and these on the box intricately tiny, so that at first glance they looked like the merest waving lines incised delicately all over the box's surface.

Not until then, following those crawling lines, did he see that the box had no opening. To all appearances it was not a box at all, but a block of carved ivory. He shook it, and something within shifted slightly, as if it were packed in loose wrappings. But there was no opening anywhere. He turned it over and over, peering and prying, but to no avail. Finally he shrugged and wrapped the canvas back about the enigma.

"What do you make of it?" he asked.

Mhici shook his head.

"'Great Shar alone can tell,'" he murmured half in derision, for Shar is the Venusian god, a friendly deity whose name rises constantly to the lips of the Hot Planet's dwellers. The god whom Mars worships, openly or in secret, is never named aloud.

They discussed the puzzle of it off and on the rest of the afternoon. Smith spent the hours restlessly, for he dared not smoke *nuari* nor drink much, with the interview so close ahead. When the shadows were lengthening along the Lakklan he got into his deerhide coat again and tucked the ivory box into an inner pocket. It was bulky, but not betrayingly so. And he made sure his flame-gun was charged and ready.

In the late afternoon sun that sparkled blindingly upon the snow crystals blowing along the wind, he went down the Lakklan again with his right hand in his pocket and his eyes raking the street warily under the shadow of his cap. Evidently the pursuers of that box had not traced it, for he was not followed.

Judai's house squatted dark and low at the edge of the Lakklan. Smith fought down a rising revulsion as he lifted his hand to knock, but the door swung open before his knuckles had touched the panel. That same shadowy servant beckoned him in. This time he did not put his gun away when he shifted it from his coat pocket. He took the canvas-wrapped box in one hand and the flame-pistol in the other, and the servant opened the door he had passed last night upon the room where Judai was waiting.

She stood exactly as he had left her in the center of the floor, white and scarlet against the queer traceries on the wall beyond. He had the curious notion that she had not stirred since he left her last night. She moved a little sluggishly as she turned her head and saw him, but it was a lethargy which she quickly overcame. She motioned him toward the divan, taking her seat at his side with the flowing, feline ease of every true Venusian. And as before, he shrank involuntarily from the contact of that fragrant, velvet-sheathed body, with an inner revulsion he could not understand.

She said nothing, but she held out her two hands cupped up in entreaty, and she did not lift her eyes to his face as she did so. He laid the box in her upturned palm. At that moment for the first time it occurred to him that not once had he met her eyes. She had never lifted those veiling lashes and looked into his. Wondering, he watched.

She was unwrapping the canvas with quick, delicate motions of her pink-stained fingers. When the box lay bare in her hands she sat quite motionless for a while, her lowered eyes fixed upon the carven block of the thing which had cost at least one life. And her quiet was unnatural, trance-like. He thought she must have ceased to breathe. Not a lash fluttered, not a pulse stirred in her round white wrists as she held the little symbol-traced box up. There was something indescribably horrid in her quiet as she sat and stared, all her being centered in one vast, still concentration upon the ivory box.

Then he heard such a deep breath rush out through her nostrils that it might have been life itself escaping, a breath that thinned into a high, shuddering hum like the whine of wind through wires. It was not a sound that any human creature could make.

Without realizing that he had moved, Smith leaped. Of their own volition his muscles tensed into a spring of animal terror away from that high-whining thing on the couch. He ground himself half crouched a dozen paces away, his gun steady in a lifted hand and his hair stiffening at the roots as he faced her. For by the thin, high, shuddering noise he knew surely that she was not human.

For a long instant he crouched there, taut, feeling his scalp crawl with a prickling terror as his pale eyes searched for some reason in this madness which had come over them both. She still sat rigid, with lowered eyes, but though she had not stirred, something told him unerringly that his first instinct had been right, his first intuitive flinching from her hand on his arm—she was not human. Warm white flesh and fragrant hair and subtle, curving roundness of her under velvet, all this was camouflage to conceal—to conceal—he could not guess what, but he knew that loveliness for a lie, and all down his back the nerves tingled with man's involuntary shudder from the unknown.

She rose. Cradling the ivory box against the sweet high curve of her bosom, she moved slowly forward, her lashes making two dim crescents on her exquisitely tinted cheeks. He had never seen her lovelier, or more hideously repulsive. For in some obscure part of his brain he knew that the humanity which she had clutched like a cloak about her was being dropped. In another instant . . .

She paused before him, very near, so near that the muzzle of his half-forgotten gun was pressed against the velvet that sheathed her body, and the fragrance of her rose in a vague cloud to his nostrils. For one tense instant they stood so, she with lowered lashes, cradling her ivory box, he rigid with prickling revulsion, gun nosing her side, pale eyes set in a narrow-lidded stare as he waited shudderingly for what must come next. In the split second before her eyelids rose, he wanted overwhelmingly to fling up a hand and shut out the sight of what lay behind them, to run blindly out of the room and out of the house and never stop until the doors of The Spaceman's Rest closed shelteringly upon him. He could not stir. Caught in a frozen trance, he stared. The lashes fluttered. Slowly, very slowly, her lids rose.

The cold shock that jolted him into incredulity then made every detail of the picture so clear that he was never to forget, no matter how hard he tried, the vividness of that first glimpse into Judai's eyes. Yet for a full minute he did not realize what he saw. It was too incredible for the brain to grasp. With thickly beating heart he stood rigid, staring into the weird face turned to his.

From under those deep-curved lashes looked out no such luminous depths of darkness as he had expected. There were no eyes behind Judai's creamy lids. Instead he was looking into two lash-fringed, almond-shaped pits of gray smoke, smoke that seethed and shifted and boiled within itself, unresting as smoke from the fires of hell. He knew then that there dwelt in the curved and milk-white body which had been Judai's a thing more evil than any devil hell's fire ever spawned. How it came into that body he never knew, but he did know that the real Judai was gone. Looking into that restlessly seething smoky blindness, he was sure of that, and revulsion surged through him as he strained at his own body for the will to blast this hell-tenanted beauty into nothingness, and could not stir. Helpless in the frozen grip of his own horror, he watched.

She—it stood straight before him, staring blankly. And he was aware of a slow seepage from the gray pits of the eyes. Smoke was curling out into the room in delicate whirls and plumes. Sickness came over him as he realized it, and an extravagant terror, for it was not the sweet-smelling, clean smoke of fire. There was no physically perceptible odor to it, but from the unspeakably evil stench his very soul shuddered away. He could smell evil, taste it, perceive it with more senses than he knew he possessed, despite the intangibility of the swirling stuff that billowed now in deepening waves from under the lash-fringed lids that once had been Judai's. Once before he had been dimly aware of this, when he had looked back as he left, the night before, to see that vague gray veiling a woman's milk-whiteness in obscurity that was somehow—unpleasant. Even that remote hinting at what he saw now in full strength had been enough to send a warning shudder through him. But now—now it billowed about him in thickening deeps through which he could scarcely make out the pale shape of the figure before him, and the grayness was seeping through his body and mind and soul with a touch more dreadful than the touch of every ugly thing in creation. It was not tangible, but it was slimier and more unclean than anything he could have named. Not upon his flesh but upon his soul that wet slime crawled.

Dimly through the swirl of it he saw the lips of Judai's body move. A ghost of a voice fluted into the grayness, a sweet, rich, throbbing thread of sound. So lovely had been Judai's voice that even the horror which stirred it now into speech could not evoke discords from a throat that had never uttered any sound but music.

"I am ready to take you now, Northwest Smith. The time has come to discard this body and these ways of seduction and put on a man's strength and straightforwardness, so that I may complete what I came to do. I shall not need it long, but your force and vitality I must have before I surrender them up to mighty———. And then I may go forth in my true form to bring the worlds under great———'s reign."

Smith blinked. There had been a gap in her words where he should have heard a name, but it had not been a gap of silence. Her lips had moved, though no sound came forth, and the air shook with a wordless cadence so deeply stirring that he felt involuntary awe—if it were possible to feel awe at the utterance of a word without sound.

That sweetly murmurous voice was whispering through the fog that had thickened now until he could scarcely see the outlines of the figure before him.

"I have waited so long for you, Northwest Smith—for a man with a body and a brain like yours, to serve my needs. I take you now, in great——'s name. In that name, I bid you surrender your body. Go!"

The last word cracked through the mist, and abruptly blindness swept over him. His feet no longer pressed the floor. He was wallowing in a fog of such revolting horror that his very soul writhed within him for escape. Slimily the gray stuff seeped through his being, crawling and sliding and oozing, and the touch of it upon his brain was a formless madness, so that the soul which shuddered from such indescribable dreadfulness would have fled into hell itself to escape.

Dimly he knew what was happening. His body was being made untenable to force his consciousness to leave it. And knowing this, realizing what its portent was, yet he found himself struggling desperately for release. The crawling ooze was a slime upon his very soul. There could be no alternative so frightful as this sickening reality. Madness was in the frightened writhing of self to escape the horror that enfolded him. Frantically he fought for release.

It came suddenly. He was aware of a distinct snapping, as of something tangible, and then freedom. On the instant those gray, crawling swaths of revulsion ceased to be. He floated free and light and impalpable in a void without light or dark, conscious of nothing but the blessed release from torment.

Gradually realization came back to him. He had no form or substance now, but he was aware. And he knew that he must seek his body again; how, he did not know, but the thought of it was a poignant longing, and his whole intangible being so concentrated upon that thought that in a moment or two the room he had left began to take shape about him, and his own tall figure swam hazily through the veiling fog. With a mighty effort he bent his thoughts upon that figure, and at last began to understand what was taking place.

He could see now with clear, unhampered vision around all points of the compass at once. Floating in nothingness, he watched the room. It was a little difficult at first to see any one thing, for he no longer had the focus of eyes to help him and the room was a wide panorama without center. But after a while he learned the trick of concentration, and saw clearly for the first time his own relinquished self, broad and tall and leather-brown, standing rigid in the midst of a sliding fog that curled about it in thick, slimy glidings which brought back memories of sickening vividness. At the feet of that brown, fog-veiled shape lay the body of Judai. Exquisitely graceful, it stretched in a glimmer of white and scarlet across the dark floor. He knew she was dead now. The breath of alien life which had been infused into her was withdrawn. Death's curious flatness was eloquent in the piteously lovely body rounding under the velvet robe. The Thing was done with her.

He turned his attention again to his own body. That horribly alive fog had thickened still more, into heavy, half-palpable robes of sliding slime that crawled unceasingly over and around the tall figure. But it was disappearing. It was seeping slowly, remorselessly, into the flesh he had vacated. Now it was more than half gone, and into that frozen body a semblance of life was stealing. He watched while the last of the gray stuff which was the Thing took possession of his lost self, waking it into a cold and alien life. He saw it seize upon the nerves and muscles he had trained, so that its first motion was the familiar quick gesture to slip the flame-gun into its holster under his arm. He saw his own broad shoulders shrug unconsciously to be sure the strap was in place. He watched himself crossing the room with the long, light steps that had once been his. He saw his own hands pick up the ivory box from the slim, pink-stained fingers of Judai.

Not until then did he realize that thoughts were open to his reading now, as clearly as words had been before. The only thoughts in the room had been the alien ones of the Thing, and until this moment they had not taken forms human enough to have meaning to him. But now he began to understand many things, and the strangeness of them whirled through his consciousness in half-incomprehensible patterns.

Then abruptly a name flashed through those thoughts, and the power of it struck him with such force that for an instant his hold upon the scene slipped and he whirled back into that void again where neither light nor darkness dwelt. As he fought his way back into the room his unbodied mind was struggling to put together the pieces of newly acquired knowledge, in which that name flamed like a beacon, the center and focus for all the patterns of the knowledge.

It was the name his ears had not been able to hear when Judai's lips spoke it. He knew now that though human lips could frame its syllables, no brain that was wholly human could send the impulses for that framing; so that it could never be spoken by a sane man, nor heard or understood by him. Even so, the wordless vibrations of it had eddied through his brain in waves of awe. And now, when its unveiled force struck full upon his unprotected consciousness, the mightiness of that name was enough to send him reeling all out of focus and control.

For it was the name of a Thing so powerful that even in his unreality he shuddered at the thought; a thing whose full might no flesh-veiled consciousness could grasp. Only in his disembodied awareness could he realize it, and he turned his mind away from that awful name even as he delved deeper into the alien thoughts that flashed before him from the creature which wore his semblance.

He knew now why the Thing had come. He knew the purpose of that which bore the name. And he knew why the men of Mars never spoke their cold god's title. They could not. It was not a name human brains could grasp or human lips utter without compulsion from Outside. Slowly the origins of that curious religion took shape in his mind.

The name had dwelt like some vast, brooding shadow among the earliest ancestors of Martian men, millions upon millions of years ago. It had come from its lair Outside, and dwelt dreadfully among mankind, sucking life from its worshippers and reigning with such awe and terror that even now, after countless eons had gone by, though its very existence was forgotten, that terror and awe lived yet in the minds of these remote descendants.

Nor was the name wholly gone, even now. It had withdrawn, for reasons too vast for comprehension. But it had left behind it shrines, and each of them was a little doorway into that presence, so that the priests who tended them furnished tribute. Sometimes they were possessed by the power of their god, and spoke the name which their devotees could not hear, yet whose awful cadences were a storm of power about them. And this was the origin of that strange, dark religion which upon Mars has been discredited for so long, though it has never died in the hearts of men.

Smith understood now that the Thing which dwelt in his body was a messenger from Outside, although he could never quite grasp in what capacity. It might have been a part of that vast composite power which bore the name. He never knew. Its thoughts when they wandered in that direction were too alien to carry any meaning into his mind. When it even turned those thoughts backward toward its origin, and the might of the name flashed through them, Smith quickly learned to shrink within himself, withdrawing his consciousness until that thought had passed. It was like gazing through an opened door into the furnaces of hell.

He watched himself turn the box slowly over between his hands, while his own pale eyes searched its surface. Or were they his eyes? Did there dwell now under his own lids the grayness of the Thing? He could not be sure, for he could not bring himself to concentrate directly upon that foggy dweller within his body. Its touch was so alien, so repulsive.

Now his hands had found some hidden opening. He could not tell exactly what happened, but suddenly he saw himself wrenching at the ivory box, with a queer, twisting motion, and the two halves of it fell apart along an uneven line of cleavage. Out of it a thick mist rose, a heavy, semitangible stuff in which the hands of his body groped as if through folds of cloth.

Sluggishly the mist spilled floorward, while from the box

he saw himself drawing a thing which cleared away a little of the mystery that shrouded so much of what had happened. For he recognized the curious symbol that had lain in the mist-filled box. It was wrought from a substance which has no duplicate anywhere on the three worlds, a translucent metal through whose depths a smoky dimness was diffused in vague curls and plumes. And its shape was the duplicate of a symbol repeated often in the wall-carvings of every Martian house. Smith had heard whispers of this talisman passed from mouth to mouth in the secrecy of space-pirates' rendezvous. For its very existence was a secret to all save those rovers of the spaceways from whom nothing is wholly hidden.

The symbol, so those whispers said, was a talisman from the old religion, used in the worship of the nameless god in the ages before discredit had forced the worship into secrecy—a thing of terrible power had any living man known how to use it. It was said to be kept in inviolable hiding somewhere in one of the canal cities. He understood now in what terror the canal-dweller with the scarred face must have gone, knew why he had not dared face the consequences of his own theft. The priests of the name were held in the more terror for the darkness of their calling.

The story behind that theft he was never to know. It was enough that the Thing had the priceless talisman now. Through his own efforts that immemorial symbol had fallen into the only hands which would know how to wield it: paradoxically, the hands that had once been his. Helplessly he watched.

His own fingers lifted it up familiarly. It was not more than twelve inches long, a thing of subtle curves and arcs. Suddenly he knew what the symbol meant. From the cloudy alienness of the mind which dwelt where his mind had dwelt, he drew the certainty that the talisman had been wrought into the shape of the written name: that unspeakable word, crystallized into nameless metal. The Thing handled it with a sort of unhuman awe.

He watched himself turning slowly round as if in an effort to orient his body with some unknown point at a measureless distance. His hand, holding the symbol, rose high. The room was full of a tense solemnity, an unbreathing hush, as if some long-awaited moment of tremendous awe and portent had been reached at last. Slowly, with stiff steps, his lost body paced toward the eastern wall, the symbol held rigidly before it.

At that tracery-incised wall it stopped, and with a gesture full of ritualistic slowness lifted the talisman and set its curved apex against an identical symbol on the wall, the carven counterpart of the name. And from that point it drew the talisman down and crosswise as if it were painting an unseen curve on the wall. As he watched that moving apex Smith realized what was happening. Invisibly, with the metal-wrought talisman following lines in the symbols on the wall, it was tracing that name. And the ritual was invested with a depth of power and a nameless portent that sent sudden terror thrilling through him. What was the meaning of it?

Cold with a bodiless chill of foreboding, he watched the rite to its close. The talisman sketched the last lines of that pattern upon the wall, completely enclosing a space that covered perhaps six square feet of tracery. And then his own tall body flourished the metal symbol like one who welcomes a caller through an opened door, and dropped to its knees before the outlined pattern.

For a minute—for two minutes—nothing happened. Then, watching the wall, Smith thought he could discern the shape of the symbol that had been traced. Somehow it was becoming clear among the painted characters. Somehow a grayness was spreading within the outlines he had watched his own hands trace, a fogginess that strengthened and grew clearer and clearer, until he could no longer make out the traceries enclosed within its boundaries, and a great, misty symbol stood out vividly across the wall.

He did not understand for a moment. He watched the grayness take on density and grow stronger with each passing moment, but he did not understand until a long curl of fog drifted lazily out into the room, and the grayness began to spill over its own edges and eddy and billow as if that wall were afire. And from very far away, over measureless voids, he caught the first faint impact of a power so great that he knew in one flash the full horror of what he watched.

The name, traced upon that wall with its own metal counterpart, had opened a doorway for the Thing which bore the name to enter. It was coming back to the world it had left millions of years ago. It was oozing through the opened door, and nothing he could do would stop it.

He was a bodiless awareness drifting through voids that held neither light nor dark—he was a nothingness, and he must watch his own body bring down the destruction of the worlds he had dwelt in without any strength to oppose a feather's weight of resistance.

Despairingly he watched a long plume of the dawning terror brush his body's bent head. At the contact that body rose stiffly, as if in answer to a command, and backed slowly across the room to where the body of Judai lay sprawled upon the floor. It stooped like an automaton and lifted her in its arms. It came forward again, walking mechanically, and laid her down under the billowing symbol that was a gateway into deeper depths than hell. The smoke wreathed downward hungrily, hiding the white and scarlet of her from view.

For an instant it writhed and boiled about the spot where she had been engulfed, and the impact of greater force struck in one mighty olow against Smith's consciousness. For across the measureless gulfs the power of the name was nearing. Whatever of energy it had absorbed from the body of Judai had brought it nearer with a long leap, so that now the might of it echoed round and round the symbol-walled room like the beat of drums. There was triumph in that beating. Remotely, in the recurrent waves of thunderous power, he understood at last the purpose of those symbols.

All this had been planned eons ago, when the Unnamable One departed from Mars. Perhaps the ages had been no more than a moment to its timeless might. But it had left with full meaning to return, and so had given more deeply than time could erase on the minds of its worshippers the need for those symbols upon their walls. Only the need; not the reason. They were to make full access into this world possible again. The remote touch which its priests kept through their shrines to the Nameless One were like tiny windows, but here, hidden among the traceries, opened a mighty gateway through which all that measureless power could sweep irresistibly when the hour came. And it had come.

Dimly he caught a vision of triumph from the mind of the Thing which stood rigid in his body before the billowing wall, a vision of other worlds wherever the symbols were graven opening like doors for the great gray surges to come flooding through, a vision of worlds engulfed and seething in one unbroken blanket of gray that writhed and eddied and sucked avidly at the bodies and souls of men.

Smith's consciousness shuddered in the void where it drifted, raged against its own helplessness, watched in horror-struck fascination the surges of billowing gray that rolled slowly into the room. The body of Judai had wholly vanished now. And the long fog-fingers were groping blindly as if in search for other food. In a swimming horror he watched his own tall body stumble forward and sink to its knees under the plumes of ravenous gray.

Somehow the vivid despair of that moment was strong enough to do something which nothing that preceded it had accomplished. The prospect of the world's destruction had made him sick with a hopeless dread; but the thought of his own body offered up as a sacrifice to the flooding gray, leaving him to drift for eternity through voids, cracked like a whiplash against his consciousness in one flash of hot rebellion that jerked him all out of focus to the scene he watched. Violent revolt surged up in him against the power of the Thing and the awful force of that which bore the name.

How it happened he did not know, but suddenly he was no longer floating disembodied through nothingness. Suddenly he was bursting the bonds that parted him from reality. Suddenly he was violently back again into the world from which he had been thrust, fighting desperately to gain access once more into his body, struggling in panic terror to force an entry against the thick grayness of what dwelt there now. It was a nauseous and revolting struggle, so close to the slimy presence of the Thing, but he scarcely heeded its nearness in his frenzy to save the body that was his.

For the moment he was not striving for full possession, but

he pushed and raged and fought to seize his own muscles and drag his body back from the billows that were rolling hungrily toward it. It was a more desperate struggle than any hand-to-hand combat, the struggle of two entities for a single body.

The Thing that opposed him was strong, and firmly entrenched in the nerve-centers and brain-cells that had been his, but he was fighting the more hotly for the familiarity of the field he sought to win. And slowly he won entrance. Perhaps it was because he was not striving at first for full possession. In its struggles to cling fast to what it held, the Thing could not oppose his subtle sliding in among the centers that controlled motion, and by jerky degrees he dragged his own body to its feet and backward, step by hotly contested step, away from the seething pattern that oozed upon the wall. Sick to the very soul with the closeness of the Thing, he fought.

He was struggling now to force it wholly out, and if he was not driving it away, at least he held his own. It could not dislodge him from the foothold he had won. There were flashes when he saw the room through his own eyes again, and felt the strength of his body like a warm garment about the nakedness of the self which strove for its possession, yet a body through which crawled and slid the dreadfulness of that sickening fog-fluid which was a slime upon his innermost soul.

But the Thing was strong. It had rooted its tendrils deep in the body he fought for, and would not let go. And through the room in recurrent thunders beat the might of the coming name, impatient, insistent, demanding sustenance that it might pass wholly through the gateway. Its long fog-fingers stretched clutchingly out into the room. And in Smith a faint hope was growing that it must have his body before it could come farther. If he could prevent that, perhaps all was not yet lost. If he could prevent it—but the Thing he struggled with was strong. . . .

Time had ceased to have meaning for him. In a dream of horror he wallowed amid the thick and sickening slime of his enemy, fighting for a more precious thing than his own life.

He fought for Death. For if he could not win his body, yet he knew he must enter it long enough to die somehow, by his own hand, cleanly; else he would drift through eternity in the void where neither light nor darkness dwelt. How long it went on he never knew. But in one of those moments when he had won a place in his own body again, and perceived with its senses, he heard the sound of an opening door.

With infinite effort he twisted his head around. Old Mhici stood in the opening, flame-gun in hand, blinking bewilderedly into the fog-dim room. There was a dawning terror in his eyes as he stared, a terror deep-rooted and age-old, heritage from those immemorial ancestors upon whose minds the name had been graven too deeply for time to efface. Half comprehending, he stood in the presence of the god of his fathers, and Smith could see a paralyzing awe creeping slowly across his face. He could not have known from the sight of that fog-oozing wall what it was he looked upon, but an inner consciousness seemed to make clear to him that the thing which bore the name was a presence in the room. And it must have realized Mhici's presence, for about the walls in tremendous beats of command roared the thunderous echoes of that far-away might, ravenous to feed again upon man. Old Mhici's eyes glazed with obedience. He stumbled forward one mechanical step.

Something cracked in Smith's consciousness. If Mhici reached the wall, all his struggles would be for nothing. With that nourishment the name might enter. Well, at any rate he could save himself—perhaps. He must die before that happened. And with all the strength that was in him summoned up in one last despairing surge he crowded the Thing that dwelt with him momentarily out of control, and fell upon Mhici with clawed hands clutching for his throat.

Whether the old drylander understood or not, whether he could see in the pale eyes that had been his friend's the slow writhing of the Thing, Smith could not guess. He saw the horror and incredulity upon the leathery features of the Martian as he lunged, and then, in blessed relief, felt wiry fingers at his own neck. Yet he knew that Mhici was striving not to injure him, and he struggled in desperation to lash the old drylander into self-defensive fury. He struck and gouged and tore, and felt in overwhelming relief the old man's strong grip tighten at last about his neck.

He relaxed then in the oncoming oblivion of those releasing fingers.

From very far away a hoarse voice calling his name dragged Smith up through layer upon layer of cloudy nothingness. He opened heavy eyes and stared. Gradually old Mhici's anxious face swam into focus above him. *Segir* was burning in his mouth. He swallowed automatically, and the pain of his bruised throat as the fiery liquid went down roused him into full consciousness. He struggled to a sitting position, pressing one hand to his reeling head and blinking dazedly about.

He lay upon the dark stone floor where oblivion had overtaken him. The patterned walls looked down. His heart suddenly leaped into thick beating. He twisted round, seeking that wall which had oozed grayness through a door that opened upon Outside. And with such relief that he sank back against Mhici's shoulder in sudden weakness, he saw that the Unnamable One no longer billowed out into the room. Instead, that wall was a cracked and charred ruin down which long streams of half-melted rock were congealing. The room was pungent and choking with the odor of a flame-gun's blast.

He turned questioning eyes to Mhici, croaking something inarticulate in the depths of his swollen throat.

"I—I burnt it," said Mhici in a strange half-shame.

Smith jerked his head round again and stared at the ruined wall, a hot chagrin flooding over him. Of course, if the pattern were destroyed, that door would close through which the One which bore the name was entering. Somehow that had never occurred to him. Somehow he had wholly forgotten that a flame-gun was sheathed under his arm during all the long struggle he had held with the Thing co-dwelling in his body. He realized in a moment why. The awful power which in his bodiless state had thundered about him from that infinity of might which bore the name was so measureless that the very thought of a flame-gun seemed too futile to dwell upon. But Mhici had not known. He had never felt that vast furnace-blast of force beating about him. And quite simply, with one flash of his ray-gun, he had closed the door to Outside.

His voice was beating insistently in Smith's ears, shaking with emotion and reaction, and cracking a little now and then like the voice of an old man. For the first time old Mhici was showing his age.

"What happened? What in your own God's name—no, don't tell me now. Don't try to talk. I—I—you can tell me later." And then rapidly, in disjointed sentences, as if he were talking to drown out the sound of his own thoughts, "Perhaps I can guess—never mind. Hope I haven't hurt you. You must have been crazy, Smith. Better now? After you—you—when I saw you on the floor, there was a—well, a fog, I guess—thick as slime, that came rolling up from you like—I can't say what. And suddenly I was mad. That awful gray, rolling out of the wall—I don't know what happened. First I knew I was blazing away into the depths of it, and then the wall beyond cracked and melted, and the whole fog mass was fading out. Don't know why. Don't know what happened then. I must have been—out—a little while myself. It's gone now. I don't know why, but it's gone. . . .

"Here, have some more *segir*."

Smith stared up at him unseeingly. A vague wonder was circling in his mind as to why the Thing that had tenanted his body surrendered. Perhaps Mhici had choked life out of that body, so that the Thing had to flee and his own consciousness could enter unopposed. Perhaps—he gave it up. He was too tired to think about it now. He was too tired to think at all. He sighed deeply and reached for the *segir* bottle.

YVALA

Northwest Smith leaned against a pile of hemp-wrapped bales from the Martian drylands and stared with expressionless eyes, paler than pale steel, over the confusion of the Lakkdarol space-port before him. In the clear Martian day the tatters of his leather spaceman's garb were pitilessly plain, the ray-burns and the rents of a hundred casual brawls. It was evident at a glance that Smith had fallen upon evil days. One might have guessed by the shabbiness of his clothing that his pockets were empty, the charge in his raygun low.

Squatting on his heels beside the lounging Earthman, Yarol the Venusian bent his yellow head absently over the thin-bladed dagger which he was juggling in one of the queer, interminable Venusian games so pointless to outsiders. Upon him too the weight of ill fortune seemed to have pressed heavily. It was eloquent in his own shabby garments, his empty holster. But the insouciant face he lifted to Smith was as careless as ever, and no more of weariness and wisdom and pure cat-savagery looked out from his sidelong black eyes than Smith was accustomed to see there. Yarol's face was the face of a seraph, as so many Venusian faces are likely to be, but the set of his mouth told a tale of dissoluteness and reckless violence which belied his features' racial good looks.

"Another half-hour and we eat," he grinned up at his tall companion.

Smith glanced at the tri-time watch on his wrist.

"If you haven't been having another dope dream," he grunted. "Luck's been against us so long I can't quite believe in a change now."

"By Pharol I swear it," smiled Yarol. "The man came up to me in the *New Chicago* last night and told me in so many words how much money was waiting if we'd meet him here at noon."

Smith grunted again and deliberately took up another notch in the belt that circled his lean waist. Yarol laughed softly, a murmur of true Venusian sweetness, as he bent again to the juggling of his knife. Above his bent blond head Smith looked out again across the busy port.

Lakkdarol is an Earthman's town upon Martian soil, blending all the more violent elements of both worlds in its lawless heart, and the scene he watched had under-currents that only a ranger of the spaceways could fully appreciate. A semblance of discipline is maintained there, but only the space-rangers know how superficial that likeness is. Smith grinned a little to himself, knowing that the bales being trundled down the gangplank from the Martian liner *Inghti* carried a core of that precious Martian "lamb's-wool" on which the duties run so high. And a whisper had run through the *New Chicago* last night as they sat over their *segir*-whisky glasses that the shipment of grain from Denver expected in at noon on the *Friedland* would have a copious leavening of opium in its heart. By devious ways, in whispers running from mouth to mouth covertly through the spacemen's rendezvous, the outlaws of the spaceways glean more knowledge than the Patrol ever knows.

Smith watched a little air-freight vessel, scarcely a quarter the size of the monstrous ships of the Lines, rolling sluggishly out from the municipal hangar far across the square, and a little frown puckered his brows. The ship bore only the non-commercial numerals which all the freighters carry by way of identification, but that particular sequence was notorious among the initiate. The ship was a slaver.

This dealing in human freight had received a great impetus at the stimulation of space-travel, when the temptation presented by the savage tribes on alien planets was too great to be ignored by unscrupulous Earthmen who saw vast fields opening up before them. For even upon Earth slaving has never died entirely, and Mars and Venus knew a small and legitimate traffic in it before John Willard and his gang of outlaws made the very word "slaving" anathema on three worlds. The Willards still ran their pirate convoys along the spaceways three generations later, and Smith knew he was looking at one now, smuggling a cargo of misery out of Lakkdarol for distribution among the secret markets of Mars.

Further meditations on the subject were cut short by Yarol's abrupt rise to his feet. Smith turned his head slowly and saw a little man at their elbow, his rotundity cloaked in a long mantle like those affected by the lower class of Martian shopkeepers in their walks abroad. But the face that peered up into his was frankly Celtic. Smith's expressionless features broke reluctantly into a grin as he met the irrepressible good-humor on that fat Irish face from home. He had not set foot upon Earth's soil for over a year now—the price on his liberty was too high in his native land—and curious pricks of homesickness came over him at the oddest moments. Even the toughest of space-rangers know them sometimes. The ties with the home planet are strong.

"You Smith?" demanded the little man in a rich Celtic voice.

Smith looked down at him a moment in cold-eyed silence. There was much more in that query than met the ear. Northwest Smith's name was one too well known in the annals of the Patrol for him to acknowledge it incautiously. The little

Irishman's direct question implied what he had been expecting—if he acknowledged the name he met the man on the grounds of outlawry, which would mean that the employment in prospect was to be as illegal as he had thought it would be.

The merry blue eyes twinkled up at him. The man was laughing to himself at the Celtic subtlety with which he had introduced his subject. And again, involuntarily, Smith's straight mouth relaxed into a reluctant grin.

"I am," he said.

"I've been looking for you. There's a job to be done that'll pay you well, if you want to risk it."

Smith's pale eyes glanced about them warily. No one was within earshot. The place seemed as good as any other for the discussion of extra-legal bargains.

"What is it?" he demanded.

The little man glanced down at Yarol, who had dropped to one knee again and was flicking his knife tirelessly in the intricacies of his queer game. He had apparently lost interest in the whole proceeding.

"It'll take the both of you," said the Irishman in his merry, rich voice. "Do you see that air freighter loading over there?" and he nodded toward the slaver.

Smith's head jerked in mute acknowledgment.

"It's a Willard ship, as I suppose you know. But the business is running pretty low these days. Cargoes too hot to ship. The patrol is shutting down hard, and receipts have slackened like the devil in the last year. I suppose you've heard that too."

Smith nodded again without words. He had.

"Well, what we lose in quantity we have to make up in quality. Remember the prices Minga girls used to bring?"

Smith's face was expressionless. He remembered very well indeed, but he said nothing.

"Along toward the last, kings could hardly pay the price they were asking for those girls. That's really the best market, if you want to get into the 'ivory' trade. Women. And there you come in. Did you ever hear of Cembre?"

Blank-eyed, Smith shook his head. For once he had run

across a name whose rumors he had never encountered before in all the tavern gossip.

"Well, on one of Jupiter's moons—which one I'll tell you later, if you decide to accept—a Venusian named Cembre was wrecked years ago. By a miracle he survived and managed to escape; but the hardships he'd undergone unsettled his mind, and he couldn't do much but rave about the beautiful sirens he'd seen while he was wandering through the jungles there. Nobody paid any attention to him until the same thing happened again, this time only about a month ago. Another man came back half-cracked from struggling through the jungles, babbling about women so beautiful a man could go mad just looking at them.

"Well, the Willards heard of it. The whole thing may sound like a pipe-dream, but they've got the idea it's worth investigating. And they can afford to indulge their whims, you know. So they're outfitting a small expedition to see what basis there may be for the myth of Cembre's sirens. If you want to try it, you're hired."

Smith slanted a non-committal glance downward into Yarol's uplifted black gaze. Neither spoke.

"You'll want to talk it over," said the little Irishman comprehendingly. "Suppose you meet me in the *New Chicago* at sundown and tell me what you've decided."

"Good enough," grunted Smith. The fat Celt grinned again and was gone in a swirl of black cloak and a flash of Irish merriment.

"Cold-blooded little devil," murmured Smith, looking after the departing Earthman. "It's a dirty business, Yarol."

"Money's clean," observed Yarol lightly. "And I'm not a man to let my scruples stand in the way of my meals. I say take it. Someone'll go, and it might as well be us."

Smith shrugged.

"We've got to eat," he admitted.

"This," murmured Yarol, staring downward on hands and knees at the edge of space-ship's floor-port, "is the prettiest little hell I ever expect to see."

The vessel was arching in a long curve around the Jovian

moon as its pilot braked slowly for descent, and a panorama of ravening jungle slipped by in an unchanging wilderness below the floor-port.

Their presence here, skimming through the upper atmosphere of the wild little satellite, was the end of a long series of the smoothest journeying either had ever known. The Willard network was perfect over the three planets and the colonized satellites beyond, and over the ships that ply the spaceways. This neat little exploring vessel, with its crew of three coarse-faced, sullen slavers, had awaited them at the end of their journey outward from Lakkdarol, fully fitted with supplies and every accessory the most modern adventurer could desire. It even had a silken prison room for the hypothetical sirens whom they were to carry back for the Willard approval and the Willard markets if the journey proved successful.

"It's been easy so far," observed Smith, squinting downward over the little Venusian's shoulder. "Can't expect everything, you know. But that *is* a bad-looking place."

The dull-faced pilot at the controls grunted in fervent agreement as he craned his neck to watch the little world spinning below them.

"Damn' glad I'm not goin' out with you," he articulated thickly over a mouthful of tobacco.

Yarol flung him a cheerful Venusian anathema in reply, but Smith did not speak. He had little liking and less trust in this sullen and silent crew. If he was not mistaken—and he rarely made mistakes in his appraisal of men—there was going to be trouble with the three before they completed their journey back into civilization. Now he turned his broad back to the pilot and stared downward.

From above, the moon seemed covered with the worst type of semi-animate, ravenous super-tropical jungle, reeking with fertility and sudden death, hot under lurid Jupiter's blaze. They saw no signs of human life anywhere below as their ship swept in its long curve over the jungle. The treetops spread in an unbroken blanket over the whole sphere of the satellite. Yarol, peering downward, murmured,

"No water. Somehow I always expect sirens to have fishtails."

Out of his queer, heterogeneous past Smith dragged a fragment of ancient verse, "——gulfs enchanted, where the sirens sing . . . " and said aloud,

"They're supposed to sing, too. Oh, it'll probably turn out to be a pack of ugly savages, if there's anything but delirium behind the story."

The ship was spiraling down now, and the jungle rushed up to meet them at express-train speed. Once again the little moon spun under their searching eyes, flower-garlanded, green with fertile life, massed solid in tangles of ravening growth. Then the pilot's hands closed hard on the controls and with a shriek of protesting atmosphere the little spaceship slid in a long dive toward the unbroken jungle below.

In a great crashing and crackling they sank groundward through smothers of foliage that masked the ports and plunged the interior of the ship into a green twilight. With scarcely an impact the jungle floor received them. The pilot leaned back in his seat and heaved a tobacco-redolent sigh. His work was done. Incuriously he glanced at the forward port.

Yarol was scrambling up from the floor-glass that now showed nothing but crushed vines and branches and the reeking mud of the moon's surface. He joined Smith and the pilot at the forward port.

They were submerged in jungle. Great serpentine branches and vines like cables looped downward in broken lengths from the shattered trees which had given way at their entrance. It was an animate jungle, full of hungry, reaching things that sprang in one wild, prolific tangle from the rich mud. Raw-colored flowers, yards across, turned sucking mouths blindly against the glass here and there, trickles of green juice slavering down the clear surface from their insensate hunger. A thorn-fanged vine lashed out as they stood staring and slid harmlessly along the glass, lashed again and again blindly until the prongs were dulled and green juice bled from its bruised surfaces.

"Well, we'll have blasting to do after all," murmured Smith as he looked out into the ravenous jungle. "No wonder those poor devils came back a little cracked. I don't see how they got through at all. It's—"

"Well—Pharol take me!" breathed Yarol in so reverent a whisper that Smith's voice broke off in mid-sentence and he spun around with a hand dropping to his gun to front the little Venusian, who had sought the stern port in his exploration.

"It's a road!" gasped Yarol. "Black Pharol can have me for dinner if there isn't a road just outside here!"

The pilot reached for a noxious Martian cigarette and stretched luxuriously, quite uninterested. But Smith had reached the Venusian's side before he finished speaking, and in silence the two stared out upon the surprising scene the stern port framed. A broad roadway stretched arrowstraight into the dimness of the jungle. At its edges the hungry green things ceased abruptly, not encroaching by so much as a tendril or a leaf into the clearness of the path. Even overhead the branches had been forbidden to intrude, their vein-looped greenery forming an arch above the road. It was as if a destroying beam had played through the jungle, killing all life in its path. Even the oozing mud was firmed here into a smooth pavement. Empty, enigmatic, the clear way slanted across their line of vision and on into the writhing jungle.

"Well," Yarol broke the silence at last, "here's a good start. All we've got to do is follow the road. It's a safe bet there won't be any lovely ladies wandering around through this jungle. From the looks of the road there must be some civilized people on the moon after all."

"I'd be happier if I knew what made it," said Smith. "There are some damned queer things on some of the moons and asteroids."

Yarol's cat-eyes were shining.

"That's what I like about this life," he grinned. "You don't get bored. Well, what do the readings say?"

From his seat at the control panel the pilot glanced at the gauges which gave automatic report on air and gravity outside.

"O.K.," he grunted. "Better take blast-guns."

Smith shrugged off his sudden uneasiness and turned to the weapon rack.

"Plenty of charges, too," he said. "No telling what we'll run into."

The pilot rolled his poisonous cigarette between thick lips and said, "Luck. You'll need it," as the two turned to the outer lock. He had all the indifference of his class to anything but his own comfort and the completion of his allotted tasks with a minimum of effort, and he scarcely troubled to turn his head as the lock swung open upon an almost overwhelming gush of thick, hot air, redolent of green growing things and the stench of swift decay.

A vine-tip lashed violently into the opened door as Smith and Yarol stood staring. Yarol snapped a Venusian oath and dodged back, drawing his blast-gun. An instant later the eye-destroying blaze of it sheered a path of destruction through the lush vegetable carnivora straight toward the slanting roadway a dozen feet away. There was an immense hissing and sizzling of annihilated green stuff, and an empty path stretched before them across the little space which parted the ship's outer lock from the road. Yarol stepped down into reeking mud that bubbled up around his boots with a stench of fertility and decay. He swore again as he sank knee-deep into its blackness. Smith, grinning, joined him. Side by side they floundered through the ooze toward the road.

Short though the distance was, it took them all of ten minutes to cover it. Green things whipped out toward them from the walls of sheared forest where the blast-gun had burned, and both were bleeding from a dozen small scratches and thorn-flicks, breathless and angry and very muddy indeed before they reached their goal and dragged themselves onto the firmness of the roadway.

"Whew!" gasped Yarol, stamping the mud from his caked boots. "Pharol can have me if I stir a step off this road after this. There isn't a siren alive who could lure me back into that hell again. Poor Cembre!"

"Come on," said Smith. "Which way?"

Yarol slatted sweat from his forehead and drew a deep breath, his nostrils wrinkling distastefully.

"Into the breeze, if you ask me. Did you ever smell such a stench? And hot! Gods! I'm soaked through already."

Without words Smith nodded and turned to the right, from where a faint breeze stirred the heavy, moisture-laden air. His own lean body was impervious to a great variation in climate, but even Yarol, native of the Hot Planet, dripped with sweat already and Smith's own leather-tanned face glistened and his shirt clung in wet patches to his shoulders.

The cool breeze struck gratefully upon their faces as they turned into the wind. In a gasping silence they plodded muddily up the road, their wonder deepening as they advanced. What had made the roadway became more of a mystery at every step. No vehicle tracks marked the firm ground, no footprints. And nowhere by so much as a hair's breadth did the forest encroach upon the path.

On both sides, beyond the rigid limits of the road, the lush and cannibalistic life of the vegetation went on. Vines dangled great sucking disks and thorn-toothed creepers in the thick air, ready for a deadly cast at anything that wandered within reach. Small reptilian things scuttled through the reeking swamp mud, squeaking now and then in the toils of some throny trap, and twice they heard the hollow bellowing of some invisible monster. It was raw primeval life booming and thrashing and devouring all about them, a planet in the first throes of animate life.

But here on the roadway that could have been made by nothing less than a well-advanced civilization that ravening jungle seemed very far away, like some unreal world enacting its primitive dramas upon a stage. Before they had gone far they were paying little heed to it, and the bellowing and the lashing, hungry vines and the ravenous forest growths faded into half-heard oblivion. Nothing out of that world entered upon the roadway.

As they advanced the sweltering heat abated in the steady breeze that was blowing down the road. There was a faint perfume upon it, sweet and light and utterly alien to the fetor of the reeking swamps which bordered their way. The scented gusts of it fanned their hot faces gently.

Smith was glancing over his shoulder at regular intervals, and a pucker of uneasiness drew his brows together.

"If we don't have trouble with that crew of ours before we're through," he said, "I'll buy you a case of *segir*."

"It's a bet," agreed Yarol cheerfully, turning up to Smith his sidelong cat-eyes as insouciantly savage as the ravening jungle around them. "Though they were a pretty tough trio, at that."

"They may have the idea they can leave us here and collect our share of the money back home," said Smith. "Or once we get the girls they may want to dump us and take them on alone. And if they haven't thought of anything yet, they will."

"Up to no good, the whole bunch of 'em," grinned Yarol. "They—they—"

His voice faltered and faded into silence. There was a sound upon the breeze. Smith had stopped dead-still, his ears straining to recapture the echo of that murmur which had come blowing toward them on the breeze. Such a sound as that might have come drifting over the walls of Paradise.

In the silence as they stood with caught breath it came again—a lilt of the loveliest, most exquisitely elusive laughter. From very far away it came floating to their ears, the lovely ghost of a woman's laughing. There was in it a caress of kissing sweetness. It brushed over Smith's nerves like the brush of lingering fingers and died away into throbbing silence that seemed reluctant to let the exquisite sound of it fade into echoes and cease.

The two men faced each other in rapt bewilderment. Finally Yarol found his voice.

"Sirens!" he breathed. "They don't have to sing if they can laugh like that! Come on!"

At a swifter pace they went on up the road. The breeze blew fragrantly against their faces. After a while its perfumed breath carried to their ears another faint, far-away echo of that heavenly laughter, sweeter than honey, drifting on the wind in fading cadences that died away by imperceptible degrees until they could no longer be sure if it was the lovely laughter they heard or the quickened beating of their own hearts.

Yet before them the road stretched emptily, very still in the green twilight under the low-arching trees. There seemed to be a sort of haze here, so that though the road ran straight the green dimness veiled what lay ahead and they walked in a queer silence along the roadway through ravening jungles whose sights and sounds might almost have been on another world for all the heed they paid them. Their ears were straining for a repetition of that low and lovely laughter, and the expectation if it gripped them in an unheeding spell which wiped out all other things but its own delicious echoes.

When they first became aware of a pale glimmer in the twilight greenness ahead, neither could have told. But somehow they were not surprised that a girl was pacing slowly down the roadway toward them, half veiled in the jungle dimness under the trees.

To Smith she was a figure walking straight out of a dream. Even at that distance her beauty had a still enchantment that swallowed up all his wondering in a strange and magical peace. Beauty flowed along the long, curved lines of her body, alternately cloaked and revealed by the drifting garment of her hair, and the slow, swinging grace of her as she walked was a potent enchantment that gripped him helpless in its spell.

Then another glimmer in the dimness caught his eyes away from the bewitchment that approached, and in bewilderment he saw that another girl was pacing forward under the low-hanging trees, her hair swinging about her in slow drifts that veiled and unveiled the loveliness of a body as exquisite as the first. That first was nearer now, so that he could see the enchantment of her face, pale golden and lovelier than a dream with its subtly molded smoothness and delicately tilted planes of cheek-bone and cheek smoothing deliciously upward into a broad, low forehead when the richly colored hair sprang back in tendrils like licking flames. There was a subtly Slavic tilting to those honey-colored features, hinted in the breadth of the cheeks and the sweet straightness with which their planes slanted downward to a mouth colored like hot embers, curving now in a smile that promised—heaven.

She was very near. He could see the peach-like bloom upon her pale gold limbs and the very throb of the pulse beating in her round throat, and the veiled eyes sought his. But behind her that second girl was nearing, every whit as lovely as the first, and her beauty drew his gaze magnetlike to its own delicate flow and ripple of enchantment. And beyond her—yes, another was coming, and beyond her a fourth; and in the green twilight behind these first, pale blurs bespoke the presence of yet more.

And they were identical. Smith's bewildered eyes flew from face to face, seeking and finding what his brain could still not quite believe. Feature by feature, curve by curve, they were identical. Five, six, seven honey-colored bodies, half veiled in richly tinted hair, swayed toward him. Seven, eight, nine exquisite faces smiled their pomise of ecstasy. Dizzy and incredulous, he felt a hand grip his shoulder. Yarol's voice, bemused, half whispered, murmured,

"Is this paradise—or are we both mad?"

The sound of it brought Smith out of his tranced bewitchment. He shook his head sharply, like a man half awake and striving for clarity, and said,

"Do they all look alike to you?"

"Every one. Exquisite—exquisite—did you ever see such satin-black hair?"

"Black—black?" Smith muttered that over stupidly, wondering what was so wrong with the word. When realization broke upon him at last, the shock of it was strong enough to jerk his eyes away from the enchantment before him and turn them sharply around to the little Venusian's rapt face.

Its stainless clarity was set in a mask of almost holy wonder. Even the wisdom and weariness and savagery of its black eyes was lost in the glamor of what they gazed on. His voice murmured, almost to itself,

"And white—so white—like lilies, aren't they?—blacker and whiter than—"

"Are you crazy?" Smith's voice broke harshly upon the Venusian's rapture. That trance-like mask broke before the impact of his exclamation. Like a man awaking from a dream, Yarol turned blinking to his friend.

"Crazy? Why—why—aren't we both? How else could we be seeing a sight like this?"

"One of us is," said Smith grimly. "I'm looking at red-haired girls colored like—peaches."

Yarol blinked again. His eyes sought the bevy of bewildering loveliness in the roadway. He said,

"It's you, then. They've got black hair, every one of them, shiny and smooth and black as so many lengths of satin, and nothing in creation is whiter than their bodies."

Smith's pale eyes turned again to the road. Again they met honey-pale curves and planes of velvet flesh half veiled in hair like drifting flames. He shook his head once more, dazedly.

The girls hovered before him in the green dimness, moving with little restive steps back and forth on the hardbeaten road, their feet like the drift of flower-petals for lightness, their hair rippling away from the smoothly swelling curves of their bodies and furling about them again in ceaseless motion. They turned lingering eyes to the two men, but they did not speak.

Then down the wind again came drifting the far echo of that exquisite, lilting laugh. The sweetness of it made the very breeze brush lighter against their faces. It was a caress and a promise and a summoning almost irresistible, floating past them and drifting away into the distance in low, far-off cadences that lingered in their ears long after its audible music had ceased.

The sound of it woke Smith out of his daze, and he turned to the nearest girl, blurting,

"Who are you?"

Among the flutering throng a little shiver of excitement ran. Lovely, identical faces turned to him from all over the whole group, and the one addressed smiled bewilderingly.

"I am Yvala," she said in a voice smoother than silk, pitched to caress the ear and ripple along the very nerve fibers with a slow and soothing sweetness. And she had spoken in English! It was long since Smith had heard his mother tongue. The sound of it plucked at some hidden heart-string with intolerable poignancy, the home language spoken in a voice of enchanted sweetness. For a moment he could not speak.

The silence broke to Yarol's low whistle of surprise.

"I know now we're crazy," he murmured. "No other way to explain her speaking in High Venusian. Why, she can't ever have—"

"High Venusian!" exclaimed Smith, startled out of his moment of silence. "She spoke English!"

They stared at each other, wild suspicions rising in their eyes. In desperation Smith turned and hurled the question again at another of the lovely throng, waiting breathless for her answer to be sure his ears had not deceived him.

"Yvala—I am Yvala," she answered in just that silken voice with which the first had answered. It was English unmistakably, and sweet with memories of home.

Behind her among the bevy of curved, peach-colored bodies and veils of richly tinted hair other full red lips moved and other velvety voices murmured, "Yvala, Yvala, I am Yvala," like dying echoes drifting from mouth to mouth until the last syllable of the strange and lovely name faded into silence.

Across the stunned quiet that fell as their murmurs died the breeze blew again, and once more that sweet, low laughter rang from far away in their ears, rising and falling on the wind until their pulses beat in answer, and falling, fading, dying away reluctantly on the fragrant breeze.

"What—who was that?" demanded Smith softly of the fluttering girls, as the last of it faded into silence.

"It was Yvala," they chorused in caressing voices like multiple echoes of the same rich, lingering tones. "Yvala laughs—Yvala calls. . . . Come with us to Yvala. . . ."

Yarol said in a sudden ripple of musical speech, "*Geth norri a 'Yvali?*" at the same moment that Smith's query broke out,

"Who is Yvala, then?" in his own seldom-used mother tongue.

But they got no reply to that, only beckonings and murmurous repetitions of the name, "Yvala, Yvala, Yvala—" and smiles that set their pulses beating faster. Yarol reached out a tentative hand toward the nearest, but she melted like smoke out of his grasp so that he no more than grazed the velvety flesh of her shoulder with a touch that left his fingers tingling delightfully. She smiled over her shoulder ardently, and Yarol gripped Smith's arm.

"Come on," he said urgently.

In a pleasant dream of low voices and lovely warm bodies circling just out of reach they went slowly on down the road in the midst of that hovering group, walking upwind whence that tantalizing laughter had rung, and all about them the golden girls circled on restless, drifting feet, their hair floating and furling about the loveliness of their half-seen bodies, the echoes of that single name rising and falling in cadences as rich and smooth as cream. Yvala—Yvala—Yvala—a magical spell to urge them on their way.

How long they walked they never knew. The changeless jungle slid away behind them unnoticed; the broad enigmatic pavement stretched ahead, a mysterious, green gloom shadowing the whole length of that laughter-haunted roadway. Nothing had any meaning to them outside the circle the murmurous girls were weaving with their swaying bodies and swinging hair and voices like the echoes of a dream. All the wonder and incredulity and bewilderment in the minds of the two men had sunk away into nothingness, drowned and swallowed up in the flagrant music of their enchantresses.

After a long, rapt while they came to the roadway's end. Smith lifted dreaming pale eyes and saw as if through a veil, so remotely that the scene had little meaning to him, the great park-like clearing stretching away before them as the jungle walls fell away on either side. Here the primeval swamplands and animate green life ceased abruptly to make way for a scene that might have been lifted straight over a million years. The clearing was columned with great patriarchal trees ages removed in evolution from the snaky things which grew in the hungry jungle. Their leaves roofed the place in swaying greenery through which the light sifted with twilight softness upon a carpet of flower-starred moss. With one step they spanned ages of evolution and entered into the lovely dim clearing that might have been lifted out of a world a million years older than the jungle that raved impotently around its borders.

The moss was velvety under their pacing feet. With eyes that but half comprehended what they say, Smith gazed out across the twilight vistas through the green gloom brooding beneath the trees. It was a hushed place, mystical, very quiet. He thought sometimes he saw the flash of life through the leaves overhead, the stir of it among the trees as small wild things crossed their path and birds fluttered in the foliage, but he could not be sure. Once or twice it seemed to him that he had caught an echo of bird-song, somehow as if the melody had rung in his ears a moment before, and only now, when the sound was fading, did he realize it. But not once did he hear an actual song note or see any animate life, though the presence of it was rife in the green twilight beneath the leaves.

They went on slowly. Once he could have sworn he saw a dappled fawn staring at him with wide, unhappy eyes from a covert of branches, but when he looked closer there was nothing but leaves swaying emptily. And once upon his inner ear, as if with the echo of a just-past sound, he thought he heard a stallion's high whinny. But after all it did not greatly matter. The girls were shepherding them on over the flowery moss, circling like hollow-throated doves whose only music was "Yvala—Yvala—Yvala. . . ." in unending harmony of rising and falling notes.

They paced on dreamily, the trees and mossy vistas of park sliding smoothly away behind them in unchanging quiet. And more and more strongly that impression of life among the trees nagged at Smith's mind. He wondered if he might not be developing hallucinations, for no arrangement of branches and shadows could explain the wild boar's head that he could have sworn thrust out among the leaves to stare at him for an instant with small, shamed eyes before it melted into patterned shadow under his direct gaze.

He blinked and rubbed his eyes in momentary terror lest his own brain was betraying him, and an instant later was peering uncertainly at the avenue between two low-hanging trees where from the corner of his eye he thought he had seen a magnificent white stallion hesitating with startled head upflung and the queerest, urgent look in its eyes, somehow warning and afraid—and ashamed. But it faded into mere leaf-cast shadows when he turned.

And once he started and stumbled over what was nothing more than a leafy branch lying across their path, yet which an instant before had looked bewilderingly like a low-slung cat-beast slinking across the moss with sullen, hot eyes upturned in hate and warning and distress to his.

There was something about these animals that roused a vague unrest in his mind when he looked at them—something in their eyes that was warning and agonized and more hotly aware than are the eyes of beasts—something queerly dreadful and hauntingly familiar about the set of their heads upon their shoulders—hinting horribly at another gait than the four-footed.

At last, just after a graceful doe had bounded out of the leaves, hesitated an instant and flashed away with a fleetness that did not look like the fleetness of a quadruped, turning upon him as she vanished a great-eyed agony that was warning as a cry, Smith halted in his tracks. Uneasiness too deep to be magicked away by the crooning girls urged him of danger. He paused and looked uncertainly around. The door had melted into leaf-shadows flickering upon the moss, but he could not forget the haunting shame and the warning of her eyes.

He stared about the dim greenness of the tree-roofed clearing. Was all this a lotus-dream, an illusion of jungle fever, or a suddenly unstable mind? Could he have imagined those beasts with their anguished eyes and their terribly familiar outlines of head and neck upon four-footed bodies? Was any of it real at all?

More for reassurance than for any other reason he reached out suddenly and seized the nearest honey-colored girl in a quick grip. Yes, she was tangible. His fingers closed about a firm and rounded arm, smoothly soft with the feel of peach-bloom velvet over its curving surface. The girl did not pull away. She stopped dead-still at his touch, slowly turning her head, lifting her face to his with a dream-like easiness, tilting her chin high until the long, full curve of her throat was arched taut and he could see the pulse beating hard under her velvet flesh. Her lips parted softly, her lips drooped low.

His other arm went out of its own accord, drawing her against him. Then her hands were in his hair, pulling his head down to hers, and all his uneasiness and distress and latent terror spun away at the kiss of her parted lips.

The next thing he realized was that he was strolling on under the trees, a girl's lithe body moving in the bend of his arm. Her very nearness was a delight that sent his senses reeling, so that the green woodland was vague as a dream and the only reality dwelt in the honey-colored loveliness in the circle of his arm.

Dimly he was aware that Yarol strolled parallel with them a little distance away through the leaves, a bright head on his shoulder, another golden girl leaning against his encircling arm. She was so perfectly the counterpart of his own lovely captive that she might have been a reflection in a mirror. Uneasily a remembrance swam up in Smith's mind. Did it seem to Yarol that a snow-white maiden walked with him, a black head leaned upon his shoulder? Was the little Venusian's mind yielding to the spell of the place, or was it his own? What tongue could it be that the girls spoke which fell upon his ears in English phrases and upon Yarol's in the musical lilt of High Venusian? Were they both mad?

Then in his arm the supple golden body stirred, the softly shadowed face turned to his. The woodland vanished like smoke from about him in the magic of her lips.

There were dim glades among the trees where piles of white ruins met Smith's unseeing eyes sometimes without leaving more than the merest trace of conscious remembrance. Vague wonders swam through his mind of what they might once have been, what vanished race had wrested this clearing from the jungle and died without leaving any trace save these. But he did not care. It had no significance. Even the half-seen beasts, who now turned eyes full of sorrow and despair rather than warning, had lost all meaning to his enchanted brain. In a lotus dream he wandered on in the direction he was urged, unthinking, unalarmed. It was very sweet to stroll so through the dim green gloom, with purest magic in the bend of his arm. He was content.

They strolled past the white ruins of scattered buildings, past great bending trees that dappled them with shadow. The moss yielded underfoot as softly as thick-piled carpets. Unseen beasts slunk by them now and then, so that the tail of Smith's eyes was continually catching the—almost—hint of humanity in the lines of their bodies, the set of a head upon bestial shoulders, the clarity of urgent eyes. But he did not really see them.

Sweetly—intolerably sweetly and softly, laughter rang through the woods. Smith's head flung up like a startled stallion's. It was a stronger laughter now, from near, very near among the leaves. It seemed to him that the voice indeed must come from some lovely, ardent houri leaning over the wall of Paradise—that he had come a long way in search of her and now trembled on the very brink of his journey's end. The low and lovely sound echoed through the trees, ringing down the green twilight aisles, shivering the leaves together. It was everywhere at once, a little world of music superimposed upon the world of matter, enclosing everything within its scope in a magical spell that left no room for any other thing but its lovely presence. And its command rang through Smith's mind with the sharpness of a sword in his flesh, calling, calling unbearably through the woods.

Then they came out of the trees into a little space of mossy clearing in whose center a small white temple rose. Somehow Yarol was there too—and somehow they were alone. Those exquisite girls had melted like smoke into oblivion. The two men stood quite still, their eyes dazed as they stared. This building was the only one they had seen whose columns still stood upright, and only here could they tell that the architecture of those fallen walls whose ruins had dotted the wooded glades had been one at variance to anything on any world they knew. But upon the mystery of that they had no desire to dwell. For the woman those slim columns housed drove every other thought out of their dazzled minds.

She stood in the center of the tiny temple. She was pale golden, half veiled in the long cloak of her curls. And if the siren girls had been lovely, then here stood loveliness incarnate. Those girls had worn her form and face. Here was that same exquisitely molded body, colored like honey, half revealed among the drifts of hair that clung to it like tendrils of bright flames. But those bewildering girls had been mere echoes of the beauty that faced them now. Smith stared with a kindling of colorless eyes.

Here was Lilith—here was Helen—here was Circe—here before him stood all the beauty of all the legends of mankind; here on this marble floor, facing them gravely, with unsmiling eyes. For the first time he looked into the eyes that lighted that sweet, tilt-planed face, and his very soul gasped from the sudden plunge into their poignant blueness. It was not a vivid blue, not a blazing one, but its intensity far transcended anything he had words to name. In that blueness a man's soul could sink for ever, reaching no bottom, stirred by no tides, drowned and steeped through and through with an infinity of absolute light.

When the blue, blue gaze released him he gasped once, like a drowning man, and then stared with new amazement upon a reality whose truth had escaped him until this moment. That instant of submerged ecstasy in the blue deeps of her eyes must have opened a door in his brain to new knowledge, for he saw as he stared a very strange quality in the loveliness he faced.

Tangible beauty dwelt here, an indwelling thing that could root itself in human flesh and clothe a body in loveliness as with a garment. Here was more than fleshly beauty, more than symmetry of face and body. A quality like a flame glowed all but visibly—no, more than visibly—along the peach-bloomy lines and smoothly swelling curve of her, giving a glory to the high tilt of her bosom and the long, subtly curved thigh and the exquisite line of shoulder gliding down into fuller beauty half veiled in drifting hair.

In that dazed, revealing moment her loveliness shimmered before him, too intensely for his human senses to perceive save as a dazzle of intolerable beauty before his half-comprehending eyes. He flung up his hands to shut the glory out and stood for a moment with hidden eyes in a self-imposed darkness through which beauty blazed with an intensity that transcended the visible and beat unbearably on every fiber of his being until he stood bathed in light that permeated the ultimate atoms of his soul.

Then the blaze died. He lowered shaking hands and saw that lovely, pale-gold face melting slowly into a smile of such heavenly promise that for an instant his senses failed him again and the world spun dizzily around a focus of honey-pale features breaking into arcs and softly shadowed curves, as the velvety mouth curled slowly into a smile.

"All strangers are very welcome here," crooned a voice like a vibration of sheerest silk, sweeter than honey, caressing as the brush of a kissing mouth. And she had spoken in the purest of earthly English. Smith found his voice.

"Who—who are you?" he asked in a queer gasp, as if his very breath were stopped by the magic he faced.

Before she could answer, Yarol's voice broke in, a little unsteady with sudden, savage anger.

"Can't you answer in the language you're addressed in?" he demanded in a violent undertone. "The least you could do is ask her name in High Venusian. How do you know she speaks English?"

Quite speechless, Smith turned a blank gray gaze upon his companion. He saw the blaze of hot Venusian temper fade like mist from Yarol's black eyes as he turned to the glory in the temple. And in the lovely, liquid cadences of his native tongue, that brims so exquisitely with hyperbole and symbolism, he said.

"Oh, lovely and night-dark lady, what name is laid upon you to tell how whiter than sea-foam is your loveliness?"

For a moment, listening to the beauty of phrase and sound that dwells in the High Venusian tongue, Smith doubted his own ears. For though she had spoken in English, yet the loveliness of Yarol's speech seemed infinitely more suited to have fallen from the lyric curving of her velvet-red mouth. Such lips, he thought, could never utter less than pure music, and English is not a musical tongue.

But explain Yarol's visual illusion he could not, for his own steel-pale eyes were steadfast upon richly colored hair and pale gold flesh, and no stretch of imagination could transform them into the black and snow-whiteness his companion claimed to see.

A hint of mirth crept into the smile that curled up the softness of her mouth as Yarol spoke. She answered them both in one speech that to Smith was pure English, though he guessed that it fell upon Yarol's ears in the music of High Venusian cadences.

"I am Beauty," she told them serenely. "I am incarnate Beauty. But Yvala is my name. Let there be no quarrel between you, for each man hears me in the tongue his heart speaks, and sees me in the image which spells beauty to his own soul. For I am all men's desire incarnate in one being, and there is no beauty but Me."

"But—those others?"

"I am the only dweller here—but you have known the shadows of myself, leading you through devious ways into the presence of Yvala. Had you not gazed first upon these reflections of my beauty, its fullness which you see now would have blinded and destroyed you utterly. And later, perhaps, you shall see me even more clearly. . . .

"But no, Yvala alone dwells here. Save for yourselves there is in this park of mine no living creature. Everything is illusion but myself. And am I not enough? Can you desire anything more of life or death than you gaze on now?"

The query trembled into a music-ridden silence, and they knew that they could not. The heaven-sweet murmur of that voice was speaking sheerest magic, and in the sound of it neither of them was capable of any emotion but worship of the loveliness they faced. It beat out in waves like heat from that incarnate perfection, wrapping them about so that nothing in the universe had existence but Yvala.

Before the glory that blazed in their faces Smith felt adoration pouring out of him as blood gushes from a severed artery. Like life-blood it poured, and like life-blood draining it left him queerly weaker and weaker, as if some essential part of him were gushing away in great floods of intensest worship.

But somewhere, down under the lowest depths of Smith's subconsciousness, a faint disquiet was stirring. He fought it, for it broke the mirror surfaces of his tranced adoration, but he could not subdue it, and by degrees that unease struggled up through layer upon layer of rapt enchantment until it burst through into his conscious mind and the little quiver of it ran disturbingly through the exquisite calm of his trance. It was not an articulate disquiet, but it was somehow bound up with the scarcely seen beasts he had glimpsed—or had he glimpsed?—in the wood. That, and the memory of an old Earth legend which try as he would he could not quite exorcise: the legend of a lovely woman—and men turned into beasts. . . . He could not grasp it, but the elusive memory pricked at him with little pinpoint goads, crying danger so insistently that with infinite reluctance his mind took up the business of thinking once more.

Yvala sensed it. She sensed the lessening in that lifeblood gush of rapt adoration poured out upon her loveliness. Her fathomless eyes turned upon his in a blaze of transcendent blueness, and the woods reeled about him at the impact of their light. But somewhere in Smith, under the ultimate layer of conscious thought, under the last quiver of instinct and reflex and animal cravings, lay a bedrock of savage strength which no power he had ever met could wholly overcome, not even this—not even Yvala. Rooted deep in that immovable solidity the little uneasy murmur persisted. "There is something wrong here. I mustn't let her swallow me up again—I must know what it is. . . . ."

That much he was aware of. Then Yvala turned. With both velvety arms she swept back the curtain of her hair, and all about her in a glory of tangible loveliness blazed out the radiance that dwelt in such terrible intensity here. Smith's whole consciouness snuffed out before it like a blown candle-flame.

Remotely, after eons, it seemed, awareness overtook him again. It was not consciousness, but a sort of dumb, blind knowledge of processes going on around him, in him, through him. So an animal might be aware, without any hint of real self-consciousness. But hot above everything else the tranced adoration of sheer beauty was blazing now in the center of his universe, and it was devouring him as a flame devours fuel, sucking out his worship, draining him utterly. Helpless, unbodied, he poured forth adoration into the ravenous blaze that held him, and as he poured it out he felt himself fading, somehow sinking below the level of a human being. In his dumb awareness he made no attempt to understand, but he felt himself—degenerating.

It was as if the insatiable appetite for admiration which consumed Yvala and was consuming him sucked him dry of all humanity. Even his thoughts were sinking now as she drained him, so that he no longer fitted words to his sensations, and his mind ran into figures and pictures below the level of human minds. . . .

He was not tangible. He was a dark, inarticulate memory, bodiless, mindless, full of queer, hungry sensations. . . . He remembered running. He remembered the dark earth flowing backward under his flying feet, wind keen in his nostrils and rife with the odors of a thousand luscious things. He remembered the pack baying around him to the frosty stars, his own voice lifting in exultant, throat-filling clamor with the rest. He remembered the sweetness of flesh yielding under fangs, the hot gush of blood over a hungry tongue. Little more than this he remembered. The ravenous craving, the exultation of the chase, the satisfying reek of hot flesh under ripping fangs—all these circled through his memory round and round, leaving room for little else.

But gradually, in dim, disquieting echoes, another realization strengthened beyond the circle of hunger and feeding. It was an intangible thing, nothing but the faint knowledge that somehow, somewhere, in some remote existence, he had been—different. He was little more than a recollection now, a mind that circled memories of hunting and killing and feeding which some lost body in long-ago distances had performed. But even so—he had once been different. He had—

Sharply through that memory-circle broke the knowledge of presences. With no physical sense was he aware of them, for he possessed no physical senses at all. But his awareness, his dumb, numb mind, knew that they had come—knew what they were. In memory he smelled the rank, blood-stirring scent of man, felt a tongue lolling out over suddenly dripping fangs; remembered hunger gushed up through his sensations.

Now he was blind and formless in a formless void, recognizing those presences only as they impinged upon his. But from the man-presences realization reached out and touched him, knowing his presence, realizing his nearness. They sensed him, lurking hungrily so close. And because they sensed him so vividly, their minds receiving the ravenous impact of his, their brains must have translated that hungry nearness into sight for just an instant; for from somewhere outside the gray void where he existed a voice said clearly,

"Look! Look—no, it's gone now, but for a minute I thought I saw a wolf. . . ."

The words burst upon his consciousness with all the violence of a gun-blast; for in that instant, he *knew*. He understood the speech the man used, remembered that once it had been his speech—realized what he had become. He knew too that the men, whoever they were, walked into just such danger as had conquered him, and the urgency to warn them surged up in his dumbness. Not until then did he know clearly, with a man's word-thoughts, that he had no being. He was not real—he was only a wolf-memory drifting through the dark. He had been a man. Now he was pure wolf—beast—his soul shorn of its humanity down to the very core of savagery that dwells in every man. Shame flooded over him. He forgot the men, the speech they used, the remembered hunger. He dissolved into a nothingness of wolf-memory and man-shame.

Through the dizziness of that a stronger urge began to beat. Somewhere in the void sounded a call that reached out to him irresistibly. It called him so strongly that his whole dim being whirled headlong in response along currents that swept him helpless into the presence of the summoner.

A blaze was burning. In the midst of the universal emptiness it flamed, calling, commanding, luring him so sweetly that with all his entity he replied, for there was in that burning an element that wrenched at his innermost, deepest-rooted desire. He remembered food—the hot gush of blood, the crunch of teeth on bone, the satisfying solidarity of flesh under his sinking fangs. Desire for it gushed out of him like life itself, draining him—draining him. . . . He was sinking lower, past the wolf level, down and down. . . .

Through the coming oblivion terror stabbed. It was a lightning-flash of realization from his long-lost humanity; one last throb that brightened the dark into which he sank. And out of that bed-rock of unshakable strength which was the core of his being, even below the wolf level, even below the oblivion into which he was being sucked—the spark of rebellion lashed.

Before now he had floundered helplessly with no firmness anywhere to give him foothold to fight; but now, in his uttermost extremity, while the last dregs of conscious life drained out of him, the bed-rock lay bare from which the well-springs of his strength and savagery sprang, and at that last stronghold of the *self* called Smith he leaped into instant rebellion, fighting with all the wolf-nature that had been the soil from which his man-soul rooted. Wolfishly he fought, with a beast's savagery and a man's strength, backed by the bed-rock firmness that was the base for both. Space whirled about him, flaming with hungry fires, black with flashes of oblivion, furious and ravenous in the hot presence of Yvala.

But he was winning. He knew it, and fought harder, and abruptly felt the snap of yielding opposition and was blindingly aware again, blindingly human. He lay on soft moss as a dead man lies, terribly relaxed in every limb and muscle. But life was flowing back into him, and humanity was gushing like a river in spate back into the drained hollows of his soul. For a while he lay quiet, gathering himself into one body again. His hold on it was so feeble that sometimes he thought he was floating clear and had to struggle hard to force re-entrance. Finally, with infinite effort, he tugged his eyelids open and lay there in a deathly quiet, watching.

Before him stood the white marble shrine which housed Beauty. But it was not Yvala's delirious loveliness he gazed on now. He had been through the fire of her deepest peril, and he saw her now as she really was—not in the form which spelled pure loveliness to him, and, as he guessed, to every being that gazed upon her, whether it be man or beast—not in any form at all, but as a blaze of avid light flaming inside the shrine. The light was alive, quivering and trembling and animate, but it bore no human form. It was not human. It was a life so alien that he wondered weakly how his eyes could ever have twisted it into the incarnate loveliness of Yvala. And even in the depths of his peril he found time to regret the passing of that beauty—that exquisite illusion which had never existed save in his own brain. He knew that as long as life burned in him he could never forget her smile.

It was a thing of some terribly remote origin that blazed here. He guessed that the power of it had fastened on his brain as soon as he came within its scope, commanding him to see it in that lovely form which meant heart's-desire to him alone. It must have done the same thing to countless other beings—he remembered the beast wraiths that had brushed his brain in the forest with the faint, shamed contact of theirs.

Well, he had been one of them—he knew now. He understood the warning and the anguish in their eyes. He remembered too the ruins he had seen in the woods. What race had dwelt here once, imposing its civilization and its stamp of quiet glades and trees upon the ravenous forest? A human race, perhaps, dwelling in seclusion under the leaves until Yvala the Destroyer came. Or perhaps not a human race, for he knew now that to every living creature she wore a different form, the incarnation of each individual's highest desire.

Then he heard voices, and after an infinity of effort twisted his head on the moss until he could see whence they came. At what he saw he would have risen if he could, but a deathly weariness lay like the weight of worlds upon him and he could not stir. Those man-presences he had felt in his beast-form stood here—the three slavers from the little ship. They must have followed them not far behind, with what dark motives would never be known now, for Yvala's magic had seized them and there would be no more of humanity for them after the next few moments were past. They stood in a row there before the shrine with an ecstasy almost holy on their faces. Plainly he saw reflected there the incarnate glory of Yvala, though to his eyes the thing they faced was only a formless flame.

He knew then why Yvala had let him go so suddenly in that desperate struggle. Here was fresh fodder for her avidity, new worship to drink in. She had turned away from his outworn well-springs to drain new prey of its humanity. He watched them standing there, drunk with loveliness before what to them must be a beautiful woman veiled in drifting hair, glowing with more than mortal ardency where, to him, only a clear flame burned.

But he could see more. Cloudy about those three figures, rapt before the shrine, he could see—was it some queer reflection of themselves dancing upon the air? The misty outlines wavered as, with eyes that in the light of what he had just passed through had won momentarily a sight which penetrated beyond the flesh, he looked upon that dancing shimmer which clearly must be the reflection of some vital part of those three men, visible now in some strange way at the evocation of Yvala's calling.

They were man-shaped reflections. They strained toward Yvala from their anchorage in the bodies that housed them, yearning, pulling as if they would forsake their fleshly roots and merge with the incarnate beauty that called them so irresistibly. The three stood rigid, faces blank with rapture, unconscious of that perilous tugging at what must be in their very souls.

Then Smith saw the nearest man sag at the knees, quiver, topple to the moss. He lay still for a moment while from his fallen body that tenuous reflection of himself tugged and pulled and then in one last great effort jerked free and floated like a smoke-wreath into the white-hot intensity in the shrine. The blaze engulfed it, flaring brighter as if at the kindling of new fuel.

When that sudden brightness died again the smokewreath drifted out, trailing through the pillars in a form that even to Smith's dimmed eyes wore a strange distortion. It was no longer a man's soul. All of humanity had burned out from it to feed the blaze that was Yvala. And that beast foundation which lies so close under the veneer of civilization and humanity in every human creature was bared and free. Cold with understanding, Smith watched the core of beast instinct which was all that remained now that the layer of man-veneer had been stripped away, a core of animal memories rooted eons deep in that far-away past when all man's ancestors ran on four paws.

It was a cunning beast that remained, instinct with foxy slyness. He saw the misty thing slink away into the green gloom of the woods, and he realized afresh why it was he had seen fleeting glimpses of animals in the park as he came here, wearing that terrible familiarity in the set of their heads, the line of shoulder and neck that hinted at other gaits than the four-footed. They must have been just such wraiths as this, drifting through the woods, beast-wraiths that wore still the tatters and rags of their doffed humanity, brushing his mind with the impact of theirs until their vividness evoked actual sight of the reality of fur and flesh, just for a glimpse, just for a hint, before the wraith blew past. And he was cold with horror at the thought of how many men must have gone to feed the flame, stripping off humanity like a garment and running now in the nakedness of their beast natures through the enchanted woods.

Here was Circe. He realized it with a quiver of horror and awe. Circe the Enchantress, who turned the men of Greek legend into beasts. And what tremendous backgrounds of reality and myth loomed smokily behind what happened here before his very eyes! Circe the Enchantress—ancient Earthly legend incarnate now on a Jovian moon far away through the void. The awe of it shook him to the depths. Circe—Yvala—alien entity that must, then, rove through the universe and the ages, leaving dim whispers behind her down the centuries. Lovely Circe on her blue Aegean isle—Yvala on her haunted moon under Jupiter's blaze—past and present merged into a blazing whole.

The wonder of it held him so wrapt that when the reality of the scene before him finally bore itself in upon his consciousness again, both of the remaining slavers lay prone upon the moss, forsaken bodies from which the vitality had been sucked like blood in Yvala's flame. That flame burned more rosily now, and out of its pulsing he saw the last dim wraith of the three who had fed her come hurrying, a swinish brute of a wraith whose grunts and snorts were almost audible, tusks and bristles all but visible as it scurried off into the wood.

Then the flame burned clear again, flushed with hot rose, pulsing with regular beats like the pulse of a heart, satiate and ecstatic in its shrine. And he was aware of a withdrawal, as if the consciousness of the entity that burned here were turned inward upon itself, leaving the world it dominated untouched as Yvala drowsed and digested the sustenance her vampire-craving for worship had devoured.

Smith stirred a little on the moss. Now, if ever, he must make some effort to escape, while the thing in the shrine was replete and uninterested in its surroundings. He lay there, shaken with exhaustion, forcing strength back into his body, willing himself to be strong, to rise, to find Yarol, to make his way somehow back to the deserted ship. And by slow degrees he succeeded. It took a long while, but in the end he had dragged himself up against a tree and stood swaying, his pale eyes alternately clouding with exhaustion and blinking aware again as he scanned the space under the trees for Yarol.

The little Venusian lay a few steps away, one cheek pressing the ground and his yellow curls gay against the moss. With closed eyes he looked like a seraph asleep, all the lines of hard living and hard fighting relaxed and the savageness of his dark gaze hidden. Even in his deadly peril Smith could not suppress a little grin of appreciation as he staggered the half-dozen steps that parted them and fell to his knees beside his friend's body.

The sudden motion dazed him, but in a moment his head cleared and he laid an urgent hand on Yarol's shoulder, shaking it hard. He dared not speak, but he shook the little Venusian heavily, and in his brain a silent call went out to whatever drifting wraith among the trees housed Yarol's naked soul. He bent over the quiet yellow head and called and called, turning the force of his determination in all its intensity to that summoning, while weakness washed over him in great slow waves.

After a long time he thought he felt a dim response, somewhere from far off. He called harder, eyes turned apprehensively toward the rosily pulsing flame in the shrine, wondering if this voiceless summoning might not impinge upon the entity there as tangibly as speech. But Yvala's satiety must have been deep, and there was no changing in the blaze.

The answer came clearer from the woods. He felt it pulling in toward him along the strong compulsion of his call as a fisherman feels a game fish yielding at last to the tug of his line. And presently among the leafy solitudes of the trees a little mist-wraith came gliding. It was a slinking thing, feline, savage, fearless. He could have sworn that for the briefest instant he saw the outlines of a panther stealing across the moss, misty, low-slung, turning upon him the wise black gaze of Yarol—exactly his friend's black eyes, with no lessening in them of lost humanity. And something in that familiar gaze sent a little chill down his back. Could it be—could it possibly be that in Yarol the veneer of humanity was so thin over his savage cat-nature that even when it had been stripped away the look in his eyes was the same?

Then the smoke-beast was hovering over the prone Venusian figure. It curled round Yarol's shoulders for an instant; it faded and sank, and Yarol stirred on the moss. Smith turned him over with a shaking hand. The long Venusian lashes quivered, lifted. Black, sidelong eyes looked up into Smith's pale gaze. And Smith in a gush of chilly uncertainty did not know if humanity had returned into his friend's body or not, if it was a panther's gaze looking up into his or if that thin layer of man-soul veiled it, for Yarol's eyes had always looked like this.

"Are—are you all right?" he asked in a breathless whisper.

Yarol blinked dizzily once or twice, then grinned. A twinkle lighted up his black cat gaze. He nodded and made a little effort to rise. Smith helped him sit up. The Venusian was not a fraction so weak as the Earthman had been. After a little interval of hard breathing he struggled to his feet and helped Smith up, apprehension in his whole demeanor as he eyed the flame that pulsed in its white shrine. He jerked his head urgently.

"Let's get out of here!" his silent lips mouthed. And Smith in fervent agreement turned in the direction he indicated, hoping that Yarol knew where he was going. His own exhaustion was still too strong to permit him anything but acquiescence.

They made their way through the woods, Yarol heading unerringly in a direct course toward the roadway they had left such a long time ago. After a while, when the flamehousing shrine had vanished among the trees behind them, the Venusian's soft voice murmured, half to itself.

"—wish, almost, you hadn't called me back. Woods were

so cool and still—remembering such splendid things—killing and killing—I wish—"

The voice fell quiet again. But Smith, stumbling on beside his friend, understood. He knew why the woods seemed familiar to Yarol, so that he could head for the roadway unerringly. He knew why Yvala in her satiety had not even wakened at the withdrawal of Yarol's humanity—it was so small a thing that the loss of it meant nothing. He gained a new insight in that moment into Venusian nature that he remembered until the day he died.

Then there was a gap in the trees ahead, and Yarol's shoulder was under his supportingly, and the road to safety shimmered in its tree-arched green gloom ahead.

SONG IN A MINOR KEY

Beneath him the clovered hill-slope was warm in the sun. Northwest Smith moved his shoulders against the earth and closed his eyes, breathing so deeply that the gun holstered upon his chest drew tight against its strap as he drank the fragrance of Earth and clover warm in the sun. Here in the hollow of the hills, willow-shaded, pillowed upon clover and the lap of Earth, he let his breath run out in a long sigh and drew one palm across the grass in a caress like a lover's.

He had been promising himself this moment for how long—how many months and years on alien worlds? He would not think of it now. He would not remember the dark spaceways or the red slag of Martian drylands or the pearlgray days on Venus when he had dreamed of the Earth that had outlawed him. So he lay, with his eyes closed and the sunlight drenching him through, no sound in his ears but the passage of a breeze through the grass and a creaking of some insect nearby—the violent, blood-smelling years behind him might never have been. Except for the gun pressed into his ribs between his chest and the clovered earth, he might be a boy again, years upon years ago, long before he had broken his first law or killed his first man.

No one else alive now knew who that boy had been. Not even the all-knowing Patrol. Not even Venusian Yarol, who had been his closest friend for so many riotous years. No one would ever know—now. Not his name (which had not always been Smith) or his native land or the home that had bred him, or the first violent deed that had sent him down the devious paths which led here—here to the clover hollow in the hills of an Earth that had forbidden him ever to set foot again upon her soil.

He unclasped the hands behind his head and rolled over to lay a scarred cheek on his arm, smiling to himself. Well, here was Earth beneath him. No longer a green star high in alien skies, but warm soil, new clover so near his face he could see all the little stems and trefoil leaves, moist earth granular at their roots. An ant ran by with waving antennae close beside his cheek. He closed his eyes and drew another deep breath. Better not even look; better to lie here like an animal, absorbing the sun and the feel of Earth blindly, wordlessly.

Now he was not Northwest Smith, scarred outlaw of the spaceways. Now he was a boy again with all his life before him. There would be a white-columned house just over the hill, with shaded porches and white curtains blowing in the breeze and the sound of sweet, familiar voices indoors. There would be a girl with hair like poured honey hesitating just inside the door, lifting her eyes to him. Tears in the eyes. He lay very still, remembering.

Curious how vividly it all came back, though the house had been ashes for nearly twenty years, and the girl—the girl . . .

He rolled over violently, opening his eyes. No use remembering her. There had been that fatal flaw in him from the very first, he knew now. If he were the boy again knowing all he knew today, still the flaw would be there and sooner or later the same thing must have happened that had happened twenty years ago. He had been born for a wilder age, when man took what they wanted and held what they could without respect for law. Obedience was not in him, and so—

As vividly as on that day it happened he felt the same old surge of anger and despair twenty years old now, felt the ray-gun bucking hard against his unaccustomed fist, heard the hiss of its deadly charge ravening into a face he hated. He could not be sorry, even now, for that first man he had killed. But in the smoke of that killing had gone up the columned house and the future he might have had, the boy himself—lost as Atlantis now—and the girl with the honey-colored hair and much, much else besides. It had to happen, he knew. He being the boy he was, it had to happen. Even if he could go back and start all over, the tale would be the same.

And it was all long past now, anyhow; and nobody remembered any more at all, except himself. A man would be a fool to lie here thinking about it any longer.

Smith grunted and sat up, shrugging the gun into place against his ribs.